Red

The Watch

Printed in the United States of America

Publishers Cataloging-in-Publication Data

Witt, Amanda Beth.
   The Watch / Amanda Witt.
   pages cm.
   Series : The Red Series.
   ISBN 978-0-9965761-0-9

1. Totalitarianism--Fiction. 2. Dystopias. 3. Dystopian fiction. 4. Science fiction. I. Series. II. Title.

PS3623.I8765 W38 2015
813.4 --dc23   2015945683

River Jude Press
www.riverjudepress.com

Cover image Pixabay, MysticsArtDesign

For Jonathan, Dante, Daniel, and John Paul

You are my sunshine

The Watch

Book One in *The Red Series*

Amanda Witt

River Jude Press

Chapter 1

When the rain stopped we left the doorway and began to run. It was dark, but the streetlights cast an electric blue glow, flickering beautiful and eerie against the wet pavement, making patterns on the drifting mist. I wished we could run in the light. Instead we ran in the shadow of the rough cinderblock wall that divided the street from the houses.

The wall had cameras on both sides, but Meritt knew which eyes were blind. He led me back and forth from the street side to the house side, through the intermittent gaps in the wall, weaving us through the web of invisible threads so that none of them ever touched us.

We ran a long way, through air that was crisp and damp and smelled like autumn leaves, and it felt good to run, to pour the tension of the past week into sweat and breath and motion. Tomorrow the tight fist of anxiety in my chest would be back, but tonight, running hard through the wet forbidden streets, I could breathe.

When the white spotlight from the watchtower swept toward us we paused, pressing against the rough wall; when it passed, we eased out and ran again. Meritt kept pace with me until the houses ended, until the street and wall ran past nothing but orchards and empty stubbled ground. Then he let loose and raced ahead, hurtling through black shadows and pockets of blue light.

I couldn't keep up with him; I didn't even try. Instead I slowed to push a stray lock of hair back under my black cap as a few belated raindrops pattered down, cold against my hot skin, and the rising breeze sent the sharp tang of fermenting windfall apples wafting past. Breathing deep, I tasted the damp night air, felt the last knots of tension relax in my shoulders, my neck. This was good. This was the happiest I ever was, out running with Meritt in the dark.

Ahead of me Meritt turned and raised a hand, trying to get me to hurry. He didn't call to me because we weren't supposed to be out this late, we weren't supposed to be here, we weren't supposed to be together, and we certainly weren't supposed to be meeting Rafe.

But I didn't want to hurry. I was tired, and he knew he was faster. It wouldn't hurt him to slow down and wait for me. So I waved back, cheerily, as if he were just waving to be friendly.

He shook his head at me, reproving. He was still moving, jogging backwards, and as we pantomimed our little argument he veered a bit, away from the wall, into the glow of the electric blue lights. They caught at the sharp planes of his face, danced in his unruly black hair, and a cold fist formed in my stomach and I stopped moving altogether.

He didn't look like himself. He didn't look like the Meritt I'd known all my life. The street was dark and empty and we were all alone, and he had turned to light and shadow, wrong-colored, frightening and strangely beautiful.

He looked like the things in the woods.

Now he was truly exasperated, spreading his arms wide—*what are you doing?*—but I couldn't move. I put one hand against the wall beside me, feeling its rough surface and the cold damp scratchiness of it, and it was hard and real and kept me upright while my vision darkened and then cleared, lightheadedness passing when I remembered that breathing was a good thing, remembered, too, that there weren't really things in the woods. Those were stories, nothing more. Bogeymen to keep people in line.

Or so I hoped.

The white spotlight swept toward us again and Meritt backed against the wall, but I was still paralyzed. The light flashed in my eyes, blinding me, and all I could do was stand frozen and try not to attract attention with any sudden movement.

We mustn't get caught. Bad things happened to people who got caught breaking the rules—prison time, cut rations, reassignment to the worst jobs. I didn't know what exactly the wardens would do to me if they caught me out after curfew, and I didn't want to find out.

Then the spotlight moved on and my eyes adjusted to the dark and I saw Meritt up ahead, looking like himself again, grimacing wryly at me. With one last adamant sweep of his arm—*come on*—he spun and sprinted toward the end of the street, toward the opening in the other wall, the outer one that circled the entire city.

After one last deep breath, feeling my head clear and my heart unclench, I started running too.

We were meeting Rafe outside the outer wall, in the broad stretch of sand and scraggly grass that marked the boundary between the city and the woods. We called that strip of boundary the wasteland, but despite the ugly name we liked the place. It wasn't the suffocating city, and it wasn't the dangerous woods.

We went there whenever we could, and this time Rafe would be there with us. He'd been one of our teachers back in school, my favorite because he was good at explaining things and, most of all, because he never treated me like an outcast or a freak. On bad days I pretended—secretly—that he was my father. If I loved anyone as much as Meritt, it was Rafe.

Slowly, throbbing through my veins, joy began to return. Meritt and Rafe, both at the same time. I felt a smile start and I leaned into the wind, running hard, while ahead of me Meritt sprinted full-out down a thin channel of shadow, his bare feet flashing, the muscles in his back moving beneath the gray uniform shirt, all of him lit in fits and starts by the blue light shifting and shining along the periphery.

That sight will always stay with me, that feeling. It was the last moment of *before*. I dream about it now, and I've dreamt it so often I can count Meritt's steps, hear the soft whistle of the rising wind, feel the last breath I drew in—too harsh, too loud—when I saw what was going to happen and had to bite back a shout, had to stop again and let him go.

She was standing in the shadows against the wall. I saw her before Meritt did, but there was nothing I could do to warn him. She stepped out when he was only a split second away, blocking his path, her white-blonde hair glinting in the electric blue lights.

In that last second before Meritt's body blocked my view, I saw that she was smiling. My own smile was still on my lips, stiff and empty, as if she had taken its soul.

Meritt skidded to a stop. He was going too fast and would have slammed into her, but he jerked sideways at the very last second and ricocheted into the wall instead. I felt the impact in my own shoulder, saw him reach up and grab his own.

She took a step toward him. He backed away, glancing around, checking his options, but he didn't look at me; he would never give me away.

Then there was noise, sounds I couldn't decipher, muted thumps and thuds. An odd electric smell simmered in the air, cast a metallic taste in the back of my throat.

4

The woman came forward another pace and the blue light shone on her face and I recognized her for certain, then—the blonde hair pulled tightly back from her face, the black warden's uniform that did nothing to hide her figure. She had been watching Meritt for months, swallowing him with her eyes when he passed on the street. I'd seen her do it; I'd told him so.

She held up a hand—*stop*—and spoke. I heard her voice but not her words.

Meritt reached up and clasped his hands on top of his head.

Staying deep in the shadows of the rough wall, I began to creep closer. I had to be careful—wardens rarely traveled alone. I had to be careful—but I made a mistake, the second one that night. My bare foot touched a cold puddle of water and the water rippled out into the light.

Someone shouted.

My heart lurched.

But I wasn't the one being shouted at, I hadn't been seen—the shout had come from the wasteland, and there was another heavy thud, and now through the gap in the wall I could see shadows thrashing, dark and confused against the pale half-dead grass. A figure stumbled into the wedge of blue light spilling from the street, the silver in his hair glinting bright and distinctive. Rafe.

I saw him, but I couldn't believe my eyes. Rafe was so careful, always so careful, and wardens never ventured out into the wasteland, so close to the woods. Even they were afraid of the woods, afraid of the stories.

The female warden beside Meritt half turned, looking toward the wasteland. Meritt could have run then, while she was distracted, and I wanted him to run but he didn't and I understood why—he'd already been seen and recognized, and anyway how could we run when Rafe was in trouble?

Not that we could do anything to help. All I could do was stand there, hiding in the shadows, feeling like a coward but knowing Rafe would want me to stay out of sight.

Rafe turned from side to side, looking for an out, but he was surrounded. The wardens edged in, tightening their circle. They gestured to each other but didn't speak.

One lunged forward. He caught Rafe from behind, pinning his arms. Rafe lifted both legs and kicked another warden hard in the stomach. The man went down, doubling over, and the warden holding Rafe lost his balance, staggered sideways, taking Rafe with him so that they both ended up on the ground.

Rafe broke free and rolled to his feet. A cry rose in my throat—*run*—but I swallowed it and the third warden sprang, lunging fast. The low buzz of a stunner rang out, the smell of hot metal intensifying.

Rafe went limp, crumpling into an uneven shadow on the ground.

Like vultures the wardens swooped in, bending over him. Still they were silent—other than that first shout, the whole thing played out voicelessly. No one wanted to attract the attention of anything in the woods.

The wardens hauled Rafe upright. His hands were cuffed behind his back and he didn't have the strength to stand. He swayed, almost fell, and they caught him and half-dragged, half-carried him out of my line of sight.

And Meritt—Meritt was shifting slightly from side to side, his hands still clasped behind his head. It took me a second to understand: He was breathing, that was all. He was breathing the way he always did when he was opening his lungs after a hard run.

Why hadn't the blonde warden cuffed him? Maybe she'd been distracted by the fight in the wasteland, but it was careless of her. Meritt could have gotten away.

Now she was gesturing toward the group in the waste-land. She was pointing at something. She was talking.

Meritt dropped his arms and shrugged.

The woman smiled.

She stepped toward Meritt and I thought she would finally cuff him. Instead she reached up and put her arms around his neck, tilting her face up to his.

I blinked hard, feeling suddenly chilled. Then I turned my back on them, and started back the way I'd come.

It was what I'd promised to do if ever we ran into trouble, and I understood why I had to do it. All the same, I hated myself. Meritt and Rafe would never have run away and left me. They were the closest thing to family that I had.

The concrete felt colder against my bare feet, harder. I was alone and it was a long way back and the streets stretched before me, glinting blue and empty, smelling of rain and wet dead leaves. I was alone and I had to remember the cameras, had to avoid the eyes, I couldn't simply follow Meritt as I'd done before—Meritt had been caught, Rafe had been caught.

What would the wardens do to them?

The wind gusted, sending pale leaves spinning across my path like living things. Leaves from the woods, from the dying trees, from the place where strange things lived.

Only stories. They were surely only stories, and I knew I was thinking about the woods because that fear was a familiar fear, easier than thinking about what might be happening to Meritt and Rafe.

I ran and tried not to stumble on stretches of crumbling pavement and tried to think of some way to help, but there was no one to tell, nothing to do, nothing except not getting caught myself—it would go worse for all of us if I too got caught.

One house had not yet gone dark, and as I ducked my head to make myself smaller and passed through the faint halo of its lighted windows, somewhere, not far away, an engine growled to life. Yellow lights flashed on and cast hazy arcs through the mist up toward the sky.

I couldn't see the car because it was on the other side of the wall, but I could track its progress by those lights. Surely it would go toward the wasteland, toward the disturbance. Surely it would go toward Meritt and Rafe, not me.

No. The headlights turned in my direction, slowly, deliberately, like the eyes of an animal stalking its prey.

I was already running fast but now I ran faster. I was a good runner but fear was making my heart race, was throwing off my breathing, and the sharp pang of a stitch bit at my ribs. A half-fallen bicycle reared up in my path, then a stack of loose cinderblocks. I veered away from the wall to avoid them, then back into its dark protective shadow. The patrol car was louder, closer. I had to make it past the corner and back into my designated area before it reached me.

Laughter rang out ahead, then a curse. I'd forgotten—three old men sat in front of a dark house drinking. Meritt and I had seen them when we came past, had swung out into the blue of the streetlights to pass them on the other side of the wall. I couldn't do that now, not with the patrol car out there.

Maybe the men were too drunk to notice a girl darting past.

No such luck.

"Look at that," one called. "Hey, what're you doing out so late?"

"Come keep us company," another yelled.

"Warden!" shouted the third.

They kept calling out, mocking, entertained. I kept running, not even glancing toward them.

I heard the bottle spinning through the air a moment before it smashed and sent broken glass skittering across my path. Jerking sideways I leapt over it, and I didn't get cut but my cap came loose, sending a cascade of hair spilling past my shoulders. That was bad. If those men caught sight of my hair, they'd know exactly who I was. They'd tell the wardens. I could make no excuse.

The thought terrified me but all I could do was go on and hope the dark was dark enough.

I was getting close. One more block of houses and I'd reach the corner by the laundry building—the southern boundary of my area. If I got caught in my own area, and alone, I'd be in trouble but not nearly as much. I only had to pass one more break in the wall where the sidewalk was exposed to the street.

I was going to make it.

But just as I stretched to leap past the opening, past the point of exposure and into the relative safety of my own area, the yellow glare of headlights poured across the gap—a second patrol car coming from the other direction.

Skidding to a halt I flung myself down and against the rough cinderblock wall, sending a burning pain across my knee, tearing the leg of my pants. I grabbed at my hair, twisted it up and shoved it under my black cap.

A car door opened. I wanted to hold my breath, but I was too winded. All I could do was hold very still and try to gulp for air quietly.

Footsteps moved toward the gap in the wall, then stopped. I'd been annoyed by the rain earlier, but now I was glad for the clouds, the hidden moon. Though the street was blue with artificial light, my side of the wall—the sidewalk side—was cloaked in shadow. As long as no one came out of the house above me, spilling light from an open doorway, I was close to invisible.

The footsteps started again, moved closer. I crouched there stock-still, muscles tensed, feeling a trickle of blood where I'd scraped my knee. And now, for a moment, I did hold my breath. The air lay still and the silence was so complete that I imagined a drop of blood rolling off my knee, striking the payment with an echoing splash, giving me away. I stared at the slanted rectangle of blue light that the gap let slip across the sidewalk, expecting any moment to see a shadow there, and then a warden.

Instead the steps resumed, receded. The car door slammed. The headlights shifted on the street and the patrol car growled away.

I didn't move. I could feel that I wasn't alone.

The white spotlight swept past, at this angle catching only the other side of the wall. For a long moment the night stretched out, sighed. A handful of leaves whispered around the corner, tumbled toward me.

I couldn't hold my breath any longer, so I let it out as quietly as I could and hoped it was quiet enough.

On the other side of the wall, someone moved, whispered. There was more than one of them, unless I'd heard only the rising wind, the leaves.

Another whisper. Not two feet away from me, on the other side of the wall.

My body screamed for me to leap up, run. My brain said no, staying put was still my best hope for escape. Don't move. Be part of the shadows, part of the night.

Then the clouds parted and the moon emerged, full and round, shining down clear and calm and bright, outdoing the electric blue lights, changing the shadows. The moonlight reached down and picked out the one part of me that wasn't pressed tightly enough against the wall—my left foot, heel braced on the ground, toes pointed up in the air. The moonlight struck it and cast a perfect shadow of its form, a foot with heel and toes, clear and unmistakable against the pavement in front of the gap.

Someone on the other side of the wall drew a sharp breath.

I scrambled to get my feet beneath me, to rush back the way I'd come. I took a step backward, turned, took one long leaping stride—and barreled straight into someone.

Meritt.

He put a hand over my mouth—not that I would have cried out—but I knew it was too late for silence, too late to hide. Someone was outside the wall, and any moment now he would step into view and pin us with his light. And unlike me, Meritt had been caught before.

All this flashed through my mind instantly, definitively. I wrenched myself out of his arms and pointed at him, then pointed back the way we'd come.

There was just time to register the quick series of expressions flitting across Meritt's face—disbelief, objection, dismay—to see him reaching to grab me and missing as I stepped beyond his grasp, pulled off my cap, shook out my hair, and plunged into the light.

Chapter 2

One of the wardens reached for his stunner and the other took a step back. I paused just long enough to register their faces—both men, that was good, it was harder to know how to maneuver if you were dealing with mixed pairs—and then I started talking.

"There you are!" I said. "I've been looking for you forever."

Go on the offensive, my friend Cynda always said, and she had more experience with wardens than any of us.

The wardens stared at me, their faces impassive. One was young. His hair was short-cropped and he had an ugly puckered scar running through his upper lip. He stood in a way designed to show off his muscles, with his chest out, his hands fisted on his hips. The other warden was bigger, softer, older—about Rafe's age, maybe—and was completely bald but had a short blond beard. I recognized him and could almost remember his name. We thought he might be Judd's father.

He asked the obvious question. "Why were you looking for us?"

"I'm lost," I said, making it up as I went. "I don't know how to get back to my dorm."

For a long moment neither warden said a word; they

just stood there staring at me. Then the one with the scarred lip reached out and took me firmly by one arm.

"Let's go," he said, and from his tone I knew he wasn't taking me home.

As he began to lead me away, the other warden, the older one, turned on his heel and walked down the shadowed sidewalk, shining his light here and there. I craned my neck to watch him, stumbling as the younger warden pulled me along, my heart in my throat.

But Meritt was safe. The older warden came back alone. He caught up to us and positioned himself on my other side, and together the two men marched me through the city. They had work boots on, so they didn't pay much attention to where we stepped. They pulled me straight through puddles and twice I stepped on sharp rocks, stumbled, was jerked upright.

The younger one was rougher than the older one, and when he figured out that my feet were callused enough not to mind the puddles and rocks—except the really sharp ones—his fingers dug into my arm. It was a stupid petty punishment, but I had bruises to show for it later, angry elongated ovals that changed from blue to purple to yellow over the course of the next few weeks, marking the ordinary passing of time as the world fell to pieces all around me.

We passed the laundry house, where soap-scented steam rose gently from the vent pipes; skirted the food preservation buildings and the infirmary, where one light burned; and made our way around the cafeteria, dark now and silent. Then we came to the center of the city, to the circle with its concentric rows of steps, to the watchtower and the door at its base. To the prison.

Even though I'd known where we were headed, the sight of the windowless door made my knees suddenly weak.

The older warden swung open the heavy outer door. It

was metal and it opened with a raw echoing clang. Inside, the long hallway smelled of antiseptic and fear, and the black-and-white tiled floor felt cold and smooth and strangely slick.

I had never been inside the prison before. There were rows of doors on each side of the hall, gray steel doors with heavy bolts. The scarred warden started to pull me down the hall toward those doors, but the older warden stopped suddenly—so that I was yanked between the two of them—and dragged me into a nearer room. That room, unlike the others, had a small mesh-covered window in its door.

"Sit," he said, pointing at a metal folding chair. Then he went back out into the hall, jerking his head to tell the other warden to follow him. Hisses and mutters followed. I couldn't hear what they were saying, but it sounded like a disagreement.

Their delay gave me a chance to scan my surroundings. The room looked clean but smelled musty, like old damp paint, and was mostly bare—a gray metal table sat straight in front of me, and two other metal chairs were folded and leaning against the wall. One bare light bulb hung from the ceiling, right above the table.

After a moment both men came into the room. The older warden grabbed a chair, opened it with a clang, and sat down a few feet away, off to the side. I had to turn my head to see him. The scarred warden took the other chair and sat down behind the gray metal table before pulling a small book with a metal cover out of his shirt pocket.

The dangling light bulb above him was glaring, but I didn't squint or look away. I didn't want to look shifty or too frightened—I didn't want them to realize I was a systematic rule-breaker who had only now been caught. I wanted them to see a first-time offender, a nobody, a girl who had stupidly gotten lost and stayed out after curfew.

"Name," the warden said, but he was already writing—

everybody knew my name—so I thought he was talking more to himself than to me. My feet were wet, the bottoms of my pants drenched, and as I watched the warden write, my teeth began to chatter. It wasn't because I was terrified—though I was—and it irritated me. This was going to be tricky enough without my body throwing out random unintended signals.

"Name," the warden said again, more sharply. He didn't look up.

I guess the formalities had to be observed.

"Red," I said. Some of the others had been given two names, but I only had one, and it was a darn unimaginative one at that.

The warden dropped his pen on the table and leaned back in his chair, making his black shirt pull taut over his chest. Ridiculous, I told myself. He was showing off, trying to frighten and impress.

"I've seen you before," he said, and his tone was flat and expressionless.

Of course he'd seen me. You'd have to be blind not to see me. I was the freak, the only person with blazing red hair in the whole city, on the whole island—in the whole world, for all I knew.

The scarred warden kept staring. Finally it dawned on me that he expected an answer.

"Oh?" I said, lamely. "Where have you seen me?"

"Anywhere you've been. Everywhere you've been."

My skin felt suddenly clammy.

He kept staring at me, tipping back in his chair. It was obviously a pose, a technique pointing out that he could relax while I was sitting bolt upright, struggling to keep from trembling. He'd probably practiced all this in front of a mirror, that flat gaze, the relaxed muscles. Ridiculous, I told myself again. He's ridiculous.

The older warden cleared his throat.

The younger one didn't look at him. "How old are you?" he said to me.

"Sixteen years, eleven months."

Then he did look over at the older man. "She's the one who was born during the ashes."

The older one nodded a confirmation. It was my claim to fame—well, that and my hair. I was the only one born during a four-year stretch when a foul-smelling ash drifted across the island, darkening the sun, blighting crops, wreaking havoc with human and animal fertility. Most women couldn't get pregnant during those years, and the ones who did miscarried. All but my mother. I'd never known her and I didn't know if she'd done something in particular that let me survive, or if she'd just been lucky.

The scarred warden was eying me speculatively. "Almost seventeen years old," he said. "I thought she was younger than that."

Everyone thought I was younger than that. It added insult to injury—all my life there had been no other children my age, and I looked even younger than I was. It had made for a lonely childhood. The young kids bored me and were frightened by me. The older kids let me tag along, at least sometimes, but they had never been my friends. Only Meritt was my friend; only Meritt had been different. He liked me and because he did, some of his friends gradually became mine as well. I owed him everything.

I would not say anything that could even possibly give him away.

The scarred warden was still examining me, his gaze running up and down my body. "Up close she looks her age," he said, in a voice that made me want to scrub with soap and water. "But now I get it. That hair—she was born during the time of the ashes, so she's damaged. She's a runt and she has mutant hair. Which is why we watch her."

That last part should have sounded like a conclusion, but he made it sound almost a question. And what did he mean? The wardens watched everyone, not just me. The cameras were everywhere. That was the way of Optica.

The older warden shrugged. "We watch her because we're supposed to."

The scarred warden studied me for another long moment, then set his chair legs down hard on the floor and looked down at his notebook.

"Employment?" he said, with the tone of someone getting down to business.

"Field A Supervisor."

The warden smirked without looking up. Supervisors got all the blame and none of the credit, which was why the older, more experienced workers usually found a way to avoid the position.

"Dormitory?"

"Girls' Dormitory H-2."

The scarred warden wrote it down. Then he looked up. The light above his head cast long shadows down his face. He didn't say anything, and I didn't like the way he was looking at me. Why was he the one asking all the questions? Was he in charge?

As his gaze lingered I felt my face begin to flush. I had to fight to keep from squirming. I had to come across as a silly stupid girl who had gotten lost—I had to seem like someone who was mostly innocent and therefore only a bit frightened, not guilty and therefore utterly terrified.

The warden tapped the end of his pen against the table a few times. "Why were you out after curfew?"

I blinked innocently at him; I was pretty good at blinking innocently. "Because I got lost," I said.

He didn't write that down. He reached in his pocket for a battered pack of cigarettes, lit one, and then settled back and stared at me again. His eyes were a pale blue, his expression flat, but that wasn't what made my throat go suddenly dry. There weren't many cigarettes left on the island and I happened to know, thanks once again to Cynda, that the wardens saved them for important occasions. To mark a particularly lucrative deal with some hapless person vulnerable to blackmail or other coercion. To celebrate some especially pleasurable arrest.

But I was nobody. I was just some girl who got lost. There was no reason for him to celebrate arresting me.

The warden smoked, staring at me with his flat eyes. Clearly he was going to sit there until I said more, but I wasn't going to say more, not until he made me. People talked too much, Cynda said. They got tangled up and gave themselves away. It was better to be as brief as possible—that way you had fewer lies to remember.

It was hard, though, to sit quietly with the wardens staring at me. The cigarette smoke tickled in my throat, made me need to cough. I managed to swallow instead. To keep myself from talking I began to count silently to myself. When I was somewhere past five hundred and thirty, the warden leaned forward and tapped out his cigarette on the tabletop, making a pile of gray ash. He carefully tucked the half-smoked cigarette into his shirt pocket and leaned back in his chair again.

"Why were you out after curfew?" he said again, exactly as he'd said it before.

This time I gave a small embarrassed shrug. "I couldn't sleep, and so I went outside to get some fresh air, and then I got lost."

He made a circling gesture with one finger. *Keep talking.*

"I couldn't sleep because of the thunderstorm," I said.

The warden scowled, but I was mindful of Cynda's warning—keep lies simple—and anyway I couldn't think of anything else credible to add. Should I say I'd gotten lost while trying to pet one of the stray cats that roamed the city? No, that was too childish sounding. It might work for the older warden, but not the scarred one. He wasn't looking at me as if he thought of me as a child.

Then it hit me. "The thunderstorm kept me awake, and then I couldn't stop thinking about the city meeting tomorrow."

That got a reaction. The scarred warden didn't say anything, but he glanced at the older warden. Did they know what the city meeting was about? None of the rest of us knew. We just knew it was bound to be bad.

The scarred warden wrote something on his paper. Then he looked up at me again. "Go on."

"I know I shouldn't have done it," I said, glancing apologetically at the older warden. "But I was scared. I *am* scared. The city meeting scares me."

"Look at me," the scarred warden said. "Not him."

I did, squinting against the light. "I was sitting on the dorm steps and I kept thinking about going to the circle tomorrow for the city meeting and about how I didn't want to go. I wanted to be somewhere else. So I sort of started walking in the other direction."

From the corner of my eye I could see that the older warden was nodding. "Toward the orchard," he said.

"Toward the orchard. And I went through the orchard, and then I sort of kept walking until I got to the gap in the wall. And then— " I took a deep breath, considered what I was about to say, and decided to risk it—"I sort of went across the wasteland to the edge of the woods."

Neither warden moved, but the room felt suddenly different. My breathing seemed too loud.

There was no rule against going to the woods—there didn't need to be—so I hadn't gotten myself deeper into trouble. With luck, I was distracting the wardens from what

I'd actually done. With even more luck, I might manage to get some precious information out of them. I'd never before had a chance to talk to wardens about the woods.

"Don't you know what lives out there?" the scarred warden said. I couldn't read his expression.

"Wild animals," I said. "Wolves and stuff."

"And stuff." He smiled without humor. "You're meant to know the stories."

"I do," I said. "But sometimes I wonder if that's all they are. You know—just stories."

The warden stared at me for a long moment, not blinking. "And what would be the point of *just stories*?" he said, his voice hard.

I chose my words carefully. "It's hard to get everything done," I said. "We don't have enough people who are strong and healthy. And if the woods were safe, we might lose good workers. Some might leave the city. They might even try to find a way off the island."

The warden crossed his arms over his chest, tipped his chair back. "So you think the city commissioners lie to keep people in the city. You're calling the commissioners liars."

"No! Not lies—just stories, for the kids, when we're little. I only wonder sometimes, because nobody I know has actually seen anyone out there. In the woods, I mean. No one has seen anyone in the woods."

I was babbling. I should never have broached the topic—but now that I had, I'd have to see it out. "I'm not saying the Watchers are liars."

"*City commissioners*," the warden corrected. "It's rude to call them Watchers."

Then he gave a humorless snort that might have been laughter, and set his chair down with a thud. "Sounds like you need a bit of review. Start with Wes. You remember what happened to Wes?"

"He gathered firewood too far north. Too near the wilderland."

"And?"

Maybe it was only a story. Still, I didn't like to say it out loud. "They sent out a search party and found him dead," I said, as evenly as I could manage. "He'd been skinned like a rabbit."

Somewhere down the hall a door shut with a clang. From the corner of my eye I saw the older warden turn toward the sound, but the scarred warden kept his gaze on me. "Now do Rosella," he said.

Rosella wasn't as hard to talk about. In fact, she was something of an inspiration to me.

"Rosella didn't like the breeding partner she was assigned," I said. "She ran away to the woods in protest."

"And what became of her?"

"She was gone for a couple of months. When she came back, she said there were things in the woods that were terrifying and beautiful, all light and shadow. Not entirely human. She went around warning people to stay in the city, away from them."

The warden nodded. "Exactly."

He seemed calm enough, so I decided to push my point. "But she came back crazy," I said.

"As a bedbug," he agreed.

"So she didn't know what she was saying. She could have been repeating childhood stories she'd been told. She might not have seen anything at all out in the woods."

I desperately wanted to believe there wasn't anything to fear out there. Sure, I'd been terrified of the woods when I was younger. I'd thought of the gaps in the walls as gaping mouths that would devour me if I wandered too close.

But now ... I wanted to believe there was a place we could go, Meritt and I, to escape from the eyes all around us.

We'd never talked about it, but I wanted to hope that when the time came for him to be assigned a breeding partner, we'd run away, go live in the woods and become part of the legends, the victims in horror stories designed to keep everyone under control, but really we'd be safe. We'd be free. We'd be the ones who got away.

"Poor lovely Rosella," the balding warden said sadly. "She was a friend of mine, once upon a time."

I turned to look at him, the metal chair creaking ominously as I moved. "You actually knew her?" She had died a long time ago.

He nodded. "I knew her," he said, running a hand over his short beard. He was watching me closely, his face weary. "The Guardians haven't been as active lately," he said. "There's a reason for that. People my age—Rosella's age—learned not to cross them. You young ones ought to learn from our mistakes. Don't think the woods are safe just because you don't personally know anyone who ran into trouble out there."

The scarred warden snorted. "*Out there*. You don't have to go into the woods to run into the Guardians. Hey—turn around. Look at me."

I did as he said.

"You're old enough to remember Chet, aren't you?"

I did remember Chet. I'd only been eight or nine when he died, but I remembered him because he had bullied some of the older children who let me tag along after them. Once he'd locked Cline in the dark food preservation cellar for fourteen hours, and another time, he'd stolen Meritt's shoes. Meritt got put in isolation for two days for not keeping up with his belongings.

There were other incidents, too, and one morning the butchers found Chet hanging from his feet in the slaughterhouse in a row of cattle carcasses. He was fifteen.

"Anyone could have done that," I said diffidently. "Chet wasn't well liked."

"He wasn't well-liked by the Guardians, that's for sure." The scarred warden's expression turned smug. "You want to know how I know it was them?"

Reluctantly, I nodded.

"I saw them come in at the northwest gap just before dark that night. Two of them."

I leaned forward. "What did they look?" I said. "Regular people?"

For a moment I thought he was going to refuse to tell me, but apparently the desire to show off won out. "Could be, but I doubt it," he said. "They were bigger than normal. Faster, too. I lost them in the blackberry fields, and I don't lose *regular* people."

Behind me the other warden shifted. "First I've heard of this," he said mildly. "Did you report it?"

"Sure. Got told to keep my head down and my mouth shut. Come daylight, the kid was dead. Come evening, I'd been made a warden."

His pale eyes glinted as he turned back to me. "So like I said, you'd best be careful, wandering around at night, talking as if the commissioners are liars. The *Watchers*."

The shiver that ran through me wasn't faked.

The scarred warden smiled. "Where did you get lost?"

The change in subject threw me off balance.

"I . . . I got turned around in the orchard," I said after a moment. "I came out of it where I wasn't expecting to be. Somewhere in the adult housing section. And then I knew it was getting close to curfew, and so I ran, and I saw some old men and tried to ask where I was but they were drunk and threw a bottle at me. Then I found you."

He was watching me with a funny gleam in his eye. I didn't know why. Everything I'd said made perfect sense, I

23

thought. The orchard was confusing, row upon row of ancient twisted apple trees, no landmarks to keep things straight. Someone could easily get lost in there. Sure, it was well past curfew, but I could easily have lost track of time when I was lost. And I'd nicely accounted for the old men seeing me.

The scarred warden tipped back in his chair, rocked gently on the back legs.

"Lost in the adult housing section," he said, and smiled as if he knew a secret joke.

Behind me, the older warden got up without a word and left the room.

Chapter 3

The scarred warden pulled out his cigarette and lit it again. He didn't say anything; he only smoked, and watched me, and rocked his chair, and tapped ash off onto the metal table, and smoked some more.

Again the smoke scratched at my throat. The room grew full of hazy gray curls that were thickest up by the ceiling, moving like living things groping blindly for a way out. There was a narrow window high up on the wall, but it was shut.

Except for that window, and the door, the gray cinderblock walls were bare and uniform all about. There wasn't anything for me to look at, and I didn't want to stare at the warden staring at me.

How would the pretend me act? Some girl who was telling the truth but couldn't help but be a little nervous that she was in the prison—what would she do?

She'd fidget. Just a little.

That was easy enough. I busied myself combing my tangled hair with my fingers, working through the knots the wind had made. I worked at it for three minutes, four, maybe longer. It felt like a long time.

"We're told to watch you," the scarred warden said suddenly, setting his chair down hard. "But we didn't need telling. That hair makes us watch."

His voice dropped to a raspy whisper. "I bet you like that."

Was he crazy? I didn't want to be watched. No one did. Nothing good ever came of attracting attention, so we all tried to make ourselves as inconspicuous as possible.

"No," the warden said. He got up and came around the table to stand over me. "Stop looking at the door. Look at me."

He was so close I had to crane my neck back to see his face. The light behind his head cast a halo. When he shifted I was blinded by the glare.

"That hair," he said. "You're a freak. You know that?"

I nodded. I knew.

He shifted and blocked the light, and the room seemed dark because my eyes hadn't adjusted, and just as they did he shifted again and blinded me again. He could give me a headache, doing this.

This time when my eyes adjusted he was examining me like a bug under a microscope. I didn't know where to look and kept focusing on the scar cutting through his upper lip, puckered and mean.

After a moment he leaned a hip against the table, smoking, gazing down at me, getting too comfortable and still standing too close, looming over me. I was small, like he'd said—just over five feet tall—and I was sitting and he was standing, and he reminded me of the bulls in the cattle yard, the heavily muscled shoulders, the flat bull-like eyes.

I wanted the other warden to come back. I didn't want to be alone with this one. He scared me—but I shouldn't let him know that. Rafe said that some animals could smell fear, that it told them you were prey. He said some animals waited to see if you'd run from them, and if you ran they knew you were prey and then they'd chase you.

I couldn't be prey. I had to stand my ground, had to be

calm, had to push back—not hard enough to get slapped down, just hard enough to not get eaten alive.

So I did the only calming thing I could think to do; I started braiding my hair. I combed it with my fingers and divided it into three bunches, and I wove them together tightly and neatly. The warden stood there—too close—watching me, smoking his celebratory cigarette, looming over me, but he didn't order me to look at him. He let me braid my hair, and the familiar motions steadied me. I wasn't prey. I was an unfortunate girl who had gotten lost, and who soon would go home to her dorm.

"I checked to see who your parents were."

Surprised, I almost dropped the braid.

The warden cocked his head, blew smoke out of pursed lips. "I searched the records. You want me to tell you what I found?"

I knew he wouldn't. But of course I wanted to know— we all wanted to know. Some people could guess, could match features and coloring and hope that they were looking at an older sibling, an aunt or an uncle, maybe even a parent. Not me. I'd never seen anyone who looked remotely like me.

"Do you want me to tell you?" the warden said again. He was toying with me, but all the same I had to answer.

"Yes," I said. "I would love for you to tell me."

The warden dropped the nub of cigarette on the floor, ground it out, and crossed his arms over his chest. "I can't."

Wouldn't, he meant. No surprise there. I fished a piece of string out of my pocket and tied the end of my braid.

"I can't tell you who your parents are," he repeated. "Even the genetic counselors can't tell you. You know why that is?"

"Because they're not allowed."

"Wrong." He smirked at me. "They can't tell you because they don't know."

He was trying to get a rise out me, trying to unsettle me, but he failed because I knew for a fact he was lying. The genetic counselors knew everything about our genetic backgrounds. That was their job, and it was an important one because on a small island like this, we had to be careful. Inbreeding could weaken us; an unfortunate convergence of genetic flaws could destroy us.

So the genetic counselors knew lineage. They knew that and much, much more—predisposition to hereditary diseases, presence or absence of various genetic markers, everything. One of the genetic counselors, Roy, had explained it all to Meritt once. It was amazing, what they could know about us from their records and our blood samples.

So I wasn't impressed by this attempt to unnerve me. In fact it made me feel calmer, to think that this was the best the scarred warden could do. Pointedly I studied my fingernails, my expression bored. I was not prey; I was a tired bored girl, waiting to be allowed to go home.

"You don't know who my parents are," I said. "That doesn't mean the genetic counselors don't know."

Slowly, mockingly, the Warden shook his head. "There's no record of anyone with your color hair—ever—and there's *no record of your birth.*"

My mouth went suddenly dry.

The warden smiled at me. It was not a pleasant smile. "That got your attention," he said. "And yeah, you heard me right. There is no record of your birth. You aren't in the books. Officially, as far as the genetic records go, you don't exist."

How could I not be in the books?

They were comprehensive, exhaustively comprehensive. This made no sense. Maybe he was lying, searching for a new way to frighten me.

"I didn't know why you weren't in the records," the

warden said. He pushed away from the table and walked a few steps, turned around, walked back. "I've been wondering about that. But now I get it. Something's wrong with you, right? The time of the ashes, all that black soot—it killed the normal ones, but not you. You're a mutant. A runt with freaky hair. But you were all we had, right? So the genetic counselors couldn't euthanize you."

I was staring at him now, horribly fascinated. I wanted to believe he was lying to me, but I just wasn't sure. If he was lying, he sure was caught up in the lie.

"For all the genetic counselors knew, you were all we were ever going to get," he said. "For all they knew, you could have been the last baby ever born. For all they knew, you were the one whose mutation made you immune to the ashes, whose blood could save the rest of us. So they had to keep you. We were in a fertility crisis. They couldn't risk eliminating the newest breeder, especially a breeder who had survived the ashes."

He stopped pacing and looked at me as if to assess my interest. He had my complete attention, and I couldn't pretend otherwise.

"So they had to keep you," he said, and now he was looking pleased with himself. "They had to keep you, but at the same time, they didn't want to be blamed for however you turned out. Because who could say what sort of mutant you would turn into as you developed, right? So they had to keep you, but you were also a big risk. And no one wanted to be on record as okaying your existence. No one wanted to be on record as planning you or keeping you."

He stood right in front of me, looking down at me, his hands on his hips.

"So they didn't write you down. And they keep a close watch on you, just in case. Because who knows what the mutant will do? Who knows what the mutant will become?"

He wasn't lying—at least he seemed to think he was telling the truth, was congratulating himself for sorting all this out. But he could be wrong.

I risked a question of my own. "But the wardens don't watch me more than they watch other people, do they?"

I made a gesture indicating that I meant all the wardens, not just him in particular, because he obviously had been watching me especially. He had been asking questions about me, checking the records, thinking about me. It made my skin crawl.

"There are cameras everywhere," I said. "Everyone is watched. It's not just me."

He gave a short humorless bark of laughter. "Everyone's watched, sure. But not like you. Where you go, who you talk to, what you say, what you do. Your birth isn't in the books, but all your days are written in them."

Maybe he was making that up—psychological torture, that sort of thing. I looked at him, trying to decide whether he was lying or telling the truth, and I saw that he was thinking about something else, that something new was flickering in his flat eyes.

"What is it?" I said warily.

"You're an unrecorded mutant, but they didn't rule you out of the breeding program."

"So I must be a harmless mutation." I tried to sound casual and unconcerned, but I managed only to sound breathless. I certainly couldn't look at him any longer.

Trying to act nonchalant, I straightened the hem of my shirt, fastened a button that had come undone on one wrist.

From the corner of my eye I could see that the warden was still watching me.

He uncrossed his arms and shifted closer still, standing right up against me. His black pants brushed my arm.

I kept my eyes straight ahead, facing the empty chair

across the table from me, trying to keep my breathing slow and easy.

"You realize that you're in over your head," he said softly. "Things are happening that you don't know about. Tonight was a bad night to be out after curfew."

He liked scaring me, and I was scared, and I couldn't fake not being scared, not anymore.

"Prison's not easy," he said. "The wardens sometimes forget you're there until you die and start to stink. Other times, you wish they had forgotten you. Does that scare you?"

I nodded.

"Good."

He bent over and looked me straight in the eye. I could smell the tobacco on his breath.

"I can keep you safe," he said softly. "I can keep them from forgetting you. Or remembering you. But you'll have to make it worth my while."

My throat closed up.

"I could even cut you loose tonight," he said. "Lose the paperwork. Make this end right here. But you'll have to give me something in return."

I tried to speak, had to stop and swallow. "I don't have anything to give you," I said, and I didn't—none of us had personal belongings. At least we weren't supposed to.

The warden reached out and moved my braid, circling my neck with his hand. It felt hot and damp against my skin.

"You have a lunch break," he said, pressing his thumb into the hollow at the front of my throat. "I can feel your pulse. I can stop your pulse, if I want to. Or, at noon tomorrow—"

The door opened with a bang. I almost jumped out of my skin. At the same instant the scarred warden straightened up and stepped away from me. He drifted casually across the room as the bald warden came in and set a white ceramic mug on the table in front of me.

"Warm milk with honey," the bald warden said, sitting down behind the table.

Then he spoke to the scarred warden. "We can't take her back yet. There's been another disturbance."

The scarred warden didn't answer, and the older warden looked from him to me, then back again.

"There a problem?" he said.

The scarred warden shook his head. His expression was closed off, remote.

"It's going to be awhile," the older warden said. "E's locked down."

Area E. The boys' dormitories. Meritt's section.

The older warden nudged the warm milk closer to me, nodded that I should drink the milk.

Though my throat felt tight with anxiety, I managed. The scarred warden leaned against a wall and watched me. The bald warden watched him.

"One of us had better get back on patrol," the bald warden said.

I didn't want to be left alone with the warden who wanted me to go somewhere, do something, at noon tomorrow. All I wanted to do at noon tomorrow was eat lunch.

After a moment the scarred warden spoke. "Children's dormitories are next," he said. "You can do them, Karl. Visit awhile with Nancy if you like. I'll hang around and keep an eye on this one."

Warden Karl seemed to consider, stroking his short beard. Finally he answered the other warden. "Nah," he said, "Not this time. My knees hurt. It's this weather. Old bones."

The scarred warden didn't answer.

"Go on," Warden Karl said, and now I heard from his tone that he was the one in charge.

The scarred warden gave a curt nod and pushed away from the wall. At the door he paused.

"Hey freak," he said, and waited until I turned. He pointed two fingers at his own eyes, and then at me.

"I'll be seeing you," he said.

Chapter 4

Afterwards, that night grew increasingly surreal. Partly it was my own exhaustion and fear, but partly it was the bald warden's doing.

"Come on," he said, once the scarred warden had departed. Then without another word he led me out the door and down the long grim hallway.

What lay behind the closed and bolted doors? I listened hard as we walked, hoping to hear Rafe's voice. Surely he must be here by now, somewhere here in the prison with me. I thought I might hear someone questioning him as I'd been questioned, but I heard only the click of the warden's heels on the tile floor. My own bare feet were silent.

At the far end of the hall we arrived at a door that led into a stairwell.

"Hope you like to climb," Warden Karl said. "Don't get dizzy."

The metal grillwork stairs curved in a spiral, going up and up. I put one hand on the cinderblock wall to keep my balance. Through little slit-like windows I caught glimpses of the moon, the night sky. The stairwell was colder than the rest of the building, and the damp cut to my bones; the metal stairs creaked, sometimes alarmingly.

Our footsteps echoed, trailing behind us, tracing our

progress. Finally we reached the top. Warden Karl pushed through a door and then we were there, in the highest room of the watchtower. The Opticon.

The circular room had a table, a few comfortable-looking chairs, and telescopes spaced at regular intervals around the windows. In the middle of the room stood a desk with a row of twelve screens that cycled from one scene to another. Views from the cameras. The ones that Meritt hadn't disabled.

One of the screens was showing the cafeteria, empty. Another was on the city circle, also empty. There was the children's dormitory, with rows of cribs and cots and sleeping children. There was one of the boys' dormitories, and the boys were moving about, climbing into their bunks, talking. I wondered whether this dorm had been the source of the disturbance, and whether it was Meritt's, but the screen changed before I could focus on any faces.

A warden wearing earphones sat in front of these screens, glancing at them occasionally, adjusting a dial, but mostly sipping something and playing cards. Solitaire. He looked over at us and slipped his earphones off.

"Hey, Zee," Warden Karl said. "Picked up a curfew-breaker. Gotta keep her here 'til the all clear. You want to get some air, I'll cover for you."

The dubious expression on Zee's face said this wasn't protocol, but he stood up and stretched. "Great," he said.

From then on I would picture that warden, that particular man, any time I saw the signs screwed into the walls beneath the cameras, the signs that said, "We Watch Because We Care."

Zee pushed open the door and left. Maybe I should have been alarmed; Warden Karl could have been up to something, could have been setting me up for more trouble.

But it was hard to think about that at the moment. I was

actually in the Opticon. Meritt was the only living person I knew, besides the wardens, who was allowed up there, and that was only because he was the one who maintained the delicate surveillance equipment now that Lonna was dead. So I couldn't worry about why I was there; I was too amazed that I was.

Warden Karl gave a short laugh. "Have you taken root?" he said.

So I went and stood near the center of the room and, there, turned slowly in a circle. I was in the middle of a circular tower in the middle of a circular city in the middle of the only land in the world, for all we knew—our circular island. This was almost worth getting arrested.

From the base of the watchtower the streets stretched out like the spokes of a wheel, lit with blue streetlights. Smaller cross streets ringed us in blue concentric circles. It was beautiful.

I'd always known Optica was carefully organized, but seeing it like this—from a bird's eye view—emphasized the precision of its design.

From somewhere beneath my feet the bright white spotlights stretched out, pointing long white fingers toward the edges of the city, probing, then moving on. Here and there pairs of tiny yellow eyes—headlights—moved along a blue line. Patrol cars, same as the one that had caught me. There were some small white lights to the south, in the area of the adult houses, but mostly the city lay wrapped in darkness.

I squinted in the direction of the homes, toward the lights that had nothing to do with surveillance. At this late hour, someone ill, I thought, or suffering from insomnia. Old men playing cards and drinking apple whiskey.

A sudden noise made me jump—Warden Karl had turned the sound up at the monitors. I heard a baby crying, and then several men talking urgently, their voices loud but indistinguishable. The warden didn't seem interested in my movements, so I went to the windows and walked all the way around the watchtower, beginning with the western side.

There were the children's dormitories, the girls' dormitories, the school, the infirmary, the cafeteria. If I squinted in the dim light I could make out the beekeeper's domain and the orchards, past the cannery and the other buildings. Most of my life had been spent in this quarter of the city.

Moving counter-clockwise along the windows, I came to the south quarter—the laundry, the genetic counseling building, the research center, the adult quarters with hundreds of houses, tiny but far more private than the dormitories.

Only the street that ran due south from the tower had a corresponding wall, which is why Meritt and I usually went that way on our runs; the wall gave us a little protection from the watchful eyes of the wardens. Sometimes we ventured through the other streets, but only on moonless nights, and only when we were feeling especially brave. On those other streets, we were completely exposed.

Beyond the lights of the adult houses, the outer city wall circled darkly around, its geometric precision contrasting with the pale moonlit wasteland of scraggly grass where Rafe had been arrested. Beyond the wasteland lay the dark ominous woods, and beyond them lay the rumor of the sea. In the farthest distance I thought I could see it shining in the moonlight, moving like a living thing.

At least I wanted it to be the sea, rolling and dancing; perhaps it was only a low lying cloud catching the moonlight. I had dreamed of the sea often but had never seen it. It was freedom, I thought. It went on so far and so wide that no one could monitor it, no one could watch every wave. It was too big even for the Watchers.

I looked back at the warden. He was still standing at the

row of monitors, watching images flash across the screens. Someone laughed loudly, without humor.

I continued my circuit, moving around to the east side of the tower. This quarter of the city was where the boys' dormitories were, and past them the industry buildings, the cattle pastures and, against the city wall, the slaughterhouse. If you walked out of the city from that direction, through the wasteland, through the dangerous woods, you reached the sea and the tidal traps and the docks where the fishermen cleaned their catches.

Supposedly the woods were somewhat safer in the east, at least in the morning when the sun was rising. Still, even there, no one went alone, no one left the path unless absolutely necessary, and no one lingered.

Then I reached the north. The clear swath of my fields spread across the middle distance. At the top of the fields lay the dark bulk of the city commissioners' compound, separated from the rest of the city by wheat, corn, the kitchen gardens, the berry fields.

I touched one of the telescopes and looked back at the warden. He was watching me now, his expression impenetrable, but he nodded permission.

I looked through the lens and saw, straight below me, the pale arc of the city circle. Two wardens stood midway up the terraced steps; I could see the color of their hair, the way one rested his hand on his belt, on his stunner. I moved my face away from the telescope and the wardens became ants, tiny dark flecks.

A chill ran up my spine. Was this how the Watchers saw us?

Tomorrow night I'd be standing down there in the circle, at my first city meeting. We hadn't had one in years—never in my lifetime. At the last one, so the older people said, the city commissioners made everyone stand on the circle steps all night long, for more than twelve hours, not letting anyone take shelter when it began to rain, not letting anyone so much as sit down, until dawn finally broke and the first rays of sun touched the watchtower and it was time to start the day's work.

It was to remind us to pay attention, the commissioners said; the boiler in the Watcher compound hadn't been properly maintained, and a pipe had exploded and badly burned someone—I didn't know who—with scalding steam.

As far as I knew, nothing had gone wrong in the Watcher compound recently. But that didn't mean the commissioners weren't angry about something.

I tilted the telescope up and the Watcher compound jumped into clarity. The buildings were cinderblock, like all the other buildings in Optica, but more elaborately built, with ridges and ledges, and arches above the door. It looked like the compound had only small high windows, but I couldn't tell for certain because there was a three-quarters-height privacy wall in front. I could understand the desire for privacy, but I wouldn't want to live in a grim dark fortress.

Behind the Watcher compound I could see the city wall, smooth and unbroken, and then the tops of the trees in the wilderland, supposedly the most dangerous part of all the woods. The Guardians might roam in other parts of the woods, the stories said, but this was where they lived.

Wait. That was odd.

Maybe I wasn't seeing what I thought I saw. It was quite far away, even with the telescope. I blinked hard, clearing my vision, and put my eye to the telescope again.

How strange.

In the rest of the city, all the streets that ran like spokes from the watchtower to the outer wall ended in gaps that opened onto the wasteland and the woods beyond. Those gaps came at precisely regular intervals—east, southeast, south, southwest, west, northwest. I'd always assumed there was a gap at the north end, too, inside the Watcher compound. Optica was tightly regulated, geometrically precise. Of course there were eight gaps, not seven, one at each main point of the compass.

But it wasn't so. Through the telescope I could see that beyond the Watchers' compound, there was no gap. There the wall was sealed, complete.

Behind me the warden cleared his throat.

"That's enough," he said, and in his voice was a warning. "Time to go."

I'd been staring too long at the Watchers.

Chapter 5

Someone grabbed my foot and shook it.

I sat up, blinking hard, feeling like I'd forgotten something urgent. Bright morning light filtered in through the high windows. I'd overslept, seriously overslept. All of the girls who worked days were already gone, and the only people in view were night workers—cleaning and kitchen workers already in bed, covers pulled up over their heads, relief workers trailing out of the showers carrying their special bags of cleansers and antibiotics, looking sleepy.

That included Cynda, who was standing at the foot of my bunk, toweling dry her honey-colored hair. "This is the second time I've woken you," she said. "I thought you were awake the first time, so I went and showered. Now you've missed breakfast, and you're about to be late to work."

Not good. Being late to work was never good, but it was especially bad now that getting reported to the wardens might mean a private visit with the scarred one.

I slid down off the top bunk, leaving it a jumble of covers—Kari's bunk below was neatly made, as always—and started for the door.

"Not like that!" Cynda said. "You look like you were up all night."

Point taken; I was undressed and to the shower room

before Cynda had finished. I couldn't risk questions or comments, not when it might make my less friendly roommates decide to lie awake and catch me sneaking in or sneaking out.

Did Cynda actually know I'd been up, or was she just talking off the top of her head? I wasn't sure. I wasn't ever sure, and it wasn't as if I could ask her.

The cold water hit me with a jolt and I shampooed and scrubbed frenetically, rinsed, toweled, and hurried back to my bunk to fish my one set of extra clothes out from under the bottom bed. I was starving, and doomed to a long ravenous morning.

Worse, I'd missed my best shot at getting information about Meritt. Almost everything useful I'd ever learned came from sitting on the edge of my bed looking sleepy and uninterested while the night workers traded gossip about conversations they'd had with various wardens the night before.

I tugged my clothes on over still-damp skin, felt a trickle of water running down my neck, and squeezed my wet hair out over the floor. Cynda—sitting on her bunk pinning her hair so it would make ringlets when it dried—raised an eyebrow. "You'd better be glad Wanda's not here," she said.

Wanda watched avidly for any excuse to report anyone—especially me—to the dorm mother. She wasn't the only one who disliked me, or the only one who tried to curry favor by tattling, but of the twenty-three girls I shared a room with, she was the one who worried me most. If she ever caught me sneaking in or out at night, there would be no discussion, no chance for persuasion or bribery. She'd turn me over to the wardens in a heartbeat.

"Sorry," I said to Cynda, mopping the floor hurriedly with my dirty shirt. Kicking it under the bed, I started for the door.

"You'll never get your hair untangled if you let it dry like that," Cynda said. "Catch."

I turned and she tossed me her comb. It was carved wood, very pretty, and had all its teeth.

"Don't lose it," she said. "It was a gift. I'll be in trouble if I can't produce it next time he comes by."

I took off down the hallway at a jog, trying to comb my hair as I went. I didn't care about tangles—not today—but if the dorm mother saw me looking disheveled, she'd send me straight back to the room, and then I'd be later still.

I hurried down the inside stairs, pushed through the outside door and into the cool morning air, and started down the exterior stairs, yanking the comb through my hair and trying not to lose my balance.

I was almost at the bottom when Estelle rounded the corner. She was one of my old people—that was what I called the handful of elderly people who had been kind to me when I was a lonely little girl, ignored or taunted by the older children.

"There you are!" she said. "I was worried when you didn't come to breakfast." Until she got too old, Estelle had been a cook, and she still kept an eye on everything in the cafeteria.

"I overslept." I was out of breath and the words came out wispily.

Estelle shook her head in disapproval. "You young ones shouldn't have to choose between food and sleep. You're growing so fast, you need plenty of both."

Plenty of both. Now there was a joke. Portion size was based on consumer size—you had to grow on what they gave you before they gave you anything to grow on—so people with fast metabolisms were at a disadvantage.

"I have to go," I said as I reached the sidewalk. "I'm going to be late to work."

"Go on, then," Estelle said, making a comfortable shooing motion. "Have a pleasant day."

Tucking Cynda's comb into my shirt pocket, I took off at a hard run.

At the corner I glanced back. Estelle was standing where I'd left her. She waved merrily, but with her other hand she was tugging at the threadbare collar of her shirt, trying to cover her throat.

That worried me—she was cold, and winter wasn't here yet. The breeze was crisp but not unpleasant, not even for me with my wet hair and bare feet.

There was nothing I could do for her, though, so I put her out of my mind and kept running. It was hard to run hungry, and I knew running would make me hungrier still, but I didn't want to be late. If the warden watching the cameras didn't notice my tardiness, any number of field workers would be happy to report me.

I reached the street that led to my fields and then had to pause to keep from getting run over by a big work truck rumbling past, its loose tailgate rattling. Four or five mechanics were sitting in the back.

If I'd thought of it in time I could have waved the driver down and maybe, if he was feeling magnanimous, hitched a ride. Now all I could do was keep running down the road behind the truck, breathing its dust, feeling faint with hunger and fear of being late, while the guys in the truck bed watched me with varying degrees of indifference and mockery.

One of them—Farrell Dean, a friend of Meritt's and by extension a friend of mine—dangled a hand casually over the side. He was holding a wrench, and when the truck hit a rough spot he dropped it. He stood up, unsteady in the rocking truck bed, and banged on the top of the cab.

The driver didn't stop, but he slowed considerably. Farrell Dean jumped out and jogged back to pick up the fallen tool.

"Better hurry," he said, snatching up the wrench and turning back. The truck was still cruising slowly along, but when he climbed back in it would take off.

I was faster than Farrell Dean, though, or at least more motivated, so I put on a burst of speed and had almost caught up to him when he grabbed the tailgate and swung himself back in.

Instantly the truck sped up. I gave it everything I had, running all out, as the men in the truck bed shouted at me, some encouraging, some jeering.

Just when I was about to give up hope, Farrell Dean stuck out a hand. I grabbed it and my shoulder jerked and my feet left the ground, and then he pulled me up and my feet found the bumper.

I clung there, panting hard, holding on to the tailgate that was already warm with the morning sun, and the men clapped and hooted and booed, and Farrell Dean kept a steadying hand on my arm.

"Throw her back!" one of them advised.

"No way," another said. "She's a field worker. We need all of those we can get."

Then the truck passed a tractor shed, where two men were arguing and waving shovels around threateningly, and the men lost interest in me.

I leaned in close to Farrell Dean and caught a faint whiff of motor oil, which probably meant he'd done someone a favor and repaired a machine before working hours. "Have you seen Meritt this morning?" I said.

He shook his head. "Not since last night. He's in isolation."

That was a relief. It meant that Meritt had made it safely back to the dorm, and isolation was small potatoes compared to prison.

I opened my mouth to ask more questions, but Farrell

Dean frowned warningly at me, jerking his head toward the other men. He was almost nineteen, like Meritt, but more solidly built and not quite as tall, with hazel eyes, a tan from working outside all summer, and a thick shock of short gold-brown hair. His fingernails were always black under the edges because he was a mechanic and no matter how much he scrubbed, he couldn't get them completely clean.

As we jolted along he shifted, leaning hard on the tailgate as if for balance, and in the process blocking me from the other men's view.

"Inside pocket," he muttered. "On your right."

Shielded by his body I reached into his jacket and found the pocket, and was rewarded with a good handful of peeled walnuts. I shoved a couple in my mouth and tucked the others into my own pocket, along with Cynda's comb, just managing not to fall off the bumper in the process. Throughout the whole operation Farrell Dean kept one hand on my left arm and the other braced on the tailgate, both in plain sight of the other mechanics.

"Thank you," I managed, mouth full. We weren't supposed to give other people our food, and we weren't supposed to carry food out of the cafeteria.

"You're welcome. Wouldn't want your tapeworm to starve."

Either Farrell Dean had a slower metabolism than most people, or he had a secret food supply, because he often slipped me bits and pieces. It was one of the things I liked best about him.

"Here's your stop," he said, letting go of my arm. "I'll be at your field this afternoon. One of the tractors has a bad ignition."

I dropped off the tailgate, stumbling but managing not to fall, and waved to Farrell Dean as the truck moved away.

This afternoon.

Until then, I'd have to wonder what had happened to land Meritt in isolation.

At least Meritt wasn't in prison, I thought, putting another lovely walnut in my mouth; but the comfort in that thought was fleeting.

Meritt wasn't in prison; but Rafe was.

Chapter 6

Under any other circumstances, I'd have thoroughly enjoyed that autumn day in the strawberry fields. In the agricultural fields the cameras were mounted high on poles, and had no microphones. That alone was always enough to make me glad I was an outdoor worker. And that day, outdoors was beautiful. The clouds had vanished and the sun, striking the wet dark furrows, raised up dancing curtains of mist. The air, sweetened by the night's rain, smelled fresh and hopeful, and as the morning wore on the sky turned a brilliant blue, so clear and cheerful I could almost believe winter would never come.

But despite the beautiful morning, I couldn't stop worrying. I found myself watching for the scarred warden's patrol car by mid-morning, and by the time the sun was almost overhead, I was a nervous wreck.

If I were just spreading straw like the rest of the field workers, being a wreck wouldn't have interfered particularly with my work. But the previous fall, after Mark lost his hand in a combine accident—he didn't let go of a corn stalk fast enough, and the roller that husks the corn grabbed his glove and yanked his hand in—they put me in charge, which meant I had the unenviable task of taking orders from my supervising farmer and trying to make the field workers carry them out. It was impossible, which was why I got stuck with it. Everyone older had some sort of pull with a warden or two, I supposed.

So there I was, trying not to worry about Rafe or think about whatever lunch plans the scarred warden had for me, while at the same time trying to get my field workers to do more than lean on their rakes and whine.

Felix and Billy kept bickering, Skye coughed like she was trying to bring up a lung, and blustery red-faced Garry, who didn't want to be field supervisor himself but who also didn't want to take orders from "some kid," kept haranguing her about spreading germs until she was in tears. Everyone else worked slowly until I turned my back, at which point they stopped for a water break, or to tie a shoe, or to whisper among themselves.

It was worse even than usual, and that was saying something. Maybe they were worried about the mysterious impending city meeting; or maybe, because I'd come so close to being late, they'd thought I wasn't coming at all, in which case they'd have napped on the straw bales until the farmer came by. I didn't really know what was wrong with them. But I did know that at this rate I was going to get chewed out by my farmer—a man I actually liked, but whose unyielding standards worried me, caught in the middle as I was.

Worse, we were never going to get the strawberries covered before the first frost, which meant a poor crop next season. And nobody but me seemed to care; nobody but me seemed to see the connection between working now, and eating later. Even Ezzie was only poking half-heartedly at the straw, singing softly to himself. He was another friend of Meritt's, so he usually took pity on me and helped me get at least some of the work done.

As I watched he stopped raking altogether, rubbing his neck and turning it this way and that.

"Pulled a muscle last night," he said conversationally. "Think I'd better take a little break."

I waved a hand, as if granting permission he hadn't requested, and turned to Skye, who was still coughing. She always coughed, and the dust from the straw was making her worse.

"You'd better go to the infirmary," I said.

Skye shook her head, too choked up to speak. Her eyes were watering and red-rimmed.

"She can't," Billy said, sounding smug. He didn't like Skye. "She's used up her quota for the year."

"Then go back to the storage shed and oil down the tools," I told her. "At least then you'll be out of this dust."

Garry threw down his rake. "That's not fair," he said, his red face turning redder. "The rest of us have to breathe it."

"Hey," Felix said. "What's he doing here?"

We all turned to look, and my heart stuttered with dread.

A patrol car was coming towards us, creeping slowly down the road like a predator stalking prey. Sunlight glinted off its shiny black metal. The patrol car's windows were tinted dark, but I knew who was inside.

My black cap was in my pocket but it wouldn't do any good, not now. He'd no doubt already seen me, and when he told me to get in the car, I'd have to do it. I couldn't run—there was no place to hide—and even if I did, Garry or Felix would be happy to grab me and win a few goodwill points with the warden.

The patrol car pulled up even with us and slowed to a stop. Through the dark glass I felt eyes fixed on me, and my back grew prickly with nervous sweat.

"Well, wonders never cease," Ezzie said, in a tone of pleased surprise. "Lunch is early today."

Sure enough, farther down the road a boxy white

cafeteria truck was trundling along. It stalled once, started up again, and finally pulled to a stop behind the patrol car, keeping a respectful distance. After a moment two workers got out and began opening the serving flap.

My team shifted, their indecision palpable; normally they'd all be rushing to get in line first, before supplies ran out, but the lurking menace of the patrol car kept them standing in place. The cafeteria truck's driver door opened and an older woman—Marta—got out. She turned to look at the patrol car, probably wondering whether it was all right to serve lunch.

And then the patrol car moved. It crawled forward a few feet, paused, then continued on, rolling past me and my group of workers, gathering speed as it left the fields and headed toward the denser city streets.

Relief made me almost lightheaded.

"Thought they were coming for you, didn't you?" Garry said, eyeing me. "What've you done this time?"

He didn't give me a chance to answer, even if I'd known what to say. He was already hurrying forward, elbowing people out of the way so he could be first in line.

Slowly, I followed, taking my usual place at the end, the rush of relief already dissipating. I was being watched; and if the scarred warden was determined to get hold of me, in time he would succeed.

Farrell Dean showed up just as I collected my lunch. Without speaking, he nodded toward the nearest tractor shed, and I headed over there, knowing he'd get his lunch and happen to wander my way as soon as he could do it casually.

Behind the tractor shed wasn't perfect. Someone could come around the corner at any moment and sit down with us, and in the distance I could see the farm workers for Area B harvesting butternut squash and pumpkins, gradually working my direction. But it was more inconspicuous than sitting on the edge of the straw trailer or trying to position ourselves between the clumps of folks scattered here and there in the field. It would also make it a little harder for the scarred warden to spot me, if he came back.

Farrell Dean came around the corner carrying his tray. He sat down in the thin line of shade behind the tractor shed, leaning against the rusted corrugated metal, and reached up to take my tray and set it down for me. I held my sandwich and stood a little away from him, in the sun. I didn't want to leave the warm sunshine, not with the gray days almost upon us.

"Meritt wasn't back by curfew," Farrell Dean said without preface, opening his sandwich and examining the small piece of meat inside. "So when the dorm father came in to do a bed check, Cline and I jumped him. Thought maybe we could confuse him enough that he wouldn't notice Meritt was missing."

It wasn't like they'd jumped an old man. The dorm father in E-1 was barely older than boys under him, was easygoing by nature, and had the tricky job of corralling the same boys he'd played with in school.

Farrell Dean looked up at me and smiled. "When the father started hollering Joe hollered back at him, and then someone jumped Joe and someone else jumped the father and we had a free-for-all going in a matter of seconds. Cline got his nose busted—it's swollen up like an eggplant, and about the same color—and Ezzie got caught in a headlock that just about decapitated him, and then some of us rushed the door and the father slammed his own hand in the door trying to keep us inside. Broke two fingers."

Farrell Dean looked a little too cheery as he described

his perspective on the night's events. I kicked at him, half meaning it, and he caught my ankle and nearly brought me down on top of him.

"Meritt had made it back to the courtyard by then," he went on, as if I hadn't almost crushed his lunch. "So he waded in with the rest of the guys and started swinging. Just in time, too, because that's when the wardens got there. They separated everybody and marched us all back inside, and the father randomly stuck some of us in isolation. He never realized Meritt had been gone."

I slid down onto the hard-packed dirt beside him, set my tray on my lap and, after a moment's reflection, scooted until we were shoulder to shoulder as a gesture of solidarity. I wasn't the only one who'd kept Meritt out of prison the night before. We ate a few bites in silence, and then I spoke. "Meritt and I went down through the south quarter last night. We were supposed to meet Instructor Rafe at the southwest gap."

Beside me Farrell Dean stiffened. "Supposed to?"

I told him what had happened, what I'd seen, but I stopped before my arrest, and I also left out the part where the female warden kissed Meritt—Farrell Dean would think the same thing I did, and then I'd have to argue against it, and it wasn't an image I wanted to hash over with him or anyone else.

When I finished, Farrell Dean shook his head. "Not good," he said. "Meritt—" He stopped.

"What?"

Farrell Dean was already thinking about something else. He scanned my face, no doubt noticing the dark circles under my eyes.

"After you saw Rafe get arrested, did you go straight home?"

Leave it to him—he'd phrased the question in a way that gave me no way out, unless I told a bare-faced lie.

"More or less," I said.

"Tell me more about the *less* part."

So I did, more or less. I left out the part about not being in the birth records—Farrell Dean was nice to me and I didn't want to give him any reason to ponder my freakiness. I also left out the scarred warden's threat or offer or whatever it was.

Farrell Dean listened to everything without asking any questions, and then turned away to set his tray on the ground. When he turned back around, his jaw was set.

"Meritt's going to be furious with you," he said. "I'm furious with you. I'm furious with Meritt, come to that. You shouldn't have been out there at all, much less turning yourself in to protect him."

I managed a shrug and took a bite of coleslaw.

"No, listen to me, Red." Farrell Dean took my chin in his hand and turned my face toward him. His fingers were warm but his eyes were cold and utterly serious. He'd never looked at me like that before. "This is not a game." His voice was hard.

I jerked my chin away. "I know it's not. I'm the one who saw Rafe get taken, remember? I'm the one who got arrested."

"Yeah, well, you don't know everything." He turned away from me and grabbed his sandwich. "Meritt treats you like a pet, takes you along for company or whatever, but he doesn't tell you everything. He's going to get you killed, fooling around like that."

I rolled my eyes, but his words stung. "How do you know what Meritt does or doesn't tell me?" I said.

He shrugged and stabbed at his coleslaw with his fork.

I was getting angry now, too angry to sit still. *Like a pet*? I slammed my tray on the ground and got to my feet.

"Exactly what deep dark secrets does Meritt tell you and not me?" I asked, making sure he heard the sarcasm.

"I don't care about Meritt's secrets," Farrell Dean said evenly. "Except when they're endangering somebody else."

I stared at him a moment. "You're bluffing," I said. "You don't know anything I don't know."

Farrell Dean shrugged again and took another bite of his sandwich.

I gave his boot a little kick. He ignored me, so I kicked him again, a little harder, this time on his leg. "Tell me." I'd lost a bit of self-assurance, and he could probably tell.

Farrell Dean chewed deliberately, swallowed. "I don't know anything you need to know," he said, and then took another bite.

But anything about Meritt was something I needed to know. All things Meritt were my concern, had been since I was little and got partnered with him at school. He could have confined himself to tutoring me in math, tolerating his chore, but he didn't. He liked me and he showed it—Meritt, respected by everyone, never mocked, never left out. He was the first person anywhere remotely close to my age who was willing to be my friend, and I was his friend too—I listened to his musings, his arguments, his jokes. I broke the rules and crept out at night because he asked me to, because we wanted to be together. It wasn't one-sided.

I certainly wasn't his *pet*.

"You're being a hypocrite," I said. "You don't have any right to criticize Meritt if you're keeping secrets, too. You're just like him."

Farrell Dean stopped eating and looked at me. "I am not."

"Yes, you are."

"Here's one big difference, Red: I don't lure you into dangerous situations."

"Nobody *lures* me anywhere," I said. "I do as I please. I'm not a child, you know."

Farrell Dean studied me, a faintly ironic expression crossing his face. "Yeah," he said. "I know."

He set his sandwich down and got to his feet, glancing as he did so at the B workers, closer now—not yet close enough to hear us, but close enough to see we were back here alone.

Farrell Dean wasn't as tall as Meritt but he was still nearly a foot taller than me, and when he took me by the shoulders and backed me against the wall, I could see nothing but him.

"Let go," I said, shrugging off his hands.

"If you want me to talk to you, be still and listen." He was showing the B workers what they expected to see, what they'd automatically ignore. We weren't supposed to indulge our personal preferences until we were past the breeding years and safely sterilized, but except for the wardens, most adults were willing to overlook a little handholding and so forth until we hit nineteen and got assigned. After that any unauthorized affection was a serious offense.

Farrell Dean put his hands on the wall behind me, one on either side of my head. He smelled like motor oil and sun, and was so close I could see the flecks of gold and green in his hazel eyes. "Why are we scarcely making it?" he said, speaking quietly and swiftly. "Why are you barefoot and practically starving?"

One of his hands dropped to my ribs, and I knew he could feel every one.

"I've been all over the city," he said. "I've made repairs in every area—agriculture, industry, medicine, food preservation, everywhere. And everywhere we're falling behind."

I was underwhelmed. "So we need to route a few more people into mechanics," I said, moving away from his hand, tipping my head back to put a little more distance between our faces. My hair snagged in a bolt on the metal wall behind me and two or three hairs came loose as I jerked my head, but enough stayed caught to imprison me.

"Here." Farrell Dean nudged my chin, turning me so he could get to the problem. "I don't mean the mechanics are behind. Everyone is."

"We always manage somehow."

"Yeah, but this year the storehouses are low," he said, and finished freeing me. "Lower than I've ever seen them."

That pulled me up short. It was late October—our stores should be at their peak. Of course, our fields hadn't had a great year. Spring had come late, and when it did come it was wet and cool.

Turning to face him, I searched his eyes, but I already knew he wasn't teasing; Farrell Dean wouldn't joke about this. A shiver ran through me as I imagined my usual hunger intensified.

"The Watchers will know what to do," I said.

Farrell Dean shrugged and began picking with great focus at the hairs I'd yanked out on the rusty bolt. I watched him, knowing he was avoiding my eyes.

"They'll know," I insisted. "The Watchers will do something."

"Maybe." He freed two or three long red hairs and wound them around his finger, while I kept up a waiting silence.

Finally he looked at me.

"We're running out of time," he said. "And the Watchers aren't making any suggestions. They're not listening to suggestions, either. A dozen different people have tried to get in to see them, and not one has even gotten past the door."

"The Watchers never let anyone in to see them," I said reasonably. "It's the rule. Nobody ever gets in to see the city commissioners."

"And in normal situations, fine. If it makes them happy

to act all mysterious, whatever. But this is not a normal situation."

A field worker gathering pumpkins shouted something to his fellow workers, and when Farrell Dean glanced over his shoulder I noticed the uncharacteristic tension in his jaw. He wasn't like this. He was always calm, always steady, always good humored, always understated.

Apparently the sight of the workers reminded him we were visible, because he turned back and braced his arms on either side of me again, and this time I stood still.

"The Watchers aren't just going to sit there and watch us starve," I said. "They must have some sort of plan."

"We'll see." He sounded as if he meant it.

"How? How will we see?"

He hesitated.

"It's Rafe," I said, and as I spoke I grew certain. "He's up to something."

Farrell Dean didn't answer, but he didn't have to. I knew I was right.

"I was there when they arrested him," I said, trying to ignore the cold finger of fear sliding down my spine. "What's going on?"

Farrell Dean shifted, but he didn't look away. "There's not much to tell. Not yet. We're still gathering information."

"*We* as in who? You and Rafe? And Meritt?" What he was saying finally hit me. "You're *spying* on the Watchers."

"Shhh." He threw me a warning look, glanced over his shoulder, then leaned in close. "Have you ever thought about how many products we have that we can't account for?" He spoke very quietly, his mouth against my ear. "Cigarettes, eyeglasses, pencils. How'd we get those? We don't mine graphite."

I had asked a nanny mother about this years ago, and the answer had seemed plausible enough at the time. The

Watchers knew how to manufacture each of those things, she'd said, but they had the city do so only in spurts, stockpiling enough for years and years, mothballing the tools until they were needed again.

Fleetingly I wondered why they hadn't kick-started the manufacture of cough medicine, given we were running short, but I was distracted by a sudden wave of guilt.

"Agriculture," I said. "We should have been working harder." It was my fault. We couldn't help the wet spring, but maybe we could have done more to make up the difference this summer.

"Yeah, you're a real slacker, Red." Farrell Dean pulled back a bit and looked at me. Though his tone was teasing, his eyes were grave. "The problem runs deeper than a bad season and your lazy workers."

"The time of the ashes?"

My supervising farmer liked to complain about how much worse the crops had been since the months of drifting ash. He thought it had messed up the soil pH, made it hard for the plants to take in nutrients.

Farrell Dean shrugged. "The time of the ashes put them out of their depth. That's how Rafe put it. They were fine as long as we could follow Plan A. Plan B—well, the Watchers don't seem to have one of those."

He was suggesting the unthinkable.

The city commissioners had always guided us—we knew no other way—and even if we did, how could we go against them? They had wardens, and stunners, and guns.

And—

"What about the Guardians?" I said.

Despite what the scarred warden had told me, I half-hoped Farrell Dean would tell me not to be silly, not to mistake bedtime bogeymen stories for reality. If he said it, I'd believe him. I'd trust him over the creepy warden any day.

But Farrell Dean nodded. "They're a problem," he said. "Still, we don't have a choice."

"This is crazy," I said, and sheltered there behind the tractor shed, blocked from view by Farrell Dean, I felt suddenly conspicuous. The Guardians—what if they could see and hear me, like the wardens but exponentially increased? I didn't want to go against the Watchers; I really didn't want to go against the Guardians.

"Surely we can hang on until spring." My voice sounded thin to my own ears.

Farrell Dean looked me straight in the eye. "We're starving," he said, and his voice was steady, which frightened me more than if he'd been dramatic. "If we don't take control away from the Watchers, some of us won't make it to spring."

Some of us. The wind rose and stirred my hair; the workers from B gathered gourds. The sky above was bright and blue, oblivious to the hungry winter that was coming.

When Farrell Dean stepped away from me, cold rushed in and settled right down into my bones.

Chapter 7

By suppertime the city's uneasiness was palpable. In the crowded cafeteria, anxiety rose around me like smoke, filling my lungs, choking me. Several times I heard "city meeting" and, once, "reprisals." The word lodged painfully in my mind, sharp and hard like a shard of glass. I looked up and down the tightly packed rows of Optica gray and couldn't see a single face that was smiling, a single person who didn't look worried or tense.

The line for food was still quite long, so I went to stand by the conveyor belt, watching for any trays with leftover scraps, more out of old habit than from any real hope that the trays would be anything but scoured clean.

After a dozen or so bare ones passed by, I returned to the back of the line and waited and tried not to think about the fact that the cafeteria's dangling bare bulbs looked just like the ones in the interrogation room, tried not to think about the warden with the scar. Instead I focused on what Farrell Dean had told me and tried to study the cafeteria, the city, with a fresh eye.

The water marks on the ceiling were getting worse. The roof needed to be repaired—and had needed it for awhile, judging by the layered patterns of stains. Routine repairs took backseat to routine emergencies—a broken pipe spewing water, an electrical outage threatening to compromise food storage, a fence disintegrating so that cattle wandered the city streets. The roof would be repaired when rain dripped into our supper, and the yellowing walls would go right on waiting for a new coat of paint. Farrell Dean was right; Optica was declining. It wasn't hard to notice really, just hard to want to notice.

A little boy picked his nose and then wiped his hand on the longsuffering wall beside the children's tables. The square floor tiles were crumbling around their edges. The metal serving table was dented and scratched. Unusable metal folding chairs leaned in a great precarious stack against the back wall.

By the time I collected my food tray I was thoroughly depressed, and apparently it showed, because one of the cooks—Alice, a woman with a calm air about her—caught my eye and nodded deliberately, reassuringly. "Everything seems worse on an empty stomach," she said. I tried to smile at her, but my face didn't want to obey.

I made my way up one aisle and down another, looking for Meritt or at least for a place to sit, listening for Rafe's name. But the muttered bits of conversation I caught were all on the same topic—the mysterious impending city meeting. All we knew was we were to gather at the city circle at eight that night and every night thereafter, until further notice.

A warden sitting across from Cynda got up and walked away, and I slid into the empty seat. Waiting for food, jostling for a chair, that was normal.

What wasn't normal was the people gathered in little knots all around the cafeteria, ignoring the cameras and talking openly about why the city meeting had been called. A few men huddled together at a nearby table, gesturing angrily. I strained to hear what they were saying, but the hum of the room blurred everyone's words.

Cynda leaned across our table and clasped one of my hands in both of hers, her long fair hair falling forward over her shoulder in delicate curls. "Ignore them," she said. "There's no point in worrying. It doesn't help."

Another warden passed nearby, eyeing her. She gave my hand one more squeeze and then let go. "Good evening, warden," she said. "Will I be seeing you tonight after the city meeting?"

The warden froze, his ears turning pink, and without answering moved away. She gave me a conspiratorial wink, and then resumed eating in her quick neat way. I took a bite as well, but the meal—I can't even remember now what it was, soup probably, or a thin stew—was tasteless in my mouth.

Across the room two girls began giggling and couldn't stop; when their laughter became tinged with hysteria a dorm mother touched them on the shoulders and led them outside. The loudspeaker announced that Physician Neil was needed at the infirmary. A group of nannies directed children to their tables, reminding the smaller ones to hold their trays level.

Someone stumbled behind me, bumping my chair as he passed. It was Farrell Dean, surreptitiously dropping a beautiful piece of cheese on my plate. Cynda smiled knowingly at him and fluttered her fingers in a wave. He nodded a greeting to her, and though he smiled, I saw in his eyes his worries about the coming winter.

A few tables away Petey, an eleven-year-old, tipped his chair too far back and crashed to the floor. His best friend, Judd, howled with nervous laughter, torn between helping Petey and leaving him to sort himself out alone. An old man as weathered and tough as a strap of leather got up from a nearby table—old Louie, one of my favorite people. He bent and untangled Petey from the chair, stood him on his feet, and dusted him off. A laundress glowered at them all, then said something to Judd that made his fists clench at his sides. Petey put a hand on his arm and Judd knocked it away, then turned and stalked out of the room, leaving his tray on the table.

The murmur of conversations rose by fits and starts until the dull roar of it pounded in my brain like an angry inescapable heartbeat. A woman sitting three down from me put her head in her arms and began to cry.

The clock on the wall said 7:30.

A little before eight, we gathered as ordered at the circle. Its western rim lay at the base of the watchtower, where a thin path led from the base of the tower down to the center of the circle, cutting through the tiered steps around it. Hundreds of people filed in and stood on the steps, each face shadowy but recognizable in the reflected glow of the blue streetlights.

I scanned the crowd, searching for Meritt—he was usually pretty easy to spot—but I didn't see him anywhere. Maybe he was still in isolation. Since he wasn't around I worked my way down and found a place in the front row, on the lowest level; tiers or not, I couldn't comfortably see over any adults standing in front of me, and nothing made me feel more helpless and claustrophobic than standing in a crowd seeing nothing but people's backs.

The city circle was crowded now. It had to be close to eight o'clock, and still there was no sign of Meritt. I was looking around again, just in case, when the door at the base of the watchtower opened and Rafe came out, alone. He stopped for a moment, blinking as if his eyes were adjusting to the shadowy blue lights. One side of his face looked swollen, though from that distance, in that light, I couldn't tell for sure. Otherwise, he seemed unharmed.

Relief brought a smile to my lips and I started to go to him, but I'd only taken a step or two when he caught sight of me and frowned.

Bewildered, I stopped in my tracks. Rafe gave a slight shake of his head, and when he began walking I thought he was coming to stand with me, that he'd been telling me not to come to him but to wait. And sure enough he walked toward me, cutting straight through the center of the circle.

But before he reached me he stopped. He stopped in the center of the circle, and he stayed there.

Someone nudged in beside me, making room where there had been none. It was Farrell Dean. He didn't look at me. His eyes were fixed on Rafe, standing there alone.

Then the spotlight came on. Around the circle every face was cast into darkness as the bright spotlight made the blue streetlights seem like nothing. For a split second I could see only that bright white light, and then my eyes adjusted, and again I saw Rafe. Everyone saw him. He was pinned in the beam.

Much as I wanted to, I couldn't escape the logical conclusion: Rafe was in serious trouble.

But the Watchers had announced the city meeting before Rafe had been arrested. How could they have known he'd be out, that he'd do something and get caught? They must have picked at random from the current crop of prisoners. I hoped that was it—I hoped they weren't angry with Rafe in particular.

At exactly eight o'clock the spotlight flashed once. The crowd, which had been murmuring quietly, fell silent.

"City of Optica."

A man's voice boomed through the tower loudspeakers, resonant and compelling. That would be one of the seven Watchers. He might have actually been in the tower, or with all their technological gear, he could have been speaking to us from their compound a mile away. "Citizens of Optica," he said. "Friends. There are cancers among you."

The voice stopped. The spotlight cut off. In the darkness the silence stretched and held.

I began to shiver, more from nerves than from cold. Beside me Farrell Dean shifted until our shoulders touched. Gratefully I leaned into him. For a long time we stood in the dark, in silence—I don't know how long, but it felt like forever. A baby began to cry and was hurriedly shushed.

The spotlight flicked back on, shifted away from Rafe, began scanning the crowd. It lingered now on one face, now on another. Farrell Dean stood steady beside me, but I took a small step away from him, suddenly afraid that I'd get him in trouble somehow.

Then I was glad I'd moved, because the light paused briefly on Farrell Dean's face and then came to rest on mine. There it stayed, longer than it had stayed on anyone else.

I could feel its heat, or maybe it was the heat of the panic flooding through me. My heart began to race; I felt my cheeks grow flushed. The wind kicked up and my hair shifted, dancing strange-colored in the spotlight, and the scarred warden's words echoed in my mind: I was watched—I, the anomaly, the freak.

Just when I grew convinced it was something more than that—that somehow they knew I'd been near the wasteland when Rafe was arrested—the spotlight moved on, over row upon row of gray uniforms, over terrified or carefully blank faces, moving faster and faster around and around the circle, licking here and there as if it were tasting us.

I began to feel sick. I had a horrible feeling Meritt was there, somewhere, and it would stop on him, that he and I would both be ordered to join Rafe in the center of the circle.

But when the manic spotlight finally stopped, it stopped on Rafe.

The voice spoke again, hushed and menacing: "There are cancers among you," it repeated. "Those who would take what belongs to all of you and abuse it, horde it, use it for themselves alone. Those who would by their words and deeds promote disunity, discord, and ultimately death. Did you think we wouldn't know? Did you think we wouldn't see?"

The light gave Rafe's gray clothes a faint blue tint; it caught at the silver strands in his dark hair and emphasized the lines on his face, making him look older than his forty some-odd years. But though he looked tired and grim, he did not look afraid.

"Instructor Rafe," said the voice. "You are a thief."

Rafe's dark eyes gave no sign that he'd heard the accusation, gave no sign, for that matter, that he was standing at the center of the entire city's attention. He stared straight ahead—straight, as it happened, at me.

"You have stolen painkillers," the voice said. "A small crime, you might say. Small pills, so easily slipped into a pocket. But value is not determined by size. Those painkillers will not be there, family of Optica, when you need them. They will not be there when you break an arm working in the field to feed Instructor Rafe. They will not be there when you go into labor to bear a child for the Family of Optica. They will not be there when a cook burns her hands, or when a mechanic loses a limb."

I felt warm breath in my ear. Farrell Dean murmured, "He makes it sound like Rafe ate buckets of the things."

The voice stopped and I was afraid that somehow it had heard Farrell Dean, that the spotlight would spring up again and pin us in its glare, but when the words resumed they continued in their former track.

"You have been tested and found wanting," it said. "You, Rafe, are a cancerous cell in our body."

They would flog him and lock him away in prison. I

wouldn't see him for ages. When he came out he would be pale from lack of sun, thin, his muscles shrunken from inactivity. That was what happened when someone seriously displeased the Watchers: you were put away, and when you came back, you were never the same.

"But perhaps—" the voice was silky now, persuasive, offering hope. "Perhaps the blame is not entirely yours. Perhaps someone else was involved."

Instructor Rafe's gaze flickered. It was the slightest of movements, almost imperceptible, but I saw it.

"Perhaps you didn't steal the pills," the voice said. "Perhaps someone *gave* them to you. Who was it, Rafe? One of the physicians?"

Rafe shook his head, and I could have sworn the tension around his eyes eased. "No," he said, his voice loud and firm. "There was no one. Only I bear the blame."

As he spoke, three black-clothed wardens marched through the prison door and out to the center of the circle. One was carrying handcuffs. He gestured to Rafe—I think he was telling him to turn around—but Rafe stared past him blankly and didn't move. The other two wardens carried handguns.

Guns?

Not stunners, but real guns. I registered this fact as the Voice again spoke: "Cancer Rafe, your sentence is death."

The crowd inhaled sharply and then everything happened very fast. Rafe moved. He swung at the nearest warden and brought him down hard, the man's head hitting the pavement with a sickening crack. The fallen warden convulsed once and lay still as Rafe turned toward two other wardens rushing in, and I was rushing forward too, not realizing I was moving until I was almost there, but just before I reached Rafe an arm went around my throat, choking me, pulling me back. Rafe's fist flashed out. The pressure on my throat vanished and everyone was shouting and the warden who had grabbed me was clutching at his own throat, and Rafe looked me in the face and yelled something over the chaos and shoved me away, toward the rows of people on the steps.

Another warden was circling around toward me, his gun pointed at Rafe, trying to get a clear shot, and now more wardens were running toward us from the prison, and I would have rushed in again, not because I could help but because I couldn't stand there and do nothing, but someone caught me and pulled me against him, burying my face in his chest, hiding my eyes, covering my head with his arms.

I knew it was Farrell Dean but I didn't care that it was him, didn't care that he was trying to protect me. I fought him but he held me too close and I couldn't get free though I struggled and kicked and bit.

Rafe's voice, sounding strangled, called out the same indistinguishable words he'd shouted before. A shot rang out. Farrell Dean's arms around me tightened.

Behind me, with a dull thud, a body struck the ground.

"Thus ends the first city meeting," said the voice, and the spotlight went dark.

Chapter 8

In the chaos and darkness Farrell Dean yanked me away, pulling me out of the throng of bodies and into the long silent streets.

"No," I said, still struggling, trying to dig in my heels, trying to stay. He was hurting me, or I was hurting myself trying to get free. "We have to go back, we have to help him."

"There's nothing we can do," Farrell Dean said. "He's dead."

But people fell down and got up all the time, that was what they did, and physicians could fix all sorts of things. Just because Rafe had fallen didn't mean he was dead.

"Don't say it," I told Farrell Dean. "Don't say it again."

He didn't say it again but he didn't let go of me, either. He kept pulling me away from the city circle, toward my dorm, and as the noise of the crowd receded so did hope. The Watchers had wanted to kill Rafe; they'd make sure the job was properly done.

Rafe was dead.

Farrell Dean's arms went from restraining to supporting, or else I would have sat down right there on the rough pavement, unable to walk, unable to think.

He got me to the dormitory steps and up them, and at the top he looked warily around before pushing open the door and guiding me over the threshold. "Stay here," he said. "Don't come out again, not tonight. Please." In the moonlight his face was unnaturally pale.

"I'll stay," I said faintly, one hand on the doorframe for support. My mind was wandering in the darkness—back to the glaring spotlight, the blood and the shouting.

"I hurt you," Farrell Dean said, touching my arm where he had gripped me, where new bruises would join the ones from the scarred warden. "I'm sorry." His voice brought me back to the present, to the cold concrete steps, and I understood that he would stand there with me all night unless I released him. His eyes were bleak, too much like my own, and I couldn't remember any words worth saying, so I reached out, brushed his hand with my fingertips, and went inside.

I was the first one back. I climbed straight up onto my bed and was reaching to pull the gray wool blanket over me when I caught sight of my feet. I had stepped in blood.

I don't remember the next few minutes, only that I was staring at a meaningless point on the ceiling when the other sisters began to arrive. They moved quietly, talking in hushed voices. I heard one or two crying.

My bunkmate, Kari, came in. I heard her footsteps on the narrow aisle beside our bunk, heard her stop, then leave. After a few moments she came back. She didn't speak—she never spoke—and I flinched when the warm wet rag touched my foot. She left to rinse the cloth and came back again, then did it two or three times more. Finally she dried my feet and pulled the covers over me, and the bed shifted as she settled into her bunk below.

Soon afterwards the lights went out, and I lay there in the darkness, stunned and disbelieving. Gradually, the knot in my chest loosened and I began to cry, hard but silently, soaking my pillow with hot tears. Around midnight, exhausted, I drifted into a restless sleep, full of dark dreams, the only light a harsh light that picked out my red hair and followed me only among the people milling around, tracking me wherever I turned. I wanted to hide the color, but all I had to dye it with was Rafe's blood. Then Meritt was standing in the city meeting circle. I was terrified, but he was laughing, and Cynda watched him laughing and then shrugged. "What will be, will be," she said, and taking a pair of scissors, cut off my hair.

I awoke the next morning numb, and fumbled through the motions of my usual routine. I dressed in clean clothes, brushed my hair, washed my face, brushed my teeth, feeling all the while somehow distant from my body, which dragged itself along while the real me hovered somewhere off to the side, incapable of believing that Rafe was gone—Rafe, the closest thing to a father I'd ever known.

I didn't want breakfast, but my feet followed habit and took me to the cafeteria. There the big room, crowded, hummed with upset voices as threatening as angry bees.

I collected a tray and wandered vaguely up and down the rows of tables, and when I came to an empty spot I sat down. A nanny mother, two mechanics, a laundress, and three women I recognized but didn't know were already sitting at the table. When I pulled out the chair and sat down, not one of them met my eyes. The laundress across from me looked almost terrified. It took me a second to realize she was terrified of *me*.

I was baffled. Then it hit me: I'd tried to defend the traitor.

I looked around the room, searching for a friendly face. Two of my old people, Estelle and Mariella, had finished eating and were making their slow, careful way out of the cafeteria. My handful of other friends—the few people who didn't much care what color my hair was—were sitting at crowded tables without empty chairs. So I shrugged to myself and reached for my spoon.

It was as if I'd flipped a switch. The people on either side of me, and the terrified laundress directly across, all got up and left. In a crowded dining hall there were three seats vacant around me.

I was a pariah.

Blood pounded in my ears. I felt as if the whole room were staring at me. They weren't, of course—I glanced around to be certain. No. No one was looking at me. They were very carefully *not* looking at me.

But no one was coming to sit with me, either. A few people were actually eating leaning against a wall rather than be seen associating with me. When I glanced their way they averted their eyes.

My face hot, I forced myself to stay put, to eat, knowing I couldn't afford to walk out and lose the calories. Fainting from hunger out in the field would definitely bring unwanted attention.

I was estimating the number of bites I had left, trying to get it all down quickly but without choking, when someone plunked a tray on the table beside me and slid into the chair. From the corner of my eye I could tell it was someone dark skinned. Cautiously I cast a sidelong glance and saw that it was Ezzie.

That surprised me. He'd always been polite, but we weren't exactly friends. When he caught my eye he nodded and then turned his attention to his bowl of applesauce.

Just a few seconds later I stood to go, and he stood as well. The people around us shot suspicious glances his way.

"You're not doing yourself any favors," I said under my breath.

Ezzie shrugged. "You've got more support than you

think. A bunch of the guys wish they'd done something last night." He winked at me. "Instead, we let a girl show us up."

He meant well, but I couldn't muster a smile.

We were halfway to the door when my heart leapt before my brain even realized what my eyes were seeing. It was Meritt, just coming in.

He had a black eye, which merely served to underscore his usual rakish air; other than that he looked healthy and whole. He was listening to Genetic Counselor Roy, and as usual drawing the eyes of everyone in his vicinity. He had an odd sort of presence, Meritt did, simultaneously self-contained and high-energy. The combination tended to make people watch him, just in case he did something brilliant and unexpected.

I couldn't speak to him with so many people around, not when associating with me could get him in trouble. I wasn't even sure he'd see me, focused as he was on his conversation. But as we passed each other his eyes met mine. He lifted his chin slightly, gesturing toward the door, even as he answered some question the genetic counselor had posed.

He'd meet me later, he was saying. The usual place, I assumed, at the usual time.

"Keep moving," Ezzie said under his breath. "Warden alert."

He was sitting at a table with a full tray in front of him. The scarred warden. The people at his table were angled away from him, eating hurriedly, silently. I was careful not to look him in the face, but I felt his flat cold stare follow me all the way to the door.

At lunch that day, Garry came lumbering over to me while I stood in line at the cafeteria truck. He'd worked hard that morning, and maybe I should have been pleased, but all

I felt was disgusted. Sure, he'd work now—now that he was afraid of being put in the city meeting circle—just not when we were facing a slow death by starvation.

"Hey freak," Garry said, jostling past a couple of people to get to me. He had yet another complaint, no doubt, and as usual it would be about something I could do absolutely nothing to remedy.

Hiding my dislike, I presented a blank face to him. Though the day was chilly he was sweating heavily, and his face, always red, looked almost purple.

"So tell me," he said, crossing his arms over his chest. "What did Rafe say to you last night?"

I mastered the urge to take a step away from him. "I don't know what you mean," I said, and I didn't.

He snorted. "He said something just before they shot him, and you were right there. What was it?"

I didn't want to think about Rafe getting shot. I'd been trying all day to think about something else, not about Rafe. But now that Garry mentioned it, I realized he was right. Rafe had called out something, just a couple of words, while Farrell Dean was pulling me away.

Felix sidled up. "You just had to get involved, didn't you?" he said to me, his whiny voice spiteful. "Why don't you just paint a bull's eye on your back and be done with it?" He'd been keeping his distance from me all morning, pointedly separating himself from whatever contagion I carried. Well, he'd be free of me soon enough. It was almost time for the field workers to be redistributed for winter jobs.

"Don't interrupt," Garry told Felix, and then stuck out an arm when I tried to walk away.

"I'm talking to you," he said. "Are you deaf?"

The people in line at the cafeteria truck glanced over and, when they saw Garry's belligerent stance, edged prudently away.

"Rafe was talking right to you," Garry said, pointing at me with an accusing finger. "I saw it with my own eyes. Soon as he knew he was going to die he started twisting away from that warden, shouting something to you. I want to know what it was."

I was willing myself to sound calm and probably failing miserably. "I couldn't hear him over all the yelling," I said, and then gave Garry's shoulder an exaggerated pat. "But don't worry. If I get in trouble the first thing I'll tell them is, *Garry had nothing to do with it.*"

Garry's face, if possible, turned an even darker purple. He was taking a deep breath, like he was about to start yelling at me, when a quiet voice spoke from up ahead. "If she didn't hear it, she didn't hear it. And I'm about to close the lunch truck, so if you intend to eat, you'd better get moving."

Garry wheeled around to see who'd dare to cross him. It was the older cafeteria worker, Marta. She had a thin, angular face and a lot of straight gray hair, and while I wouldn't have thought she could stare down Garry, lo and behold she did just that. He snatched up his tray, spluttered something—I didn't exactly catch it, but I was pretty sure he was cussing at us both—and stalked heavily away.

I was alone now, except for the three cafeteria truck workers. The two younger women had their backs to me— whether intentionally or not, I didn't know.

"Thanks," I said to Marta as she handed me a plate.

She nodded briskly and put one hand on her hip. "Hold on," she said. "Lena, Terri—do we have any more ham sandwiches?"

"No," one said sadly, eyeing my food. "That's the last."

"Maybe B Truck has extras. Why don't you two go see?"

The two girls vanished instantly.

Marta watched them go, then leaned across the truck counter toward me. "I couldn't hear what Rafe said either," she said. "But like that idiot Garry, I'm pretty sure Rafe was trying to tell you something. You or the boy."

"I can hear him call out, in my mind," I said. "But it's just sound. It isn't words."

"I understand. Don't worry about it. But—" she lowered her voice, tucked a strand of gray hair behind her ear. "There might be another way."

I waited, not understanding.

"Rafe knew anything was possible, once the city meeting was announced," she said. "He would never put all his eggs in one basket."

I stared at her. "You think maybe he left a message?"

Marta gave the smallest of nods and ran a wet rag over the counter.

Could that have been why we'd been going to meet him? Because he wanted to tell Meritt something?

"Maybe at the school, maybe at his house," Marta said, because of course she didn't know we'd been going to meet him in person.

"He wouldn't put anything in writing," I said. "Too dangerous. The wardens might find it. Rafe was careful. He was always careful."

Marta nodded. "Exactly," she said. "He was careful enough to make contingency plans. And if he left a message, he wouldn't have left it in plain sight. It will take someone who knows him well to find it."

Then, with a brisk nod, she pulled down the serving flap and left me facing a rusting metal wall.

By the time the city siren sounded to end the work day, I was weak with hunger. Even so, the memory of being ostracized at breakfast made me dread the cafeteria. Maybe I'd go by the dorm and shower before dinner. I'd end up getting the dregs of whatever we were having, but at least by then there'd be plenty of empty spots at the tables.

On my way to the dorm I caught a movement out of the corner of my eye. I knew what it was without looking—Petey and Judd horsing around—though I couldn't believe they were playing their usual games, not after what had happened last night. For a second I was appalled, disgusted with them, but then I imagined them behaving like the laundress at breakfast this morning, white-faced with fear. This was better.

So I mustered a little energy and strolled down the street as if I hadn't noticed their dash from doorway to doorway. I pretended to be utterly absorbed in the goings-on around me: I took in the weary-looking physician carrying two large boxes into the infirmary; the dorm mother sweeping the front steps of her dormitory; a knot of older women moving slowly toward the cafeteria, helping each other over uneven places and up steps.

The way they clung to each other gave me the uneasy feeling that if one slipped, they'd all go down in a heap, shattering hips and arms and who knows what all.

I was trying to see if any of my old people were in the group when Mariella caught sight of me. Her face lit up and, daringly, she let go of the arm she was holding for balance and waved gently in my direction. Heads turned; they all saw me, all smiled, all lifted their hands in greeting, all swayed unsteadily.

I smiled and waved back, the pain in my heart easing just a little. My old people weren't hiding from me. They never had. They'd always made time for me back when I was a lonely little girl. They'd told me stories, taken me for walks, watched me play in the dirt in the yard of the children's dormitory, listened to my secrets. Sometimes they touched my hair wonderingly, but they never called me a freak.

They moved carefully on, and I watched them until they were safely inside the cafeteria. Then I started down the street again.

Finally I was within range, and my stalkers pounced. They leapt out from the shadow of the prison house, shouting something incomprehensible, grabbing my arms and spinning me in a circle, their own arms and legs flying in all directions. "We got you!" they yelled. "We win!"

A passerby edged around us, shaking his head disapprovingly.

"Did you see us?" Petey asked anxiously as we stumbled to a stop. He was a thin boy, eleven years old, with an oddly round face.

"If I'd seen you, would I have let you catch me?"

Judd saw through my evasion and snorted. "Yeah, you would. You keep thinking we're babies." Judd was twelve, stockily built, and blond. I had been his partner at school, after Meritt left, so he wasn't afraid of me and my odd hair, like most of the younger kids were.

"Don't cheat for us," Petey said. "If you see us, you have to tell. Otherwise how can we get better?"

I considered this. "Okay, I saw you," I said. Petey's face fell. "But just barely. You moved faster than everyone else on the street, and that caught my attention."

"Right, blend in," Judd said, "You're so very good at that, Red. Thanks for the tip."

He shot me a smile before he ran off. I hoped being seen with me wouldn't get him and Petey into trouble.

When I finally got back to my dormitory, the bathroom was blessedly empty, except for Meri, who was never one to chatter. In a dorm room full of girls, I liked that about her. She wouldn't be here much longer; she'd just turned nineteen, and soon would be moved to the adult quarters—assuming, of course, we survived that long.

As I stripped my clothes off in the steamy shower area, I wondered who she'd be assigned to. There was quite a crop of guys who'd recently turned nineteen or soon would—Ezzie, Cline, Joe, Harding, Errol, Farrell Dean. Though I didn't want Farrell Dean for myself, I couldn't picture him with Meri. Or with anyone, actually. And when Meritt was assigned . . .

I ducked under the spray, turning my face up to it, wishing I could wash away whatever the future held—because whatever it held for me, it wouldn't be Meritt. Not if we couldn't escape to the woods.

Meri might get him. Though there was no guarantee Meri would be put with a young man, because there were more girls than boys her age. She could get put with a reassigned older man. That happened a lot. And sometimes the genetic counselors reassigned one of the older men to a new breeder, even if there were younger men available. I didn't know why.

But I did know that Meri at least had a chance at the boys her own age, and I didn't. I was two years younger than they were. They'd all be assigned long before I turned nineteen. And I'd be turning nineteen all by myself, because after Meri's age group came the big empty gap with nobody but me in it. So I'd get put with some reassigned middle-aged man. Someone I didn't know well, or worse, someone I did. Felix, for instance. Or—the thought made me shudder—Garry. I could be forced to live in the same house with blustering red-faced Garry, just him and me, alone together, for years and years.

Or I could be assigned to the scarred warden.

That was when I remembered the camera—or, rather, remembered who could be watching me through it.

I'd have leapt for a towel, but I was covered with soap.

Instead I turned further away, feeling my face flush red with embarrassment. The camera had always been there, and I'd always ignored it. What else could I do? I had to bathe.

But now I'd seen that bank of monitors in the watchtower; I'd seen actually seen a man watching us through those little mechanical eyes.

And worse, now I knew the scarred warden watched me especially.

I would ask Meritt to disable that camera as soon as possible. He'd taught me how to interfere with the sound, but visuals were harder to mess up, at least if you wanted to make it look accidental. Surely we could find a way to sneak him into the dorm, or find a legitimate electronic issue for him to deal with in here.

"Nice to have hot water for once," Meri called, startling me. She never made small talk. "I sure needed a good shower today. I had blood all the way up to my elbows."

It was true that her skin was pink from scrubbing—she worked in food preservation, which was a pretty messy job. But it dawned on me that she wasn't really talking about cleanliness; terse, efficient Meri wouldn't bother to make chit-chat about something like that. Maybe, in light of my ostracization this morning, she was talking to me just to let me know she was a friend.

"What did you do today?" I called, testing my theory.

Meri turned off her shower and reached for her towel. "Cut and cured beef strips."

"So are we all set for winter?"

It was a clumsy question, and when Meri turned toward me she glanced up at the camera, even though she knew the sound of my shower running would mask our voices, as long as we kept them low.

"You know the saying, 'waste not, want not?' With the beef sausage, nothing went to waste. We had to use everything we possibly could, and we're still only at about half our usual quota."

"That cattle illness in the spring?" I'd heard about it all the time, but hadn't paid much attention.

She nodded. "Coccidiosis. We lost a lot of calves. Too many."

"What about our other meat supplies?"

She shrugged and began toweling her hair. "Fishing is a little thin; poultry ... well, disappointing; and pork had a scour epidemic back in May. The wet spring."

I thought of the rot problem we'd had with the early potatoes, and the sorry crop of cherries thanks to a late freeze. I didn't have to tell Meri about that. Word had gotten around. And the entire first cut of alfalfa was pretty much worthless.

For a long moment we were silent, pondering how much devastation a single unusually wet, cool spring could have. "It seems like there should be some way to make up the difference," I said finally.

Meri shrugged, twisting a dark strand of hair around her finger. Then, wrapping the towel around her, she walked under the camera as if leaving the room. When she was directly below it, she reached up and twisted the wire that Meritt had taught me controlled the sound.

She knew. Meri knew how to mess up the sound.

I stared at her, and she met my eyes levelly. "We didn't have much margin to begin with," she said. "So much of what we have goes to the Ws."

To the wardens, the Watchers, and to the watcher assistants. I had no idea how much the Watchers and their assistants ate, but I knew how often the wardens went back through the serving line.

Meri wasn't looking at me anymore; she was eyeing the sign beneath the camera—"We Watch Because We Care." But she hadn't left the room.

"Why do you think they do it?" I said, keeping my voice down, averting my face so the camera wouldn't see my moving lips.

"Do what?"

"Watch us all the time."

She shook her head; she didn't know.

"I just keep thinking how much easier it would be if they weren't watching us," I said. "And really I can't figure out why they are. So many cameras, so many wardens, all the time. It just all seems so unnecessary. Like swatting a fly with a sledgehammer. Like we're all dangerous criminals or something."

The wire uncurled back into its usual shape. I shut off the shower, snatched a towel, and hurried to where Meri stood beneath the camera, putting a finger to my lips as soon as I was out of its sight.

Meri nodded and put one arm around my neck. She was damp and hot from the shower, so hot she felt feverish.

"You shouldn't have tried to help Rafe," she said. Her voice was a mere breath. "But I wish it had worked."

Blinking back tears, I nodded and pulled away.

Meri studied me. I guess she saw something that made her decide to trust me, because she leaned in close again. At the same time she reached up and started scraping her fingernails against the wall just beneath the camera, creating sound cover. It was another trick of Meritt's.

"A couple of weeks ago, one of the mechanics accidentally cut a couple of wires when he was patching a leak in the roof of the food preservation building," she said, so quietly I could hardly hear her. "He tried to fix them but just made matters worse, and electronics hasn't gotten around to replacing them yet. So in the meantime I've been hiding food."

It took me a moment to understand what she was telling me, and then a startling image filled my mind: Farrell Dean, our best mechanic, playing the bumbling incompetent. *Gathering information*, he'd said, as if he'd been doing nothing more.

"I can only skim off a little," Meri murmured. "But if the Watchers don't know we have it, maybe it'll help. Maybe it'll keep us alive."

Then she turned and left the room, leaving me to get my mind around this conspiracy I'd been totally oblivious to.

Hurriedly I toweled off, staying in the small blind spot under the camera, and pulled on my pants and shirt.

In the bedroom Meri was sitting cross-legged on her bunk, yanking a comb through her hair. I couldn't ask what I wanted to know, not with the live camera above us, so instead I went back to the shortage problem. "What's wrong with poultry?" I asked. "Did they have disease issues?"

"Nope. Predators."

"Raccoons?"

Meri frowned. "No," she said. "Something's coming in from the woods."

"What, a wolf? A fox?"

"I don't know." Meri glanced up at the camera. "It isn't a secret," she said. "It's just that nobody likes to talk about it. It's creepy. Last week they started posting a round-the-clock watch, but whatever this thing is, it's slipped past them twice already. And it doesn't just steal a chicken or two—it rips the heads off dozens and dozens of them."

"Sounds like a weasel," I said, sitting down beside her, the thin mattress sagging beneath my weight.

"Except weasels don't paint pictures on the walls using chicken blood."

I shivered. Meri was right—that was creepy.

"What sort of pictures?"

Meri glanced around warily, and I found myself doing the same. "Stick figures," she said. "Stick figures fighting, chasing each other, cutting each other's throats. And lots of sketches of eyes."

I lowered my voice to a whisper. "It doesn't sound like a Guardian." If such things existed.

Meri nodded. "Too random. And too stupid—the Guardians are supposed to be smart. Smarter than we are."

"So if it isn't a Guardian, what is it?"

Meri shook her head. "I don't know."

"So the streets aren't safe at night." I was thinking about the night workers, about Cynda. About my own forays into the darkness.

Meri eyed me narrowly. "I don't want to scare you," she said, "but listen—whatever it is, it's awfully good at getting into secured areas. Indoors might not be much safer than out."

I thought about the gap in the western wall, only orchards and beehives between it and the dormitories where the girls and children slept. Lovely.

Now I could add insomnia to my growing list of problems.

Chapter 9

That evening after supper I was standing out in the eastern wasteland, just beyond the slaughterhouse, huddled against the city wall.

We usually met later than this, but at eight we'd have to go to the city meeting, so I was hoping Meritt would come now. This was our preferred meeting spot because, although the slaughterhouse camera was active, it had been malfunctioning and Meritt, conveniently, hadn't had time to fix it.

While I waited I pressed against the city wall, my eyes fixed on the woods fifty yards away, dark and ominous in the fading light. The path the fishermen took to the sea cut an insubstantial gap into the gloom of undergrowth and overhanging trees. Staying on it wasn't enough to keep you safe, not in those dark woods. You had to go in the daylight, and travel in company.

"Hey," a voice said softly, and Meritt was beside me.

He joined me against the wall, bracing one foot on it behind him as if at any moment he might push away and be gone. His dark hair fell over one eye and he shoved it back as if it irritated him. It was getting too long, but it wouldn't occur to him to cut it until someone ordered him to, and fewer and fewer people were ordering Meritt to do anything. He was too valuable to the city, too crucial to electronics—

indispensible, really, if the Watchers wanted to keep watching. Only the wardens and maybe the genetic counselors ranked higher than Meritt these days.

The collar of his coat was turned up—he had a coat, though it was patched in two places and pulling loose at the seams—and he was wearing his boots. He didn't wear them when we ran, not usually, because they were heavy and noisier than bare feet. He was already tall and the boots made him taller still, so that when I leaned a little against him, using his body to block the wind, my head was below the top of his shoulder.

For a long moment we were silent, standing there side by side. I don't know what Meritt was thinking, but I felt almost faint with relief. He was here; he was safe. I could feel the rough fabric of his coat against my cheek, sense the pent-up energy humming in him. He burned fast, old Louie once said, fast and bright and unpredictable.

And he had made it through that entire terrible day without getting himself locked up or whipped or shot. He was here and we were alone, away from prying eyes, away from the Watchers and the wardens and all the people who stared at me because I was a freak, and at Meritt because he was not.

I was so glad to be there with him that all the things I'd thought to say, all the questions I wanted to ask, seemed suddenly unimportant. All that mattered was that he was safe and there with me, leaning against the wall with his hands in his pockets, breathing the same air I was breathing, looking out into the woods where we couldn't go, not if the Guardians were real.

Though—and this was a new thought for me—Meritt might be able to get what he wanted. He was increasingly important to the city, and there were ways—everyone knew there were ways, unstated and illegal but definitely possible.

Surely, somehow, we would always be together.

Thinking about that, I shifted away from his shoulder and looked up at him. He was gazing out at the trees, the angular lines of his face etched stark in the dying light. The bruise beneath his eye was a purplish blue. His expression was remote, intent; but he didn't have the anxious air of thinly veiled panic that so many were wearing that day.

I couldn't read the thoughts passing behind his gray eyes, of course, but as I watched him I realized I knew that expression. He was planning. He was strategizing three moves ahead, as he always did in any game we ever played. He wasn't a victim. He wasn't prey. He wasn't afraid.

As I stood there studying him, some of the fear ebbed out of my own blood.

"Meritt?" I said, and waited until he glanced down at me. "Is it all going to be all right?"

It was the question I always asked him whenever anything big or small was troubling me.

Meritt looked at me for a moment, at first absently, then really seeing me, the taut lines of his face easing as if he'd just remembered I was there and was glad of me.

"Depends on your definition of all right," he said. Then he smiled at me, not quite his usual jaunty grin but almost, and I smiled back at him. It was the answer he always gave, and he finished with the rest of the formula. "According to my definition, sure. One way or another, it'll all be all right."

And then he reached out to tug the end of my braid, and Farrell Dean's words came rushing in on me.

Farrell Dean was wrong—I knew he was wrong—but I had to make sure.

And anyway I wanted answers; I wasn't going to be left in the dark, not at such a time as this.

"Meritt, I need to ask you something," I said.

He raised his eyebrows, curious but unconcerned.

"Okay. What?"

"Do you know why Rafe wanted you to meet him that night?"

Meritt held my gaze for a moment. "Not exactly," he said, and then bent to pick up a small rock.

"Inexactly, then."

Half smiling, he shook his head and flung the rock toward the woods. "If I can't be exact, I won't be anything at all. Speculation's a dangerous game."

"So is ignorance," I said. "I got arrested for being out that night. Don't you think I have a right to know why we were there?"

Meritt didn't answer. He was watching the woods, where a handful of birds were fluttering up, twittering protests, disturbed by his stone.

"I know what's been going on," I said. "I know that Rafe was conspiring against the Watchers, and that you are, too."

At that he turned, his face startled and amused. "Me?" he said. "Come on, Red. You know I always play to win, you've complained about it often enough. Mere mortals against the Watchers are not what I'd call winning odds."

I stared at him. "This isn't funny, Meritt. Rafe's *dead*."

A flash of pain crossed his face. "I know."

"I can see why Meri needs to hide food," I said, laying all my cards on the table. "I can even see why you and Farrell Dean need to spy on the Watchers, if the only alternative is starving. But I can't figure out why Rafe wanted those painkillers."

Meritt actually looked a little worried; I knew more than he'd expected.

"Did he tell you?" I said. "Do you know why he had them?"

"Maybe he didn't have them. Maybe he was set up."

"No, I think he had them," I said. "I saw his face. But I

can't figure out what painkillers have to do with keeping us from starving this winter."

Meritt picked up another rock and flung it into the woods. He didn't say anything. Every time he threw a rock something clinked softly as he moved—the tiny screwdrivers he always carried in his pockets, the tools of his trade.

"I saw Rafe's face," I repeated. "I was right there, just a few feet away. And you know what was odd? He didn't look worried until they suggested someone else might be involved."

Meritt reached for yet another rock and I stepped between him and the trees, blocking his aim, the scruffy grass and sand shifting unevenly beneath my feet.

"Do you hear what I'm saying? Rafe didn't want to give anyone away. He didn't want to give *you* away. You were the one he was meeting the night he got arrested." I hesitated and then went on. "He died protecting you."

A shadow passed behind Meritt's eyes while he stood there looking at me, tossing that stupid rock from hand to hand. His expression was unreadable, but I knew I was right. Rafe had died protecting him.

My legs began to feel shaky and I sank down to the ground, turning so my back was toward Meritt and the wall, not the looming trees. I could smell them, the pines and the cedars—a smell I always associated with Meritt, with our secret forays outside the city walls.

After a moment Meritt dropped the rock and sat down beside me. He pulled up a few tufts of rough grass, tossed them up to see which way the wind was blowing. "Rafe knew he was going to get punished regardless," he said, watching the dry blades go spinning away. "All he did was choose not to take anyone else down with him. He was practical."

"He was brave. He didn't try to sell you to buy mercy for himself." My voice trembled on the words.

Meritt propped his elbows on his knees, observing me as he did from time to time, as if I were a particularly curious alien from another world. The wind stirred his dark hair and he shook it out of his face, his eyes still on me. Then he reached out and tugged gently at my sleeve.

"Tell me about your interrogation," he said.

I ran my fingers across the nubbly brown grass. "It wasn't bad," I said, pushing away the memory of the warden with the scarred lip. "They gave me warm milk and took me up in the watchtower. I pretended to be a silly girl."

"Which you're not." Meritt's expression darkened. "It could have been much worse, Red, and it was my fault. I led you right into trouble. I didn't mean to, but I did, and you kept your head and got out of it, and got me out of it too. You did good."

"I didn't get you out of all of it," I said, and let the implicit question hang in the air. Meritt met my gaze but I couldn't decipher his expression. He could make his gray eyes as blank as slate.

When he didn't speak, I tried again. "How did she know you were going to be there?"

"She didn't."

"Someone knew," I said. "At least, someone knew Rafe was going to be there. The wardens were waiting for him. Meritt—why didn't they arrest both of you?"

Meritt shook his head. He started to say something, then stopped, his lips pressed tightly together.

"I can take a hint." I braced my hands on the rough grass, started to get up. "If you don't want to talk to me, I don't want to be here."

Meritt reached out and grabbed my sleeve again, pulling me back down.

"I always want to talk to you," he said. "Sometimes I can't, that's all."

"Won't, you mean."

"Shouldn't. Or can't, because you won't stop arguing long enough to listen." His grin flashed and then was gone, and he began speaking quickly, the way he sometimes did, so quickly and in such a low voice that I had to listen hard to keep up.

"I knew there might be trouble the other night. There always might be trouble when we're out, you know that, it's just the way things are—but not that, never that. I had no reason to think the wardens were that sort of threat, no reason to think Rafe would get killed. The Watchers don't do things that way. Or they didn't. A healthy man is a valuable resource, not something I'd expect them to waste."

He still had hold of my sleeve, but he was looking out at the dark trees, not at me. The fading light washed his face of color, deepened the darkness of his near-black hair and brows. Light and shadow, a study in contrasts. My Meritt.

"I wouldn't have taken you with me if I'd known what was going to happen, and I was glad I was way ahead of you, glad you stopped in time and didn't get caught. I was thinking about that, about you, hoping you'd have the sense to stay out of sight."

He shot me a quick glance and I knew he was thinking of how, at the city meeting, I'd failed to do just that.

"So I was distracted, and it took a minute to catch on that the warden was stalling me. She didn't want me out in the wasteland when Rafe got arrested. She didn't want the other wardens to see me. That was when I knew something really bad was going on—" he met my eyes again, looked away. "Otherwise she'd have let me take whatever I had coming. Flogging, a few days in prison, whatever. And then she said—"

He broke off abruptly and dropped my sleeve, still turned toward me, but with his gaze fixed somewhere over my shoulder. This was quintessential Meritt, quite capable of vanishing to chase some mental rabbit trail, right in the middle of his own sentence.

"Go on," I said after a moment. "Tell me what she said."

He looked at me, his eyes unreadable. "Just that someone like me could get in a lot of trouble unless he had connections."

I thought about this. "What did she mean, 'someone like you'?"

He shrugged. "You know, reckless, taking risks, that sort of thing."

I started to press him for her exact words, but I didn't have the heart. I'd felt sick when I saw the blonde warden waiting for him, reaching for him, and nothing he had said made me feel any better. If the wardens, the Watchers, took the best of everything, why not this, too?

Meritt apparently guessed my thoughts. "When exactly did you take off?"

"Just after the kissing started."

He didn't look away. "Then you saw that it stopped as soon as it started. I ended it."

"Maybe she doesn't think it's ended."

"What are you implying?" he said sharply. "I told you: I ended it."

I got up, and this time he didn't stop me. The tufts of grass felt rough under my bare feet. "I'm not implying anything. I'm saying, straight out, that wardens have done this exact sort of thing before."

"What sort of thing?"

It was a trick he had, a way of avoiding unpleasant conversations. Lots of times it worked, when the other person—me—felt uncomfortable saying out loud something awkward or frightening.

Well, I was uncomfortable, and I was frightened, and I

wasn't going to spell out what wardens too often did. But I wasn't going to let the matter drop, either. Not this time.

So I gave him a pointed look. "You know exactly what I mean," I said. "Do you really want me to get explicit?"

It backfired. Meritt was nobody's fool, and he knew me well. He got to his feet, his eyes like ice, the way they got when he was very angry.

"Has a warden been messing with you?"

This was not the way the conversation needed to go. Meritt wasn't exactly what I'd call the chivalrous sort, but if he knew the scarred warden had threatened me, there was a good chance he'd decide to do something about it—if for no other reason than that messing with me was, indirectly, messing with him. And I didn't want him getting hurt because of me.

So I rolled my eyes. "Please," I said. "You're the one who was kissing a warden."

Meritt's expression turned neutral.

I pressed my advantage. "Over-age wardens have done it before," I said, making myself think only about the blonde, and not about the scarred warden. "You know that. It happens all the time. They do a favor for someone under nineteen and then cash it in."

Involvement with someone under nineteen was less risky for the wardens. With someone over nineteen, someone who had already been assigned, the warden got two years in prison. But if the target was under nineteen the warden only got a slap on the wrist, a "documented reprimand."

I drove the point home. "You're not nineteen yet," I said. "You've got, what, almost five months left? That's plenty of time for an over-age warden to get whatever she wants."

"I'm not a relief worker," Meritt said irritably. "And 'over-age' makes it sound like she's got one foot in the grave. She's, what, twenty-eight, thirty?"

"That's past the female breeding age," I said. "She's been sterilized. And don't say 'relief worker' like it's a dirty word. They didn't choose the job. They got assigned, just like you did."

He didn't answer. Now he was doing that thing I hated, staring over the top of my head, making me feel two feet tall and invisible. At least he wasn't quizzing me about the scarred warden—though perversely, part of me wished he hadn't been so easily distracted. It made me feel frighteningly alone with that problem.

It also made me sure that I was right about the blonde.

"You might as well face facts," I said, giving up any effort at sounding calm. "Wardens take the best of everything. And that's you, Meritt."

He waved that off impatiently, threw me one scalding look, and then, jamming his hands in his pockets, turned away. He moved fast. In a heartbeat he was out of reach, stalking away from me, down the wasteland.

All the anger drained out of me. I stood there alone, shivering and tired, watching him stride away, and told myself I deserved it for being an idiot. I'd been so happy Meritt wasn't still locked up, and now he was angry, and it was almost time for the city meeting, and there was no telling when we'd find time to meet again. Why had I picked a fight? Meritt could have been killed, like Rafe. So what did it matter if a pretty warden kissed him? What would it even matter if he'd enjoyed it? It was quite possible she had saved his life.

Kisses didn't matter. This was Optica. Nothing important could be allowed to matter.

Far down the wasteland, Meritt stopped, his back to me. After a long moment he turned and came back, angry stride easing into an amble, his eyes fixed on the ground in front of him, his hands still in his pockets. I stood quietly, leaning against the wall and watching him, tall and angular and loose-limbed. After the long gray day the sun had decided to peek out just in time to set, and now it filtered through the trees and brushed him with warmth, his hair, his skin. For a heartbeat I let myself imagine a world where I could have the colors I wanted, where practicality and consistency didn't mean everything had to be neutral tones, where red hair wasn't freakish, where we were allowed to choose where we worked, who we loved, whose children we bore.

Meritt lifted his eyes and looked straight into mine, and his expression changed.

"Don't, Red," he said softly, stepping close. He cupped my face with one hand and ran his thumb across my cheek. "Don't cry."

I hadn't realized I was.

Chapter 10

Eight o'clock.

We stood in the concentric circles of the city circle, a field of gray dotted here and there with black-clothed wardens. Five people stood in the middle of the circle, their backs to one another, facing out.

We couldn't tell who they were; the angle of the floodlights reduced them to silhouettes. The rest of us were fully exposed, our faces washed pale in the glare of the artificial light.

"Family of Optica," said the voice, the same one as before. "There are cancers among you."

The voice paused. The lights stayed on, but the silence went on too, and despite the crowded square, that silence felt empty. It made me want to yell out.

Cline was standing beside me tonight, his nose swollen and discolored from the fight at the boys' dormitory. He was big and solid, built like a brick wall, a match for the bulls he worked with at the cattle yard. But though he was there beside me I felt exposed and alone.

The voice spoke again, now hushed and menacing: "There are cancers among you," it repeated. "Those who would take what belongs to all of you and abuse it, horde it, use it for themselves alone. Those who would by their words and deeds promote disunity, discord, and ultimately death."

A tense ripple spread through the crowd as the spotlight shifted. We were now in darkness, and the five in the center blinked in the sudden glare as the spotlights turned on them. One woman—a very beautiful woman—and four men.

"Seamstress Lavinia," said the voice. "Step forward."

The woman took one step forward, two. Her jaw was clenched, but she held her head high. Her hair, long and dark, flowed over her shoulders like a cape.

"Mechanic Dane, Engineer Win, Butcher Ross, Shoe-maker Larry."

The men stood still as their names were called.

"Seamstress Lavinia has been released from the breeding program and is free now to choose her companions. If you'd like to compete for her affections, step forward."

Despite myself I turned toward Cline. "But—" Sharply he shook his head, his eyes fixed on the tableau in front of us. He was right. Of course I shouldn't speak. But what did the Voice expect the men to do? If they stepped forward, they'd be confessing to quarreling, to disrupting the Family.

The men clearly knew this. They stayed put, their feet firmly planted, their hands clasped behind their backs. Or were their hands tied?

"What? Not one of you wishes to compete for Lavinia?" The voice laughed without humor.

The men stood still. The butcher, a heavy-jowled man, was facing me, and in the light of the spotlight something glistened on his cheek.

"Seamstress Lavinia," said the voice. "You have been tested and found lacking."

This time five wardens in black uniforms came out. One stood in front of each man, and one went to Lavinia. He didn't do anything; he simply stood behind her.

"Your beauty has been the cause of dissention and

strife," said the voice. "It has betrayed the City of Optica. Your sentence is death."

Lavinia turned and walked straight at the warden. He took a step back and she brushed past him, striding toward the edge of the circle with her head held high. For a heartbeat it felt, amazingly, as if they might let her go.

A shot rang out from somewhere outside of the circle, and Lavinia fell, her long hair pouring across the gray pavement like oil.

For a moment, no one moved. The echo of the shot hung in the silence. Then three of the four men yelled and leapt forward toward Lavinia, the butcher vomited all over a warden, and the crowd shouted, swayed, and began to break rank. "So ends the second city meeting," said the Voice over the chaos, and the spotlight went dark.

Afterwards the dormitory was in a state—girls crying, girls staring blankly at the gray walls, girls trying to be practical or comforting. The dorm mother had not put in an appearance, which wasn't surprising. We'd seen less and less of her lately.

"Lavinia had three babies," my bunkmate Kari said, so quietly that most of the room didn't hear her. "That's a record. You'd think it would buy her some mercy." Kari worked in the postnatal ward. She meant that three babies was a record since the time of the ashes. Optica still hadn't fully recovered from it, apparently, because pregnancies were few and far between, and many of the babies didn't survive to term.

I saw her point. Why Lavinia? As far as I knew she was just a pretty woman, pretty and quiet.

"Who was her breeding partner?" Meri asked.

"Butcher Ross," Cynda said. "But what does that matter? They'd both been released from the program."

"It matters because the Watchers killed her," I said, my voice rising. "Everything about Lavinia matters because they killed her."

Apparently I sounded like I was about to lose it, because all eyes in the room turned in my direction, and Cynda wrapped her arms around me, making little shushing noises. I didn't want to be confined—I was angry, not weepy—and I elbowed out of her grasp as Liza climbed up onto a top bunk from an angle, so the camera couldn't see her, and with a pencil gouged behind it at the wires. She didn't just twist them; she ripped them right out, her frizzy hair bouncing in time with her efforts.

"You are going to be in so much trouble," Wanda said gleefully.

"Try it, Wanda," Shawna said. "Tattle on Liza, and ten of us will testify that you're the one who sabotaged the camera." Around the room, a dozen or so heads nodded. Shawna was a live-and-let live sort of person, and often ended up acting as the peacekeeper of the dorm.

Wanda said nothing, but the look in her eye told me Shawna had moved to the top of her hate list. Just under me, that is.

"Go ahead," Liza said to me, settling down cross-legged on the top bunk. "What were you saying about Lavinia?"

I collected my thoughts. "The Watchers were trying to make those men turn on Lavinia," I said. "And they tried to make Rafe turn in whoever was helping him."

Cynda shrugged, as if to say she didn't follow my point, so I went on. "They say the city meetings are to punish us for disunity, but it's almost like they're designed to create disunity, to turn us against each other."

Bizarrely, Lea, the youngest girl in my dorm, began to laugh. "Lavinia was going to get shot no matter what the men did," she said, and tears began streaming down her cheeks.

"They couldn't make matters worse. They couldn't make matters better. They couldn't make matters worse."

She might have gone right on seesawing between better and worse, but she was sobbing and laughing at the same time now, gasping out her words.

With no warning Cynda hauled back and slapped her. "Get a grip on yourself, Lea," she said. "Take a deep breath and hold it."

Lea looked stunned, but managed to do as Cynda said.

"One deep breath. Now another. I have to go to work soon, and I can't leave you hysterical."

A circle of girls formed around Lea, all attempting to comfort her, patting her shoulder, offering her water, saying soothing things. It soon became clear, though, that the attention wasn't helping. Maybe Cynda ought to slap her again. Or I could. I couldn't think of any comforting words, that was for sure, and anyway I had no interest in playing nursemaid.

Liza didn't either. She threw Lea an exasperated look and then, bizarrely, began to clap—not like she was applauding, but slowly and loudly until everyone was staring at her. Everyone—even Lea—turned toward her. Liza wasn't particularly pretty, with too-large hands and feet, a beaky nose, and that sandy-colored frizzy hair; but she was smart and decisive, and when she had something to say, she made sure people listened.

"Red hit the nail on the head," she said, when she saw that she had our full attention. "The Watchers want the people in the city meeting to turn on each other. They want us to sell each other, sacrifice each other, do whatever it takes to stay alive."

Shawna was nodding, and Meri looked thoughtful. Before they could say anything, though, Wanda jumped in.

"That's not true," she said. "The Watchers are showing us where we're weak. That way we can become stronger."

Liza snorted. "Look at how people have been acting since Rafe got killed. Avoiding each other, whispering about each other. Afraid of each other. And now, with Lavinia, it'll be ten times worse." She nodded decisively. "Something's definitely hinky."

"Hinky?" Meri said sarcastically, stretching out on her bunk. "Where do you get that idea? We had a terrible spring, something's killing our chickens, we're running out of food, and the Watchers' solution is to kill a woman for being beautiful. All very logical."

"We're running out of *food*?" Lea moaned.

"No, we are not," Cynda murmured soothingly. "She's just giving an example. A *what if.*"

"*What if* the Watchers are completely illogical," I said. "*What if* there's no rhyme or reason behind the things they do."

"Wanda," Shawna put in. "If anyone gets in trouble for anything that's said tonight, we'll know who to blame."

Wanda glowered at her. "Red can get in plenty of trouble without any help from me," she said.

"Unfortunately, that's true," Cynda said, throwing an apologetic look my way. "You really ought to be more careful., Red."

Wanda perked up at this unexpected ally. "Exactly. Red disrupted the first city meeting, and that definitely breaks the rules about orderly assembly."

"We aren't supposed to have anything to do with people who break rules," Lea said, looking at me uneasily.

"Then go away," I told her. "Remove yourself from my bad influence."

"But it's after curfew. I'd be breaking *that* rule."

"Red puts us in an impossible position," Wanda agreed, looking around at the other girls. "She was a lightning rod even before the city meetings, and now she's downright unsafe to have around. That hair is like a target, painted right on her head."

"Now you're just being mean," Shawna said.

"It's mean to state the obvious? To say that Red stands out?" Wanda looked at me with a dark glint in her eye. "If you ask me, *that's* the reason for the city meetings. The Watchers are tired of people who call attention to themselves. I mean, Rafe was everybody's favorite instructor. And Lavinia was gorgeous. They stood out and they knew it. They thought they were better than everyone else."

"That's ridiculous," Liza said.

Wanda ignored her. "And neither one of them was anywhere near as bad as you, Red, with that hair—"

"It's not like she chose that color on purpose," Shawna put in.

"—And we all know they watch you more than anybody," Wanda concluded.

"They do not!" By this point it was more wishful thinking than anything else, but I protested anyway.

Cynda shifted. "Well, actually, they do watch you more," she said. "Warden Rick told me. They keep special records on you."

Baffled, I stared at her. Why hadn't she told me that before? She was my best friend, next to Meritt, of course.

"Of course they keep special records." Wanda ran a smug hand over her own unremarkable dark brown hair. "They're afraid she's got some mutant disease from the time of the ashes. She has that hair, and something obviously stunted her growth. She's a runt mutant."

I didn't dignify that with a reply, but Liza did. "If Red is what you get from the time of the ashes, then ashes are medicine you could have used, Wanda."

Wanda looked baffled, then offended. "If you think a runt mutant—"

Liza talked over her. "She's prettier than I am, too, Wanda. I'm just saying Red may be small and redheaded, but she does have some things in her favor."

"Meritt certainly thinks so," someone muttered.

"Farrell Dean, too," Wanda announced. "She'll probably get both of them pulled into a city meeting. She's probably the next Lavinia."

"Don't be stupid," Liza said sharply.

"She misbehaves and she's a mutant."

"Anyway I wouldn't say that Red is stunted," Shawna said. "She's on the low end of normal, that's all."

Wanda shrugged that off. "Whatever you call it, they aren't going to want her in the breeding pool," she said.

An uneasy silence filled the room as Cynda's pretty face went blank. Several girls shook their heads reprovingly; even Lea pulled herself together long enough to throw a chiding look Wanda's way.

We didn't know why Cynda had been sterilized—the genetic counselors wouldn't tell her what the problem was, not even whether it was something that might have hurt her children but wouldn't affect her, or whether it was a disease she'd develop as she aged. They told her it wasn't productive for her to know things she couldn't do anything about.

Not many things bothered Cynda, but that did. She wanted to know.

"The genetic counselors are very careful," Wanda said, relentless, with the self-righteous air of a person who sees herself as brave enough to state an unpleasant truth. "They don't want us to be weakened by compromised genes."

"Save it for the cameras, Wanda." I went to Cynda and put a hand on her shoulder. "There's nobody but us watching you now."

Wanda turned on me. "I'm surprised they haven't already put you in a city meeting," she said. "You're a freak and a public nuisance. If you cared at all about fitting in you'd at least cut your hair short. I mean, look at you, flaunting it like that. It's almost down to your waist."

Cynda came to my defense. "Red does try to keep it tucked away in her cap when she's out in public, but I don't think she realized how sensitive you are about how dull your hair looks by comparison. Red, to spare Wanda's delicate feelings, could you be sure to start wearing your cap round the clock?"

Wanda looked livid, but Lea was the next to speak.

"Cutting her hair wouldn't help," she said. She was still splotchy from her hysterical crying jag and had a terrible case of the hiccups, but she was determined to make her point. "It'd still be that color. Unless she shaved her head bald." Fixing her gaze on me, she started crying again. "Please," she said. "Please, Red, you have to do it."

I waved Lea off, trying to sound nonchalant despite the note of terror in her voice. "Don't be silly—I'm not going to shave my head."

"But they'll *kill* you!"

"A bald girl. It's not like she'd be less noticeable that way," Liza said practically, and Lea began to wail.

"Lea, hyperventilating will not help matters." Cynda looked stern. "If you can't control yourself, I'll have to slap you again."

Lea gave a little jump, but she stopped crying and, after a moment, sagged back against Cynda's comforting bulk.

Wanda's two best friends, Joy and Linni, had been oddly quiet through all this, but now one of them spoke up.

"She could dye her hair," Joy said.

Linni nodded in agreement. "Good idea. She should dye it."

"With what?" Meri sat up and looked interested.

Joy made a thinking face. "Oh, I don't know. Boiled tree

bark? Or—listen, don't orange and purple make brown? So she could use blackberries."

Linni tittered.

"She'd attract flies," Joy went on, "but it would be worth it, right?"

"Oh yeah," Wanda said, giving a satisfied smirk. "That would be worth it."

"It would be worth it," Linni echoed.

I decided to ignore them.

"I vote that she sticks with the cap," Shawna said, as usual trying to de-escalate. "That's probably a safer bet than trying to dye her hair. If it ended up purple, she'd really be in trouble."

By now, every girl in the room was staring at me.

"Forget my hair!" I said. "Who cares about my hair? Two people are dead, and there's another city meeting tomorrow."

Lea let out a wail. Cynda glared at me.

Wanda nodded smugly.

There I went again, causing trouble.

Chapter 11

My lungs burned. I was desperately trying to keep up with Meritt, but he was too fast, hurtling toward the wasteland as if he didn't know death waited there. I tried to call out, to warn him, but the habit of silence and secrecy was too strong.

He was lost.

When I stepped in something wet I knew it wasn't rain. It was thick and dark and smelled metallic, and when I stopped, the puddle widened, darkened, held me fast.

Then wardens came out of nowhere, pointing their guns at me, and in the split second before I felt the bullets I tried to shout that Meritt was lost so that maybe someone would find him, but no one who cared was around to hear.

Then Rafe picked me up and I was limp and heavy and he carried my body to the sea. He wanted to wash away the blood, and only the sea could do it.

And then I was alone, lying on cold sand, and Rafe was wading out deeper and deeper, trying to wash off the blood, and the waves crashed against us, separated us. They carried him away, though he struggled to stay with me, and I was alone.

With a start I sat up, heart pounding. The room was

pitch black; someone was snoring gently. The cameras I couldn't see seemed pointed straight at me.

I lay back down, not expecting to sleep, but exhaustion claimed me almost instantly. And as soon as I slept I dreamed again. I was standing in the circle at a city meeting but it was Meritt, not Farrell Dean, who was dragging me away from Rafe. In real life Farrell Dean had held my face against his chest, trying to calm me, trying to keep me from seeing Rafe die, but in my dream Meritt didn't do that. Instead he put his hands over my ears to stop me from hearing Rafe's dying words. *It's better you not know*, he said. *I like having you for a pet.*

This time when I sat up, I knew I wouldn't sleep again.

How much of the night was left? I wasn't sure. I might have been able to guess if I could have seen the moon, but heavy blinds blocked out the night. Not that I would have had it any other way. If it weren't for the blinds that darkened our room and blinded the cameras, I'd never be able to sneak out to meet Meritt.

I pushed back against the wall and pulled my knees up to my chest, moving carefully so I wouldn't jostle the bunk and disturb Kari.

It felt like the middle of the night. It felt like it would be a long time until dawn. Well, I knew one thing I could do to pass some time. I would make myself remember what Rafe had said, whether Meritt wanted me to remember or not.

No, Meritt wasn't trying to keep me from remembering; that was only my dream.

Taking a deep breath, I closed my eyes. Carefully, knowing it was going to hurt, I put myself back in the city meeting circle. I saw Rafe come out of the watchtower door. I squinted against the spotlight. I heard the impossible death sentence. I felt the warden grab me—he was choking me, but Rafe stopped him with a strike to his throat. I was struggling against Farrell Dean as he wrapped me in a bear hug and turned me away from Rafe, from the gunshots. I strained my ears to catch Rafe's words, but they echoed and doubled back on themselves and were nothing but the inarticulate sounds of my own grief.

I opened my eyes. This was no good. The harder I thought, the more garbled Rafe's words became.

Suddenly restless, I couldn't bear the thought of sitting there quietly tormenting myself and waiting for morning. How could everyone sleep so peacefully, when all around us the world was more full of weeping than we could understand?

That was what old Louie sometimes said, and he was right, though I hadn't truly understood it until now. He started saying it back when I was little, when no one would play with me, and he'd take me on his lap and tell me I was different because I was a fairy child—which even then I knew was silly, but it was better than thinking about the many ways I was a freak. I'd sit there with Louie and maybe a couple of the old women, and he'd make up some story about adventures I supposedly had had. The stories were all different, but Louie always started them in the same way: Come away, oh fairy child, to the waters and the wild. Come and let me hold your hand, for the world's more full of weeping than you can understand.

Louie was a sweet old man.

And I couldn't stand to sit there, alone and awake in the dark crowded room, any longer.

Gently I swung down from my bunk and felt around on the floor for my clothes. In the darkness I pulled them on, paying careful attention to my cap, making sure it covered every single hair. Then slowly, scarcely breathing, I eased across the room, telling myself I was silence. I was night.

Lea sighed and turned over, but no one else moved. The

cadence of a sleeper's breathing went steadily on; the snorer never paused. Even Shawna, who was an irritatingly light sleeper, was still and quiet.

The metal door was cold and heavy. I opened it just far enough to slip through, then held it so it would close slowly, without its usual telltale thud.

At the bottom of the stairs I did the same thing with the outside door, flinching as the cold air hit me in the face. It smelled like frost and made all my senses feel fully alert, honed sharp.

The moon was high in the sky and more than three-quarters full, bathing the city in light that was almost as bright as day and yet cooler, more remote. The bright moonlight made it a little harder for me to travel the streets unobserved, but I could manage. I'd done it before.

There was a cinderblock pillar on either side of the door, braces that held up the narrow roof that protected the entry area. I stepped behind one of the pillars, the same way I always did, and scanned the streets.

No one was in sight. The spotlight swept across the city, probing the shadows cast by the moon, but it revealed no movement anywhere.

Still I hesitated, leaning against the rough pillar, studying the moon-washed buildings and empty streets. I'd never gone out alone with no one to meet. I'd always gone out to meet Meritt.

But now Rafe was dead. I'd always pretended he was my father, and if my father was gone, then I had to grow up.

So I slid from shadow to shadow, keeping track of the cameras Meritt had taught me to avoid, ignoring the ones he said were dummies or defective. I behaved exactly as I always did, telling myself with every step that this was no different from any other night. I knew the routine. I knew the safe path through the dark.

By the time I passed the slaughterhouse with its metallic scent of blood, and crept out the western gap into the wasteland, I half-expected to see Meritt waiting for me right where he usually stood. He wasn't, of course. The wasteland lay bare, its ugly tufts of grass twisted flat against the sand. Meritt had been here just a few hours ago, though. He'd been here with me. I could practically see us, quarreling, reconciling. I saw him touching my face, wiping away my tears, stroking my hair.

The memory of us, of him, made me feel less alone. I leaned against the outside of the city wall, where Meritt and I always leaned, and felt the emptiness, the silence, gently opening places in my mind that had been tightly shut. I could smell the pine trees and taste a distant salty hint of the sea. I could hear the wind rustling high in the evergreens, stirring now and then the dying leaves that drifted, one by one, to the ground.

It was because there were too many people, I decided. The city was fraught with thoughts and emotions, with fear and anger that were almost palpable, choking me when I breathed, squeezing out any space for thought or memory. In the dormitory someone was always crying, being comforted or ignored. Out here it was just me, alone. Out here I could think.

But thinking too hard seemed to scare the memory of Rafe's words away, so I let my mind drift, out into the woods, into the water beyond.

Beyond Optica. What was out there? Were there other islands, other people? Once when I mentioned the idea to Cynda, she said, "And maybe there are talking animals, too. And maybe a giant duck will carry us to a happy place where the sun shines every day." She'd put her arm around my shoulders. "This is where we are, Red. This is what is. Optica."

Still I couldn't help thinking about it, and a breeze

passed over and the shadows of the trees gesticulated, seemed to beckon me.

I was afraid of the woods, but now that there were predators inside the city, the wild things of the forest seemed less terrifying. It wouldn't be hard to let myself creep slowly toward the trees, to let their shadows cloak me as I moved across the open expanse of wasteland.

Before I knew it, I was fifty feet beyond the wall; I had never been so far from Optica. What was a few feet more? Quietly, slowly, I edged closer and closer to the woods.

And then I was in them, only a few steps beyond their border, but already it felt a world apart. The city smelled all of pavement, people, chemical cleansers. These trees smelled fresh and somehow hopeful. Despite everything I knew and had heard about the wilderland, that scent made me feel safer. Then, too, the trees were so tall; that meant they must be quite old, and it seemed to me that if they could endure that long, if the earth had kept feeding them all those years and the sky had kept bringing them sunshine and rain, then maybe there was something in the world that might help us endure as well.

I knew I was too far from the beach to hear the sea, at least at ordinary times, but that night felt extraordinary, so I stood very still and listened for the distant sound of waves along the shore until the night insects among the trees grew accustomed to my presence and began to sing again.

Then I emptied my mind and listened still longer, focusing my gaze on the night sky above the city, clear for once and spangled with a million stars. And the longer I looked, the more stars there seemed to be, as if some were timid and were peeking out only after careful consideration, after they got used to me and saw I was no threat.

I gazed upward for so long that I began to feel untethered from the earth, as if I were rising up toward the tiny lights far and away. If I moved my hand away from the rough bark of the tree, I could fly.

That was when I heard the voice.

With a start I came back to myself, my feet firmly on the ground. Wardens didn't usually patrol behind the slaughter-house, near the gap where I'd slipped out—it smelled bad, and it wasn't in a heavily populated area—but once or twice Meritt and I had narrowly missed being spotted by an unu-sually thorough warden. One of those must be out tonight, checking each and every sector.

At least I hoped it was a thorough warden, and not a la-zy one. What if I got trapped out here indefinitely while some slacker lounged by the gap smoking and dozing?

The voice muttered again, unintelligible, and my blood froze. It wasn't inside the city; it was behind me, in the woods.

Pressing my back against the rough bark of the tree I looked wildly around, peering into the dark woods, across the wasteland at the gray city wall. I saw no one, no unnatu-ral movement, nothing but the swaying shadows of the trees in the night wind.

I wanted to make a dash for the city but was afraid to move. If I stepped out into the wasteland he—it?—would see me. I remembered the stories of people returning from the woods without hands, or skinned alive, driven insane.

A cloud rolled out from behind the tops of the trees, and I stood there, helpless, and watched it cover the moon, leav-ing me stranded and blind. I could still hear, of course. I could hear twigs snapping, leaves rustling. Some animals could see in the dark. Could Guardians, or whatever this thing was?

The moon drifted back out and I frantically scanned my surroundings. I saw trees; I saw the pale wasteland; I saw the city wall; but I saw no one, no person, no animal. I peered into the darkness for so long that my shoulders began to ache with tension and my eyes stung dry and prickly from not blinking.

But I hadn't imagined the voice—I'd heard it. I was sure.

Then I heard it again. It was still quiet, but this time perfectly distinct.

"Red!"

Who would be outside the city in the middle of the night, calling my name? There was only one possibility.

"Meritt?" I called, very quietly.

"Red!"

My blood froze. The voice was louder this time, and much closer, and it sure wasn't Meritt. It wasn't any voice I knew. It was guttural, half-choking on my name.

I flung myself toward the safety of the city, stumbling over the tufted wasteland grass, urging myself not to fall, and the voice cried out again, louder, nearer still, calling my name pleadingly, so close I was afraid to look back, afraid I'd see it reaching out to grab me, and then I reached the gap in the wall and hurtled inside, not pausing to check for wardens or spotlights, not caring if they caught me.

I hit the pavement of the city and kept running, skidding around the corner of the slaughterhouse, smelling blood and death and fear, hoping the wall would stop my pursuer, hoping he wouldn't follow me into the city and chase me down and kill me in the street and paint pictures on the slaughterhouse wall with my blood.

Behind me the voice cried out once more, distantly and in tones of despair, "Red."

Chapter 12

"Family of Optica," the Voice said, and Judd, standing next to me, spoke the rest with him. "There are cancers among you."

"Shhhhh." I glanced warily around at the rows of faces. Judd's father might be a warden—might, if we'd guessed right—but that wouldn't protect Judd, not these days.

He glared at me for shushing him but stayed quiet during the rest of the lecture, while the wardens led Stuart, a butcher who'd recently lost an arm in an accident with the sausage grinder, into the spotlit center of the circle. Then wardens brought out an elderly man and stood him a few feet away from Stuart.

It was Louie.

I must have gasped. "Shh," Judd said, and in the reflected glow of the spotlight his face was unnaturally pale and pinched.

The wardens set a heavy bag of grain on the ground near Louie, and a bucket of water on the ground near Stuart.

The Voice didn't give us its introductory lecture. It didn't ask the men any questions. It didn't explain to us what the men had done wrong. Instead, a warden lit a match and touched it to the bag of grain. Then, unbelievably, he reached out and lit the sleeve of Louie's shirt.

A cry, hastily muted, went up from the crowd. Butcher Stuart didn't hesitate. With his one good arm he grabbed the bucket and flung the water over Louie. Before our lungs could release our collective sigh of relief, the Voice spoke.

"Butcher Stuart has failed the test," it said. "Cities do not survive on sentimentality."

As the last word echoed over the stunned crowd, a shot rang out. Stuart fell.

In the circle, Louie ran a disbelieving hand across his eyes. Then he knelt, slowly and awkwardly, beside Stuart's body and touched his neck, feeling for a pulse. When his shoulders sagged, we knew he'd found none. I thought he'd get up then—I was afraid he'd stand up and the warden would shoot him next—but Louie stayed on his knees. Clasping his hands together in front of his chest, he bent his head. His lips moved.

Then the spotlight cut out and all was black.

After a long paralyzed moment, when the lights didn't come on and the Voice didn't speak, people began moving silently, leaving the circle. Beside me Judd was craning around, peering into the darkness. Then he leaned toward me and breathed noisily in my ear. He was only twelve, but already he was taller than I was.

"Have you seen Petey?" he said.

I shook my head.

"Stuart was Petey's dad," Judd whispered. "We think."

Late that night, afraid but determined, I made my way through the streets to Rafe's house, avoiding the live cameras, staying in the shadows, trying not to think of all the ways I could get caught. I was in danger from the girls in my dorm, if any woke and found me gone; in danger from the cameras winking at me from the walls; in danger from patrol cars;

from the scarred warden; and from Zee, the warden in the tower, peering at me through the telescopes, following the pointing finger of the spotlight.

Unless Zee was busy drinking hot milk and whisky, playing Solitaire.

That thought made me angry. He sometimes watched and sometimes didn't, so even when I had privacy, I didn't know that I did. I'd never know whether there were watchers in the tower, or if they were only in my mind.

The adult houses near Rafe's were all dark, all quiet. His house was on the end of a row, so though it was crowded on three sides with other small dark houses, to the west were only the bee fields and then the orchards. That would have been helpful to Rafe, I thought. It would have made it easier to slip out unnoticed.

I stood against the western wall of his house a long time, watching for wardens, but the street remained quiet. In the narrow strip of sky between the eaves of two houses I could see only a single bright star, and a rhyme one of the nanny mothers had taught us came back to me—"Star light, star bright, first star I see tonight, I wish I may, I wish I might, have the wish I wish tonight." It wasn't the first star I'd seen that night, and besides, stars were burning balls of gas that couldn't grant wishes. Still I said the rhyme in my mind and added, "Please, star. Please help me remember what Rafe said."

The door to Rafe's house swung open at my touch; I crept inside and stood very still, ready to run, holding the door just barely ajar. I had to be as careful as possible, though I didn't think anyone else had been assigned to this house yet, and it didn't feel like anyone else was breathing in the darkness. The room felt hollow.

When I was as certain as I could be that I was alone, I pulled the door quietly shut and, after a moment's thought, swung the bar down to lock it. If someone tried the door and found it barred they'd instantly know that someone was inside, but if I didn't bar it, anyone could walk right in.

I'd never been in any of the houses before, and I wasn't sure what to expect. In the dark, I felt my way around, avoiding the shadowy shapes of furniture, the deeper darkness of the walls.

Exploring didn't take long. The tiny house consisted of only two rooms, the main one where I'd come in, and a small bathroom.

Some of the window shades were open. I pulled them down, and found a towel to cover the gap where one shade wasn't quite long enough to completely block the window. I was afraid to turn on the overhead lights, and I had no flashlight, of course—only wardens had those—but I had managed to pocket a candle from the emergency supply in the dormitory storeroom, and now I lit it, carefully shielding the flame with my hand, keeping even its small light away from the windows.

The main room contained a couch, a double bed with a gray blanket, and a small table with two chairs. A stack of books and papers sat on the table, and I went straight over. If Rafe had left a message, that seemed like a possible hiding place—tucked in a book, buried in lesson plans.

The top book was a history of Optica. It was an important book, because our history had passed out of living memory some fifty years before, after some sort of electrical storm had caused widespread illness and amnesia. I wasn't surprised to see the book here. Rafe had been particularly interested in our missing past and had spent a lot of time talking to the old people, asking questions, trying to help them remember what had happened.

He'd even spent time in prison for that. The wardens said he was unsettling people.

The books beneath the history were less interesting, though still important—we didn't have many books, and the ones we had were passed around among the handful of instructors. There was a book of mathematical proofs and explanations, and a book about logic and logical fallacies. Neither had any notes stuck between the pages.

Next I fanned through the stacks of papers, releasing the familiar smell of the schoolroom, of chalk and paper and sweaty children. All the papers were written in Rafe's own hand, in the decisive and efficient half-cursive, half-print that I'd seen a million times on the blackboard.

At first I thought all the papers were lesson plans; then I realized that a few of them turned personal.

"What is it that makes me want privacy?" he'd written on the bottom of a grammar lesson. "How can I even imagine it? My students imagine that we adults have privacy, but wardens knock at my door at all hours. They come in, they run their hands under the sheets, they check the bottoms of the chairs, and then they vanish again—until the next day, or the next hour. And even when they aren't here, they know things they couldn't know unless they were here, which means they could be watching even now, as I write this. They snatch my thoughts out of the very air. Do they watch everyone as closely as they watch me? They are everywhere and nowhere."

Hastily I let the pages fall, hiding those words. Watching *now*? I hoped not. Meritt had never said anything about cameras in the adult houses.

But maybe Meritt didn't know everything.

And yet Meritt probably *did* know everything about surveillance; he maintained it all.

But I hadn't warned him that I was coming here. If he'd known, maybe he would have warned me that there were cameras.

After sitting there frozen in panic for who knows how long, I had a marginally helpful thought: There was no point in worrying now. If I'd been seen, I'd been seen.

Again I looked down at the pages in my hands. I would take Rafe's words away with me—not to read, but to destroy. They were private, weren't they? One of the only privacies Rafe had ever had. Even if wardens had already been here, even if they'd already read these pages, destroying them would be my gift to Rafe. That's what I would do.

But now I had to concentrate on why I was here.

I stood in the center of the main room and considered. If Rafe had left a message, maybe it wouldn't be in a book or under the mattress. He knew wardens searched such places. So he'd hide his message in a way that they wouldn't understand. He'd make it so that even if they saw it, they wouldn't know what they saw. The question was whether I would.

Rafe had been fond of me, enough that I had even dared to wonder, against all the evidence of our very different appearances, if maybe I really was his daughter. Progenitors had more information than children did—they at least knew how old their children were, and sometimes they knew the gender, if the mother managed to catch a glimpse in the delivery room—so finally, in a fit of courage, I'd asked him.

He had looked at me for a long time. "Lonna's pregnancies were well before your time," he'd said finally.

"And you were never assigned to anyone else?"

"No," he said. "But if it's any comfort, Red, I wish you were mine. I'd be glad to claim you."

Yes, Rafe cared about me. I had no doubt about that. But he'd never told me about what he was doing, about the spying and the hiding of food and the mysterious stealing of painkillers. So if there was a hidden message, it probably wasn't intended for me. I might look right at it, and not recognize it for what it was.

Pushing away that discouraging thought, I set to work. Not expecting to find anything, I flipped up the mattress, felt among Rafe's clothes, his towels, his bedding, looked under the bottoms of the chairs in case Rafe had written something there. I felt like a warden, but I kept looking anyway.

I found absolutely nothing. I saw nothing that seemed odd or out of place.

Where else could I look?

There were three things on the wall: a calendar, a sketch of Lonna, and a map of Optica that Rafe had used to teach us geography.

The calendar was heavily marked, but nothing on it seemed significant—notes about when and where the moon rose and set; comments about the tide; and, of course, his plans for what he intended to teach each day at school. One day in April was marked, simply, Lonna. It was, I thought, the day she died. It had been some sort of electrical accident at work. She'd still been training Meritt, but he hadn't been with her when it happened. He and Rafe had found her afterwards. She had died alone.

I studied her picture on the wall. It was amazingly like her. Had Rafe drawn this himself, or had someone else drawn it for him? Sometimes we doodled in the sand in the schoolyard, but there wasn't enough paper for us to practice real drawing. Someone had, though. Someone could draw quite well.

The only thing left to examine was the map. Gently I reached out one hand and touched it, remembering sitting in school, listening to Rafe going on about the difficulties of mapmaking.

"When you're in the middle of a forest, all the trees seem tall," he'd said. "Distance is skewed by your own physicality, by whether you're tired, lonely, energetic. In mapmaking, feelings count for nothing. It's all measurements and geometry. It's all brain, not heart. But even brains sometimes fall prey to illusion."

He'd had us try to make our own miniature maps on our small chalkboards, then sent us out into the city in pairs. One partner was blindfolded and led about until thoroughly lost, then freed and told to find the way back to school using the little map.

Staring at Rafe's map, there in the flickering candlelight, I remembered being blindfolded, feeling Meritt's hand in mine, holding tight to my map with the other. We had walked a long time, but I hadn't known whether we'd gone a long way, or whether he'd led me around in circles.

When he let go of my hand I stopped in my tracks, afraid he had run away and left me alone and lost in some distant part of the city.

He was two years older, after all, and a boy. Sometimes he thought things were funny that I didn't. So I stood there in the darkness, seeing only a strip of gray concrete beneath the edge of the blindfold, picturing myself searching for him down unfamiliar streets, lost and terrified.

It felt like forever to me, but it was probably only a few seconds before Meritt untied my blindfold, pulled it free, and revealed his big joke: the blood-filled slaughterhouse yard. He was hoping to make me shriek, but I was so relieved he hadn't abandoned me that a bunch of cow blood didn't seem like a big deal.

I think I managed to impress Meritt a little, that day. He never knew how frightened I'd been. Only Rafe knew that.

He knew, because when the other kids left school that day, I stayed behind to talk to him. I didn't have anything to say, not really, but I was always looking for some reason to prolong my time with him. That day, what I said was, "Will we have another Lost Child day, or was today the only one?"

Rafe had been taken aback—I think he'd forgotten I was

so much younger than the other kids, more liable to be frightened by being turned loose in the city.

"Lost child," he said, putting an arm around my shoulders and pulling me close. "Is that how you felt?"

And that was it.

That was it!

I took a deep breath, wanting to shout, wanting to tell someone. That was what Rafe had said just before he died: *Lost child.*

It was a message only I would understand. Nobody knew about that but the two of us, Rafe and me. What did he want me to remember about the Lost Child day?

I thought back to that incident, five years before. After I'd been unimpressed by the bloody slaughterhouse yard, I'd managed, with a good bit of winding and doubling back and sheer blind luck, to get us back to school. Then Meritt and I had switched places. I had blindfolded him, and wandered randomly around until we ended up at the blackberry fields.

Was there anything significant about either of those places? The slaughterhouse lay on the eastern wall, near the safer woods. It smelled metallic and salty, like blood. The camera was unreliable. I couldn't see what any of that had to do with Rafe.

But the fields didn't, either. As a farm worker I knew there was nothing there—just rows of aggressive blackberries with their sharp thorns that left stinging cuts on our faces and arms, their fruit that stained the bottoms of our feet purple. They grew so fast you could practically see it happening; they were a blessing and a blight. They had nothing to do with Rafe.

Shutting my eyes, I imagined myself back into the Lost Child day. I was small, looking up at Rafe. His face was troubled because he'd intended it as a fun outing for us, but he could see that something in the experience had shaken me.

He had started to say something, then stopped, shaking his head. Then he took hold of my shoulders and pulled me into his arms. That didn't happen very often, and I felt startled and pleased. Rafe's shirt was rough under my cheek, like my own was rough on my back. He smelled like chalk dust and musty books and himself. He seemed very large and warm, and for once I felt completely wanted, completely safe from jeers and jostlings and accidental injuries that had been carefully planned.

When he spoke I heard his voice rumble in his chest, where my ear was. He said, "Red, remember this: You're never a lost child if you have a map in your hands or in your head."

And now I opened my eyes.

There on the wall of the empty home was the map Rafe had used to teach us geography. It was a large square of paper, carefully framed in wood. At the top it said, "A watched city is an orderly city."

The motto struck me as odd, now, and I wondered whether Rafe had put it there as his own private joke, or maybe to make it look like he believed in everything that was Optica. Because he hadn't. Even years ago, before the city began failing and Rafe began spying on the Watchers, years before when I was just a kid in school, Rafe had said things that made us ask questions.

Holding the candle up, I studied the meticulous portrayal of Optica. There was my dormitory. There were my fields, with the Watchers' compound above them, and the wilderland beyond that. I found the watchtower in the middle, saw the circle beneath it, even the tiered steps carefully rendered in impossibly thin lines. Every street was drawn, every building, right down to every little house. Rafe—or whoever had made this map—had included every detail.

He had even, I saw now, marked the cameras. Surely

that was what the tiny x marks meant. Yes, there were the two in the school, and the wide-lens in the schoolyard marked with a double x; and there was the one at the slaughterhouse.

What was I looking for? What had Rafe wanted me to see?

I studied top to bottom and left to right. I began finding the places where things had happened to Meritt and me. I traced the lines of the streets where I'd run with him that memorable night, noted the exact spot where I'd been caught. There was the gap where the blonde warden had stopped Meritt; there was the wasteland where Rafe had been arrested.

Something caught my eye.

Rafe—or whoever the mapmaker had been—had drawn a tiny, almost invisible circle on the outer side of the city wall. I looked at the rest of the wall; tiny circles appeared regularly. There was one outside the eastern wall, near the slaughterhouse. But I knew that area well, had spent hours out there with Meritt, and I couldn't remember anything there worth marking with a circle.

Lifting the candle, I examined the map again, this time turning my attention to the inside of the city. After a little while I spotted another tiny, faint circle under the watchtower. I went on searching for the tiny circles until I thought I was going cross-eyed, and counted nine more before my stinging eyes made me stop.

What were they? I had no idea.

I rested my eyes for a few minutes, and then tried again. I was just on the cusp of giving up when I noticed something else, a mistake that until just recently I would have considered completely unremarkable: On Rafe's map the wall was open between the Watcher compound and the wilderland. But I knew the wall there was unbroken—I had seen it through the telescope in the watchtower. The Watchers were walled off from the Guardians.

My heartbeat sounded suddenly loud in my ears. I didn't know whether it was from hope or fear.

Rafe was careful. Rafe had drawn this map—and I was sure, now, that he had drawn it with his own hand—with incredible accuracy and care. So if the discrepancy meant what I thought it meant, at one time the wall beyond the compound had opened to the wilderland. And that made sense. The Guardians protected the Watchers, enforced their commands.

But then something had changed, a falling out perhaps, and the openings in the walls had been filled in. And if the Guardians were no longer allies with the Watchers, there was at least a small chance that they would help us.

There was another possibility, of course. Maybe the wall was sealed because something mad or evil out there had killed the Guardians, or the Guardians themselves had gone mad, and nothing was safe from them.

Who would be brave enough—or foolish enough—to go into the woods to find out?

I shivered, remembering the guttural voice from the night before, the voice from the wilderland, calling my name.

Chapter 13

Anxious to find Meritt and tell him what I'd discovered at Rafe's house, I went to breakfast early. It was a misty morning, touched with pale pink light—one of those strangely delicate mornings that sometimes come just before a hard frost.

Though I was out far earlier than usual, the streets weren't empty. Small groups of people clustered here and there, huddling into themselves against the morning chill. A boy on the edge of the circle nearest to me surreptitiously snickered. I approached one group—cautiously, given my pariah status—in time to hear a woman say, "It's not just this one. It's most of them."

She was standing beneath a camera. I followed her gaze and saw that someone else had been slipping through the shadows on the streets of Optica the night before. Someone with access to black paint.

The sign under the camera now read, "We Watch Because We SCare."

The cafeteria was full of gray-faced, frightened people. If they'd seen the altered signs, they were afraid to laugh at them.

After waiting by the door for ages I went through the

line and got my food, and then settled at a table with old Louie and Cline, where I could see the entrance. Two people at the table promptly got up and left, but the rest stayed put. I guess they figured they were already eating with Louie, who'd actually been put in a city meeting, so what did I matter.

Louie patted my hand when I sat down. "I don't want to talk about it," he said, and I nodded.

"Neither do I."

"Then let's discuss a more pleasant topic. You, for instance, are getting prettier every day." He winked. "Though that's only to be expected, given you're a fairy child."

Cline's face took on a look of such pained incredulity that I almost smiled.

Louie chatted on in the same manner, saying nothing important, but somehow steadying me just the same. And all the while, I was watching and waiting. How was I going to stand it if I had to go all day—and possibly all night—without being able to tell Meritt what I'd found?

Eventually Louie wandered off to cheer up someone else and left me to Cline's silence. I was finishing my toast—still keeping one eye on the door—when Farrell Dean slid into the seat between us and rolled a hardboiled egg from his tray to my own. His face was flushed and his eyes sparkling, unlike pretty much everyone else in the room.

Maybe it was the contrast between him and all those gray-faced and cowed people, or maybe I was annoyed with Meritt for not being there when I needed him; in any case, I smiled at Farrell Dean with more warmth than I intended, and he went abruptly still and quiet.

Cline glowered at me—he seemed to think I was an embarrassing habit Farrell Dean should have the willpower to break. I smiled sweetly at him, knowing it would irritate, and turned my attention back to Farrell Dean.

If I could have told him about the map I would have—I

was itching to tell someone—but there were too many people around for that sort of conversation. I settled for teasing him a little.

"You're looking fit this morning," I said. "Sleep well?"

He cast a sideways glance at me, his eyes wary. "As always," he said.

"Have sweet dreams?"

"Not really, no." He turned sideways in his chair and looked at me directly. "I dreamed about you."

I stuck out my tongue at him and he laughed.

The textile worker directly across the table was smiling benevolently at us. At least we'd managed to distract one person from the stress of the day.

"So what happened in this dream about me?" I said, rolling the egg on the table to crack its shell.

"Actually, it was a nightmare."

"A nightmare? No way. Not with me in it—I'm a fairy."

"Since when?"

"Since Louie said so. Ask Cline."

Cline made a disgusted noise.

"Can you tell just by looking?" Farrell Dean began considering me narrowly, leaning back and forth to see me from different angles, presumably looking for signs of fairy-dom. "Do fairies have wings? Fancy hair? Are they pretty?"

Cline dropped his fork in exasperation; the textile worker flinched, startled, then recovered and smiled at us again.

"Fairies are smart," I informed Farrell Dean. "That's their key characteristic—they're smarter and braver than other people give them credit for being."

Farrell Dean nodded, miming deep thought. "The Red in my dream was smart," he said slowly. "Too smart for her own good, in fact. And too brave, and too stubborn. Plus she had terrible taste in men. Does that sound like a fairy to you?"

I frowned; Cline smirked. The textile worker looked back and forth between the three of us.

"And in my dream this fairy—or whoever she was—kept dancing on the edge of a cliff." Farrell Dean pointedly met my eyes. His tone was still light but his face was grave. "That's where the nightmare came in. I knew I was too far away to catch her if she fell."

For a long moment the table was silent.

"Maybe the fairy didn't need to be caught," I said. "Maybe she could fly."

Farrell Dean smiled, but his eyes were serious. "Maybe she thought so," he said softly. "But it was only a dream."

The textile worker waited to see if I'd reply. When I didn't, she stood up and collected her tray. "Young people are so resilient," she remarked as she turned to go.

I got up as well, and pushed my metal chair back up to the table.

"I'll be at your field sometime today," Farrell Dean said in a low voice, every trace of joking gone. "We need to talk."

"About what?"

He glanced over at Cline, who nodded, his face set and grim.

"About Meritt."

"*Warden,*" Cline muttered.

I turned, and found myself face to face with the scarred warden.

"Time to go," he said.

"What do you mean?" I tried to back away from him, but Farrell Dean had stood up and was right behind me. He put a protective hand on my shoulder.

The warden looked at him over my head. "This has nothing to do with you," he said. "She's field supervisor, and she's late."

I wasn't. I knew exactly how much time I still had. But

arguing would do no good, and I wasn't going to drag anyone else into trouble as well.

"He's right," I said hurriedly, glancing back at Farrell Dean. "I'm going."

"Red—" Farrell Dean began.

"Take her tray," the warden told him. "Clean up her mess."

Then he took me by the arm and started pulling me after him.

"Hey—" Farrell Dean said. "Wait a minute—"

I glanced back over my shoulder, casting a beseeching look at Cline. He nodded and, without a word, stepped in front of Farrell Dean, blocking the narrow aisle with his bulk.

When I glanced back again, from the end of the aisle, Cline was gripping Farrell Dean's shoulder and whispering something in his ear. Farrell Dean's gaze was fixed on me, his face white.

As for the scarred warden, I hoped he was only trying to scare me—surely he wouldn't make me go with him now, when I really was supposed to be at work, when I'd be missed and reported.

But I grew less hopeful as he pulled me toward the door, staying so close that I could feel his breath on my hair. I wanted to believe he was only toying with me, but with each step I felt less and less certain. If I was late to work, after all, I'd be the one in trouble; and if I blamed him, if I complained, no one would pay any attention. He only had to say that he'd taken me in for some infraction.

What would happen if I ran for it as soon as I got outside? I was fast, though maybe not faster than he was—and anyway where could I go? Even if I escaped this time, he'd catch up to me sooner or later, and it would be worse then. Or he might pay me back by going after my friends—and Meritt and Farrell Dean certainly couldn't stand up to malicious scrutiny, not if they'd been pulling stunts like the one that got Rafe killed.

But if I went with him ...

As I reached the door, still trying to find a way out of my quandary, two figures appeared at the entrance to the kitchen. I saw them out of the corner of my eye, but didn't pay any attention. They'd be kitchen workers, finishing up their first shift; they always came out about now, ready to take a break before starting lunch. They couldn't help me. Nobody could help me, except maybe another warden, and why would one of them take my side against one of their own?

I had started to push the exit turnstile, leaning into it—I had to run, I couldn't meekly hand myself over to this man—when someone spoke.

"Oh, Red, I'm glad I caught you," she said. It was Marta, the kitchen worker who drove the lunch truck. "I need to talk to you about the number of Field A workers—there's a miscount somewhere, and I don't know if it's on our end or yours, but your field is requiring more meals than we've rationed for you."

She looked at the warden, then, as if she'd only just noticed him.

"I'm sorry, warden, we're blocking your way," she said, taking my arm and leading me around him, toward the kitchen door. That swinging metal door with its scuffed gray paint seemed like the most beautiful thing I'd ever seen. I didn't look at the warden—I kept my eyes firmly on that door. Marta pushed it open and we stepped inside. The door swung shut behind us. Steamy heat from the big sinks where workers were washing pots enveloped me. It made me feel faint, or maybe I was faint from relief.

The scarred warden hadn't followed us. Apparently he wasn't yet prepared to make a scene, was willing to bide his time till a more opportune moment.

The kitchen workers were folding their aprons and filing toward the door we'd just entered. Marta eased us around the stragglers, one hand still firmly on my arm, and pulled a clipboard from the wall.

"Here," she said. "Look over those names, and tell me who's missing."

I met her eyes. Not by so much as a flicker of an eyelash did she indicate that she knew she'd interfered with whatever the scarred warden had planned for me.

But I had to wonder. The list had all the proper names.

The day went downhill from there. Farrell Dean never came to my field, and wasn't at supper, and Meritt didn't come to supper either. I searched for him at the city meeting, but if he was there I never did spot him. I ended up standing with my silent bunkmate, Kari, who wasn't really quite as silent as she seemed, at least not that night. She hummed, just barely audibly.

Maybe it was a holdover from her work in the postnatal ward; maybe she hummed to the newborn babies. Or maybe she just found it comforting. In any case, she did it all through the city meeting, so quietly that sometimes I couldn't hear it but could only sort of feel it. It didn't bother me, but it didn't comfort me either. I wished it did.

That night, the Watchers put Judd and Petey in the circle.

"One of these boys stole a pair of boots," the Voice, echoing out of the darkness, announced. "Our surveillance team caught both of them at the relevant place in the relevant time frame. But which boy was it?"

They looked so young, standing there in the glare of the spotlight. Judd was shaking his head. Though the night was chilly, his face was red and beads of sweat stood out on his forehead. Petey looked petrified with fear.

"Each boy has two choices," the Voice said. "He can confess and ask for mercy; or he can stay silent and maintain his innocence. But there are consequences. If one boy confesses and the other stays silent, then the one who confesses will be executed for stealing. If neither boy confesses, or if both boys confess, they'll both be executed."

A wave of nausea hit me. They were so young, they were best friends, and they would both die unless one volunteered to die alone.

Rain began to fall, not heavily, but each separate drop cold and sharp, stinging my face. I didn't raise a hand to protect myself; no one did. In the harsh glare of the spotlight we stood frozen, appalled, watching Petey and Judd sort through the dilemma. Their faces fell into expressions of despair as they realized there was no way out, no way for them both to survive.

"Time is up," the Voice announced. "I will count to five. At five, your decision has been made."

Two wardens stood behind the boys, guns at the ready. Judd turned his head and looked at his younger friend. Petey was terrified, all skinny arms and legs and big frightened eyes. He was staring fixedly straight ahead, as if he couldn't believe this was happening to him.

"One," said the Voice.

"This is stupid," Judd said loudly, indignantly. "Nobody stole any boots."

"Two."

"We're friends," he said to the crowd, to all us voiceless, useless people.

"Three."

"They're trying to make us enemies." He wasn't talking to us anymore. He was talking to the universe, pleading for someone, anyone, to be fair, to put this impossible situation right again.

"Four."

Petey's lips moved. "Shut up, Judd," he said.

"Five."

Petey stepped forward. "It was me," he said. "It was only me."

Then the bullet hit him and he fell, the single shot all but swallowing Judd's cry.

The spotlight went off.

"Stay in your places," the Voice said.

Uneasily people shifted; we'd never been made to stay before.

After several tense minutes the spotlight came back on. Judd and Petey were gone. Instead Ronnie, a cook who had been badly burned in a kitchen accident some years before, was standing in front of a bucket of water. On one side of her lay a full crate of candles. On her other side stood Opal, a laundress in her late fifties, a gentle, quiet woman everybody loved.

"A double city meeting," someone behind me breathed, her throat sounding thick with dread.

I couldn't take my eyes off the bucket of water. This was the way Louie's city meeting had started—the city meeting in which Petey's father, Stuart, had died.

Sure enough, the warden lit the crate of candles and then touched his match to Opal's shirt.

Ronnie didn't hesitate. She threw the water over the candles, and within seconds Laundress Opal was a mass of shrieking flames. She dropped to the ground and rolled, trying to put out the fire, but it wouldn't go out.

Around the circle people were crying out, pressing their hands over their mouths in horror. In the front row a man stepped forward, tearing off his shirt, and I knew he intended to smother the flames. Before he could reach the writhing woman, however, the warden raised his gun and shot her. He must have made that decision on his own, to spare Opal the agony of burning to death, because after he did it he looked around nervously as if expecting to be condemned himself.

"Congratulations, Warden Eli," the Voice said. "You have shown compassion. Cook Ronnie has not, though she herself has suffered burns and knows how painful they can be."

"No," Ronnie said, backing away from the warden. "No!"

"Candles are meant to burn," the Voice said smoothly. "People are not."

And Cook Ronnie was shot.

Chapter 14

When the dazed crowd broke up, I found myself moving in the direction of the slaughterhouse, my body shaking but my feet moving steadily and away from the flow of people. I wasn't going out into the wasteland, not after hearing that voice calling my name, but I could hide in the slaughterhouse doorway beneath the broken camera and have some privacy.

I couldn't face going back to the dormitory just then, back to a room full of frightened girls, and I still had plenty of time before curfew. These days most of the girls were sound asleep by curfew, hiding under the covers, escaping the only way we knew. Maybe I'd risk staying out late and hope Wanda didn't stay up to notice.

The cold sharp pellets of rain were still falling, but I didn't care. Why were they doubling up on executions? Poor Opal—burning was a terrible way to die, the worst. And Petey was so young.

He hadn't stolen any boots, of course he hadn't. Why would anyone steal something he couldn't wear without getting caught? The Watchers were lying, making excuses to do horrible things to us.

But why? It made no sense.

I stepped around the beginnings of a puddle, still

hearing the distant noise of the city meeting behind me. Petey had been so brave. Judd would be feeling terrible right now, mourning his friend, wishing he'd stepped up and saved Petey. He'd probably also be feeling glad to still be alive, and that would make him feel even worse. Would he go straight back to his dorm? I supposed he would; there was nowhere else for him to go. Surely someone there would take care of him—Farrell Dean, if he'd turned up. Or maybe Ezzie.

The rain went from stinging to a downpour. By the time I reached the slaughterhouse my clothes were drenched and my hair streaming. It suited my mood, cold and grieving, helpless and alone.

I thought I'd be alone, there at the slaughterhouse. No one besides Meritt and me came there this time of day, and I hadn't seen him alone for what felt like forever. But when I arrived Meritt was there, a lanky, immediately recognizable shadow leaning against the slaughterhouse door.

Farrell Dean was always nudging me, rumpling my hair, throwing an arm around my shoulders, but Meritt hardly ever did more than touch my sleeve or tug at the end of my braid. That night, though, he reached out without a word and pulled me to him. He was wet from the rain but his body still felt warm, and I stood there, my face against his chest, feeling his arms around me, feeling him breathe, and gradually I stopped shaking.

Meritt released me then, but he still didn't move away. He kept one arm around my shoulders and we huddled in the darkness in the doorway, sheltered from the rain, our faces close together, and I didn't say a word about Petey and Judd. Instead I told Meritt about going to Rafe's house, about seeing the map and remembering the words "lost child."

"Rafe wanted us to see that map," I said at the end. "That's his message."

Meritt's arm around my shoulders loosened. "You did

good," he said, and his voice in the darkness sounded oddly relieved.

"What, you expected me to screw things up?"

"Of course not. I'm glad nothing happened to you, that's all. I don't like you being out alone. It isn't safe."

I gave a short harsh laugh. "Nothing's safe," I said, thinking of Petey falling, of Judd's horrified face.

"True. But some things are less safe than others."

Waving that off, I went back to my discovery.

"So what do you think those circles on the map are? One's right outside the wall, close to where we usually stand."

"I don't know." Meritt removed his arm from my shoulders. "Let's go look. Show me where it is."

But I hesitated, thinking about being out in the wasteland in the dark, remembering the voice in the woods. "Do you think that's safe?"

Meritt looked down at me, and in the darkness I saw the flash of his crooked grin. "Nothing's safe," he said, echoing my own words.

It would have been natural, then, to tell him about my recent experience in the woods, about the voice that called my name, but somehow it was too much on top of the horrors of the evening. I didn't want to talk about it. It edged too close to my dream that we could run away together, Meritt and I. It meant we could have no escape.

Meritt was watching me, or at least his face was turned toward me in the dark.

"Is there something you're not telling me?" he said. "You've never been particularly afraid of the wasteland before. And I'll be with you, just like always."

I half shrugged and looked away. "It's just ... what if someone's out there? Watching us from the woods? Meri says something has been coming into the city lately, killing chickens. Something that isn't an animal."

For a long moment Meritt was silent. He turned his face toward the pouring rain and leaned one shoulder against the door, tilting his body toward me.

"The woods are dangerous," he said. "I'm not going to tell you otherwise. You wouldn't believe me if I did." He pushed off the wall and took hold of my shoulders, turning me so we stood face to face. "But I can promise you this: As long as you're with me, you're safe. Nobody's going to hurt you if you're with me. I won't let them."

He meant well, and part of me felt comforted. Most of me, though, was old enough to know he was making a promise he couldn't possibly keep. He just wanted to find one of those circles, and would tell me anything to get me to show him the spot.

But it was true enough that we needed to find those circles, if we were to ever understand Rafe's dying message, his plan. And even if Meritt couldn't keep his word, I couldn't help but be a little touched by his uncharacteristically firm reassurance. He wanted to protect me; he wouldn't risk me needlessly. That, I believed.

I shot a silent *I told you so* Farrell Dean's way.

"All right," I said to Meritt. "Let's go."

Slipping out of the slaughterhouse doorway into the cold rain, we covered the short distance to the wall and the opening onto the eastern wasteland in a few seconds.

Outside, the woods rose up, dark and deep. I kept one hand on the wall's rough surface as I walked a few paces south, trying to picture Rafe's map in my mind, wondering whether he'd been precise about distances.

"Somewhere right in here," I said finally, uncertainly. "I guess."

But I hadn't been able to tell, from Rafe's map, how high up on the wall the circles were supposed to be. For a long moment we stood side by side, gazing at the wall. It seemed like an impossible job, to find something we'd never noticed before, and find it in the dark, in the rain.

Without a word, Meritt started at the top of the wall. I started at the bottom, and we patted and stroked and felt along the rough wet cinderblocks until our hands touched. Then we moved over a couple of feet and did it all again. It was tedious work, and cold, with the rain running in our eyes and down the backs of our collars, and every now and then—despite Meritt's promise—I couldn't resist glancing over my shoulder at the woods.

"Meritt," I said after awhile. "Have you seen Farrell Dean today?"

Above me he paused, then started moving again. "No," he said cautiously.

"Why do you say it like that?"

"Maybe because last time I saw Farrell Dean, he threw a punch at me."

It was my turn to pause. "Why'd he do that?"

Meritt nudged me with his knee. "Because I'm reckless and selfish and take stupid risks, and one day I'll get you in trouble and then I'll regret it but it'll be too late, et cetera, et cetera. Same thing he's always saying. He just punctuated it with a punch this time."

I didn't know what to say. They shouldn't be fighting each other, not with Rafe gone, not when they were working together against the Watchers. I didn't want to be the cause of trouble, but then the problem wasn't me, was it? It was Farrell Dean.

"It's no big deal," Meritt said, sounding cheerful. "Farrell Dean's feeling tense and he needed to take it out on somebody. Now me—when I need to hit somebody, I go for Harding, or maybe even Cline. That's like bringing a building down on top of you. You don't worry about anything but survival after that."

"So you haven't seen him at all today."

He turned away from the wall. "No. What's up?"

"He said he needed to talk to me—" I didn't want to mention that he wanted to talk about Meritt, and I sure didn't want to mention that he'd almost gotten crossways with a warden on my account—"but then he never came to the field."

Meritt lost interest. "Don't start worrying yet," he said, turning back to his search. "Things come up, especially for him—he's a good mechanic, and some people kick up a fuss if they get sent someone else."

We kept searching. The rain stopped, and that was good, but somehow without the rain I felt colder. I was shivering hard, trying to stop my teeth from chattering, when Meritt gave a quiet exclamation.

"What?" I said. "Did you find it?"

"Yeah, but I don't know what it is. It's smooth. I think it's a metal panel. It's small—just a square inch or so."

I stood beside him as he poked and prodded. Whatever it was, it was quite high on the wall, well beyond my reach.

"It opened," he said. "The panel slid back." He tapped gently. "Underneath it feels like glass." Keeping his hand on the mysterious thing, he turned toward me.

"Red," he said softly. "It's a camera lens."

I stared at him. Had someone been watching us groping around tonight? But no—the cover had been closed.

Meritt pulled a small screwdriver out of his pants pocket and turned back toward the wall.

"What are you doing?" I hissed, alarmed.

"Taking it out," he said. "It's dead."

"How do you know?"

"It's not wired to anything." He pried the camera out and pushed the cover back over the gap.

Holding it up, he turned it this way and that. "It's no

use," he said. "Too dark." Carefully he tucked it in his shirt pocket and returned the screwdriver to its place, then turned to me. In the darkness I could just make out his grin.

"Let's go see Rafe's map," he said.

"Now?"

"No time like the present."

The streets were eerily silent. We saw no headlights, nor any indication that wardens were patrolling.

"Why should they bother?" Meritt said when I mentioned the unusual stillness. "They think we're all cowering in our beds."

I shook out of my head the night's gruesome city meetings—Petey falling, blood pooling around his head, Judd's roar of anguish and anger, the laundress going up in shrieking flames—and focused on the present moment.

"This might not be safe," I said in a whisper as Meritt reached for the door to Rafe's house. "Rafe thought someone was watching him in here. Do you know anything about that?"

Meritt stared at me, his face blank in the blue streetlights. His hair was still wet, plastered to his head, and it made the bones of his face stand out starkly. It gave him that unfamiliar look again, beautiful but strange, and for a moment I stared at him as blankly as he was staring at me.

"Cameras in the adult houses," I said, reminding myself as much as him. "Wardens and Watchers?"

He shook his head. "No," he said, pushing open the door. "No cameras in the adult houses. I'm sure of it."

I'd left the candle and a couple of matches under Rafe's bed. Now I lit the candle and pointed Meritt to the map on the wall.

"I remember this," he said, going to stand in front of it.

"But as a kid I didn't realize how detailed it was. Everything's exactly proportional. It must have taken him forever."

Carefully Meritt lifted the map down from the wall and over to the table. As he went to lay it flat, something pattered out, landed with tiny plinks on the floor.

I fell to my hands and knees, groped along the cold concrete.

"What is it?" Meritt said.

"The thing that got him killed." I held out my hand, palm up. Three tiny white pills. "Painkillers."

Meritt took one, held it up in the candlelight. "Not exactly," he said, his gray eyes sparkling. "Sedatives."

I gave him a look, but he didn't notice. "Why did Rafe have these?" I said.

Meritt didn't answer. He sat down at the table, took the other two pills out of my hand, and with infinite care wrapped all three in a small piece of paper and tucked it into his pocket.

"You wouldn't have those pills if it weren't for me," I said, getting to my feet. "Tell me what's going on."

He looked up at me. "I'd rather you trusted me on this," he said.

"And I'd rather you trusted me. I thought we were friends."

Meritt leaned forward and pulled the map toward him. "You're my best friend, and you know it," he said. "Show me the other circles—"

"Then why don't you trust me?"

Meritt didn't even look away from the map. "I do trust you. But you have to trust me, too."

I didn't answer. After a long moment Meritt sighed and looked at me. I still didn't say anything, and neither did he. He tipped his chair off its front legs and began rocking it up and down.

Finally he spoke. "The other night, when you got picked up? If you'd known why I was meeting Rafe, would you have been able to play innocent as well as you did?"

"I would never give you away," I said, and my words caught hard in my throat. "Not ever."

Meritt looked alarmed. "Don't cry," he said, and his chair legs thumped hard on the floor. Reaching out, he took me by the arm and pulled me down onto his knee. "I know you wouldn't give me away. Not intentionally. But you might give away that you weren't giving me away, and then we'd both be in danger, not just me, but you too. Sometimes ignorance is the best defense."

As he spoke he collected my wet hair at the base of my neck, his hand warm on my skin. I wanted to lean into him; I wanted to be held.

Instead I pulled my hair out of his hand and stood up.

"Tell me what's going on," I said. "If you won't tell me, then the next time I find something out, I'll deal with it on my own. Or I'll tell Farrell Dean. In any case, I won't be coming to you."

Meritt's expression hardened. "Farrell Dean," he said. "So that's what this is about."

"No. This is about us. You and me. This is about you treating me like a child."

Meritt shook his head, looking irritated.

"You are," I said. "Rafe trusted me—he told *me* where to find those sedatives."

"Because he had no choice," Meritt said. "You were the one who happened to be there when he got the chance to speak."

"*Happened* to be there? I went to him, Meritt. I tried to save his life." The memory brought tears to my eyes. "Why can't you take me seriously?"

Because I was small and young and looked younger

than I was, because I had stupid freaky red hair—but I didn't say any of that. It sounded whiney, even to me. Someone who deserved to be taken seriously wouldn't list the reasons why she might not be.

Meritt's expression softened, but he didn't pull his punches. "Don't delude yourself," he said. "Rafe and Farrell Dean wanted to keep you in the dark—they were in complete agreement about that—and I was the one who disagreed. Who's been sneaking out with you three or four nights a week for, what—two years now? Me, that's who. So you've got no business being mad at me. If you can't be mad at Rafe because he's dead, then save your indignation for Farrell Dean."

"I don't care about Farrell Dean," I said. "I – ."

Meritt met my gaze but didn't say anything.

My face grew hot. We had never spoken of what was between us. "I thought you were different," I said finally, and my voice broke on the words.

A faint flush rose on Meritt's cheeks, but the uncompromising expression in his gray eyes didn't waver. He wasn't going to tell me. He was going to take my information and share it with Farrell Dean and tall-older-Meri and who knew what others, and leave me out.

Speechless with frustration, my chest tight with distress, I turned away and headed for the door. I didn't walk slowly. I didn't hesitate. I wasn't bluffing.

What did it mean, that I was walking away from Meritt? I didn't know. He was my best friend. I loved him. I couldn't even remember how it felt to not to love him. But something terrible was happening in Optica, and if there was a solution, I wouldn't be left out. Not without a protest. Not when he was endangering himself.

My hand was on the doorknob when he spoke.

"They were for me."

I turned, surprised.

"Yeah," Meritt said, running a hand through his hair. "That's right. Rafe got the sedatives for me."

"You're not sick." I was too startled to move away from the door.

Meritt looked startled too, and then regretful, and then something else.

"Not like you mean," he said slowly. "It's not a physical illness ..."

"Stop it, Meritt. You aren't sick in any way at all."

"It was worth a shot," he said with a shrug, flashing me a grin that quickly vanished.

"No, don't get mad again, Red. Listen—here's how it's been. For the past few months I've been working on rigging the connection to the compound so I can spy on the Watchers from the tower. It took awhile because I could only work on it when I got called to the compound, and then only for a minute or two at a time, when the wardens weren't hanging around. So I brought Farrell Dean in and coached him through it so that when he got called out there he could do some of the work, and then I'd pick up where he left off next time I got called, and so forth and so on. You see?"

I nodded.

"So last week we finally finished it. We've got the compound part in place, and I can get into the watchtower easily enough—something's always malfunctioning up in the Opticon, they're always calling for me. But the warden won't ever leave while I'm there."

I was shaking my head, moving back toward him. "No, no, no," I said.

"Yes, yes, yes. It's perfect, don't you see? There's only one warden up there at night. He always drinks hot milk and whiskey. I can slip one little pill into the bottle of milk, and once he drinks it he won't know anything else until morning. It'll work. I know it will work. *Rafe* knew it would work."

There was no point arguing with him. It would only convince him he shouldn't have told me.

"So was it the pills all along?" I asked. I was standing directly in front of him now. "Was that what Rafe wanted us to find? Not the circles, not the map itself?"

Meritt's eyes went distant, abstract.

"Both, I think," he said after a moment, focusing back in on me. "Whatever these other cameras are, they're significant." He gestured toward the sketch of Lonna on the wall. "I bet that's why she died. I bet she found something."

"You mean they killed her? Electrocuted her and made it look like an accident?"

"Maybe. Or maybe she tried to check it on her own, and electrocuted herself. In either case, if she knew something, then her getting killed lost us six months."

His matter-of-fact tone made me blink. We'd known Lonna; Rafe had loved Lonna; how could Meritt talk about her possible murder in such analytic terms?

"You sound like you're talking about chess," I said. "This isn't a game, Meritt."

He made an exasperated gesture. "I never said it was. I said it was a shame Lonna died before she could tell us what she'd found, and if she were standing here, she'd say the same thing. Stop spoiling for a fight."

He'd wrong-footed me, and I wasn't sure how, and anyway a sudden fit of shivering kept me from answering.

"You're soaking wet," Meritt said, as if he'd only just noticed, which he probably only had.

"So are you," I said.

"I'm not turning blue. Go see if you can find some towels. See if the hot water's working. You could even take a shower, if you want. It might make you feel better."

"Don't patronize me." My voice was firm, but I had to fight not to smile back at him when he grinned at me.

I turned my back on him in an attempt to maintain a non-amused, adult demeanor. Of course the most adult thing, I thought then, would be admit that he was right: there was no point in standing around freezing. So I went to the bathroom in search of towels, and once there I couldn't resist checking the water. It was, in fact, hot.

The temptation was enormous—I was so cold, and I could so easily imagine the comforting warmth, the tenseness in my neck relaxing, the shivering stopping.

I stripped off my wet clothes, dropped them on the floor, and ducked under the running water. It wasn't a particularly safe thing to do—a warden could show up at any moment—but it felt safe enough. I was in Rafe's house, and Meritt had suggested it.

So I stood there in the dark, blissfully warm, feeling my shoulders relax, and the muscles in my face, and the tight fist of anxiety in my chest, and I let myself pretend that this was our house, Meritt's and mine. We lived here in the circle of Rafe's protection, and we trusted each other, and we were happy.

And no one would ever tear us apart.

Chapter 15

"Red?"

Meritt's voice jolted me awake. I'd dozed off standing under the warm water, leaning against the tiled wall.

"Coming," I said. I turned off the shower, dried off, and pulled on my clothes. They were still wet and cold, but I felt much better. In fact, I felt triumphant: Meritt had caved. He'd brought me in on his secrets.

Meritt was sitting at the table, examining the camera by candlelight. "This is high-tech stuff," he said. "Way beyond our cameras. It's another discrepancy to add to Rafe's list."

"Like pencils," I said, remembering what Farrell Dean had said. "And eyeglasses."

Meritt shook his head. "More like our power system."

The system ran off of the sea, somehow—no one was quite sure how. Meritt and Farrell Dean had bored me many a time speculating together about how it actually worked.

"We don't know things we *should* know, given the things we do know," Meritt went on. "We have peculiar technological gaps."

"Is it because of the Guardians? Did they tell the Watchers how to do certain things?"

"Maybe," Meritt said, noncommittal, fiddling with the camera.

150

"They really do exist. That's the only explanation for the gap by the Watcher compound being sealed."

Meritt gave me an odd look. "Of course they really exist," he said. Then he gestured at the camera again. "That panel that covered it—it must be motion-sensitive. That would let it stay closed unless there was something to see."

"What's to see in the wasteland? The other cameras, the ones inside the city, those make sense. But who goes to the wasteland?"

Meritt cocked an eyebrow.

"I know we go there," I said. "But who else?"

"I don't know. People. Where else is there to go, if you don't want to be seen by the Watchers?" But he was still fixated on the technology in his hand. "See how tiny it is, compared to the regular cameras? And it seems to be functionally wireless. Must use some sort of radio signal."

Hurriedly I put my hand over the glass. "If it doesn't need wires, does that mean it's working right now?"

He pushed my hand away, fiddled with the camera. "I don't think so," he said, pulling out a tiny piece. "See this? It's corroded."

He moved the candle closer to the camera, studied it some more.

"Maybe it wasn't the Watchers who put these up," I said, and Meritt looked at me, suddenly wary.

"Three of the circles are in the Watcher compound," I said. "Maybe someone's been watching the Watchers, and watching us when we were in places the Watchers couldn't see." I shivered. "It has to be the Guardians. Don't you think?"

Meritt shrugged and his eyes slid away from mine, went back to the tiny camera.

"They might help us, Meritt," I said, but before I finished speaking he was shaking his head.

"Even if they hate the Watchers' guts, it doesn't mean they'd help us."

"What exactly do you think they are?" I wanted him to say they certainly weren't animal-like creatures with poor drawing skills and a taste for chicken blood—or guttural voices calling my name—but he merely shrugged again.

"Do you think they're human?"

"They do inhuman things," he said, still looking at the camera.

"If our technology came from the Guardians, they must be smart. Like we are, I mean, or more than we are. Not like animals."

Meritt didn't answer.

"Don't you even have a guess?"

"Sure." He glanced up at me. "My guess is they're flight-less birds with the heads of men and tails like lions."

I crossed my arms over my chest. "Not funny," I said. "I'm serious, Meritt. Who are they? What are they? And what if they're angry that we took their camera?"

Meritt didn't seem concerned, at least not about that. "Nobody's taken care of this device for a long time," he said. "I'm guessing nobody cares about any of these cameras any-more." His voice went quiet. "Maybe nobody even remem-bers they exist."

"I wonder how Rafe found them," I began, but my words were cut off by a sound.

Someone was trying the door.

Meritt and I stared at each other. The door rattled again.

Meritt jumped to his feet and in two steps was at the wall, re-hanging the map.

There was no other exit besides the door—not unless we could get a window open and get away before the warden walked around the house.

He was probably doing that already. He'd know someone was here—he'd be calling for backup. They could be coming from all directions.

We were caught.

A scene flashed through my mind: Meritt, standing in the center of the city meeting circle.

"Meritt," I said. "Hide in the bathroom."

"No," he said, turning to me. "*You* hide."

"You've been arrested five times to my one."

"No."

"I don't know how to spy on the Watchers from the tower. You do."

"Shhh," he said, ignoring my argument and pulling me by the arm toward the bathroom.

I yanked my arm free.

"I won't hide. I've already seen Rafe die, and I'm not watching the same thing happen to you."

For a heartbeat Meritt stared at me, frowning. I could see calculations passing through his mind. Then he bent over me, kissed me on the lips, and was gone. I didn't even feel it until it was over.

Hurrying to the door, I unbarred it, opened it just a crack. Please not the warden with the scar, I thought. Please not him.

"Hello?" I called uncertainly, my heart pounding.

Out of the darkness a form materialized from around the corner of the house. It came closer, and the beam of a flashlight shone in my face, blinding me. This was it. At the very least I'd be put in prison. Surely, surely they wouldn't put me in the city meeting—I wasn't stealing anything, I wasn't causing discord, it probably wasn't even past curfew yet, but this was Rafe's house, the traitor Rafe—

"Blast it all," a gruff voice said. "I thought it might be you."

It was the bald, bearded warden. Warden Karl.

Without another word he pushed me into the house and closed the door. His round face was grim and his eyes looked hard and strangely tight, as if he'd looked into a too-bright light and hadn't yet recovered.

Judd, I thought, more sure than ever that Warden Karl was his father. What had this man suffered, watching Judd in the city circle that night?

He glanced around the room, noting the candle burning low on the table, the open books.

"You want to explain?" he said shortly, crossing his arms over his chest.

I nodded. "I came to say goodbye."

His look became, if possible, even more disapproving. "You think Rafe cared about you?"

"I know he did."

"So you think he'd want you getting in trouble?"

I didn't have an answer for that, but the warden didn't wait for one. Instead he began strolling around the room, turning over the books and then moving to the wall, where he studied the sketch of Lonna, then took another few steps and stood in front of the map. His eyes narrowed. Reaching up, he touched a point with the tip of his finger.

"That's where we're standing," he said. "Right there. And there's the city circle."

It could have been a threat, but I hoped it wasn't. He was Judd's father, and I was Judd's friend, and Petey had saved Judd's life with his own. We couldn't talk about it, couldn't commiserate, but we could look at the circle on the map and hate it.

I stepped up beside him and peered at the map as if for the first time.

"There's my dormitory," I said, pointing. Hinting. *Let me go home.*

The warden turned and faced me. I couldn't read his

expression. His decision might depend on whether he'd found me on his own, or whether the warden in the watchtower had seen something and sent him out to investigate. Whatever happened, as long as he didn't decide to search the house, Meritt at least would be safe.

"Here's how this works," the warden began. "The warden handcuffs you. He takes you to the prison and sticks you in a cell. He files a report that gets sent to the Watchers. Best case scenario, you don't see the sun for three months, and various wardens end up in charge of your well-being from one shift to the next. One warden at a time, if you get my drift."

Unfortunately I did.

"That's the best case scenario. Worst case scenario, you end up in the city circle tomorrow night, or the next day, or the next. That's what would be happening to you, if most any other warden had walked through that door tonight. That, or else he would have offered you a deal you couldn't refuse. Do you understand what I'm telling you?"

I nodded.

"I won't be able to cover for you again," he continued. "I have obligations. Do you understand?"

Again I nodded, certain that he was referring to Judd.

Warden Karl studied me for a long moment, his face unreadable, the skin around his eyes still tight and angry. "I'll take you back to your dorm now, if you're finished with your good-byes."

A third time I nodded mutely, afraid that a spoken word from me, any word, would break the spell of good fortune.

Warden Karl turned, and I followed, and neither one of us so much as glanced toward the bathroom as we headed out the door.

Chapter 16

All the next day I watched for Farrell Dean, and all day long I was disappointed.

It was just as well. I wanted to say "I told you so" about Meritt—he definitely was taking me seriously, wasn't treating me like a child or a pet—and that was sure to rub Farrell Dean wrong, and the last thing I needed to be doing was making things worse between those two.

As the day wore on, though, I began to get truly worried. Farrell Dean had never stood me up before, had never been late even by a minute. Now he was a full day late, and more. I supposed he could be coping with some huge mechanical issue, but wouldn't he at least come to meals?

When blustery Garry started chewing out Felix for taking the best hoe, I didn't immediately rush to break it up. Instead I took the opportunity to edge close to Ezzie.

"Have you seen Farrell Dean lately?" I said.

Ezzie shook his head, his dark eyes worried. "His bunk was empty last night," he said. "Nobody knows where he is— at least, nobody's saying. I was hoping you knew something."

Mutely I shook my head, and a hard cold fear began to grow in the pit of my stomach. Farrell Dean had tried to interfere when the scarred warden accosted me in the cafeteria. If he was in trouble because of that, if he was in trouble because Marta had stepped in and asked me to look at the lunch truck list, depriving the warden of his prey—

For all I knew, Marta might be missing, too. For all I knew the scarred warden was punishing everyone who stood between him and me. It was a terrible thought.

It was better, though, than the alternative. If the Watchers had found out that Farrell Dean was spying on them, there was nothing I or anyone else could do to help him.

That night they put a plump, elderly nanny mother in the circle center and lined up a whole row of little girls in front of her. They made her call out the children's names— Nevada, Savannah, Olympia, Denver, Helena, Dakota, Geneva, Florence, Cheyenne. I was afraid the Voice was going to order the wardens to kill the children, but instead he asked the nanny why she had chosen these names.

"Well, I've named so very many children," the nanny mother began, her brow furrowed with worry. She seemed quite old and fragile, and I knew she wanted to keep the children out of trouble but couldn't fathom from what direction the trouble might come. Nor could the rest of us. The names meant nothing that I could see—they were just sounds, signifiers, a way to identify the little girls.

"Sometimes it's hard to think of new names. These just came to me, and I used them," she said.

The Watcher kept asking questions. Had she ever known anyone called by one of these names? Was she sure about that? She made them up herself? No one helped her? Had she ever heard those names before, in another context? Had she read them somewhere?

The city meetings were getting increasingly bizarre.

Pinned in the glare of the spotlight, the nanny mother

seemed as baffled as the rest of us. She stuck to her initial answer, but after repeated questions of the same sort finally said, "They came into my head, that's all, and I thought they sounded pretty, special." Beside me, Meri sighed heavily; sure enough, the Watcher pounced.

"Special? You wanted to give these children special names? Pretty names?"

"Yes," agreed the nanny mother, though her face turned gray as she realized her mistake. We weren't supposed to play favorites; we weren't supposed to treat anyone differently from anyone else.

The nanny tried to rectify it—or maybe she was only trying to protect the little girls. "They were such very ordinary children," she said. "I didn't think special names could hurt them."

I thought her answer was clever, but they shot her anyway.

Meritt materialized beside me as I was making my way out of the circle in the dark.

"I'm doing it tonight," he said softly. "You want to come?"

It was too dark to see his face clearly. "To the watchtower?" I whispered.

"Yeah. Pill's already in the bottle of milk."

If Warden Karl caught me again, there'd be no talking my way out of it this time, but I couldn't let Meritt go it alone. "I'll come," I said. "When?"

"Midnight. Don't forget your cap."

"Where should I meet you?"

"As luck would have it, the camera behind this building will be shorting out just before midnight," he said, and was gone before I could ask him how he could possibly have managed that.

That night, I thought I'd never get away. All the girls sat up late discussing the city meeting, except for Cynda and the others who were at work. Everyone else huddled together on creaking bunk beds, trading theories, getting up to check and re-check that the green wire had not been re-attached to the camera. They had more to say about this city meeting than any of the others, and I wasn't sure why. Maybe they were getting used to being terrorized, at least enough that they could think and talk instead of weeping and getting hysterical.

"What do you think, Red?" Liza said. "Why her?"

I was sitting cross-legged on my top bunk, alone and a little apart from everyone else, trying not to look impatient but also doing nothing to keep the conversation going. "Just another way to freak us out," I said. "No rhyme or reason."

"But Red, why would they need to *freak* you out?" That was Wanda, of course. "That nanny was playing favorites," she continued. "They had a perfectly good reason to discipline her."

Liza snorted. "Oh yeah. A bullet to the head. That'll teach her a lesson."

"Killed for picking pretty baby names," Shawna said musingly.

"It's as bad as Lavinia, killed for being pretty," Meri said, and then other voices went on, picking up the discussion, arguing. But I had heard something else.

"What did you say?" I leaned over the edge of my bunk to look down at my bunkmate. Kari was sitting with her arms wrapped around her knees, and at my question she hugged herself more tightly, looking as if she wished she'd kept silent.

"It's okay," I whispered, swinging down to sit beside her. "Nobody else is listening. I thought you said, 'she wasn't killed for being pretty.'"

Blushing, she nodded.

"Why'd you say that?"

Kari glanced around uneasily, but no one was paying us any attention. Liza and Wanda were going at it, each gathering supporters as she went.

Kari leaned a little toward me. "I work in the postnatal unit. And Lavinia was a seamstress, and one of the other seamstresses had a baby last week, so she was in postnatal."

She broke off, and I nodded encouragingly.

"This other seamstress said that Lavinia sort of ...." Hastily Kari let go of her knees and waved a hand. "Not like the Watchers mean," she said, and then once again stopped.

I had no idea what she meant. "Go on," I said, maybe a trifle less patiently than before. This was like pulling teeth.

Kari flushed an even deeper red, but pushed on. "None of the seamstresses really thought about it, because Lavinia was so quiet. But after she died they were talking about how she'd been such a good listener. She didn't say much, but now and then she asked just the right questions ..."

"Like Rafe, back when we were in school," I said.

Relieved, Kari nodded. "That's it," she said.

"You mean that she didn't say anything negative herself," I went on, "but she asked questions that got people to thinking, and talking."

Kari nodded. "And when they talked—"

She looked at me hopefully, and so again I waded forward. "And when they talked, they realized they didn't trust the Watchers. Is that what you mean?"

Kari nodded again. She pulled on a strand of hair, then took a deep breath. "And Mechanic Dane—he was ..."

"One of the men in the city meeting with her. I know."

"He told someone else I work with that those men weren't fighting over Lavinia. He said that he ... that she and he ... "

"They had an understanding?"

Kari nodded. "They had put in a request to live together. Those other men sort of hung around, because she was so pretty. And, well, Butcher Ross was very fond of her. He was sad she didn't want to stay with him. But there wasn't any conflict. He was just sad. That's what Dane said, anyway."

"You overhear a lot, don't you?" I said, and Kari looked like she wanted to hide under the covers.

"It's okay," I said. "I listen, too—though maybe not as well as you do."

Kari smiled faintly. "I blend into the background better," she said.

"Have you heard anything about the others who've been in city meetings?" I was thinking about Louie. He had caused trouble in his time. And Judd definitely had a rebellious streak. But they hadn't died, so either the city meetings had somehow gone wrong, or I was off track. I probably was, since I really couldn't fathom why naming a baby Denver would get someone killed.

Kari was considering my question. She tucked her smooth dark hair behind her ears and then smoothed her blanket. Finally she looked at me. "Sometimes names are forbidden," she said.

I waited.

"I don't know why. But certain names come up again and again—different people suggest them—but when that happens, we're supposed to reject the name and write in another. Call the baby something else."

"But why? What's wrong with the names?"

Kari shook her head, looking perplexed. "They don't mean anything," she said. "I don't know why people even come up with them. Paris, that's one. Plato. London. Jesus. Elvis."

We stared at each other. "Are those boy names or girl names?" I said.

"Both. Either. I don't know. There are others, but I can't think of them right now."

"Did the nanny mother who died suggest those names?"

Kari shook her head. "Yes. No. I suppose maybe sometimes . . . but other people did, too. And the names she died for aren't on the forbidden list."

Two bunks over, Lea had started crying again. Most of us had long ago given up on keeping Lea calm, but Linni abruptly stopped echoing everything Wanda said, and bent over the girl.

"Why don't you get in bed?" she said. "I'll tuck you in and tell you a story, like the nanny mothers used to do."

Lea nodded and moved to her own bunk, which, as bad luck would have it, was next to Kari. Wanda's beady little eyes followed Lea, and when she saw me sitting with Kari, she leaned over and whispered something to her minion Joy.

"Let me know if you think of anything else," I told Kari, and climbed back up to my bed.

Over by the door Shawna spoke up. "There's no point in driving ourselves crazy trying to figure out the Watchers. I'm going to sleep." I threw her a quick glance but she carefully avoided my eyes, turning over and pulling her blanket up around her neck.

To my relief the rest of the dormitory followed her lead, and soon the room was silent. The dorm mother never came in to turn off the light, so eventually Liza did it.

I waited until everyone was lying still and breathing evenly. Then I waited until Meri got up for her requisite al-most-asleep-and-realized-she-had-to-go bathroom visit. Then I waited until Linni began snoring softly, and until the girl in the bunk beside her poked her so she'd roll onto her side. Then I counted to one thousand.

Finally I was confident no one in the room was awake except for me. Cautiously I eased out of my bunk, found my coat on the floor, and crept across the room.

From the bottom bunk nearest the door, Shawna waved at me as I passed.

Chapter 17

I needn't have been in such a rush. I waited for Meritt for ages, shivering in the darkness, seeing now and then the headlights of a patrol car flashing across the cafeteria yard.

The Watchers were systematically weeding out rebels—that had to be the method behind their terrorizing. Louie hadn't died, but maybe Butcher Stuart was a troublemaker too, so the Watchers were happy whichever died. Judd and Petey? That one I couldn't figure out, nor the nanny mother.

And if the Watchers were killing off rebels, why didn't they announce what they were doing? It seemed like that would make people more likely to behave.

I stood there shivering, trying to make sense of things, until finally Meritt arrived. He didn't come all the way to where I waited, but gestured from across the yard, and I left the shadows and followed him to the foot of the watchtower.

At the prison door, I whispered, "You're sure there's only one warden?"

"One upstairs," he said. "We'll have to avoid any others."

Great.

Meritt swung open the door and slipped inside.

I followed, anxiety a tight band around my lungs. The long tiled hallway was deserted, but lights shone from beneath two of the doors.

Swiftly we hurried down the hall to the stairway door at the far end. Meritt was opening it—he was inside, and I was just behind him—when we heard it.

The crack of a whip, and the sharp hard exhalation of someone in pain.

I looked at Meritt. He gestured to me to come on and started up the stairs, walking as softly as he could so the metal grillwork wouldn't creak and echo. I could be quieter; I was lighter, and I was barefoot.

I started to follow him, but the whip cracked again and I hesitated, peering down the empty hallway. It must be nearby—must be the lighted doorway just a few yards away. I took one step toward it, two.

A man's voice, calm and deliberate, spoke.

"You might as well tell me now," he said. "While you have a little skin left."

"Nothing to tell." The voice was hoarse, but I knew it. Farrell Dean.

I shut my eyes as the whip cracked again.

Behind me I heard the main door to the prison begin to open. In two steps I was at the stairway, through the door, running softly up and up, listening for the sound of pursuit behind me. No sounds came. Whoever it was hadn't entered the stairwell.

I could hardly think straight. Were they beating him because of me—because of the warden with the scar? I couldn't bear the thought, but the alternative was even worse. If they were beating him because of the spying and sabotaging, they'd call him a traitor, a cancer.

We had to get him out.

Though surely they wouldn't kill him, not their best mechanic. Optica needed him.

My thoughts were racing when I pushed open the door at the top of the stairs, the door to the Opticon observatory.

Meritt was already inside, bending over a slumped warden, the same one from the night I'd been there before. Zee, that was his name. Meritt had him under the arms and was hauling him away from the bank of equipment, propping him in one of the comfortable chairs.

The door didn't have a lock, but it opened inward, so I took hold of another chair and dragged it across the door. It wouldn't stop anyone for long, but it would buy us a few seconds. To do what, I didn't know—we were completely cornered up here.

"Meritt—" I began, intending to tell him about Farrell Dean, but he cut me off.

"Let me concentrate," he said. Swiftly he pulled his small tools from his pocket and began to work, removing a cover, changing settings by flipping miniature switches. Then he sat down and began typing on the keyboard. One of the screens went dark, then flared green. Lines of incomprehensible words and numbers began to scroll down it.

"They won't be meeting this late," I whispered, glancing at the warden, but Meritt merely waved at me to hush. He put on the headphones and typed a command, watched the scrolling text, typed another. His eyes lit up.

"Got it," he said, gesturing for me to come closer. He pulled one earphone away from his head and I heard voices. Then he touched a key and the voices stopped.

"I recorded them from earlier," he said, looking up at me. "You know how the general system works, right? The Watcher compound has a bank of screens identical to this one so they can see all over the city, and they can also watch whoever is here."

I glanced around uneasily.

"They aren't watching us now," Meritt said. "They're all asleep." He pointed to a screen showing a long table and seven empty chairs, and, at the far end of that room, a bank of screens like the one in front of me. As I watched, that image flipped to a different scene: the city circle, empty in the moonlight.

"Besides, I've spliced in a loop from yesterday. If anyone looked now, they'd see the warden sitting there playing cards."

Meritt looked at me, making sure I was paying close attention. "So here's what we've done. I put together a voice-activated application and recording camera component. It piggybacks on their central computer. I had to loop it so I wouldn't use too much—never mind about that. The main thing is, just now I remote accessed it, and now I'm going to play back whatever it caught this evening. And next time it'll be even easier—I've set up a shortcut, do you see? All I'll have to do next time is this." He tapped three keys. "Great, isn't it?"

Behind us the warden was snoring gently. I turned so I could keep an eye on him. "Meritt," I began again, determined to tell him about Farrell Dean, but then the top left screen filled with the same table and chairs we'd seen a moment before. Now, however, the chairs were filled by seven people dressed in white.

Immediately—to my later shame—I forgot all about Farrell Dean. These were the men and women who ruled my life, the men and women who watched every move I made, and I had never before seen them. These were the Watchers.

I leaned forward over Meritt's shoulder and studied them. There were four men and three women. They all sat on the same side of the table. The men sat together to the left, and the women sat together on the right.

Except for their white clothes, they looked completely ordinary—more or less like anybody else in Optica. They were all older, with white hair or gray hair, and some had backs bent slightly with arthritis. They didn't look terribly wise or even terribly important. They just looked like people.

A plump woman with short gray hair was chuckling. "Did you see their faces?" she said, leaning forward. "They were completely baffled. They have no idea where those names came from. They think the nanny made them up. The nanny herself thinks she made them up."

"The past bleeds through," another woman said, languidly stroking a finger across the table in front of her. "Memories don't stay buried. That has always been a problem. It's one more reason to euthanize the old ones."

"And a very good reason," the plump woman said. "We can't afford memories, especially not now."

"How many more city meetings before we do it?" This was a short, round man.

"One or two more should be enough," another man said. He had a very long face and was looking at a paper on the table in front of him. "Except for the redhead that first night, nobody has lifted so much as a finger. They're completely cowed. But it's best to be sure."

"That redhead is a problem, and in more ways than one." This was a man who looked so old I was surprised he could sit upright. "One of the wardens has been asking rather nosy questions about her."

Meritt glanced over his shoulder at me, raising an eyebrow. I grimaced, repressing a shudder. He still didn't know about the scarred warden, and I wanted to keep it that way.

"We always knew she raised dangerous questions," the plump woman said. "How could she not, with that hair?"

The old man frowned. "She was a practical joke," he said. "One that has never been funny. We should have disposed of her long ago. An accident, an illness. It would have been safer that way."

I froze, one hand on Meritt's shoulder.

"Absolutely not," said the woman on the end, her voice

sharp. To my surprise I recognized Marta, the woman from the cafeteria truck. She was a Watcher?

Hastily I scanned the other faces again; no, I didn't recognize anyone else.

"No," the languid woman agreed. "We were obligated to give her a chance. Joke or not—and you're no doubt correct about that—she was, nevertheless, our best hope for subsequent subjects. There have been so few."

"She's still our best hope," Marta said. "And therefore well worth the risk. Meritt certainly would agree."

Meritt? I shot him a glance, but he shrugged and kept his eyes on the screen.

"At the risk of stating the obvious, Meritt isn't here," the old man said, waving a hand at the room. "And if he were, and we explained the situation, he'd certainly understand that at this point the girl is far more trouble than she's worth."

"I agree," the plump woman said. "Enough is enough. And we've kept a close eye on her. We'll have her records, if we ever need them, though at this point that seems highly unlikely."

"Exactly," said the long-faced man. "At this point the number one priority is our survival. Not the redhead, not the records, not anything else. And I really don't think anyone at all could possibly disagree. Lives are at stake."

"All this discussion is pointless," the languid woman said, and yawned. "We all know that one way or another, the redhead won't be a problem much longer."

"I'm going to keep saying this until the rest of you show sense." Marta was angry. "It is essential that we keep her."

"But why?" the plump woman said, spreading her hands. "She's nothing but a waste of resources, a loose end, a loose cannon."

"She's undisciplined," the round Watcher agreed.

"Quite," said the very old man. "And if Optica is to

survive, it must recapture its original discipline, its original efficiency."

Marta threw up her hands in exasperation. "Efficient? Optica? We never had to worry about that. We certainly never had to worry about being self-sustaining. That was never the point. People like Estelle, Louie, all of them—including the redhead—they were the point."

"Yes, Marta, we know," said the plump woman, rolling her eyes. "Please recall that we were on this council long before you came along."

Marta smiled a little grimly.

"Which means you just might be too close to the problem," she said. "Or a bit too attached to your role. Whereas I, as a relative newcomer, have retained a little healthy distance."

"And what do you think we should do?" the round man said. "Give up all our secrets? Announce that for whatever reason we've apparently been left on our own to sink or swim, and we're sinking?"

Marta shook her head. "Of course not. There's no need to cause a panic. But I do think these city meetings are worse than pointless. You're deliberately wasting some of our best resources."

"We're not wasting anyone. We're disposing of trouble-makers," the long-faced man said. "We must address this present crisis, and to do so we must rid ourselves of those who would, for whatever reason, stand in our way. The ones who would be sentimental and thus destroy us."

A murmur rose around the table; heads nodded in agreement.

"The ones who might have saved us," Marta said. "The ones who had the brains to help us out of this predicament, and the ability to lead the others, and the charisma to keep them calm. You don't have any of those abilities. You aren't city managers. That's only the mask we have to wear. If you persist in confusing your role with reality, we may all die."

Voices rose over each other, arguing. Most of what I could make out was directed at Marta.

"We are agreed."

At the sound of this new voice, a shiver ran up my spine and the rest of the Watchers fell silent. It was the Voice. He was sitting at the center of the row of Watchers.

He was a heavyset, brutal looking man, old like the rest of them but still powerfully built. He looked around the table. "We will have one more city meeting," he said. "One more to make sure there is no one left who would dare to balk at the euthanizing of a few old friends."

Except for Marta, the other Watchers were nodding.

"The people are sufficiently cowed," the Voice said. "And confused as well. They have lost the war without most of them ever realizing there was one."

"That one city meeting didn't go as we expected," the very old man said, his tone querulous. "The little boy who confessed wasn't the one who was supposed to die. Who'd have thought he'd be so brave?"

"He served our purpose well enough," the Voice said. He looked up and down the table; all eyes were on him. "Our last city meeting will be the one involving the cook."

"That one was my idea," the short-haired plump woman said happily. "It can't go wrong."

I was beginning to really, really dislike that woman.

"This is the best way," the languid woman said to Marta, reaching out to pat her hand. Marta moved hers away.

"Truly," the languid woman said. "It makes perfect sense. City meeting first, and then we can proceed to the euthanizing. You know quite well that's the only way we'll make it through the winter. And then, once we've survived until the next growing season, we can reassess our long-term goals, though even you must admit they're probably irrelevant at this point. That's something we must learn to face. It isn't easy, I know, to see one's life work come to naught."

Marta didn't respond.

The Voice went on to summarize their plans. A group of people would be collected in the Watcher compound—people too old to do hard manual labor, people who had been in the infirmary more than twice in the past year, people who had suffered injuries that continued to limit their labor, and people who didn't meet weight requirements.

"That will dispose of our heaviest burdens," the Voice concluded. "The old, the ill, the injured or disabled, and those with inefficient metabolisms."

The very old man nodded, his face pleased. "And if she's still around, that will take care of the emotional redhead. One way or another, she'll be out of the way."

The languid woman raised a warning finger. "Euthanasia isn't punishment, remember. It's mercy. A good death instead of a slow, miserable starvation. Some people might survive this winter's strict rationing. People like the problematic redhead wouldn't."

Meritt muttered something under his breath.

"And do we have statistics yet?" the round man was asking. "How many will be euthanized?"

"One hundred and twelve who are dead weight," the Voice said. "Another sixty whose productivity does not compensate for their needs."

They were going to kill me, me and a whole host of other people who didn't meet their strength criteria—including my old people, the ones who'd had time for a lonely little girl. Mariella, who took me for walks. Estelle, who talked to me about cooking as if I'd have a chance to try it myself. And Louie—he'd escaped once, but he wouldn't escape this time.

"So a bit over ten percent of our population . . .. Is that

sufficient for the rest of us to survive the winter?" the long-faced man asked.

"We believe so," the Voice said.

"The productive citizens might be a bit unnerved," said the long-faced man. "But it's easy enough to recover from a done deed. And they'll know, by then, how necessary it was. They'll see that they survived only because the others died, and they'll thank us for saving them. They'll thank us for bearing the weight of the decision ourselves."

"And by then we'll have the angelic Meritt," the languid woman said, and Meritt leaned closer to the screen. "He'll distract them. They'll be meek as lambs, seeing that one of their own is on the city commission. Such a good idea—we should have thought of it earlier."

"We did," the Voice said. "But there are, as you well know, considerable risks."

"Has he been approached?" the very old man asked.

"Yes," the Voice said. "We have been pursuing that option and are pleased with preliminary reports."

"In other words, he's smart enough to see he has no viable alternative." That was Marta.

"He'll virtually eliminate the possibility of any future uprising," said the plump woman, just as the very old man said, "He'll minimize the possibility of trouble from other quarters."

"Indeed." The Voice sounded bored. "That is the plan. But negotiations are not complete. As we know, he has divided loyalties. He will have to make an unmistakable gesture of good will before we concede anything. He will have to bind himself to us irrevocably. Once he does, however, he will serve our purposes well enough." He looked around the table. "Other business?"

No one spoke. "Meeting adjourned," he said.

Chapter 18

Meritt began disengaging whatever he had set up. "Well, it worked," he said, keeping his eyes on the screen. His face was very white against his dark hair. "Farrell Dean can be proud."

The present danger flooded back. "Farrell Dean—" I began, but Meritt spoke over me.

"He installed the final components in the Watchers' conference room when he repaired their heating a couple of days ago. Did it perfectly. It's not so far out of his skill set, of course. He's a great mechanic, and I explained to him how—"

I cut him off. "Farrell Dean is downstairs, Meritt. He's the one they were beating."

Meritt stared at me. "We've got to get out," he said, and began keying still more rapidly, his fingers flying. "He knows too much."

"He won't tell them anything," I said. "But we have to help him—they were beating him. They might kill him."

Meritt shot one glance in my direction. "He won't want to talk. But even the best of us can be broken."

I shook my head. "Not Farrell Dean. Not when it comes to— "

"Not when it comes to you?" Meritt laughed shortly. "Moot point, Red. Farrell Dean doesn't know you're up here.

He only knows about me. And if they catch me, they catch you."

"He won't give you away, either," I said. "We have to help him."

Meritt stood up, went to the sleeping warden, and began dragging him back over to the desk. "Everything's negotiable, Red. Farrell Dean might not trade your life or mine to save his own, but what if they stack the deck?"

"He won't tell." I went to help him prop the warden at the desk, shifting his arm so he wouldn't have a crick in his neck when he woke up.

Meritt laughed softly, but his face was wry. "Do you have half the faith in me that you have in Farrell Dean?"

"More," I said, looking straight into his eyes. "You know that."

For a heartbeat Meritt looked as if he would say something, but then he shook his head, turned, and headed for the doorway. "Come on," he said. "Hurry."

Silently we raced down the stairs. At the bottom we paused, leaning against the wall by the door, listening, hearing nothing. Meritt opened the door a crack; the hall was empty. I could see the door to Farrell Dean's cell. It was bolted now, and no light shone from under the door.

"Let's go." Meritt took my hand and pulled me along with him.

When we got to Farrell Dean's door I dug in my heels and wrenched my hand away. By the time Meritt regained his grip on me I had unbolted the door.

"We can't help him right now," he hissed. "He'll be chained to the wall."

"We have to try," I said.

Voices stopped our argument, voices and footsteps. They weren't close yet, but they were coming from the direction of the way out—the only way out.

Meritt shut his eyes. He looked pained, not terrified. When he opened his eyes his face was resolute.

"My turn," he said, pulling open Farrell Dean's door and shoving me inside. "When it's quiet again, get out of here. And Red—" his voice sounded strained—"We can't be seen together anymore. It's too dangerous."

I opened my mouth to protest, but he leaned over me and kissed me. Then the door swung open, swung shut again, and he was gone.

"Rhoda?" I heard him call. "Is that you?" His voice faded; he was walking away from me.

Rhoda. Was she the blonde Warden?

"What are you doing here?" a man said.

Meritt said—calmly—"Let go of my arm."

"I'll let go when I feel like it. Answer the question. Why are you here?"

"I'm looking for Rhoda."

"Now? Past midnight?"

Meritt gave a grim laugh. "You'd rather I came at noon? Announcing to the whole city that I'm talking with the Watchers? No wonder Optica's in trouble. You telegraph every move."

Another voice said something. His tone was concerned, but I couldn't catch his words. I hoped they were far enough away not to notice that Farrell Dean's door was unbolted.

"All right then," the first voice said. "Come with us." Footsteps moved away down the corridor. I could hear Meritt talking, his voice fading as they moved away.

My heart pounding, I hesitated by the door. Meritt would want me to get out now, as soon as he had the wardens out of the hallway, safely distracted. But I couldn't go yet, not without checking on Farrell Dean. Maybe Meritt was wrong and he wasn't chained; maybe I could get him out.

It was pitch black in the cell. The thin line of light

coming from beneath the door seemed to make the darkness thicker. Keeping one hand on the wall I began to edge my way around the room. I could hear someone breathing jaggedly, painfully. The air smelled coppery, like blood.

"Farrell Dean?" I whispered. No one replied.

I edged a little further. My foot bumped something and I knelt to touch it. A foot. It didn't move at my touch. I felt along him, trying to get oriented. He seemed to be lying on his face on the floor. His right leg was stretched out—the one I'd bumped—and his other leg was bent. He was shirtless and waves of heat came off his skin, as if he were radiating pain.

Careful not to touch his back, I found his arms. The left one was chained to a metal ring in the wall. His face was turned away from me.

I stepped carefully over his chained arm and made my way around him, so we'd be face to face.

"Farrell Dean?" I found his hair, smoothed it back. It was wet—whether with sweat or with blood, I couldn't tell, and through all my fumbling, he hadn't moved.

"Farrell Dean," I said again. "It's Red. Can you hear me?"

He drew a jagged breath, shifted slightly beneath my hands.

"I'm here," I said. "We're going to help you."

"Get out," he said. His voice was hoarse. "It's not safe."

"I'm going, but I'll be back. We'll get you out of here."

He didn't answer.

"Farrell Dean?"

My blood was pounding in my ears; I couldn't hear him breathe, couldn't feel any movement except what might have been my own. I felt for his neck, tried to find a pulse. He was so warm but I couldn't find a heartbeat, and his neck was slick with blood, it had to be blood, there was too much for it to be sweat.

I took him by the shoulder and shook him. "Don't die," I

said, and it came out a sob. "Don't die, Farrell Dean, please don't die."

His right hand came up and grasped my wrist. "Red," he said. "I'm not dying. It just hurts like the dickens. Stop jolting me all around."

Weeping now, I found his cheek and kissed it. He sighed heavily.

"Go," he said. "Go *now*."

"I'm going. But I won't let them kill you, Farrell Dean. Meritt won't let them. We'll get you out."

He didn't reply but his hand moved on my wrist, letting me go. I kissed him once more, then did what both he and Meritt wanted me to do. I left.

Chapter 19

Outside the watchtower I huddled in the shadows, trying to think clearly. Adrenaline was coursing through me, and anger. So they'd beat Farrell Dean bloody, would they? They'd twist Meritt, use him for their own ends. They'd kill us off, Skye with her cough, sweet old Mariella, all my old people, anyone who wasn't strong and compliant.

We'd see about that.

It was very late, but there was no way I would go back to my dormitory and to bed. I hadn't saved Rafe the night he'd been arrested—I hadn't even known he needed saving until it was too late. I wasn't going to make the same mistake twice. I wasn't going to go back to my dorm to discover later that Farrell Dean was the next city meeting victim.

But who could help me get him out? Cline was his closest friend, but I couldn't get into the boys' dormitory without being caught. And even if I could, he might not come with me. He didn't like me or trust me. And even if he'd come, he couldn't get Farrell Dean out of the prison, not with the wardens there, not with the chains. No one could.

Without coming to a conscious decision I started moving silently through the dark streets of the city. Every building was dark, even the laundry, though hot mist billowed hazily from its vent pipes, vanishing quickly in the crisp clear air. It had turned colder, less humid. The blue lights were free of their usual blurry halos, and the white spotlight cut cleanly through the streets.

I reached the end of the buildings and made my way through the dark meadow. I could see the shadowed forms of bee hives clearly enough on this cloudless night, and it was chilly enough to make the bees sleepy. Even so I slowed, went cautiously.

Beyond the bee fields, in the orchards, the ancient twisted apple trees threw wild shadows. On the ground a few rotting, wormy apples spread a surprisingly potent scent. Sometimes deer came in through the gap in the outer wall to eat the fallen apples, but even they wouldn't want the mushy nubs left on the ground now.

When I reached the gap that opened onto the wasteland I hesitated, just for a moment. Then I thought about Meritt and Farrell Dean, about my old people, and I stepped out into the exposed space and crossed the pale thin grass to the edge of the trees, where again I stopped.

I'd never been outside the wall on this side of the city. As far as I knew, no one had. Not only did I have to go into these trees, I had to keep going and bear north, toward the frightening wilderland.

My heart began to pound. Despite my best intentions, I couldn't lift a foot to step into the trees. The Guardians weren't just stories; Meritt said so. If I went into the woods, I might well get killed, by them or by something else.

But I was going to get killed anyway, soon enough. And I knew what I had seen: the gap behind the Watcher compound had been open once, and now was sealed. Surely that indicated first an alliance—the Guardians supporting the Watchers, as we'd always been told—and then a disagreement. I had to focus on the slim possibility that the Guardians were intelligent beings, unhappy with the Watchers, and willing to help us overthrow the Watchers, or at least make them listen to reason. I had to focus on getting help for my friends.

I could do this; I could. I just needed a moment to compose myself.

The night was silent and still, and the stars shone calmly overhead. But the trees didn't feel welcoming, like they had the first time I'd ventured into them, over on the other side of the city by the slaughterhouse. I hoped I was imagining the menace; I hoped it wasn't something real, something waiting for me in the woods. The thing that had called my name, or something else. If the Guardians killed me, fine. That was a risk I was willing to take. But I didn't want to get killed by a wolf, or by some crazed chicken-vandal, before I'd even found the Guardians.

The ominous feeling didn't abate, but nothing jumped out at me, and I couldn't stand there at the edge of the wasteland forever. Meritt was in trouble; Farrell Dean was chained in prison; Rafe was dead.

Taking a deep breath, I plunged into the darkness between the trees.

I half thought a voice would start calling my name, but in the woods the world felt quieter still, hushed. The ground was uneven beneath my bare feet, strewn with fallen limbs, rocks, and sharp-edged pine cones.

Before I went any further I bent and, feeling carefully so I wouldn't cut my hands on a sharp twig or razor-like bramble, found five or six egg-sized rocks. I stuffed most of them in my pockets and kept one in my hand, a small weapon, but better than nothing.

It was hard to go quietly. Drifts of dead leaves blanketed the ground, rustling underfoot. I avoided them as best as I could. The tops of the trees obscured the sky, but I thought the moon must have risen, for though the trees were growing more closely together, I could see a little more clearly. Or maybe my eyes finally had adjusted to the darkness.

For an hour or so I picked my way through the woods. I walked long enough that I actually began to feel tired instead of terrified. The ground out here wasn't as level as the ground inside the city, and the repeated uphill, downhill trudge made my legs burn.

Then a sound—or not so much a sound as a shift in the air—made me freeze. Was something there?

And then I saw it—ahead of me, just over a small rise, the silhouette of a creature on all fours, larger than a dog, larger even than I thought a wolf should be.

It slunk around a tree and disappeared, then came back into sight a few yards from where I stood paralyzed. There it paused and sniffed the air.

The hair on the back of my neck prickled. Should I run? But then it would surely chase me, and I doubted I could out-run it. Should I stand still and hope it wouldn't notice me? Could it climb trees?

It lowered its head to the ground, sniffed, and then raised its face in my direction. The night was so dark I couldn't get a clear look at it—wolves were large wild dogs, distant relatives of the dogs the cattle workers used, but something about this creature didn't feel dog-like. The shape of its head seemed wrong and I couldn't see a tail.

I tried to remember what I had been taught about bears. Weren't bears either black or dark brown? This thing was definitely light in color.

After a long moment I thought might kill me from fear alone, the creature shook itself as if awakening from a dream, stood up on its hind legs, and sniffed the breeze again.

When its face turned away from me I threw my rock in-to the underbrush.

In a heartbeat the creature dropped to all fours and was

gone, pounding after the sound. I hurried in the opposite direction, quickly but as quietly as I could.

How long I ran I don't know, but it was long enough that my legs grew shaky. Finally I stopped and listened so hard that I forgot to breathe, but I heard nothing. I started walking again, still listening, but the only sound was an occasional hoot-owl, the first so close I nearly jumped out of my skin. Maybe I'd startled it before it startled me.

The trees were now thickly matted with undergrowth. Large rocks, boulders really, began cropping up time and again whatever path I took. I had to go slowly, circling those boulders, squeezing through low-slung branches, stopping to untangle my legs from clinging vines. If there had ever been a path, I'd lost it long ago. All I was pretty sure of was that I was still bearing north, or at least northwest, away from the city and toward the wilderland.

Maybe I was already in the wilderland; I didn't know. All I knew was that I had to keep pressing on in the same direction or risk going in circles all night long.

Eventually I found myself confronting an enormous fallen tree, its top twice as high as I was tall. I couldn't go under it—dense undergrowth filled the space. To the left was a mass of twisted blackberry bramble, and to my right was a large boulder and more dense growth.

I'd have to climb over the tree. But in the middle of the night, exhausted as I was, it seemed too daunting a task.

I decided to rest for a bit before tackling it. I thought again about the strange wild creature and wished I could climb a tree and rest up there, but the trees around me were either giant, their lowest branches unreachable, or young striplings with branches too thin to support even my weight. And anyway, for all I knew, the thing could climb.

Huddling down at the foot of a tall pine, hiding in the shadows of the undergrowth, I leaned back and shut my eyes.

The wind rustled some dying leaves nearby, and the thought came to me that if I lay down here and didn't rise, soon enough I'd be buried under autumn leaves, hidden by the forest. Vanishing without a trace wouldn't be so bad. It would be clean, somehow, my blood on nobody's hands but my own.

For a long time I sat there, resting my eyes or opening them on the dark. I was too tired by then to feel afraid, too tired to feel sorry for myself, too tired to think or even to listen for creatures in the night. I merely sat there, feeling the wind on my face, smelling the piney trees.

Soon I would get up and go on; I would keep trying. I'd go still deeper into the woods, on and on as long as it took, until I found the Guardians. If they didn't kill me before I could say a word, I'd ask them to help us.

In my exhausted state I'd actually begun to drift into sleep when something jerked me awake—a voice, saying my name.

"Red?" it muttered.

I held very still, not even daring to breathe.

A form had clambered onto the fallen tree from the other side, and now stood perched on top. It was large and there was something wrong about it, something deformed.

"Red," it said again. "Red, red, red, red, red."

It had a man's voice, but the cadences were sing-songy and blurred, like those of a small child.

"Redder . . ..redder . . ." it said. Then it snuffled and leapt down from the tree, landing only a few feet away from me. I couldn't move. There was only one clear thought in my head: Coming to the woods had been a very, very bad idea.

"Redder . . .redder . . .redder . . .reddest!"

The thing leapt at me—it was a large man with a long tangled beard. He grabbed at me and then I moved, shrieking and scooting away, avoiding his hands, crawling on my hands and knees, trying to get my feet under me so I could run, but he caught me around the waist and lifted me off the ground. He was strong, and so large, and in a heartbeat I had been flung over his back and was gasping for breath, his shoulder digging painfully into my stomach.

As he hauled me over the fallen tree I raised up, struggling against him, but he gripped me tightly around the legs and tipped me further back so that I banged my chin against his lower back and bit my tongue. He stank of smoke and muck, and the rough fabric of his shirt scraped against my face as he began to move faster, in a sort of staggering half-trot. I cried out again but he gave me an impatient shake, and I imagined how easy it would be for him to swing me around and slam my head against a boulder. I could imagine all sorts of horrible deaths—and anyway there was no point in calling for help out there in the lonely woods.

My more immediate danger was that, as he loped along, I was jolted with every stride, hard enough that at this rate I'd be too dazed to take any useful action by the time he stopped. There was no good position, but I found that by bending myself against him, crossing my arms over my chest and holding my head in my hands, I could minimize the damage.

The dark woods went by in a blur, sideways and upside down, rocks and trees and thick patches of undergrowth. I don't know how long he carried me, but it felt like I'd been dangling over his back forever when we came to a clearing and he stopped, and with no warning he swung me off his shoulder and dumped me on the ground, putting one heavy foot on my stomach to hold me in place.

My head swam—the clearing circled dizzily around me—but finally it stilled, and there in the clearing, in the light of the waning half-moon, I finally got a good look at my captor.

He stood crookedly, with one shoulder dipping down

and the other rising high, and when I saw his face any hope I had of appealing to his better nature vanished. Behind his wild beard his mouth hung open loosely, and his pale eyes were vacant. He must be another luckless soul, driven insane by whatever it was in the woods that had driven Rosella mad, the difference being that this one didn't drift around helpfully warning people to stay out of the wilderland, or harmlessly warbling unhinged melodies about lost love.

After a moment of staring vacantly ahead, he raised his chin and bellowed, "Red! Red redder reddest!" I had a horrible feeling that he was calling his friends.

Then he looked down at me, lifted his foot from my stomach, and prodded at me with his toe. I didn't know why he was doing that, but when he kicked harder and began to make frustrated sounds, I rolled to my hands and knees. He grabbed my arm and yanked me to my feet. Then, holding tight to my arm, he began to slap at me, not hard but hard enough, patting at my legs, my chest, my back, turning me this way and that, his hot foul breath in my face.

"Red redder reddest," he muttered, and a line of spit ran down into his filthy beard.

Terrified and revolted, I turned my face away from him—and my heart leapt.

There in the moonlight, at the edge of the clearing, was another man, just barely out of the shadows. Unlike the thing holding me, he was normal looking—or, rather, better than normal. Beautiful wouldn't be putting it too strongly, if a man could be called that. He had long fair hair—in the moonlight I couldn't tell whether it was blond or silver, or how old he was except to say he was definitely a grown man, far older than me—and he was tall and straight, with broad shoulders, and dressed in clothes covered in a pattern of dark and light that made him blend in with the shadows and moonlight.

"Have you been hunting, Caliban?" he said. His tone was clear and amused, as if he were humoring the creature. "What have you found?"

My captor took me by the shoulders and shoved me out in front of him.

"Red," he said. "Red girl." And he yanked off my cap and let it fall to the ground.

The other man nodded. "Like moth to flame," he said quietly, his eyes on me. "Cover it up again, there's a good girl."

I bent and picked up my cap, and as quickly as I could, twisted my hair up and hid it.

The man in the distance remained rooted where he was, looking at me consideringly. He was clean and handsome, and had every appearance of sanity. I wanted to call out to him for help, but there was something dangerous in his aspect, something I couldn't quite put my finger on, so I stayed quiet.

"Are you out here alone?" he said finally.

There didn't seem to be any point in lying, so I nodded.

He untied something from his waist and tossed it towards us. It fell right at my feet—a small leather bag, the top pulled together in a tight gather.

"A treat for Caliban," the man said. "It's been a long time since you've had a treat, hasn't it, Caliban?"

My captor snatched up the bag. Then he began slapping at my back, almost hard enough to knock me off my feet.

"You've dusted her off very nicely," the man in the distance said. "Now let her alone before you break her."

The hands stopped pawing at me. I could feel him standing behind me, but he wasn't restraining me any longer, wasn't holding onto my arm or any part of me.

"Come to me, girl," the man said. "He'll let you. He knows you're mine."

"Then he's mistaken," said another voice.

I swung around but couldn't see who was speaking. "Lieutenant Jensen! Bring the prisoner to me."

The man behind me grabbed me up, flung me back over his shoulder, and began hurrying toward the edge of the clearing in his stumbling, halting gait—not toward the beautiful man but a quarter turn away from him. "Red redder reddest!" he said excitedly.

"Well done," said the voice, and my captor jerked to a halt in front of a bank of shadows. "Set her down."

I was unceremoniously dropped onto the ground like a sack of grain, and when I got to my feet I found myself face to face with an old man who was wearing the same sort of splotchy clothing as the handsome younger man.

"Don't make any sudden moves," the old man said in an undertone, then raised his voice. "Jensen! Cover my retreat."

The man stood up as straight as he could, clutching the leather bag to his chest. "Sir!" he said, then turned and trotted off, stuffing the bag into his shirt as he went.

"Come." The old man didn't look at me. He said that one word, turned, and set off into the woods.

I looked back over my shoulder, towards the handsome man, but he had vanished. Taking a deep breath I did the only thing that seemed possible: I followed the old man deeper into the woods.

He moved swiftly for someone his age, and quietly. I had to hurry to keep up, and more than once stepped on something sharp or hard, but I was afraid to pause for fear of losing him. He made several sudden turns for no reason that I could see, and twice reached out and without a word pulled me up behind him into the branches of a tree, where we seemed to be waiting or hiding.

The first time we did this I saw nothing. We waited for awhile, then climbed down and went on. The second time, however, the enormous four-legged wild creature—or another like it—came and snuffled around the base of the tree. The old man was beneath me, and I hoped he knew how to fight the thing off if it began to climb.

But it didn't climb. After sniffing all around the tree on all fours, the creature stood up just like a man and peed on the tree.

The sight, combined with the pungent ammonia smell, made me gag, but I fought the reflex back for fear the thing would hear and come scrambling up the tree after me.

Then it walked away on two legs, and as it walked I could no longer tell why I'd ever thought it was an animal. It looked just like a naked, dirt-encrusted man.

We stayed clinging to the tree for a long time, so long that I began to wonder whether we would stay there until daylight. Finally, though, the old man climbed down and dropped to the ground and I followed, carefully avoiding the place where the creature had marked the tree.

We walked on, and soon it seemed like every few steps there was another large boulder. Some we went around, others, because they lay in a narrow path hemmed in by bramble-choked woods, we climbed over.

My adrenaline rush had by now long faded, so I concentrated on following the old man's steps, on keeping up without falling or making noise. I tried to move like him, a secret creature of the night. I lost all track of time.

At some point I became aware of a faint hissing noise—I thought I had been hearing it for some time without noticing. It seemed to come from everywhere and nowhere. But the clouds had covered the moon again, and I could see very little, even less than I might have because it was dark enough now that I didn't dare gaze about lest I trip in the darkness or lose the old man.

I was only a step behind him, skirting an especially large

boulder, when he spoke to me for the first time since we'd begun the trek. "Come inside," he said.

At first I couldn't tell what he meant. Then I realized that what seemed to be a shadow on the sloping rock wall behind him was a hole almost as tall as I was.

I followed him to it. It was the opening to a cave.

Though I'd been following the old man through the woods for ages, I was reluctant to be trapped with him in a cave somewhere deep in the wilderland. Then again, I didn't want to be outside alone if the wild man who'd abducted me showed up again. There was also that mysterious hissing noise, louder than ever now. So, deciding the old man was the least scary of three scary things, I followed him inside.

Once in the pitch blackness of the cave I changed my mind—the old man was a certain and present danger, and the wild man and the noise only possible future ones. So I turned back, creeping quietly, and pressed myself against the cold stone wall beside the opening, trying to see out into the darkness, trying to see if it was safe to creep out there and away alone.

Behind me came the sound of a match being struck and a sudden glow of light. I turned and saw the old man setting a lamp in the middle of the floor of the cave, saw too that the cave wasn't a bare hole in the rock, but a home.

One part of the rock-walled room was crowded with stacks and stacks of short metal cylinders with paper labels, and the rest of the wall space was lined with stacks and stacks of books—more books than I had ever seen, more books than I knew existed. In one corner stood a pallet-like bed with a bright cover, and at its foot a large rectangular box with hinges.

For a hole in a rock the place was quite civilized. How long had this man been out here, fending for himself in the woods?

In the lamplight the man still looked very old, at least as old as the Watchers, but he also looked wiry and strong. His face was deeply lined from his nose down to the corners of his mouth, and around the corners of his eyes, and he had no hair except for a silvery gray stubble that matched the uneven stubble on his chin. His eyebrows were silver and his eyes were a startling bright blue. As I studied him, he opened a tin container and took out a handful of dried apple slices.

"Hungry?" he asked. I nodded and he brought the apples to me, along with a cup of water from a covered bucket on the floor; then he went back and took out apples and water for himself and sat on the end of his pallet, eating.

The apples were sweet and satisfying, the water cold and fresh, and I finished them quickly. I stood there turning the empty cup over in my hands, waiting for the food to hit my bloodstream and stop my trembling, and as it did I began to realize exactly how exhausted I was—so exhausted, I couldn't go one step further, not unless some new burst of fright sent more adrenaline coursing through my veins.

The old man ate another piece of apple. He hadn't so much as glanced at me, since he'd handed me food and water.

Cautiously I slid down to a sitting position, resting my back against the rocky wall. Safe or not, and whether I wanted to or not, I had to rest. Worse, safe or not I'd soon be asleep. My eyelids were heavy and my limbs too relaxed, and the hissing sound outside didn't help. Now that I was sitting still and not hurrying through the woods, I could hear a rhythmic quality to it, a soft and gentle shushing. It rose and fell, rose and fell, pulling at my tense muscles, unwinding the tight cords in my neck and shoulders, lulling me to relax.

Without thinking I reached up and pulled off my black cap. The old man gave a sharp intake of breath. He looked startled, and then pained, and then—and this was oddest of all—tender.

When our eyes met, he spoke. "Jensen spoke truer than he knew," he said, in a quiet and musing voice. "Red indeed."

His words made perfect sense, coming as they did when he'd seen my hair, but somehow I felt he was changing the subject.

"What is her name?" he said.

My heart leapt in panic and I scanned the cave, trying to see who he was speaking to—someone hidden in the shadows, or behind the books. Someone else to fear.

I could spot no one, and no one answered him. His eyes were fixed expectantly on me.

Maybe in my exhaustion I'd misheard him. Maybe he'd only asked me my own name. After a moment's further lingering uncertainty, I answered. "My name is Red," I said.

The old man shut his eyes and began to laugh, a long lilting cackle that raised goose bumps on my arms. He laughed so hard he cried, holding his stomach and rocking. He made no move toward me or I'd have been gone, out of the cave and into the night, regardless of whatever else was out there.

After what seemed like a very long time his cackles subsided. He wiped his eyes on his sleeve and shook his head, still smiling. "Red in hair and Red in name. Jensen was twice right. That's a record."

"Does he know me?" I ventured.

The old man's forehead furrowed. "No, no. Not like you mean. Knowing is pretty well beyond him now. Sometimes he doesn't know me. Most of the time he doesn't know himself. Fortunately he remembers being scolded for eating people, so he decided to give you as a gift to appease his gods."

I didn't follow everything he said, but the part about Jensen eating people was perfectly clear. The skinned man on the steps of the circle flashed into my mind, and the man missing his hands.

"How old are you, Red Girl?" the old man asked, pulling up his feet so that he sat cross-legged on his pallet.

"Sixteen. Almost seventeen."

"Seventeen years old ... how time does fly. A lifetime for you, the blink of an eye for me. Where do you work?"

"In the fields."

"Who are her parents?"

I stared at him. Was he still talking to me?

"I don't know," I said.

He began laughing again, that cackling, disconcerting laugh. "Of course not," he said. "The joke's on me. But it isn't funny, so we'll try again." He eyed me narrowly. "She needn't be afraid."

I discovered that, without realizing it, I had begun edging toward the doorway.

"No, no, she needn't be afraid," he said again. "I don't eat children. Or adults, for that matter. Nor do I give them to Angel for playthings."

"Who is Angel?"

"You saw him," the old man said. Now I was *you* again. "He's pretty, but pretty is as pretty does, and he does wicked things, so he isn't pretty at all."

I blinked hard. I was so tired, and so frightened, and the old man's words were hard to follow.

"So Angel is the handsome man, and Jensen is the—" I caught myself, not wanting to give offense—"the one who caught me. And who are you?"

He cocked his head, as if listening.

I listened too, but I didn't hear a thing.

"I agree." He uncrossed his legs. "There can be no harm in telling her, so long after the ashes. And surely she deserves that much." More quickly than I would have expected for a man of his age, he got to his feet. I braced my hands against the ground, ready to push myself up and away, but he made

193

no move toward me. Instead he stood in the center of the cave, beaming at me, his teeth crooked and discolored but his blue eyes bright and clear.

"She will please allow me to present Joint Special Ops Commander Thomas Anthony the Third," he said, and made an elaborate bow. When he straightened back up, he was looking at me expectantly.

"That's a very long name," I said politely, and he cackled with laughter again.

"It is," he said. "She may call me Tom. But in front of Jensen she must call me Sir. If she fails I will let him eat her."

I decided I'd call him Sir all the time.

Suddenly his smile faded and his face grew stern. "Does Red Girl know what time it is?"

I shook my head.

"Long past bedtime, that's what time. Her mystery parents would never forgive me for chattering on like this. She's a young thing and must be worn to a raveling." As he talked he moved around the room, gathering blankets, even a pillow, and bringing them to me.

"Clearly she likes the threshold," he said. "It's safe enough. Jensen and Angel have never come close to finding this one, and they all know traps are set. So she may sleep on the brink if she wishes, and breathe the fresh air, and dream of the sea."

How could he know that I often dreamt of the sea?

"I will wake her for breakfast—no," he interrupted himself. "I will wake her to wash and then have breakfast. She has blood on her hands and face. Not hers, I take it, for she appears to be uninjured, at least in body. Mind and soul we cannot so easily say." He winked at me.

Then he leaned in close, so close and so intently that I pressed my head back against the hard stone wall and hoped I hadn't made a terrible mistake in trusting him this far.

For a long heart-stopping second he held my gaze with those strange bright blue eyes.

"She shall have no fear," he said, and his voice was calm and authoritative and completely sane. "Tonight she may sleep in peace."

There was no chance of that happening, I remember thinking.

It was the last waking thought I had.

Chapter 20

I woke at dawn parched with thirst. Sitting up, I pushed my hair out of my eyes and looked around. The cave was empty, a wash of thin almost-morning light laying a path from the entrance across the dim dirt floor.

Scrambling to my feet I went to the bucket and lifted its wooden cover. It was full of water, and the cup I had used the night before was sitting on the ground beside it. I drank and drank, and only when I finally paused for breath was I awake enough to wonder where the old man had gone.

His pallet bed was neatly made, the extra blanket crisply folded at the foot. Mindful of my status—prisoner or guest, in either case I thought I should behave well—I folded my own bedding and set it on the floor beside his pallet. Then I crossed to the entrance of the cave and cautiously went outside, shivering a little in the gray early dawn.

When I rounded the big boulder that hid the entrance to the cave, I stopped cold. I couldn't believe my eyes. There it was, shushing gently, rolling in and rolling out, shimmering and shifting in the receding darkness like a breathing, living thing. I had slept beside the sea.

I couldn't see the end of it—maybe once full daylight came I would. Or maybe it would still stretch beyond my sight, miles and miles of sea rolling on forever.

The thought of so much open space took my breath away, made me feel as if I were standing on the edge of the world. I had never before been more than a few yards beyond the city walls.

The sand went stretching alongside the waves in a long expanse. It was darker where the waves had washed over it, lighter closer to me. It was mostly clean and bare, strewn here and there with long whips of kelp, ugly and strangely familiar, like giant hairs pulled out by their roots.

The air smelled organic, a strangely pungent smell for so much open empty space. It reminded me of the compost piles we kept for the vegetables, piles of decomposing fish heads mixed with rotting leaves and eggshells. Then a salty breeze picked up, blowing in from the sea, and the smell faded, and the wind stirred my hair just like it stirred the shifting darkening waves.

A little ways down the beach the old man was bent over, putting driftwood on a small fire. The smoke was invisible in the gray light, but I could see the orange flickering flames, and my mouth watered as the smell of woodsmoke and cooked fish reached me.

The old man stood up, caught sight of me, and gestured for me to come to him.

My first few steps took me across a thin stretch of yellowed grass. Then I reached the clear pale sand, which shifted up between my toes, strangely warm on this cool morning. And then I went from dry sand to wet sand, which took my footprints, then erased them.

"Good morning," the old man said as I drew near.

"Good morning." He was odd and interesting, but at the moment the vast expanse of water before me was more so.

"The sea whispers," I said. "It sings."

"Oh yes, she sings. Day and night, she sings in her chains."

I gazed out at the wide expanse, at the low-lying clouds just beginning to be rimmed with gold, at the gently shifting waters and the smooth bare sand. The sea. I was finally seeing the sea.

For a long moment I stood there, yearning, held back by some invisible tether. Maybe it was the old habit of unfreedom, or maybe I was afraid to do anything that might upset my strange host.

"For goodness sakes, go," the old man said. "Bathe yourself. Be sure to wash the bloodstains from your hands and face. Breakfast is only fish, but we do what we can to stay civilized."

I looked at my hands, at Farrell Dean's blood, and wondered whether he'd survived the night.

"Go wash," he said again.

I started toward the water, but then uncertainty hit me and I turned back toward Sir Tom. Did he really mean for me to walk into the sea? How deep was it, how wide—

The old man met my gaze and pity flashed across his face, replaced almost instantly with a sort of amused affection. "Go on," he said. "It won't swallow you whole. The tide's coming in." Pointing to a neat pile of fabric near his feet, he added, "Here's a fresh change of clothes for you. I'll turn this way, toward the north, and you bathe that way, toward the south, in privacy." And he turned away from me.

I tasted those words. In privacy. I said them aloud to see if they changed the world, brought the Watchers upon me again. Slowly I turned in a circle. No cameras. No wardens. No Watchers. Not anywhere.

It was a strange feeling—exciting but also dizzying. If no one could see me, would I vanish?

I stepped cautiously into the foamy low-rolling waves. They were cold but silkily caressing, and coy in the way they rushed at me, then hurried away, then came back again. My next few steps brought me knee deep, and I began to feel the pull of the water, its buoyancy and its power.

When I was hip deep—still wearing all my clothes—I glanced over at the old man. He had rolled up his pants legs and waded out into the water, his back to me, and was pulling some sort of basket out of the sea. I had never seen the tidal traps our fishermen used, but maybe this man had something like them.

I couldn't swim, but I wasn't afraid. The water was alive, moving beneath me, lifting me off my feet but always shoving me toward shore and safety. It splashed in my face and I licked my lips; they tasted salty. Rafe had told us the sea was salty, that it shouldn't be drunk no matter how thirsty we were.

The sand shifted slyly beneath my feet; small green plants waved around my toes, tickling. Shells peeked out from beneath the sand; I tipped my face up toward the sky and reached down for them, the waves licking at my chin. I came up with a handful of shells and wet sand, and when I rinsed the sand away and lifted the shells up to the strengthening morning light, I saw that the larger ones glowed inside, pink and white and purple.

"Red Girl," called the old man. "Did your instructors never mention the word hypothermia? Get to the fire and get warm." By then he was sitting on a piece of driftwood a little north of the fire, his back to me still, fiddling with one of his traps—repairing it, I thought.

When I waded to shore I realized that although the deepening pink and gold light looked warmer than the gray dawn had, the wind had risen; it was cutting through me.

Hurriedly I pulled off my sodden clothes, dried myself with the towel the old man had laid out for me, and pulled on the fresh clothes—of a thicker and warmer fabric than I was used to and in splotchy browns and greens, like the clothes he wore. They were big, but he'd left a canvas belt as well. I ran it through the belt loops on the pants and cinched it up.

"Are you decent?" he said.

"I'm dressed." My teeth chattered when I spoke.

The old man got up off the driftwood and turned around.

"Blue lips with red hair," he said with a wink and a smile. "Very fetching." He pointed at a blanket on the sand, and I picked it up and wrapped it around my shoulders.

"Sit," he said. "Rest by the sounding sea." He nodded at the fire. "There's still warmth in the embers, but I must let the fire die now. Angel will be watching for us. "

Slowly my shivering subsided and I began to work at rolling the pant legs up to ankle length. Every few seconds I paused, looking out at the waves. The sparkling water went on as far as the rose gold sky. What was on the other side of it? Did it have another side or did it go on forever without touching land, until it came back to the other side of our island?

"You like the sea," the old man said, with that same amused look of affection he'd had before. He was missing some teeth, and the ones he had were yellowed and uneven. The effect was to make him seem a bit unstable, though so far that morning he'd seemed perfectly fine.

"It's odd," I said. "But I feel as if I've been longing for the sea all my life."

That made him cackle. "What do they long for, as I long for ..." Grimacing, he closed his eyes. "What do they long for, as I long for a swift salt scent of the sea once more? One soft scent of the sea ... salt scent of the shore ... ah." He opened his eyes.

"That was lovely," I said.

He looked at me uneasily. "No," he said. "It was not. It should be lovely, for the lovely Edna wrote it. But I neglected to invite her along, and in consequence I am condemned to mangle her lovely lines."

His bright blue eyes were beginning to look dim and vague.

"Is that breakfast?" I asked to pull him back, pointing to the spit of fish above the glowing embers.

It was as if I had called him from a long distance, as if he could barely make out my words. His forehead creased; his expression was perplexed. But after a moment his eyes brightened and focused. "Breakfast, of course! Do you like fish?"

"Yes, very much," I said. I liked anything even remotely edible, but as it happened, his fish was the best fish I had ever tasted. I was even hungrier than usual, and the fish was plentiful and fresh and almost too hot to handle, smoky and crisp and delicious, and I was sitting on a piece of driftwood in the open air beside the rolling, murmuring sea. It was without a doubt the best meal of my life.

Tom—*Sir* Tom to me—sat watching me eat, smiling benignly and a little vaguely. His sleeves were rolled up and I could see the muscles in his arms, ropy but strong. He might be old, but he wasn't feeble.

Rested, warm, and with both our stomachs full, I decided it was as good a time as any to press onwards with my mission.

"May I ask you a question?" I said.

Sir Tom nodded and looked exaggeratedly attentive.

"Besides you, Jensen, and Angel, is there anyone else living in the woods?"

The old man looked away. He watched, expressionless, the last few wisps of smoke rising from the red gold embers. Then he sighed heavily and met my eyes.

"It is not as simple a question as Red Girl assumes," he said. "But to answer its spirit rather than its letter: We three are the only living souls awake in the woods who still possess a remnant of humanity."

A shiver ran up my spine.

Sir Tom was waiting—not expectantly, it seemed to me, but with resignation.

"You mean there are living things that once were human?"

He nodded. "Got it in one."

"Last night—at first I thought it was an animal . . ."

He nodded again.

"He was human?"

"Was, is. It's a tricky line to draw. But as best as I can tell, their memory of humanity has fled."

"Something from the woods comes into the city and draws pictures," I said. "With chicken blood. But I guess that could be Jensen."

Sir Tom raised his eyebrows. "Ah. Chicken blood art. That's one even I have never seen. You're right, however, to raise the question. Is the ability to imagine, to create art, a sign of humanity?"

Maybe that was interesting to him; to me it was just creepy.

"And then of course there's language," he said, poking at the near-dead coals with a stick. "We too make noises when we laugh or weep, but words are for those with promises to keep."

I really did not know how to respond to that.

His expression shifted, became contrary. "Birds do not make promises," he said, and it sounded like a retort. "I never saw a wild thing sorry for itself, but I also never saw a wild thing who understood it was betrayed. Have you?"

He actually seemed to expect an answer.

"No," I said, hoping that would suffice.

It did. The old man nodded vehemently. "Lawrence always was a self-congratulatory old fool," he said. "There's a place for pity, and for self-pity too, long as you don't drown in it. We can't all shrug off every wound with nary a flinch of pain. And we can't learn empathy unless we too have felt the heat 'o the sun, and the furious winter's rages."

I wondered how long it took for the wilderland to turn a person insane. Maybe I'd better hurry up.

"You said only a few living souls were awake," I said. "Does that mean some people are asleep?"

Sir Tom blinked hard several times, clearly disoriented. Then he nodded, but made no other answer.

"The ones who are asleep—" I was groping for words— "Are there many of them? And how long will they sleep?"

Maybe they hibernated like bears. If that was the case, I sure wanted to be far from the woods come spring.

Sir Tom's face was sober.

"A fair number sleep," he said. "Those who died in the time of the ashes, and those who died later, of causes natural and unnatural. All total, twenty-three souls are sleeping in the woods, waiting to be awoken by the trumpet at the end."

Sleeping? But Sir Tom had slid over from talking about sleep to talking about death. So the wild things in the woods couldn't really be woken, could they? Not by a trumpet— whatever that was—or by anything else. And at the end of what?

Feeling unnerved, I picked up a long stick and poked at the fire. The old man turned his face toward the sea and stared fixedly at the horizon.

When the wind kicked up and set the sea frothing, making me shiver and reminding me that time was short, I decided to try a different approach, a more direct one.

"Sir Tom," I said, and waited until he looked at me. "Have you ever heard of the Guardians?"

The old man let out a cackle and leapt to his feet,

gouging a deep channel in the wet sand. When he charged toward me I flinched back, scuttling on the sand like a crab on my heels and bottom and hands.

"She's heard of the Guardians, has she?" I lost my balance in the soft sand and fell, half on my side and half on my back, and the old man stood over me, eyes wild. "Of course she has heard of the Guardians. Bogeymen, monsters under the bed, goblins gobbling up bad little boys and girls, keeping them bounded in their nutshell."

He was biting off his words and his blue eyes were flaming, and I didn't like him towering above me. I scrambled to my feet and backed away, sand prickling everywhere my skin was bare, catching in the wind and threatening my eyes.

"Guarding the guarded for the watchers watching the watchers," Sir Tom said. "Watch*makers*, making watches without any sense of time or tide or wisdom, presumptuous idiots, full of sound and fury."

I took another step backwards. If I ran would he chase me? How fast was he?

"Signifying nothing!" he shouted, and then he spun around and stalked away, talking loudly as he went, waving his arms, shaking his fist. At me? At the wind, the sea, some demon seen only by himself?

He went twenty yards away, thirty. Only then did I realize I'd been holding my breath.

And he kept going. Fifty yards. His boots left marks in the wet sand. The wind whipped my hair into my face and I fought it back, watching the old man go. Where was he going? The beach stretched out in front of him, long and unbroken, until it hit a steep wall of rocks in the distance.

Eighty yards or so. Ninety. He looked small now, small and unthreatening. The first rays of sun hit the sand and set it sparkling, as if it were strewn with tiny bits of glass. I felt small, alone there on the beach, small and helpless. Was he going to go away and leave me here? If he did, then what would I do?

The woods were so dark and thick they seemed impenetrable. There was underbrush, thorny and twined. And there were traps, he had said.

If I could get through all that, I probably could find my way back to Optica—all I had to do was walk straight in and keep going until I hit the wasteland and the city wall—but there was no help for me in Optica, where Farrell Dean lay chained and Meritt was caught in some dangerous game with the Watchers, and where I'd be weeded out before winter. And somewhere in the woods were the wilderland creatures, those sniffing, prowling wolf-like men. I didn't want to face those things again, and I didn't want to be caught by Caliban, Jensen, whoever or whatever he was.

Maybe the other man would help me find the Guardians. Angel. Could I find him, if I went back into the woods?

If I hadn't been so frightened I might have cried.

Down the beach the old man was so far away that he looked as if he'd stopped moving entirely. I squinted. Was he moving? Was he still walking away?

He wasn't. He'd turned. He was coming back toward me, across that long expanse of wet sand, making a second set of footprints beside his first.

The wind shifted, blew smoke from the dwindling fire into my eyes. I blinked hard, tried to bring the old man's face into focus. Was he calm now? Sane?

As he got closer I was pretty sure he looked calm. At least, he wasn't berating the wind anymore. All the same, I got ready to make a run for it.

I brushed the loose sand off my hands and face and planted my feet firmly, plotting a path. I'd go straight toward the firmer sand, the wet sand, and I'd run up the beach beside the waves and then, when I'd put enough distance between us, I'd cut across the soft part to the tufty yellowed grass.

But when the old man drew near me, there was something like tenderness in his eyes, and regret.

"Forgive me," he said gently. "You asked a reasonable question. You deserve a wholesome reply. Red Girl, meet the Guardians."

And he bowed, touching one hand to his chest.

Chapter 21

Words failed me.

Sir Tom smiled, his expression wry. "Apparently reality doesn't live up to fiction," he said.

"*You're* a Guardian?"

He nodded. "I was Chief Guardian for thirty-five years," he said, and wrinkled his nose as if he smelled something bad. "Now I'm the only one."

"The only one?" I sounded like an idiot, but I couldn't help it. All those nightmares, the stories, the legends—that was all this one old man?

Sir Tom shrugged apologetically. "The others are dead or witless, including poor soul-sick Jensen. I'd not call him a Guardian, not anymore. Would you?"

I made a helpless gesture.

"As for Angel, he never should have been a Guardian. Any military man can tell you that conflicts of interest are the deadliest sort of conflict. Angel pulled some strings and set the puppets dancing, moved some pieces on the chessboard, and claimed he was playing the game he was ordered to play, and not his own. But who's to say?" He shook his head sadly. "Not I."

I couldn't follow what he was saying about Angel; I was too busy thinking about what his revelation meant. The

Guardians were humans. Nothing more. And Sir Tom, old and cryptic and half insane, was more or less the only one. It was far from all I'd imagined, all I'd been told.

What did it mean for Meritt, for Farrell Dean, for the others in danger?

It meant the Watchers had no one to back them up, and that was good. We might be able to do something, might be able to fight back, save the city, if we had only the Watchers and wardens to face, and not some unknown power. But it also meant there was no one to come to our aid. The Watchers and wardens had guns, stunners, handcuffs, cameras, patrol cars, prison cells. We had nothing, and more than a hundred of us were about to be euthanized. What a stupid word. We were about to be killed, that's what was going to happen.

Could we come out here and survive on our own in the woods, by the sea? I didn't know. Winter was coming, and most of those about to be killed were weak already.

I thought of gentle Mariella, so very old. She wouldn't live long in a cold cave, and she couldn't hunt or fish. She needed a bed in a heated building, needed food prepared and set down in front of her. Could those of us who were stronger feed those who were not? And what food was there, besides fish? Could we catch enough fish to survive?

"You're shocked and disappointed," Sir Tom said. He didn't look hurt, just sympathetic. "Of course you are. Oz behind the curtain is always a disappointment, and I can't even claim to be a bad wizard, much less a good one. And I suppose you're asking yourself the question I've been asking myself all these years." He lowered his voice confidentially. "What do Guardians guard?"

"I thought you guarded the Watchers," I said tentatively. "They told us you did. That you enforced their rules, protected them."

"Ah. You thought we were glorified wardens, more or

less. An understandable mistake. But wrong." He waited, nodding encouragingly at me.

"Well ... if you don't guard the Watchers, then what do you guard?"

"Nothing."

I stared at him.

"We guard *nothing*," he repeated, giving me a knowing look. "Not since the watchmaker died. For he's long dead—or at least long gone—and all that remains are the watchers and the watched, and guardians guarding nothing but an abandoned clock ticking out its last few ticks."

Whatever that meant, it didn't sound good.

Before I could figure out how to phrase another question, Sir Tom's head jerked to one side. Then he cocked it, listening, squinting as if straining to hear.

"No," he said, and he wasn't looking at me. "It was not my idea, true. But I watched. I watched the ants behind the glass, and reported, and followed orders regarding their care and feeding. I let myself be made a demigod, and the gods I obeyed were graven idols."

His eyes went to me, and he lowered his voice and shielded his mouth with a fist, as if pretending to cough, clearly trying to keep me from hearing.

"And now, you see, she has come to me. The one to whom, above any other, I owe a debt. Gullible old fool that I am and was."

He shut his eyes as if he couldn't bear the sight of me. Then, keeping them shut, he lowered himself down onto the wet sand, slowly, carefully, and went completely silent. His knees were bent and his elbows rested on them. His hands were loosely clasped. He sat there for a long time without moving.

I couldn't stand it. I had so many questions, but I was terrified of setting him off again.

Eventually I edged closer. He didn't move, didn't look at me. "This watchmaker," I said. "Who was he? What did he want? Why did he send you out into the woods?"

Sir Tom's head jerked up and his eyes opened. He opened his mouth, too, and his lips moved, but no sounds came out.

Finally he flung out his arms. "The admiration of a grateful nation? Knowledge for its own sake?"

For some reason that sent him into another cackling fit. He clutched his stomach and laughed like a maniac.

Which he apparently was. I was out here in the middle of nowhere with a raving lunatic.

In fact—at this thought I backed away from him, but slowly, so he might not notice—what if he wasn't a Guardian at all? What if he was just another person driven mad by the Guardians, like poor Rosella?

That had to be the case. The Guardians weren't just ordinary people; they were legendary, mysterious, powerful. Sir Tom and Jensen must be outcasts from the city, crazy people who'd never made it back in, who had somehow survived out here among the wild animals and those half-human things.

And Angel? I didn't know what to make of him.

The old man had stopped cackling and was watching me. "This much is clear," he said, and I really, really hoped something clear was coming. "You asked about the Guardians. Does that mean we are what brought you out into the wilderland alone?"

Cautiously, I nodded.

"It must be bad," he said. "It must be very bad in the city, if you felt driven to come out here looking for the monsters."

I looked at him more closely. Quiet authority had returned to his voice. He actually sounded sane.

"It is bad," I said.

"Tell me."

A minute earlier I couldn't have imagined having a coherent conversation with the man. But what was I supposed to do? I had nowhere else to turn. And surely it wouldn't hurt to tell him, even if he wasn't a Guardian, even if he could do nothing to help us.

"We don't have enough food to make it through the winter," I began, edging a little closer to the fire, now nothing but glowing red embers. "So the Watchers are going to kill those of us who consume more than we produce. The sick, the underweight, the injured, —"

Suddenly embarrassed, I hesitated. He smiled a little grimly. "The old," he concluded. "Though the Watchers, presumably, are exempt."

He stayed calm, and though I'd much rather have been talking to someone a good bit more stable, it was a relief to tell anyone outside of Optica about the problems there, to describe the city meetings to someone who wasn't traumatized by them or endangered by them, to talk to someone I didn't have to comfort, who wouldn't try to bolster me with false reassurances.

Sir Tom nodded while I talked. He didn't seem surprised by anything I said—at least until I got to the part about Meritt spying on the Watchers.

"Young Meritt," he said softly.

"Do you know him?"

Sir Tom's gaze went distant. "Knowing another is more difficult than we like to believe," he said. "In the end we will know fully, even as we are fully known. But here, faces are veiled. Not entirely, of course. But some veils are thicker than others."

Of course he didn't know Meritt. Meritt would have told me if he'd met a lunatic who thought he was a Guardian.

"But that name I do know," Sir Tom said, his eyes focusing again. "Yes. I most certainly know the name. Young

Meritt has nerve, if he's willing to spy on the Watchers up close and personal."

"Yes. He's very brave."

"Some young men have more nerve than brains, and some have more brains than nerve."

"Meritt has plenty of both."

Sir Tom looked at me sharply. "So that's the way the wind blows," he said. "Well, well."

My face began to feel hot and I changed the subject. "Apparently the Watchers watch me in particular," I said.

"Naturally." To my surprise tears filled his eyes.

"Because of my hair—" I began, but he gave a short bark of incredulous laughter.

"Hair has nothing to do with it," he said. "What? Do you think they're beauticians?"

My face grew hotter still—but at least the old man wasn't crying any more.

He studied me with his brow knitted. "I'm too blunt," he said apologetically. "I had a way with the ladies once, but that was many years ago."

"It's okay," I said. "You can be blunt. I want to know the truth. If it's not because of my hair, what is it? Why do they watch me?"

"They watch you because they can," he said, and then he screwed his eyes shut. "I will go no further," he said, and he wasn't talking to me. "I will not. Going further means dashing hopes or raising hopes, and neither will I do."

"But—"

He opened his eyes. "Some doors, once opened, can never be shut. And some doors, once shut, can never be opened."

I couldn't believe it—he wouldn't tell me?

Maybe he wouldn't tell me anything because he didn't have anything to tell. He was like one of my old people spinning a yarn, except without the good grace to finish the story or even say it was all make-believe.

"I will do no more harm," he said. "I can live with no more. But I will tell you this: Red Girl wouldn't be in the fix she's in if it weren't for me. And I'd fix that fix if I could, but I can't, because not a soul alive can turn back the clock."

A deeper shadow passed over his face. "Break, break, break, on the cold gray stones, o sea. But the tender grace of a day that is dead will never come back to me."

More rhyming. Wonderful.

I had an idea. "Even if you can't turn back the clock, can you do something to help me now? In the present?"

He brightened. "Now that is an interesting thought," he said. "I've been pondering it since you showed up on my doorstep last night, like the ghost of Christmas Past draped in long red hair instead of chains. But it's been a long time since I've reconnoitered, a very long time indeed. Longer than you've been alive."

He was on the wrong track. I had been trying to think of a tactful way to get him to lead me to the real Guardians, but he sounded as if he intended to help me fight the Watchers himself.

He tilted his head, gazed at me. "Are the wardens well armed?"

"They all have stunners, and there are some real guns, but I don't know how many—I've only seen a few."

"Is anyone else armed?"

"Not that I know of."

"No one? Not even after all these years? That is a pity."

He bent and sketched a big circle in the sand.

"Does Red Girl know where the active cameras are?" he asked. "Not the secret ones, and not the blanks, but the ones the Watchers watch? Last I checked they were here."

Taking a stick, he drew a rough city map, and then

marked the active cameras. And he was right—he knew exactly which cameras were dummies, and which were active.

"Meritt has disabled a few of the active ones," I said, and pointed out which.

But my mind was on his earlier words. "The secret cameras?" I said. "What do you mean?"

He looked up at me.

"The ones in the wasteland," he said. "They're hidden, as are the ones in the Watcher compound. We didn't guard the Watchers, but naturally we had to watch them. And it was essential that we maintain the perimeter."

He was talking about the circles on Rafe's map, about the camera Meritt and I had found.

"What do you mean, the last time you checked?"

He wasn't particularly interested in answering—he was studying the map on the sand—but he replied, absently, "The stockade has a monitoring system. I disabled it long ago, when I finally realized what we'd done. Until then we saw whatever the Watchers saw, and more. The streets, the dormitories. Each cell in the prison. That lazy old warden sitting in the tower playing Solitaire. The wasteland, where people tried to hide from watching eyes."

There was no way he could know all that if he were making everything up.

"You really are a Guardian," I said. I couldn't quite believe it.

He glanced at me wryly as he got to his feet. The tactless morning sun caught every wrinkle in his creased face, sparkled in the stubby silver hair on his head, but though it made him look older it did not make him look weak.

Turning toward the water, he scanned the horizon. There was nothing out there—nothing but water, sky, the curve of the earth.

"Hubris, old man," he said, but his voice was calm. "Emancipating an entire city is not an easy thing for one old man and one young girl to do. Impossible, if the city does not want to be emancipated."

His head turned just slightly to the left. "And if it does?"

Now he turned slightly to the right. "Some ills are beyond your power to fix."

"But not all."

"Guilt impairs your clarity of thought."

"Restitution is a legitimate desire."

"Restitution, or restlessness? Old Ulysses heading out to sea one last time?"

"Better than to rust for want of use."

It really sounded as if he were talking to someone else, impossible as that was. Which was worse, I wondered—an old man who argued with himself, or an old man who talked to invisible beings?

Whichever he was doing, I knew which side of the argument I was on.

"Please help us," I said. "My friends are going to die."

For a long moment Sir Tom stood there with his back to me, facing the sea. Perhaps the argument continued in his head, but if so, he gave no sign of it. He simply stood there, perfectly still, gazing away from me, across the wide gray sea.

Finally he turned. "I am weary of watching," he said. "This will take time and consideration. We will not accomplish any large success today or tomorrow or tomorrow's morrow."

"But you'll help?"

His blue eyes were troubled. "I will try."

Chapter 22

We had almost reached the cave when Sir Tom fell. At first I thought he had stumbled, lost his balance; then I saw the red bloom of blood on his thigh and, an instant later, heard the shot.

Before I could react he had gotten to his feet and was shoving me across the shifting sand and into the cave, back against the wall in a shallow indentation. "Stay here," he said.

Though his leg was bleeding profusely he moved fast. He crossed the room and, from behind his pallet, brought out a small gun. Then he crossed the cave again and handed it to me.

"Shoot anyone who tries to come in," he said, showing me the trigger. "This isn't a bad wound, but I must stop the bleeding."

He went to the back of the cave, took down a clay pot, and opened it.

"Watch the door," he said sharply.

I tore my gaze away from him and fixed it on the cave opening. Beyond I saw wind-blown beach, waves, a trail of blood drops clumping in the sand, and nothing more. Shadows moved here and there, but I thought they were shadows of the trees behind us, above the great boulder.

Behind me I heard humming, snatches of song. Then

the old man began to mutter to himself. I hoped he wasn't drifting into one of his fits of confusion. I hoped he wasn't more badly wounded than he thought.

I was just considering risking a glance at him when I glimpsed movement out of the corner of my eye.

"Someone's out there," I said, and raised the gun.

For a long moment nothing happened. I felt my heart beating hard, heard the old man take a harsh breath behind me, saw the wind ripple the sand like waves.

Then a man strolled up to the cave opening, for all the world as if he were in the city visiting friends, and my heart leapt into my throat.

"Don't come any further," I said.

It was Angel. In broad daylight he was every bit as handsome as I'd thought, and I wondered later whether that was what kept me from shooting him. At least, if it had been Jensen, I'd probably have shot him on sight.

Behind me the old man barked out a command. "Hold your fire, Red Girl," he said.

"A bit late," Angel said, looking amused. "If she intended to shoot me, she'd have done it already." In the sun his eyes were a silvery grayish blue. His hair was wet, molded to his head, and his clothes were dripping, darkening the sand. He had stopped just outside the entrance, about ten feet away from me, and made no move to come closer. Now that he was near I saw that he was quite tall, six and a half feet or more, taller than anyone I'd ever known.

"He's unarmed," I said.

"He's more dangerous unarmed than your wardens are armed," Sir Tom said, moving up to stand beside me. He was holding a gun as well, a larger one than mine.

Angel inclined his head; I thought he was acknowledging the compliment, but he might have been greeting Sir Tom, now that he was in sight.

"So you swam from the cliff," Sir Tom said. "You're a better swimmer than you used to be."

One corner of Angel's mouth curved up. "And you're more careless than you used to be," he replied. "It won't be any fun to hunt you, Tommy, if you're as easy to track as this. You left a swath as big as a city road on your way here last night."

"Getting old, I reckon," Sir Tom said, without a hint of undertone, but my face flushed; I knew I must be the one to blame. "And anyway, I must not be as easy to track as all that, if you ended up having to swim for it. As a matter of curiosity, Angel, to what do we owe the honor of this visit?"

Angel spread his hands as if the answer were obvious. "I want the girl back," he said, and looked at me, his gaze lingering on my hair. Then his eyes met mine and the look in them made me take a step back.

"She's mine, Tommy," he said. "She was brought to me, bought by me, and she belongs to me."

I raised the gun again. Maybe I would shoot Angel after all.

The old man waved a hand at me without looking around. "Don't mind him," he said. "If wishes were horses, he'd have a cavalry. Now, Angel, where is Jensen? Up in the big spruce to the north?"

Angel shrugged. "Probably. If that was as close as he could get. He doesn't like your traps. He's seen what they can do."

"Lucky for me," the old man said, "And lucky we moved into his range before you were quite here. Three minutes, four. A thinner line than that lies between life and death. Now put your hands above your head and back up. Slowly."

Angel raised his hands and did as he was told. The old man followed him, but did not step out of the cave. At the entrance he called loudly, "Lieutenant Jensen!"

Distantly, a voice cried, "Sir!"

"Cease and desist. Await further orders."

"Yessir!"

Sir Tom nodded at Angel. "It's a hindrance to you, having a soldier who prefers another man's orders to your own."

There was no trace of a smile on Angel's face. "He'll obey me well enough when you're dead," he said.

"You'd best be sure of that," Sir Tom replied. "Jensen unleashed is not a pretty sight." He shifted and caught his breath, and I remembered his wounded leg.

Angel nodded toward it. "You'd be dead right now, if I wanted you dead. Many a time I've held your life in my hands."

"Back at you. Now, Angel, let me tell you exactly what is going to happen now. You are going to turn around and swim back the way you came. I will tell Jensen to wait for you at the stockade. If you do not arrive to meet him in one hour, he will initiate detonation."

Angel's face darkened. He lowered his hands, and the old man didn't complain. "That's the height of recklessness, even for you," he said. "Think of the people in the city."

"You think of them. It's in your hands to prevent it."

"It would kill Caliban."

"Collateral damage. You're intimately familiar with that term."

Angel looked directly at me. "You heard him," he said. "This man is dangerous, and he is not your friend. But he won't force you to stay with him if you wish to go." A flash of irony crossed his face. "He professes, at least, to be a proponent of free will."

Sir Tom shifted uneasily. Angel kept his eyes on me. "Will you come with me?" he said.

The glance that had unsettled me earlier was gone; his expression was calm and direct. Standing there near the half-crazy old man, Angel looked young, strong, sure, and above all, sane.

"Don't be afraid," he said. "Caliban was shooting at Tommy, not at you."

I wavered.

"I'm the one you came looking for," he said softly. "I'm the Guardian who can help you. That's why Caliban brought you to me. We'll go to the stockade, and you will be safe there. The stockade is a real building, not a cold damp cave. Once there we can discuss your situation and find a way to help your friends. That's what you want, isn't it? To save your friends from the Watchers."

I began to feel, strangely, as if I'd known this man a very long time. He seemed familiar and new, all at once.

"Come," he said, holding out his hand. "Come with me to the water."

The words came before I had decided what to say. "I can't swim," I whispered, and felt my face flush.

Angel smiled faintly and let his hand fall to his side.

"You don't have to swim. Tommy will let you walk away. Right, Tommy?"

Beside me the old man sighed. "If you want to go, I'll not stop you, Red Girl. Though I strongly advise against it."

"I'm sure the young woman duly notes your objection," Angel said gravely, still looking at me.

I didn't know what to do. He seemed competent and strong, and much more like I'd imagined the Guardians to be, albeit only human.

The old man, though—his ramblings frightened me sometimes, but he looked at me so fondly, as if he knew me and liked me. Not many people in my life looked at me like that.

"Are you ready?" Angel said.

Without really deciding, I shook my head. I only meant

I wasn't ready yet, that I needed another moment to think, but Angel took it differently.

"Then I'll come back for you soon. Be ready for me." Without another word he turned and strode away.

I didn't know whether to be disappointed or relieved.

Chapter 23

The old man stepped farther out of the shadows and turned toward the south.

"Jensen," he called. "Attention!"

Sir Tom gave his instructions and dismissed Jensen, then turned back toward me. He was limping, but only slightly, and a white bandage was wrapped around his left thigh, over his pants.

"The best laid plans of mice and men gang aft a'gley," he said. "And those were not the best laid plans. Then again, they were no doubt the best Angel could manage, given that Jensen is all he has. An unreliable weapon, at best."

"He obeys you," I said. "But he would have killed you."

The old man shrugged. "Not if I told him not to. Hence the distant tree, you see. Angel was trying to keep him out of my range of command."

He went into the cave and came back almost immediately with a pack on his back and a long gun slung across his shoulder. He reached down and picked up something from the ground—my damp clothes and black cap, folded in a tight bundle.

"Let's go," he said, tossing the bundle to me. "We must get you back to Optica before Angel returns."

I wasn't at all sure Optica was a better risk than Angel.

Sir Tom caught my expression and sighed. "He's pretty, Red Girl, but he's bad."

"What's so bad about him?"

Sir Tom looked reluctant, but he answered. "He toys with people, for one. He's lost his paradise and can't stand to think that anyone else might manage to find some scrap of happiness themselves, so he pulls off their wings and watches them writhe. Have you heard of Rosella?"

I nodded.

"That's why I want you out of the woods until I can give him something else to think about."

It took us about two hours to reach the city. We had seen no sign of anyone, not of Jensen or Angel or the wild men, only birds and rabbits and squirrels.

Near the edge of the western woods, almost in sight of the wasteland, Sir Tom eased himself down on a rock at the foot of a tree, his face drawn. The bandage on his leg was tinged pink with blood. He pulled a canteen of water out of his pack and offered it to me, then handed me a piece of venison jerky, which I devoured ravenously. A handful of dried fruit followed.

We had not talked at all during our journey, but it seemed he had been planning.

"Change back into your own clothes," he said. "Mine are better for the woods, but they'll draw attention in the city. At nightfall bring anyone you trust. Male or female, either one, but they must have strong nerves and be quick on their feet. Young Meritt worries me, but if he feels about you as you feel about him, I reckon we can make do. I'll meet you here. Wait for me if you arrive first."

I nodded.

"Don't expect miracles, Red Girl," he said. "This is a mighty endeavor, and a difficult one. We first must retake the stockade from Angel. That is what these friends of yours will help us do. Once we have weapons and supplies, and the shelter of the big stockade, we can consider how best to approach the city. Do we remove the endangered ones first? Or do we begin more ambitiously, overthrowing the Watchers and their wardens? And here's a question for you: How many in the city will stand with us? How can we separate the wheat from the chaff?"

I thought about that, but didn't have an answer.

"Lots of people are upset with the Watchers," I said. "If Rafe were alive, he'd know exactly who. And he could persuade them."

Suddenly I missed him so much it hurt. He had thought through all this, no doubt; he would know the answers to Sir Tom's questions; he was the one who should be leading us.

"Rafe is gone," Sir Tom said, but his tone was not ungentle.

I nodded, made myself think. "Meritt and Farrell Dean might know who would be on our side," I said. "If I can get to them. And I know one warden who might help us. They almost killed his son."

Sir Tom nodded.

Taking my clothes, I turned to go.

"Whoa, soldier. You haven't been dismissed," Sir Tom said, checking me with a hand on my arm. "Don't get caught," he said. "And Red Girl—"

He lifted my chin so that I looked him in the eye. His expression was severe. "Don't go into the prison," he said. "Do not, and I repeat, do not go after the other boy. You got lucky last night, but you won't get lucky again."

I tried to hold his gaze, but mine slid away.

"You have been missing all night and half the day," Sir Tom said. "You will have been reported. If you get caught now, Red Girl, they will kill you. No question about it."

He held my eyes until I nodded.

"I am not exaggerating," he said. "No one who has met the Guardians can be allowed to live. The Watchers can't let their bogeymen be exposed. So whatever you do, don't get caught."

Chapter 24

I didn't get caught. It was worse than that.

For hours I prowled around trying to spot someone I trusted. It proved difficult, finding the handful of people who fit the requirement—people I trusted, with strong nerves, who were quick on their feet—without being noticed by anyone else.

I had my black cap on and knew all the tricks to avoid the cameras or the eye of anyone in the watchtower surveying things from the windows. What I was afraid of was other people on the streets, not just the wardens, but the regular people. Sir Tom had said I'd have been reported; I wasn't sure what that meant, but it was possible that everyone had been told to keep an eye out for me, and I knew there were some people who would be all too happy to turn me in, and more who would be afraid not to.

Taking my cues from the old game with Petey and Judd, I did my best to blend in, to act normal, walking with purpose but without hurry along the streets. It was best, I decided, to walk behind a group of people—far enough back that they wouldn't particularly notice me, but not so far back that I stood out as a girl alone. I slipped in and out of doorways, marched purposefully around buildings, and several times hid my face by bending over as if searching for a splinter in my foot. The sky was a spiritless gray, and after a couple of hours I began to lose heart.

Twice I caught sight of girls from my dorm, but first it was weepy Lea—not exactly a person with strong nerves—and the second time it was Cynda, but she was with Wanda the Watcher Defender.

Once I saw Ezzie from a distance, but I didn't know him well enough to be certain we could trust him. And anyway he was driving the tractor to the big farm shed and there was no way for me to reach him, crossing the wide empty field, without drawing attention to myself.

All afternoon went like this. Though the sky was cloudy and I couldn't see the sun, I knew when it set because the gray became darker. Twilight lasted a long time, this time of year, but it would be dark soon enough, unless the clouds cleared. This wouldn't be a problem in the city with its blue electric lights, but I didn't like to think how the orchard and wilderland would feel in pitch blackness.

Finally, shortly before supper, when the streets would become too crowded to be safe, I turned a corner and spotted Cline scraping his boots outside the slaughterhouse.

I glanced around; he was alone.

Casually I walked up to him as if it were any other day, as if I were any other person, as if I had every right and reason to be there.

"Hey," I said, leaning against the building wall. Cline looked up at me, just for a heartbeat, then went back to scraping his boots.

"They've got Farrell Dean," he said.

"I know. He's pretty beat up, but he's alive. I went and saw him last night."

Cline shot me another look. His nose was back to normal size, but traces of his black eyes remained as yellow bruises against his pale freckled skin.

"Is that why we're supposed to turn you in if we see you?" he asked. "Because you sneaked into the prison?"

I shrugged. "I don't think so. It's probably because I went to the wilderland last night and met with the Chief Guardian. We have a plan. I need your help collecting a group to steal guns and then overthrow the Watchers and save the city."

Cline stood up straight, his face incredulous. I couldn't help but grin.

Cline's face went suddenly blank. "Warden behind you, heading north," he said. "Walk past me—act natural—and go into the slaughter yard."

I did as he said, moving as casually as I could. The yard smelled metallic but wasn't too gory. I picked my way around a few puddles and crept into the shadow of the back doorway to wait for Cline where I'd so often waited for Meritt.

A few minutes later he joined me. Cline was a big guy, stockier than most boys his age, strong from working cattle. His pale blond hair had been cut recently, and the top of his forehead looked white where it had been protected from the sun. I noted this while he stood studying me, no doubt weighing his dislike of me against the urgency of the situation.

"You're telling the truth?" he asked me finally. "This isn't a sick joke?"

I shook my head. "I wouldn't joke about this. And you know Farrell Dean has been up to something."

Cline nodded. "But how is this plan of yours going to get him out?"

That, I didn't know. "Every minute the Watchers are in charge, he's vulnerable," I said, feeling my way as I spoke. "But if we can take control away from the Watchers, we should be able to get him out."

Unless they had already killed him for refusing to speak,

I thought. Or unless the wardens killed their prisoners in the chaos when we tried to take the city, or he died of his injuries without any further assistance from his interrogators.

And unless the insurrection failed miserably and the whole of us got slaughtered. Standing by the slaughterhouse, the thought took on a visceral quality in my imagination that I could have done without.

Judging from Cline's face, similarly dark thoughts were running through his mind. But after only a moment's reflection, he nodded. "I'm in," he said.

That was the break I needed. Cline agreed to talk to some others in the cafeteria at suppertime—Ezzie would do it, he said, and Joe and Harding, and of course Meritt. All boys, Cline insisted, all almost nineteen. They'd be stronger and they'd be less likely to be frightened by the woods, or by Jensen.

"And guys won't be impressed by the glamour man," he noted, giving me a dirty look I thought was entirely unfair. Describing Angel merely as tall and fair-haired, without mentioning his beauty, would have been about as helpful as describing Ezzie as having dark hair without ever mentioning his dark brown skin.

"Angel might be okay," I said. "He might be on our side."

"Or he might not be," Cline retorted. "And the old guy's clearly the one in charge, if anyone is. We have to go with that. Stick with the plan, Red."

When everyone else left for the city meeting, Cline and the others would make their way out to the apple orchard. I would be waiting there, out of sight, to lead them to Sir Tom.

It was a good plan, but it didn't work.

I did my part, the easy part. In the dying light I went to the orchard to wait among the twisted trees. It seemed like forever, but it could only have been a couple of hours that I waited out there, pacing around, avoiding the bees that hovered around the fermenting windfall apples. For a little while I sat, listening to my stomach growl, trying not to think about how impossible our task seemed, but sitting somehow made waiting harder. Then I tried to find apples that weren't too far gone, but there was a reason the pickers had left these; most were worm-eaten and mealy, disintegrating into a slimy mass in my hands. I only managed to find a few edible bites.

A light rain began to fall and the bare-branched trees offered no real shelter. Fortunately it was one of those rains that was more a thick falling mist than real rainfall—we never got truly stormy weather until late November. So although I grew damp I wasn't wet through or particularly cold; it was the waiting that was bad, the long anxious time alone.

Finally, just before eight o'clock, Ezzie came running into the orchard, peering around in the gloom, trying to find me. As soon as I saw him I stepped out from behind the trees, smiling, so glad to see someone, to not be alone, but when I saw his face I knew something was terribly wrong.

He skidded to a stop on the wet grass. "Farrell Dean," he gasped out, panting hard. "Farrell Dean's in the circle."

The ground swayed beneath me, righted itself. Without a word I began to run, and Ezzie ran with me. This couldn't be happening. Farrell Dean was the steady one, the reliable one. I couldn't imagine the world without him.

We ran back through the orchards in the heavy mist that suddenly made me feel like I was drowning. When we'd skirted the beehives and reached the lit city streets we slowed to a brisk walk, trying not to attract attention.

Why was Farrell Dean in the circle? Had he confessed? Had they beaten him again, gotten something out of him, or had all the damage been done before I'd seen him last night?

Meritt had said Farrell Dean could be broken, made to tell everything, but I didn't believe it. He was loyal, Farrell Dean. He had integrity; perhaps only I knew how much.

The streets were almost empty now, the electric blue lights reflecting off damp bare pavement. Everyone was at the city meeting. Around us the mist drifted in heavy waves, muting sound, making strange halos of the streetlights.

We slunk around the watchtower near the base, in the deep shadows. I scanned the crowd frantically.

"Where's Meritt?" I said. Meritt would know what to do, would have an idea. I had none, had no idea what to do, how to save anyone from that horrible circle.

Ezzie shook his head, didn't answer. His eyes were fixed on the center of the circle, on Farrell Dean, Judd, and two other boys who stood in the glare of the watchtower spotlight. They weren't bound, and the wardens watching them were not standing particularly close. Ever since the snipers had been instituted, the wardens stayed back as much as possible.

The boys stood facing one middle-aged woman. The cook, I thought. My brain seemed to be moving in fits and starts, unreliably, because I remembered the Watchers' discussion of this city meeting before I realized exactly who the woman was.

It was Cook Alice. She still looked calm enough, but even in the washed-out electric lights I could see spots of color high on her cheekbones, and her chest rose and fell quickly with her shallow breaths. I wanted to help her, but I was helpless, I was hidden in the dark, and my head was throbbing.

I had to stay calm, had to get a grip on myself. I was watching Cook Alice's chest rise and fall, rise and fall, and I was breathing with her, faster and faster, in danger of hyperventilating. Now that would be real useful, I told myself viciously. Faint, call attention to yourself, get everyone shot.

Forcing myself to breathe more slowly, I tried to make sense of the scene—was it better for Farrell Dean that there were others in the circle as well? Did that give him more of a chance?

I hated myself for the thought, for wanting someone else to die instead of him. And instead of Cook Alice. And instead of Judd. This was twice in the circle for Judd—how could that be? How unfair—how monumentally unfair—to put him there twice.

Like last time, Judd looked furious. Farrell Dean didn't look angry. He looked pale and self-contained, as if he might be having to concentrate very hard to stand up straight. He was still in pain from the flogging, of course. Had he had any food or rest? I willed him to look my way, half believing that even in pitch blackness Farrell Dean could find me, but his eyes stayed fixed on the ground a few yards in front of him.

The other two boys, a little older than Judd but still a good bit younger than me, shifted uneasily from foot to foot, casting sideways glances at each other, at the crowd, and my heart swelled with worry for them, too.

The loudspeakers crackled to life. "Family of Optica," said the hated Voice. "There are cancers among you."

What were we going to do? I searched the rows of people, spotting friends here and there, but no one was moving to stop this horror—all the faces looked stunned, all eyes were fixed on the spot-lit scene, strangely softened and unearthly in the misty drifting rain.

The Voice boomed out, "Stealing food for favorites, betraying the Family of Optica." In the circle, Cook Alice shook her head firmly.

Where was Meritt, Cline, anyone who could help—but how could anyone help? It would be just like Rafe all over again.

A warden stepped forward and, bizarrely, handed Cook Alice a gun.

"We know which boy you have fed," the Voice said.

"And you know, Cook Alice. But the rest of the family does not know. You have five seconds to consider. Then you will walk up to the guilty boy, put the gun against his head, and pull the trigger. You have one bullet. If you do not shoot him—if you choose instead to shoot yourself or someone else—all four boys will die, and so will you."

Suddenly I saw it. It was there in the straight line of the nose, the steady eyes, in the constant understated kindness to me. Cook Alice was Farrell Dean's mother.

Her hands were shaking. The mist swirled around her like a living thing. She held the gun in front of her, pointed down at the ground, and it wobbled in her grasp. Her face, always so cheerful and calm, was agonized.

I couldn't just stand there and watch this.

Ignoring Ezzie's protest, I started around the curve of the tower base, toward the circle, toward Farrell Dean. I would die, I knew I would die, but at least my death would be a protest—

Someone grabbed my arm, hard, and spun me around, knocking my shoulder roughly against the prison wall so that pain ran through me like an electric shock. It was Cline. His expression was grim and freckles stood out sharply against the unnatural pallor of his face. He started to say something but the Voice drowned out his words.

"And now the countdown will begin," it said.

Cline bent and pressed his mouth against my ear. "Meritt's going to create a diversion," he said. "Get to Farrell Dean, get him away. He won't want to go but he might do it for you."

His mother. He wouldn't want to leave his mother.

The Voice was counting. Five. Four.

"I'll get her," Cline said. "Tell him that. Tell him I'll get Alice."

Three. Two. As the Voice said one, the lights went out.

We sprang into action. I rushed straight to Farrell Dean, thankful I'd been focused on him, could find him even in the dark. As I reached him I felt Ezzie and Cline shove past, sensed them begin to struggle—with wardens, with the other victims, I didn't know. All around us people were shoving, yelling. A woman screamed.

"This way," I said to Farrell Dean, pressing my mouth to his ear to be heard over the uproar, pulling at him frantically. My eyes were adjusting to the darkness but that meant other people's eyes were adjusting as well, meant wardens, the snipers, might begin firing at any second. But Farrell Dean was immovable as stone, too heavy for me to budge.

"They'll kill her!" he said, pulling roughly away from my grasp. Over his shoulder the mass of bodies separated briefly, shifted.

"Cline has her," I said. "Let's go."

Farrell Dean looked at me once, intently, and then it was as if he suddenly saw me and knew me. "I promise," I said. "Cline has her. He'll take care of her." And then Farrell Dean was helping me fight our way through the panicked crowd.

Miraculously we made it out of the chaos and past the watchtower, into the silent streets. Even the electric blue lights were out, and it was very dark. Behind us the uproar continued unabated.

Cautiously we made it past the cafeteria, past the girls' dormitories, running blind in the darkness, moving as swiftly as we dared, holding to each other's sleeves, hands, stumbling now and then but never falling. I was glad I knew the streets so well, glad I had explored them with Meritt so many nights.

We had made it to the edge of the meadow where the beehives stood when behind us the blue streetlights flickered, came on. I risked a backwards glance; the watchtower spotlight was back as well, stretching its white probing finger north, sweeping counterclockwise, towards us.

"Hurry," I said, pulling at Farrell Dean's sleeve, but there was nowhere to hide. In a heartbeat the spotlight was washing us in its relentless white light, illuminating every inch of the meadow, every hive, every stone. I hoped no one was watching—surely their attention would be on the circle, on the chaos there.

As the light passed on, leaving the darkness blacker than before, Farrell Dean staggered. I caught his arm to keep him from falling, and as he regained his balance I felt him take a deep wincing breath.

"It's not much further," I said. "We just have to make it to the woods."

The heavy clouds parted, showing bright stars, and in their light he turned a startled face toward me.

"It's okay," I said. "I've been there, I've met someone— the head Guardian—and he's going to help us."

Farrell Dean shut his eyes briefly. When he opened them he looked at me, not like Cline had done, as if I might be crazy or lying, but as if I'd said something perfectly sensible.

"Let's go," he said.

Chapter 25

We had to go more slowly through the meadow, avoiding the hives, feeling for each step in the darkness that felt darker every time the stars shone and then vanished again.

Farrell Dean was breathing shallowly, cautiously, as if every inhalation hurt. I could only guess at the extent of his injuries. Broken ribs? Weakness from loss of blood? I couldn't imagine what it must have taken for him to move as fast as he had through the city streets.

What would I do if he fell? He must outweigh me by sixty or seventy pounds. I wasn't strong enough to carry him, probably couldn't even get him back on his feet if he went down.

I found myself talking in my mind to the First Star—yes, I know, stars are burning balls of gas. But I talked to the First Star anyway, telling it I knew it was back there somewhere behind the clouds, and begging it to keep Farrell Dean going, to keep him on his feet until we reached safety.

In the orchard the trees were twisted shadows, hardly visible through the darkness and shroud of mist. Even the spotlight couldn't reach cleanly through their tangled forms. Eventually the waning moon would show, unless the clouds covered it, and walking would be easier, but we'd also be more exposed. By then, I hoped, we'd be safely with Sir Tom.

When we neared the gap in the wall I stopped. "We'll wait for the others here," I said, not wanting to leave the camouflaging shadows of the apples trees. If Sir Tom wasn't out there yet, I didn't want to cross the wasteland vulnerable and exposed and with an injured man to protect.

"Try to rest," I said, and Farrell Dean carefully lowered himself to the ground and sat, unsupported, because his back couldn't bear leaning against a tree. I wanted to ask him about what had happened to him in the prison—I wanted to know how many times they'd lashed him, and whether his wounds had been treated in any way, and what they'd asked him, but all of that would only make him focus on the pain.

"How long have you known about Alice?" I said instead.

Beside me, in the darkness, Farrell Dean shifted.

"A long time," he said. "She told me as soon as I was old enough to keep a secret."

"Cline knew, too." It came out sounding petulant, which surprised me, but come to think of it, I was a little peeved. Apparently lots of people had been keeping secrets from me.

"He figured it out," Farrell Dean said.

A muffled noise made us both go very still.

"That must be the others," I whispered. Surely it was, but it wouldn't do to get careless now.

Farrell Dean began, slowly and painfully, to get to his feet. I put a hand on his arm. "Stay here," I whispered. "I'll go check it out."

After a heartbeat he made a resigned gesture.

"I'll be careful," I said, before he could tell me to, and I began picking my way through the twisted trees toward the sound, but veering to the left of it, flanking it.

As I drew closer and slowed to a walk I could tell that someone was moving through the orchard—more than one someone.

I crept closer, until I saw movement among the shadowy trunks of the apple trees. Whoever it was came carefully, trying to be quiet, but the darkness and the trees made it hard. As they drew nearer I heard a murmur—a female voice.

Only when they were almost to me did I see that their clothes were gray, not the black of wardens. Then, finally, I recognized them. It was Joe and Harding—the ones Cline had chosen—and with them, Shawna and Liza.

Trying not to startle them, I called out softly.

Shawna and Liza hurried to me, exclaiming quietly, asking questions; Joe and Harding hung back. A look passed between them that I couldn't read, but guessed it had to do with the presence of the girls.

Sure enough, Joe—dark haired and slight, not tall, but known for being tough and quick with his fists—tilted his head apologetically.

"Followed us," he said shortly. "Our fault."

Harding nodded grimly. He was a big sandy-haired guy—not as big as Cline, but in that range, and strong. "We started to send them back," he said. "But then we figured, the city's gotten as bad as the woods these days." He glanced at Shawna, who smiled sheepishly at me, and suddenly I understood.

Liza shook her frizzy hair out of her face and spoke, her voice, as ever, practical and brisk. "You need us. You know you do," she said. "And, listen. We'd best not hang around here. It's pretty chaotic back there but someone still could have seen us go."

And so I led them to where Farrell Dean waited. When we reached him Harding and Joe huddled in close, muttering under their breath, and he nodded and replied equally quietly. Shawna and Liza stayed with me.

I glanced at Shawna out of the corner of my eye; I'd been so busy being glad she was keeping my secret that it hadn't even occurred to me to wonder whether she had a secret of her own. Had she slipped out at night, after I did? Was she that sly? The thought made me nervous for a moment, but then I decided that in this situation, slyness was all for the best. More power to her.

Something about the way Liza held herself told me she and Joe were not a couple; she was self-contained, somehow, while Shawna kept glancing Harding's way. And when Joe left Farrell Dean and came over to me, she didn't seem gravitationally drawn to him, the way I knew I was with Meritt.

"Where's this friendly Guardian?" Joe asked.

I nodded toward the woods.

"Does he have a place, a house or something? Someplace safe? Because Farrell Dean's in no fit state to go much further."

I'd been trying not to think about that. The place I knew about—the cave by the sea—was a long way away. I didn't think Farrell Dean could make it that far. But maybe Sir Tom had someplace else, someplace closer.

Before I could explain all this to Joe, we heard a shout—not close, but closer than anyone should have been. Joe and Harding glanced at each other.

"You girls stay here," Harding said, and they were off.

Liza rolled her eyes. "Oh, please!" she said. "We'd be quieter than they are."

Another yell split the silence, and though I couldn't make out the words I knew the voice. Without a word or a thought I started running, ignoring the questions Liza flung after me.

How many times had I crossed this orchard today? The trees still did not seem familiar; they reached out of the mist and grabbed at my hair with small branches, their shadows mingling with solid trunks until I couldn't tell which was which. I kept dodging what I thought was a trunk, only to discover I was dodging a shadow and running into a trunk. It felt as if it took forever to reach the voices. They were at the edge of the orchard, almost to the city proper.

Harding and Joe had stayed back, ten or twelve yards away from them, hiding in the shadows and the trees; I stopped there too, trying to make sense of the scene. There was so little light, so many twisted shadowy forms between us and them.

First I saw a light-haired boy whose back was to me; it had to be Judd, whose shout I'd heard.

He was facing off with someone—an adult—someone wearing black, and whose bald head gleamed in the darkness. Warden Karl?

Warden Karl—if it was indeed he—was talking in a low voice, a voice meant to be soothing. His hands were up soothingly as well, showing that he held nothing. Then everything happened very quickly.

The warden moved, lurched sideways, and at the same moment Judd raised his arm.

"Judd has a gun," Harding said, and I leapt forward, shouting.

"No!" I cried. "He's your father!"

A gunshot drowned my words and the warden fell—surely not Karl, surely not—didn't Judd know? Everyone talked about it, when we played our guessing games. Surely Judd knew.

Sick at heart I kept moving, hurrying to Judd, who now was running forward, away from me, straight to the fallen warden.

The warden wasn't dead. He was getting to his feet and turning, looking behind him on the ground, where another body lay. He bent over the body for a moment, and then stood upright.

"That's torn it," he said to Judd, putting his arm around

the boy's shoulders and glancing at me over the boy's head. He didn't seem surprised that I was there.

"Is he dead?" Judd's voice was too high.

"Yes," Warden Karl said. "He's dead."

"He was going to shoot me," Judd said. He was shaking. "He raised his gun and he shoved you out of his way and I had to, he was going to—"

Warden Karl was shushing him. "You did fine," he said. "You did great. But now we'll have to hide you somehow."

I could tell from his face that he couldn't think how to do that. Wardens who weren't in the breeding program didn't have houses of their own; they lived in the barracks together.

"He wasn't the only one who saw you take that gun from Alice," Warden Karl said to his son. "There were at least three more who went other directions, trying to cut you off. You gave them quite a run—I was proud of you, boy—but now that we've stopped they'll find us soon enough. We need to get moving again."

He was talking to Judd but his mind was elsewhere, searching for a way to save his son.

Judd was crying now, tears running down his cheeks. "I killed him," he said. "I just wanted him to go away, but he wouldn't. He wouldn't leave."

Warden Karl nodded, his face grim. I looked toward the form lying awkwardly on the ground, but couldn't tell who it was. The scarred warden's face came into my mind, the one who had threatened me. Was it him?

"And I used up the only bullet," Judd said plaintively.

"What were you planning to do with it?" Warden Karl asked.

Judd looked at me, and then down at the gun in his hands. "I was going to give it to Red," he said. "I thought she could use a gun."

Warden Karl nodded again. "Because she's in trouble.

Because she's your friend. She's always been your friend, hasn't she? Since she was back at school with you. She helped you with your sums."

Judd nodded and they both gazed fixedly at me. I knew Warden Karl was trying to distract Judd, and I tried wildly to think of something helpful to say, but I couldn't think—ridiculously, I felt paralyzed with embarrassment. Here we were, on this horrible city meeting night, with a dead man lying on the ground a few feet away—a man that Judd, a twelve-year-old boy, had killed—and Judd and his father were standing there silently, staring at me.

The back of my neck prickled. Somewhere out in the darkness Harding and Joe were staring at me, too.

Then Judd broke the silence. "At the city meeting you went to Farrell Dean," he said, and before his eyes dropped I saw a flash of something.

"He was hurt," I whispered.

Judd nodded. "I know," he said, but his eyes were still lowered. "He needed help and I didn't, and so you helped him—and I saw the gun, and I took it away from the cook, and I wanted to help you so I followed the way you'd gone."

"You did great, Judd," I said, drawing closer.

"I followed, only they were following me, so I had to weave around to lose them, and I wasn't sure exactly where you'd gone and then they were too close . . ."

Behind me Joe stepped into the meadow, out of the shelter of the trees, and cleared his throat. "Best be off," he said to me. "It's not safe here."

Warden Karl eyed him sharply, then turned to me. "You've got someplace to go?"

I nodded. "Outside the city." I didn't know what else to say, how much to trust him. And even if I did trust him, as Meritt had said, even the best man could be broken.

Warden Karl seemed to be thinking the same thing,

because he flung up his hand. "I don't need to hear any more," he said.

Beside me Judd sniffed, then faked a cough, trying to hide that he was crying, now that Joe was there.

I came to a decision. "Judd should come with us."

Joe glanced over sharply.

"It's not like it's safer for him in the city," I said.

Warden Karl's face was inscrutable. He stood looking at me, running his hand absently along the top of his stunner. Then he gave one decisive nod. "Off with you, Judd," he said, putting a hand on his son's shoulder. "Take care."

Judd hesitated, looking up at Warden Karl. Joe reached out and took the boy by the elbow. "Let's go," he said, and with one last glance at his father Judd melted into the darkness.

I couldn't see Harding but I was sure he was still there, waiting for me in the trees. I couldn't tell whether Warden Karl knew he was there or not. He stared at the darkness where Judd had vanished, then sighed and looked at me. "If you protect him half as well as you protect Meritt, he'll be okay," he said.

I kept my face a careful blank. "I'll take good care of him," I said.

The warden smiled approvingly at my evasiveness, and then his face hardened. "Promise me," he said, and he looked like wardens usually looked, focused and dangerous. But I wasn't afraid of him. We were on the same side.

"Yes," I said, looking him straight in the eye. "I'll take care of Judd. I promise."

Chapter 26

The moon wasn't up, but by now the clouds had begun to clear so that the stars overhead provided a little steady light.

When Harding and I got back to our little group, we found it had grown in our absence. Meritt wasn't there yet, but Ezzie was lying sprawled on the ground near Liza and Shawna, panting hard as if he'd been running for a long time. Cline was standing in front of Farrell Dean but with his back to him, guarding him, and Cook Alice was kneeling on the ground beside her son, talking quietly.

As I watched, Alice reached out and began unbuttoning Farrell Dean's shirt. When she pulled it open, he winced but shifted so she could ease it off his back. His injuries were bound to be ugly, but encouraged by her calm, pleasant expression, I drew near. When I went to kneel beside her, however, I noticed the tears on her cheek and caught the murmur of private conversation between mother and son.

Feeling awkward, I muttered something—as if I had recalled a pressing matter—and backed away, an all too familiar pain shooting through me.

Judd and his father, Farrell Dean and his mother. People were drawn to their own flesh and blood. They sought it, looked for it in the shape of a jaw, in mannerisms, in the sound of a voice. They wanted connections, physical connections, the magical echoes of themselves in other bodies, other lives. I wanted it. But my parents, if they were living, had never sought me out, and I'd certainly never seen anyone who looked like me. It wasn't just the hair, as Wanda was so fond of pointing out. Someone in my genetic background must have been small, too, unless I really was a mutant freak.

Ashamed of my envy and loneliness in this moment of shared danger, afraid Farrell Dean would glance up and read it in my eyes—and I didn't begrudge him his mother, I didn't, I only wanted my mother too, whoever she was—I turned away.

A few minutes later Cline came to where I was sitting alone beneath an apple tree.

"What are we waiting for?" he said, stopping just a bit too far away, as if I might be contagious.

He knew exactly what we were waiting for, but because he disliked me, he wanted to make me say it. Fine.

"We're waiting for Meritt," I said brusquely.

To my surprise Cline looked uncomfortable. He shifted on his feet, glanced over his shoulder as if wishing for help. Then, reluctantly, he looked at me. "He isn't coming, Red."

"What? Why not?" Surely Meritt knew that going to the Guardians—the Guardian—was our only hope. He'd heard the Watchers talking, same as I had. Why wouldn't he come?

The look in Cline's eyes was suspiciously like pity. "He was up in the tower," he said. "You know that. That's the only way he could have cut the lights like he did."

In the Opticon, at the top of the watchtower, above the prison. With only one way out.

"There's no way he could have escaped," Cline went on, and I wanted to cover my ears. "They've got him."

I felt my jaw set stubbornly. "Do you know that for a fact? Did you see them catch him?"

Cline didn't answer that question.

"If you want to wait here until the Watchers find you, then wait," he said. "But don't take the rest of us down with you. Tell me where to find that Guardian. Give me a message so he'll know we're from you. Or don't. But the rest of us are going."

He meant it.

And he was right. We had to go, and Meritt wasn't coming. He'd been trapped. Would they kill him? Of course they would. And why would they wait? He could be dead already. Meritt might be dead.

Hundreds, thousands of images of him filled my mind. Meritt bent over my school desk, helping me with work; Meritt laughing, grinning his crooked grin; Meritt in the darkness, in the sunlight, in the wasteland, under the electric blue lights, shoving his dark hair out of his face, his gray eyes alight, distant, focused, teasing. Meritt leaning toward me, kissing me so quickly I didn't feel it until he was gone.

Hot tears filled my eyes, ran down my cheeks.

"Hey," Cline said, gruffly but not unkindly. "Save it for later."

But I couldn't do this without Meritt. I wasn't brave enough, old enough, wise enough. I needed Meritt. I needed Rafe. We all needed Rafe, but he was dead too.

"Listen," Cline said. "I don't know what they'll do to Meritt, or when. But we aren't any use to him dead. Help me get the others someplace safe, and then maybe we can figure out a way to help Meritt."

Unexpectedly, he stepped forward and held out his hand. I reached up and took it, and he pulled me to my feet. Instantly he released me—he might get cooties—and stepped back.

"Good," he said. "Now all you have to do is get us to the Guardian."

Chapter 27

In the distance an owl hooted. An image of the wild men rose in my mind, and I pushed it away. An image of Meritt falling, shot and bleeding, took its place. I pushed that away, too.

Cline was gathering everyone together. He would take the rear, he had said, to help stragglers and to watch for trouble, and I was to lead the way. I watched Farrell Dean as he got to his feet, his mother helping him, and then slowly—having put it off as long as I could—I went to join the group.

"This way," I said, and pointed, and we headed for the gap in the wall.

At the gap I went through and had begun to cross the wasteland when I realized I was alone. Turning, I saw that the rest of the group had paused at the gap.

I'd forgotten. Most of them had never been outside the wall.

As I watched, Joe and Harding came forward. Those two had cut trees in the eastern woods, the safer woods.

Then Farrell Dean, whispering some word of encouragement to his mother, led her out; he'd probably been outside of the walls with Meritt or Rafe. Slowly, hesitantly, the rest followed.

Silently they joined me. The wasteland glowed pale and

cold in the starlight, eerie, but not as eerie as the shadowy trees with mist twining around them like ghosts.

Once we were deep in those dark trees I had to stop again to get my bearings. Exactly where had I left Sir Tom? We'd parted in the daylight, and the woods looked different at night. I took a few steps forward; the whole group moved with me, right on my heels.

"Stay here just a minute," I whispered, and walked a few yards. Yes. This was the way—just over there was the rock where Sir Tom had sat down, and I'd changed clothes behind that smaller tree.

I gestured. The others joined me and we quickly covered the short distance to the meeting place. There was no sign of Sir Tom, though on the large rock a streak of dark blood told me this was indeed the right place.

"He's not here yet," I said, stating the obvious. "But he'll come." I hoped.

The others shifted uneasily, looking around, gazing up at the tall trees, the patch of sky. No one wanted to sit, to rest. Shawna, Liza, and Alice stood close together beside Sir Tom's rock. The guys paced back and forth in a sort of ragged patrol of the area. They looked twitchy, like cats waiting to pounce on something. Even Farrell Dean, clearly in pain, was managing to focus on the shadows and the trees.

At least Judd wasn't thinking about the dead warden anymore; like the other guys he was pacing, staring into the darkness.

When a twig snapped nearby, Cline and Harding moved before I could even see what had made the noise. They charged into the underbrush, Ezzie, Joe, and Judd right behind them. Alice grabbed Farrell Dean and stopped him from following; Shawna and Liza huddled closer together.

We heard struggling, grunts, the thud of a fist on flesh, an infuriated scream. I was edging toward the sounds when

Ezzie reappeared, followed immediately by the rest of them. They were dragging something that was digging his fingers into the ground, trying to claw himself back into the shadows, now and then letting out a tangled, angry stream of nonsense.

Jensen.

"He bit me," Cline said angrily, stepping on the small of Jensen's back and pinning him flat to the ground, though still he thrashed and struggled—uselessly, because the others were now pinning him down as well, kneeling on each of his arms and legs.

"Don't hurt him!" I said.

"Red redder reddest!" the man cried, hearing my voice, straining to turn his head toward me. "Red redder reddest!"

"What is this?" Cline asked. "One of the wild men? How does he know your name?"

"No, this is Jensen."

"The wild men are worse than *this*?" Cline lost his balance and Jensen screamed.

"Stop!" I said. "Don't hurt him. Help him up."

"No way!"

"Yes—" How to explain while Jensen was listening? I didn't even know how much Jensen understood. "He gets a little confused sometimes, but he's loyal to Sir Tom."

"Sir!" roared Jensen, struggling harder. "Sir!"

Cline looked unconvinced.

"Sir Tom won't like it if we hurt him," I said.

Cline considered this, glancing around at the other boys. They shrugged. "He doesn't have a weapon," Ezzie said.

Cline snorted.

From behind me Farrell Dean spoke. "We've got him outnumbered."

"Jensen," I said, drawing as close as I dared. I made my voice as crisp as I could. "Lieutenant Jensen! Hold still!"

He stopped struggling. Cline threw an incredulous glance in my direction.

"Jensen, we're going to release you. Stand to attention!"

After a moment's hesitation, the boys stepped off Jensen's body. Cline reached down and hauled him to his feet.

"Attention!" I said again, firmly, and—to my amazement—Jensen put his feet together, straightened his back as much as he was able, and saluted. "Red redder reddest!" he said.

Judd smothered a laugh.

"Jensen!" I said crisply, glaring at Judd. "Have you seen Sir?"

Beneath his shaggy, filthy beard, Jensen's lips moved. No words came out.

"He's crazy," Cline said softly.

"Sir," Jensen said uncertainly, slumping. "Sir?"

"Sir will be here shortly, Jensen," I said. Very shortly, I hoped—and what was I going to do with Jensen in the meantime?

Inspiration struck. "Jensen!" I said. He stood straighter again. "Your orders are to find Sir Tom!"

Jensen saluted but didn't otherwise move.

"Find Sir!" I said again. "Bring Sir here!"

Again Jensen saluted.

Farrell Dean spoke quietly in my ear. "I think he's waiting for you to dismiss him," he said.

"Jensen! Dismissed!"

Jensen spun and took off at a trot through the woods. Within seconds he was out of sight.

The others stared after him, then turned and stared at me.

"Pretty impressive, Red," Ezzie said, grinning. "Too bad you couldn't get the field workers to obey like that."

"Maybe if I'd pinned them to the ground first," I said

dismissively, though in truth I was pleased with myself. I'd kept Jensen from getting hurt, and maybe regained a few points with Cline—he'd never like me, but I wanted him to at least respect me, not think I was just a silly weepy girl.

"Now what?" said Cline, rubbing one hand with the other.

"Now we wait," I said.

Alice spoke up. "How bad is the bite?"

Cline turned his hand over, studying it in the moonlight. "I don't think he broke the skin," he said. "He startled me, that's all. He fights like a girl."

Liza heaved a pointed sigh. "He fights like an *animal*," she said.

We gathered near Sir Tom's rock, with our youngest and our injured in the center and the rest of us circled around them, facing out, keeping watch.

What if Sir Tom's leg had gotten worse? What if he couldn't walk, couldn't come meet us? What if he'd sent Jensen with a message, and we'd terrified the poor creature into forgetting his mission? Or what if Sir Tom had died? After all, he was wounded.

And then there were the wild men—how many of them, I didn't know. But I was pretty sure they'd try to kill us if they found us. The guys had managed to pin Jensen, but they might not be as successful with those wolf-like creatures.

Beside me Joe cleared his throat and I jumped. "Ahead and to the right," he said softly.

A low fern was swaying gently, though there was no wind.

"What was it? Did you see?" I spoke as softly as he.

"No."

I was in clear view; if it had been Sir Tom, he'd have seen me and shown himself. Or if it had been Meritt, if he'd gotten free and come looking for us—

My heart leapt, but reality rushed in fast and hard, and I had to blink back tears.

On the other side of our little circle Farrell Dean's mother called out, "Who's there?"

I turned to look but Joe grabbed my arm. Where the fern had moved there now stood a tall and imposing figure, hair shining in the moonlight. Angel.

And who was behind us? Who had Alice seen?

"Good evening," Angel said. I felt movement behind me, people turning toward his voice, and I hoped someone had the sense to keep watching the other direction.

"I see you found me. And you brought friends. That's very good." His voice was gentle, civilized, and just like that, with those few words, I felt again the strong sense of familiarity, of—strangely—safety. Wouldn't it be okay to go with Angel? He had never tried to hurt me. And I only had Sir Tom's word for it that Angel was responsible for Rosella's madness.

Then Angel stepped forward, further out of the undergrowth, and I saw that he held a long gun in both hands, nose pointed at the ground midway between us.

"Keep him talking, Red," a voice said, so softly I could barely hear it. It was Cline, from the other side of the circle.

My mind promptly went blank. I was supposed to make small talk with Angel?

"*Talk*," Cline hissed.

I said the first thing that came to mind. "One of my friends is injured," I said.

"I have medical supplies." Angel said gestured toward the north. "Come this way."

"No," said Farrell Dean. "We're not going anywhere."

Angel raised his eyebrows.

"Let me be blunt," he said. "If you don't come with me, you won't last the night. There are things in these woods that would make your blood freeze."

I felt the group behind me move closer together.

"I'm supposed to meet Sir Tom," I said.

Angel nodded. "You're worried that going with me will hurt Tommy's feelings. I respect that. Perhaps we should pretend that I captured you."

He must have seen something in my expression, for his own grew softer. "He's told you stories about me," he said. "Lies. The truth is, many of your people have come to me willingly. They left your city and sought me out, and I helped them as best as I could."

I'd never heard anything about that. Some stories said that not everyone tried to escape from the Guardians once they'd been caught by them. But seeking them out? As far as I knew, I was the first to willingly come to the Guardians. I didn't know whether Angel was telling the truth or lying.

Angel was still talking. "Tommy tells only what is useful to him," he said. "He leaves out details of his own sins and regrets, and exaggerates mine. I will not hurt you. If I wanted to hurt you, I'd have done so long ago."

"Long ago? What do you mean?"

He didn't take his gaze from mine. "You must be very hungry, to be reduced to eating wormy apples while waiting for your friends."

"You were watching me?"

"No. I was watching over you."

I took a step out of the circle, toward him, but at the same instant he jerked around and pointed the gun at someone behind him.

"Split up!" Cline shouted, and everyone began to move, plunging wildly in various directions. I didn't move—I didn't know what was behind Angel, or whether to run away from him or to him.

"Stay close," Sir Tom called. "Split up but stay close."

He stepped out from behind a tree, his leg bandaged, his

long bulky gun aimed at Angel's head. "So, Angel" he said. "Are you ready to surrender?"

Angel laughed. "There's a fine line between optimism and insanity," he said, and then he turned and vanished into the dark woods.

Sir Tom shrugged. "Come back, all you people," he said. "Red Girl, tell them I'm safe."

"He's safe," I said, and if I sounded a bit unenthusiastic, Sir Tom didn't comment. I went to meet him and slowly, more cautiously, the rest of our group came as well.

Sir Tom nodded encouragingly at them. "Don't you worry about Angel," he said. "I've set Jensen to following him. He'll let us know if he heads back this direction."

Then he turned to me. "If we may postpone introductions, Red Girl, we'd best be on our way." He looked at Farrell Dean. "Can you walk?"

"Yes," Farrell Dean said. His face was frighteningly white.

"Good man," said Sir Tom. Shifting his gun to his other hand, he dug in a pocket and pulled out a small silvery package, which he tossed to Farrell Dean. "Unwrap that and get yourself around it," he said. "It'll give you a little energy."

Farrell Dean pulled off the silver to reveal a dark square. "What is it?" he asked.

Sir Tom gave a bark of laughter. "Chocolate. A great delicacy of which you hitherto have been deprived. Food of the gods, young man. Giver of instant energy. It won't heal wounds or mask pain, but it will get you through the next little while."

He glanced in my direction. "The next little while could be a bit tricky," he said. "Everyone stay close."

Chapter 28

We didn't go in the direction I expected, north toward the sea cave. Instead we headed further south, into denser woods.

It wasn't easy going. My feet were tough from being barefoot for so long, but there were many rocks and sharp branches. Fortunately Judd and I were the only ones without boots, and I actually didn't mind the pain. Now and then it made me think about something other than Meritt.

I was frightened for him, but when I thought about it, I couldn't believe he was dead. Though I felt panicked at the thought of leaving him further and further behind, I didn't feel a permanent absence. Then again, I also didn't feel as if Rafe were permanently absent, and he was most certainly dead and gone.

A pinecone cut into my heel and I stumbled. Just ahead of me Farrell Dean soldiered on silently, his mother and Cline never far from him. His shirt was tied around his waist, and in the mottled and shifting light of the rising moon I could see thick welts and gashes on his back. Some looked scabbed over, but some oozed fresh dark blood.

We reached a wide rocky section. I tried to pick my way carefully, but there seemed no good place to set my foot, and the rocks were small and sharp. After wincing through two or three steps, I paused, trying to think of a solution. I wished I had something to tie around my feet, but all I had were the clothes on my back.

Ezzie tapped my shoulder and then squatted down in front of me. After a moment's hesitation I climbed on and put my arms around his neck, careful not to strangle him, and he hooked his arms behind my knees.

Up ahead Sir Tom was saying something to Alice. She nodded and turned to Farrell Dean.

"This part is a bit challenging," Sir Tom told the rest of us. "But we're almost there."

He pointed to a steep upward slope on our right. "I have a cabin at the top," he said. "It's easy to defend because it's hard to get to."

That was an understatement. The slope was loose dirt and pine needles—no rocks, no handholds. It looked impossible to climb.

Sir Tom walked a few steps to a large tree and slapped its trunk. "I will bring up the rear," he said. He gestured toward Joe. "You look like a climber. Am I right?"

Joe nodded.

"This young man will go first," Sir Tom said. "Follow him up the tree. Climb as he does. After a bit you'll see a rocky ledge on the right. You'll have to stretch a bit, but once you get to the ledge, you'll be able to climb the slope to the top."

As Joe started up the tree, Sir Tom lined up the rest of us according to some plan in his head: first Alice, then Farrell Dean, Cline, Liza, Harding, Shawna, and Judd.

"You're my lookout," he said to Ezzie, and turned to me. "And you stay right with me. Angel is altogether too interested in you for my peace of mind. Even these two lovely young women did not distract him, and they're rather more his usual taste." He meant that Liza and Shawna were tall and more grown-up looking. At his words they looked uneasily at each other and moved a little closer to the boys.

"Have no fear," he said as he cupped hands and gave Joe a boost onto the first branch. "I will not surrender any of you to Angel."

They didn't look particularly reassured.

Sir Tom sent us up at regular intervals. One by one my friends grasped the lowest branch of the tree and vanished into the darkness above. I could hear occasional murmurs— Joe warning about a tricky patch, Alice urging caution, a sudden thud and scramble as someone leapt from the tree to the rocky ledge.

Finally Sir Tom pointed at me. "You next," he said, and then turned toward where Ezzie had been keeping watch. Something in the old man's face made me follow his gaze. Ezzie was gesturing silently at three forms—four—crouching on a large boulder just visible through the trees. From here they were merely shadows, dark forms silhouetted against the pale rock behind them. As we watched, one of the crouching figures stood.

"Up," Sir Tom said shortly, but before I could move someone spoke from the branches above.

"I can't!" The voice was high with anxiety, and it took me a second to realize it was Shawna.

Harding said something in response, but she cut him off. "No, I can't! It's too far."

"Brace yourself against the trunk," Harding said, his voice louder. I shot a glance toward the wild men; sure enough, they had turned toward us, were sniffing the air.

"Get good and steady, and then jump. I'm right here. I'll catch you."

"I'll fall!"

The wild men were sliding down from the boulder.

"Get going," Sir Tom said. I reached for the lowest

branch and he boosted me unceremoniously up, the rough bark scraping my arms. The branches felt sturdier than I'd expected, but all the same I was careful to stay close to the trunk as I began to climb, hurrying to get out of the way so Ezzie and Sir Tom could get up too. I glanced back to see if they were coming.

Below me Ezzie was reaching for the lowest limb. Sir Tom was behind him, standing on the ground, facing away from the tree.

There was a flash of movement, and then he was slamming the butt of his gun against a human face—ugly, vicious, with strangely long and pointed teeth, but human. The wild man covered his face with his hands, blood pouring from between his fingers, and howled in rage or pain; above us Shawna shrieked as if in answer.

Sir Tom turned away and swung at another creature. Why didn't he shoot? He had a gun.

Ezzie was in the tree now but he wasn't climbing. He was crawling out on a lower limb, toward Sir Tom. As Sir Tom knocked the second creature to the ground, a third came out of nowhere and lunged at Sir Tom's back, and Ezzie locked his arms around the branch and swung down, kicking the wild thing, knocking it off its feet. Before Ezzie could pull himself back up the first wild thing lowered its bloody hands from its face and leapt for Ezzie's dangling legs. I screamed a warning and Ezzie jerked away, almost falling, kicking at the crazed thing scrabbling and snarling at him.

A cracking sound split the air—not a gunshot, because Sir Tom was grabbing a limb, pulling himself up into the tree fairly far from the trunk, his gun slung over his shoulder. Ezzie gave one last violent shove and the wild man fell away.

"Climb!" Sir Tom said, and I looked up and caught a glimpse of Judd, quite high now, moving fast. I followed him as quickly as I could, glancing down only to make sure it was

Ezzie breathing hard behind me, not a wild man. Sir Tom, I could see, was right behind him.

A flurry of anxious voices came from above. Judd said something I couldn't catch. Shawna was crying and talking at the same time. Harding yelled a warning. Then the tree seemed to shudder. A large limb crashed down, breaking smaller limbs as it fell, catching against another branch just below the place where I stood clinging to the trunk.

"I'm thinking we've about had enough drama," Ezzie said dryly.

But our trouble wasn't over. There was Judd, standing safely on the rocky ledge; and there was the white exposed wood where the limb to the ledge had broken off. Now it was just a stubby projection, a foot or two long, reaching nowhere near close enough to the ledge.

I stared at Judd across the gap, and he stared back at me round-eyed, his blond hair standing on end. I could hear the others scrambling up the slope above him.

"What happened?" I said.

"Harding came back to help Shawna. Both of them on the limb—and he's so big . . ."

"You went across it after it cracked?" He could have been killed.

"That finished it off. I'm sorry, Red. I thought it would hold."

"Is anyone injured?" Sir Tom called from below.

"No, Sir," Judd said. "At least, not bad. Shawna twisted her ankle or something. They're getting her up the slope."

I looked down at Sir Tom, waiting for direction. The rocky ledge was about fifty feet above the ground. Now, with the limb gone, it was impossibly far away from the tree.

"Go on up to the next branch, Red Girl," the old man said.

Clinging to the trunk I climbed to the next good branch

on that side of the tree, several fee higher but not nearly long enough for my taste.

"Ease on out," Sir Tom said. "Young man, clear the way." Judd disappeared from view. Cautiously I crawled out, above the broken branch, my palms slick with nervous sweat. Now I could see the ledge again; I was more or less above it, but it was a long way down.

"Go as far on the branch as you can, Red Girl," said the old man from beneath me. "Get a good grip, ease off the branch, and then drop."

I did not like this, not at all.

"You can do it, Red," Ezzie said, his voice sounding oddly strained.

What choice did I have? I took a deep breath and lowered my legs off the branch, balancing on my stomach. Cautiously, I shifted my weight and let more of me slide off, the bark of the limb pulling up my shirt and scraping at my skin, until I was dangling in thin air, held up only by that slender limb.

I was afraid to let go. What if I hit the ledge and rolled off? The ground below was a long way down, and if the fall didn't kill me, the crazy things who'd attacked Tom and Ezzie probably would make me wish it had.

"Go!" Sir Tom ordered.

I let go. There was a split second of falling when I thought I had missed the ledge, but then I landed hard and fell to my hands and knees. I didn't roll off the ledge, and as best I could tell, nothing was twisted or broken. Hurriedly, my heart pounding, I scrambled away from the edge and up the slope, and immediately Ezzie dropped from the high limb to the ledge behind me. He landed on his feet, staggered, and fell against the slope of the hill.

Sir Tom was right behind him, landing smoothly in a crouch just a couple of feet from Ezzie. He grabbed Ezzie under the arms and pulled him to his feet, then hurried us up the slope before I'd had time to catch my breath.

"Go, go, go," he said, urging me forward. He still hadn't let go of Ezzie.

The slope was doable but still not easy. Though rocks and thick roots were plentiful, the soil was loose and every handhold had to be checked. More than once a handful of dirt broke free and sprayed down into my eyes. Half-blind and coughing from the dust, I had to focus completely on putting one hand in front of the other, on not making a mistake that would send me sliding back down.

At least it would be hard for the wild things, too, I hoped. How well could they climb? And why was Sir Tom rushing us now—were they chasing us?

That thought gave me enough energy to claw myself up the rest of the steep slope, finally pulling myself over the edge, where I collapsed onto my back, panting, my eyes watering and stinging with dust.

When my heart stopped pounding in my ears, I sat up. Nearby the others were moving around, talking in low, worried voices. Shawna said something about blood—her voice was thick with tears, but she sounded like she was giving orders.

"Use this," Sir Tom said.

Ezzie was lying on his back, his arms flung wide, his fingers twitching. Harding was bent over him, ripping his pants leg open.

Shawna took a small jar from Sir Tom and brushed Harding aside. She touched Ezzie's leg and he cried out. Harding braced Ezzie's arms to hold him still, and Cline and Joe stepped forward and held his feet. They were pinning him to the ground, just like they'd pinned Jensen.

I got up and went to get a better look. Ezzie's left leg had four long red angry cuts, running from just above his knee almost to his ankle. Shawna was sprinkling the gashes with yellowish powder from Sir Tom's jar. A burnt smell reached me; Ezzie cried out again; beside me Liza turned her face away.

Then Sir Tom's voice rang out.

"Carry him inside," he said, and I raised my head and finally noticed my surroundings. Sir Tom was standing at the door of a tightly built cabin made of whole logs. It stood in a narrow, rocky clearing, from which the land dropped sharply away on all sides. Below us on three sides were trees.

On the fourth—with the moonlight shining on it—was the sea.

Chapter 29

"We scare because we care," Ezzie said. "Unless the berries are ripe." He muttered something else, turned on his pallet, and grew quiet.

I looked at Sir Tom.

"We treated his wounds immediately," he said. "This will soon pass."

The scratches from the wild man's claws oozed a foul-smelling pus that Shawna kept drawing out and wiping away with a cloth soaked in warm water and some sort of reddish orange cleanser. The bucket sat beside the fire, on the stone hearth, staying warm.

Shawna's ankle was swollen, but she didn't seem to notice. She kept talking soothingly to Ezzie as she tended his wounds, wiping away pus, rinsing the cloth in the bucket, wiping away more pus. She was wearing long green surgeon's gloves from Sir Tom's medical supplies, and disgusting though Ezzie's injuries were, she'd stayed perfectly calm the whole time, even when Ezzie had screamed wildly and accused her of being a secret warden. Seeing her now, I couldn't believe she had panicked in the tree.

"Do not *ever* touch the wall," Ezzie said. "It will eat your fingernails."

"He's completely off his head," I whispered to Sir Tom.

AMANDA WITT

Sir Tom shrugged. "Delirium isn't dangerous," he said. "As long as he doesn't do himself any harm, and we won't let him do that."

The others—warm, fed, doctored, and wrapped in Sir Tom's blankets—all seemed to be asleep despite Ezzie's ravings. All save Cline, who was taking the first guard shift. He sat just outside the threshold alone, facing the slope, a gun in his hands.

Though the cabin was too small for this many people, it really was a remarkable thing for one man to have built alone. Or maybe this had been built long ago, before all the other Guardians had fallen asleep or become less than human.

The cabin had two small windows covered at the moment with waxed cloth. It contained a table and chairs, and plenty of supplies stacked along the walls—metal cans that, I now knew, held food, boxes of medicines and ammunition, and folded piles of blankets and clothes.

There was even plenty of water. Sir Tom had rain barrels, but he'd also rigged a bucket on a pulley system to catch the fresh water from a spring he'd discovered trickling out of the cliff below.

Most importantly, situated as it was, no one could get to the cabin easily, and certainly not without making noise when leaping onto that rocky ledge. That was the only possible way up, and a pile of large rocks at the top of the slope showed how Sir Tom intended to deal with trespassers.

It was perfect. It was the refuge we needed. I should have been thrilled.

Actually, I should have been asleep, like the others. But I was too worried.

"Ten little Indians," Sir Tom said now, taking another puff on his pipe. His chin was speckled with gray stubble, just like his head, and his eyes had a faraway look. He and I were

264

sitting at the table, sleeping bodies lining the wooden floor between us and the fire. Judd was lying right at my feet.

"Red Chief has brought me ten little Indians to fight Custer," Sir Tom said, "and we can hope she shall never need ransoming."

I shut my eyes. I was so tired. If my mind would stop spinning, I was sure I could fall asleep sitting bolt upright, even with Sir Tom talking to himself and dropping unsettling little remarks into the conversation every little bit.

"But among all the little Indians, I have none named Meritt."

My eyes flew open.

Sir Tom was looking at me intently, puffing away at his pipe. The smoke curling blue around his face, the smell of tobacco, recalled to my mind the scarred warden smoking in the prison house the night Meritt ran down the electric blue streets, that night when we last were as we had always been.

"Red Girl is worried about him," the old man said.

I nodded, blinking hard to keep the tears from forming in my eyes.

The old man studied me, his face inscrutable in the firelight. After a long moment of silence he tapped his pipe on the hearth and shook his head.

"There are more things in heaven and earth than you have dreamt of in your philosophies," he said.

Impatiently I lifted my hands. "What does that mean?"

He grinned, showing his gapped teeth. "It means you never know, Red Girl. Young Meritt could be alive, or he could be sleeping. It is not up to us. It may not even be up to the ones who think they hold his life in their hands, though there we run into deep water—destiny, freedom, fallen man and fallen angels, sleeping and waking, the quick and the dead and the quickening dead . . ."

I stared at him blankly, and he laughed.

Judd threw out an arm and cried out in his sleep. I leaned over, pulled the blanket more snugly around him, and kept my hand on his chest until he sank into calmer sleep. When I sat back up in my chair the old man spoke as if there had been no interruption.

"Until we know for certain what has happened, it's best to think and act as if young Meritt is living still."

I had just begun to feel a little heartened by that comment when he added, "Otherwise you may grieve when there's no time for grieving."

"He is still alive," I said flatly.

When he saw my expression he smiled again, this time a bit wryly. "That's the spirit," he said. "There will always be time to grieve later on."

This was very frustrating. I wanted to argue that he wasn't making sense, that I couldn't act as if Meritt was fine unless I really believed he was fine. But Sir Tom was still rambling on.

"By grieving too soon when there is no need," he said, "you may create the need to grieve later. Self-fulfilling prophecies have a way of fulfilling themselves."

While I tried to untangle that, wondering whether he was very wise or very crazy, he got to his feet and handed me a blanket. "Try to sleep," he said. "Tomorrow is a busy day."

Judd spoke in my ear. "You must choose," he said.
Farrell Dean spoke the same words. "You must choose."
Then Meritt. "You must choose."
Then Angel. "You must choose."
And Rafe shook his head. "There is no map," he said. "You've lost my map."

Someone stroked my hair away from my forehead and

the sea came in, the tide rising, the tide falling, and I sank into its waves and drifted away.

It was black, black as the darkest night I'd ever seen. Then a thin slice of pale light split the darkness. A form went out; another came in, felt cautiously around, lay down. The changing of the guard.

Warden Karl shook his head. "Promises are promises," he said.

"They're too young to remember, these children."

I lay still, trying to orient myself, sorting out dream from reality.

Sir Tom laughed softly. "*They're* too young? You're only a youngster yourself, Alice, and a most lovely one at that."

This must be reality. I'd never have dreamed the head Guardian *flirting* with Farrell Dean's mother. He must be forty years older than she was, at the very least. I opened my eyes just a slit and peered up at the table where they sat.

Alice smiled gently at Sir Tom's comment, but didn't otherwise acknowledge it. "Those were terrible times," she said. "The ash was so thick, some days, we could barely breathe. And dirty! Everything was filthy all the time. We gave up trying to wash sheets; wetting them down just made matters worse, made mud. The crops hardly grew—our stores dwindled away to nothing—and so many fell ill. Some who lived still aren't the same; you can hear them rattle when they breathe. Pregnant women miscarried. I lost my second baby then, and never conceived after. That was a terrible, terrible time."

Sir Tom nodded.

"What was it like out here in the wilderland?" Alice asked, and I looked at her more sharply. Her expression was just as always, serene and matter-of-fact. She sounded like she was chatting with an old friend, not with a Guardian, that creature of legend and mystery.

"Oh, it was bad for us, too," Sir Tom said. His voice was level but his eyes seemed to be looking far away. "And because I couldn't leave it alone, because I couldn't stand not knowing what had happened, I made matters worse. Curiosity didn't kill the old cat, just his men. Or worse."

Alice said nothing, just sat there patiently with her hands in her lap, and eventually Sir Tom went on.

"I sent troops to reconnoiter," he said. "Should have known better, but didn't. Didn't know what it was, the black cloud, the dust. And the ones I sent, the ones who went to explore, they came back sick. Sicker by far than those of us who stayed."

Alice murmured sympathetically. "Sick in their lungs?" she asked.

"In their minds," Sir Tom said. "Heart and spirit." He began to fidget, tapping his fingers on the table, on his knees, and I hoped Alice's questions wouldn't provoke him into one of his fits of insanity—or into playacting insanity. I was beginning to suspect that sometimes he exaggerated his confusion.

"It doesn't sound like the same thing that affected us in the city," Alice said thoughtfully. "The ashes and dust affected us physically, but not in any other way. Did your men tell you what they'd seen? What they'd found?"

He shrugged. "Devastation. Death. Not that they explored exhaustively. They felt themselves sickening, and they came back."

"So they picked up some sort of illness, in the place the ash came from."

"An illness, a contamination, something," Sir Tom said. "But something not that simple, either. I've come to think of it like this: You know when you're sick with something minor, a cold or a little virus, and the muscle you sprained weeks before begins to ache again?"

Alice nodded.

"The virus didn't cause your muscle sprain," Sir Tom said. "But when the virus came, it sought out weaknesses in your body. That's what I speculate happened. Whatever it was, this contamination, it found their weaknesses. It nurtured seeds that had been planted long before."

"Seeds of wildness? Of violence?"

Sir Tom would say no more. "I can only speculate," he said. "It's not for me to judge. All I know is, my lieutenant was the best of my men. Even with the illness, he still is. He's confused, but he's never taken to preying on people, like the others who got sick did. Some bit of him remembers that he's human even now."

He looked back up at Alice.

"That was when the Watchers sealed the wall," he said. "Just in the one place, right behind their compound. They laid traps for my poor men, too, though they never caught a one of us. Bureaucrats versus trained soldiers? They were always more likely to blow themselves up than to do us any harm."

"The place the ashes came from," Alice said. "Where was that?"

He looked at her uneasily, jiggling one foot up and down. "The mainland," he said. "A big place. Could be someone still there, somewhere, though I doubt it. Since the time of the ashes we've never heard a single word. It's just been my men and me, going here and there in our little worlds, listening to the clock tick slower and slower each day."

The main land? I mouthed the strange phrase. What was it to be a main land? As opposed to what? A minor land?

I wanted Alice to ask about the mainland—who else and

what else was out there?—but instead she changed the subject.

"This afternoon—is there no other way?" she said.

Sir Tom sat silent for a moment. "You don't like it," he said. "I don't like it myself, but I do believe it is the best way to ensure her safety. Perhaps the only way. And the time of year is right—gentle winds, no sudden storms."

Beside me on the floor Farrell Dean muttered something, and I shut my eyes and made my breathing steady and deep, lest his mother look at him and see I was awake.

"Still, it's very dangerous," Alice said.

"But she is very brave. And she's in danger regardless. She's what he wants, Alice my dear. What he thinks he deserves, what he thinks he requires. And that is not an envious position to be in. Do you remember Rosella?"

My heart began to pound. Why did he always have to bring up Rosella?

"Oh, yes. Of course I remember her." Alice's voice was sad. "She had the most beautiful long dark curling hair. And she was a sweet woman. Sweet, and a bit fey somehow."

"As if she knew she'd never make old bones?"

"That's exactly it. She told me once that she didn't expect to grow old."

"People who feel that way can be a little headstrong."

"I suppose they think that if their time is short . . . yes, Rosella could be a little reckless. Obviously. She went to the wilderland, after all."

"With that in his background—you see my point, I'm sure. I'd like to give him the benefit of the doubt, but the stakes are terribly high. We need to get the girl away."

"My son will want to go with her." Alice's voice was steady, but I heard the competing undercurrents. Pride. Worry. Relief.

"If he could climb that tree last night, he can do it. He

can row. And if I had my druthers, he's the one I'd choose to go with her, because I can count on him to protect her."

Row? It was too much. I sat up and opened my eyes. They both were watching me, and Sir Tom was smiling.

"Even with his injuries, the two of them can row around to the other side of the island," he said, still speaking to Alice as if I couldn't hear. "It won't be easy, but I'll medicate him first, and they're both young and strong. And there's no other boat, so there will be no pursuit. You can see, dear woman, that ultimately they'll be safer."

"You can't be sure of that," Alice said.

Sir Tom shrugged in acquiescence.

I got up and went to the table. "What's the plan? Where are we going?"

Sir Tom reached out and took my hand. "Come away, oh human child, to the waters and the wild."

A chill went down my spine and I pulled my hand away. Those were Louie's words, but different. Fairy child, Louie always said.

Sir Tom nodded at me. "You've heard it before, have you? 'With a fairy, hand-in-hand, from a world more full of weeping than you can understand.'"

His eyes fill with tears. Then he laughed, too loudly, and around the room people began to stir.

Chapter 30

"Hunting, they called it," Sir Tom said, rubbing a hand meditatively across his grizzled chin. "When they could still talk. They made no distinction between animals and humans."

He was briefing us, telling us where the stockade was located, telling us about the Guardians who had gone rogue after the time of the ashes and begun mauling and killing at random. I still didn't know whether one of them was the chicken vandal, or whether that was Jensen.

"Main thing is, you want to avoid them," Sir Tom said, as if any of us needed that particular warning. "It isn't all that hard to do. They aren't really dogs, even if they try to run around like them. They only have a human sense of smell and hearing."

As for the stockade, Sir Tom had not seen inside of it since he'd lost control of it six years earlier.

"I came down with a bad bout of flu," he said. "Angel couldn't take me down, but a little bitty bug could and did, and Angel seized the moment."

Based on its earlier state, though, Sir Tom thought the stockade should still be well stocked with everything we would need—weapons, medicines, food.

"It was intended to support thirty-plus Guardians for

five years at a time," Sir Tom said. "Not that we ever had to go that long between supply drops. And Angel and I both live off the land as much as we can, so the canned goods and MREs should be largely intact."

"Exactly who dropped the supplies?" Farrell Dean asked. "And why? And from what?"

"That's a fascinating tale for another day," Sir Tom said, frowning. "Today we focus on our plan. That's rule number one: Focus on what is at hand. Distracted leads directly to dead."

He was going to teach us to shoot. Then we would retake the stockade. Once we had the stockade, we'd have a fortress from which to launch our attacks, and a refuge for the old and the weak if we needed to bring them out of the city before emancipating it. We would have a nearby place from which to send out spies to locate and persuade sympathizers in the city, perhaps even among the wardens. We might even have functioning communication devices and monitoring capabilities, if Sir Tom could fix what he'd undone, or if Farrell Dean could bring something he'd learned from Meritt to bear on the problem.

The only barrier was Angel.

I cleared my throat. "Do you think we could negotiate with him? Maybe he'd join forces with us." I looked at Sir Tom, trying not to see the bandage on his leg. "I know you don't get along with him, but—maybe he's lonely, out here with no one to talk to. And what if he ever got sick, like you got sick, or injured? He could die out here, with no one to help him. Maybe we could persuade him that he'd be better off in the long term, if he'd agree to work with us now. And it would definitely better for us if he were on our side."

Cline snorted. "Red's always had a weakness for a pretty face," he began.

Farrell Dean shook his head, and Cline subsided.

"It's a legitimate question," Farrell Dean said. "We can use all the help we can get. Sir Tom, what do you think? Red can be pretty persuasive."

A look passed between Liza and Shawna that I couldn't read, but which nevertheless made a flush crawl up my neck.

Sir Tom seemed uncomfortable; he looked everywhere but at me. Obviously he didn't like my suggestion, but surely it was a reasonable one. Angel very well might help us. We hadn't exactly had a chance to establish what he was like, what his intentions toward us were—Sir Tom kept sweeping in, talking about Rosella, preventing me from even having a full conversation with the man.

Sir Tom looked helplessly at Alice, and she stood up.

"Red," she said, coming over to where I sat, kneeling on the ground in front of me. "I heard him last night. He sounds sincere. But you don't really know him."

"You don't know him either."

"That's true. But I do know of him. And what I know is not good. He has done things in the past that are simply un-speakable."

What else had Sir Tom told her about Angel, I wondered. And then I was back to the question of how could we be certain Sir Tom was reliable.

"Couldn't I at least try to talk to him?" I said. "I don't think Angel would hurt me."

I didn't know how to convey the odd feeling of familiarity that he gave me, and I didn't want to try to explain it, given the scorn on Cline's face. If I gave him any excuse, he'd make me sound completely superficial and unreliable.

Alice searched my face. "Angel might not hurt you," she said. "But what about everyone else? If he did agree to work with us, you'd be trusting him with their lives." And she gestured at the rest of the room, at my friends who sat staring uncomfortably at us.

"What do you think?" I asked them. "Does Angel scare you?"

For a long moment no one spoke. Then Ezzie shifted, cleared his throat. He was alert and in his right mind this morning, and the cuts on his leg had stopped oozing and begun to scab over. But something about him worried me. He was a little too bright-eyed, a little too antsy. It wasn't natural, not after the harrowing day he'd had, the injury, the restless night. The rest of us were dragging. Why wasn't he? Maybe he still had a little fever.

"Angel scares me like a cobra," he said. Everyone else nodded agreement with him.

Only Shawna, among the lot of them, even looked ambivalent. She lowered her eyes and put one hand on Ezzie's calf, feeling, I supposed, for heat or swelling. Her eyes were puffy from lack of sleep. She had sat up all night with Ezzie.

"Cobra's a perfect analogy," Liza said, nodding approvingly at Ezzie. "Hypnotic and deadly."

Again, the others nodded—all but Farrell Dean, who stared straight ahead. Taking no sides.

For a long moment I waited, but no one said anything else. "All right," I said finally. "I'm outnumbered. We won't try to negotiate with him. But I don't want you to kill him either."

Sir Tom threw up his hands. "I don't want to kill him either, Red Girl. Never have. Else I could have done it many a time, these long years past."

So it was settled.

With a bit of muttering from Cline we worked out a plan to distract Angel, to draw him away from the stockade so we could snatch it up while his back was turned.

I would be the bait.

Chapter 31

"I don't like this," Farrell Dean said, looking down at the empty beach. He must have been talking to Cline, because he sure wasn't talking to me.

It was early afternoon, and he hadn't spoken directly to me all day long, had avoided looking at me or even being in my vicinity. I might have been invisible, except then he'd at least have bumped into me a time or two by accident. He was only with me now because Sir Tom's plan demanded that we wait together in the woods at the edge of the beach. Some thanks for saving his life at the city circle, I thought irritably. What on earth was wrong with him?

"I don't like Red doing this alone," Farrell Dean said.

"She won't be alone," Cline said. "I'll be watching, and Sir Tom and Ezzie are watching. If there's trouble, we'll step in right away."

Farrell Dean looked over his shoulder at the dense woods, where filtered sunlight made uneasy, shifting shadows. "I hope the others don't run into Jensen or the wild men," he said. The others were stationed near the stockade, ready to occupy it while Angel was gone. "And I hope Alice is okay."

Honestly, I had never in my life seen Farrell Dean worried, and now he didn't seem able to stop.

"Alice is fine," Cline said. "And it's time. You'd better go."

Farrell Dean nodded and turned to me, looking directly into my eyes for the first time all day. He still didn't speak to me, but he looked so tense that my indignation evaporated. Maybe his peculiar behavior had nothing to do with me.

After all, he'd been through a lot, and his back was probably hurting. And he had, as his mother had predicted, insisted on being the one to wait for me in Sir Tom's hidden boat.

The plan was this: After I distracted Angel awhile, I'd climb down the cliff to the hidden boat below—"escape down the cliff," was how Sir Tom put it, making it sound as if Angel would try to grab me and tie me up, which I thought was unlikely. Then Farrell Dean and I would row up the coast, land, and rejoin the others at the newly retaken stockade.

I smiled at Farrell Dean, trying to look reassuring. His expression didn't ease, so I reached out and laid my hand against his cheek. It felt rough, sandpapery under my fingers, because of course he hadn't been able to shave, not for several days.

For a second or two he didn't move. Then he reached up and covered my hand with his.

Cline cleared his throat impatiently and Farrell Dean released me and stepped back. Cline stuck out his hand and Farrell Dean started to shake it, but then they pulled each other into a brief embrace. What was that about? They weren't acting like themselves. I wasn't afraid of Angel, but they were scaring me.

"See you at the boat," Farrell Dean said to me. Then he turned and walked into the woods.

We watched him go, the woods dappling the light that fell on him, glinting in his hair. He moved a little stiffly because of his injuries, glancing warily around him as he went, and my heart seemed to clench up. Something was going to go wrong. I could feel it. We had a good plan—I knew we did—but everything suddenly felt out of joint. The day felt false like the sunlight was false, unexpected and unreliable this time of year.

Farrell Dean vanished from sight into the shadows, and the instant he did, Cline rounded on me. "Can't you let him alone?"

"What are you talking about?" I said.

Cline smirked, batted his eyes, and reached out and touched my cheek, as I'd touched Farrell Dean's.

I jerked away from his hand, and Cline dropped back into his normal cynical expression. "You should keep your hands off of him," he said. "It isn't right."

"Isn't *right*?" I said incredulously. "He's my friend. You just hugged him, and I didn't even do that."

"Come on, you know what I mean," Cline said. "You lead him on." His voice was low but it cut like glass. "You've always led him on. You make him think he has a chance, but he doesn't, not with Meritt around. Meritt, his friend. Couldn't you even pick on two guys who weren't buddies?"

"This isn't the right time for this," I began, but Cline spoke over me.

"I know exactly how you play him. Everybody knows. You encourage him just enough to keep him at your beck and call. Poor sucker probably thinks he stands a chance now that we're out of Optica and Meritt's dead—and Meritt probably is dead, regardless of what you want to think—regardless of what any of us want to think, because he was our friend too, not just yours. And how do you suppose Farrell Dean feels about that, being half glad that Meritt died? And died saving Farrell Dean's life?"

My face felt hot and I was beginning to tremble. I'd known Cline disliked me, but this—he downright hated me. He thought I was a terrible person.

"And if Meritt's dead and Farrell Dean ever does have a chance with you, you'll make him pay. You'll punish him for not being Meritt. You'll make him wish he'd died instead, which is exactly what would have happened if the Watchers had had their way. He'd be dead—he was the one, you know? The actual guilty party."

Tears welled in my eyes and began streaming down my cheeks, and still Cline went on.

"So maybe you're thinking it's his fault that Meritt's dead, but it isn't. If anything it's yours. Farrell Dean was always worrying about you going hungry, afraid you'd get sick, afraid you were malnourished. The food he took, he took for you. So if you want to blame someone for Meritt's death, blame yourself. Don't blame Farrell Dean."

"Leave me alone!" I cried, and turning away from him I started to run, out of the woods, onto the exposed beach.

I ran toward the water, slanting toward the promontory, trying to control my tears, trying to block out the images of Meritt dying, of Farrell Dean avoiding my eyes, trying to forget the loathing in Cline's voice, the accusations he'd thrown.

I got a stitch in my side—it must have been the crying, because I'd hardly run any distance at all. I stopped, gasping for breath.

It wasn't true. None of it was true. I wasn't responsible for Meritt's death. I wasn't responsible for Farrell Dean and his mother being put in the city meeting. I wasn't.

An image of Cynda crossed my mind, her wink, her knowing smile when Farrell Dean slid something onto my plate. Did she think I was using Farrell Dean? And Shawna and Liza, that glance when he said I was persuasive—but they were my friends, and Cynda was my friend, surely they couldn't be my friends and think terrible things about me?

Abruptly my surroundings came into focus. I was almost to the promontory where the boat was hidden; just ahead, on the last stretch of sandy beach before the rocks took over, I could see the two rocks that marked the trotline. Blast Cline! I didn't have my net and bucket, no place to put the catch from the trotlines. Under the heat of Cline's verbal onslaught I'd left them on the ground at his feet. Had I already screwed up the entire plan?

Looking around, I saw no sign of anyone. The thin strip of sandy beach was bare of footsteps, save my own. The tide was high; soon it would turn, the waves beginning to think about going back to their home in the sea.

What should I do now? Go back for the bucket? Lurk around here? Build a sand city? Sure. That would look real natural. But I had to do something to make me look credible when Angel showed up. If he showed up.

What a letdown it would be, if we went through all this and then he didn't even come. We'd have to come up with some other way to capture the stockade, or repeat this again and again until Angel finally showed.

The sun went behind a cloud and the wind kicked up, making me shiver. The sea was still beautiful, but it didn't look welcoming any more. Without the sun it looked secretive, shifting, sinister.

"My poor child."

I almost jumped out of my skin. I spun around wildly, looking for him—there, beside the big rock, wearing as usual his camouflage clothing. He was standing about twenty feet away, and his gun was slung over his shoulder.

"He doesn't understand you at all." Angel's face was sympathetic.

My cheeks grew hot. He'd overheard Cline's accusations?

"Don't be embarrassed," Angel said. "You're a beautiful girl, and men react to you. You can't help that. You aren't responsible for how they feel about you, for what they do for you."

Behind him the trees swayed gently in the wind. I glanced at them, thinking of Sir Tom and Ezzie hidden somewhere, wondering who else had heard Cline's words. When I looked back, Angel had come quite a bit closer to me. Startled by his sudden proximity, I backed away.

"Shhh," he said soothingly. "Don't be afraid. I only want to talk with you."

I shot a glance up the beach; no one was in sight, just the sand and rocks, the tall trees and the shadows.

"He doesn't understand you," Angel said. "But I do. I know what you want, what you need. And I can give it you."

"That's quite a promise." My voice broke on the words.

Angel shrugged. "It's simple enough. You want Meritt. I can take you to him."

The world spun wildly around me, trees and sky and sea in one wild tumult, then slowly grew solid again. Angel had not moved—if he'd come at me then, I couldn't have moved in time.

"Is he alive? Where is he? What happened to him? Is he hurt?"

Angel laughed and held up a hand as if to slow my questions. "He's fine," he said. "Would you like to go to him now?"

I had taken two steps toward him before I thought.

"How do I know this isn't a trick?" I said, stopping.

Angel studied me gravely. "You don't," he said. "But it isn't. You'll find the outcome well worth the risk."

And why not risk it?

Even if Angel was lying, if I went with him it would distract him long enough for the others to take the stockade. Wasn't that what mattered? Even if he was lying it would just be me who got captured. Even if he killed me—which he wouldn't—it would just be me. The others would take care of the old people, would change life in the city. They didn't need me for that. Farrell Dean might miss me but, as Cline had said, he'd be better off without me tormenting him.

Then I remembered that Cline was watching, Cline and Sir Tom and Ezzie. I couldn't see them, but they were there. And they had guns. They wouldn't let me go with Angel, and they might kill him if I tried.

"I can't go with you right now," I said softly, and despite myself my eyes were drawn to the sunlit shadowy woods, to the figures I couldn't see but knew were present.

Angel's eyes narrowed, became cold and dangerous and unreadable, and sudden panic welled up in me. What had I done?

Desperately I tried to think of a way to keep his mind on me, not on the men in the woods, not on his now-vulnerable stockade.

"I'll meet you later," I said in an undertone.

"Where?"

"The western gap. Where we met last night."

He nodded and his eyes went back to looking benevolent, but then he began walking toward me, holding one hand out as if to tame a wild thing.

"It would be better if you came with me now," he said. "If Sir Tom suspects you are sympathetic to me, he will watch you closely. You might not be able to get away again, and then Meritt would wait and you would not come to him. Think how disappointed he will be."

But I had seen the coldness, the calculation, though they were hidden now. Angel could shift so quickly.

Besides, how could this man possibly take me to Meritt? He had to be lying. Meritt was either dead or locked up in the prison, in the city, surrounded by wardens. I had almost sacrificed our entire plan out of stupidity, out of childish wishful thinking.

I backed away for a few steps.

"You think I'm lying to you," Angel said. "And I can't prove otherwise. I can't prove that I can take you to Meritt, though in fact I can and will. But I can tell you why I want to take you to him."

Something in his tone halted my retreat. He was no longer cajoling; he was speaking matter-of-factly, as if he had dropped the act and was now dealing straight with me.

"I've seen the two of you out in the dark together," he said. "I know that you care about him and he cares about you, and I know that the Watchers won't let you be together." He smiled. "Believe it or not, I'm not too old to sympathize."

"You watch us?"

He nodded. "Many a night I've seen you avoiding the cameras, slipping outside of the wall. He teaches you how to be invisible. You give him something to look forward to, after a long frustrating day."

It should have been good news—he wanted to help us, and he was strong and not insane—but I felt chilled down to my bones, violated. Those were my most private memories, those nights spent running the dark streets with Meritt. They were the closest thing to freedom I had known. They were *mine.*

And he had been watching us.

"But why?" I said. "Why did you watch us?"

Angel shrugged. "Old habits are hard to break."

I stared at him blankly.

He spread his hands as if stating the obvious. "It was my job. Someone had to keep an eye on the experiment."

The experiment. The word seemed to grow in my mind, crowding out everything else.

Angel's expression changed. "You didn't know," he said, and now he sounded concerned. "Tommy didn't tell you that Optica was a research trial?"

It took a moment to find my voice. "No."

"I'm sorry," he said. "I would have broken it to you more gently had I realized."

His expression turned wry. "And I should have realized," he said. "Of course Tommy didn't tell you. He feels too guilty about the part he played. He wants to be the hero. He wants to save the city. Am I right?"

I nodded.

"Afterwards, that's when he's no doubt planning to tell you. After he's paid his debt. When you're so grateful to him that you'll do anything for him, give him anything. Even forgiveness."

I heard his words but they didn't penetrate. All I could focus on, at that moment, was the term *experiment*. In school we dissected small animals, mixed chemicals in test tubes. That was what I thought of when I heard the word. How could we be that? In my mind I pictured an entire city in a petri dish.

"You don't mean an actual experiment," I said, groping for words.

"But I do," Angel said. "State-of-the-art, if you find that any comfort. Cutting edge. No expense spared." His voice was heavily ironic, and I didn't know why, and I didn't care.

"Tommy was involved from the beginning," he said. "His job was security—keeping the subjects corralled, providing back-up for those pretentious paper pushers you call the Watchers, liaising with them and the administrators on the mainland. Now that it's all gone sideways Tommy's guilt-stricken—that happens, you know, when people discover they've backed a failure. They suddenly develop a conscience."

"What sort of experiment?" I said.

But Angel was distracted now, frowning and glancing to his left, toward the bank of dark trees.

I followed his gaze and saw movement. Sir Tom or Ezzie

had blown their cover, I supposed. Well, at least that wasn't my fault.

"There's no time," Angel said, and began to stride toward me. "Let's go meet Meritt."

I stood there and watched him come. I was a practical joke, the Watchers had said. A subject.

An experiment.

Angel saw that I wasn't running and he smiled, but not at me. It was a secret smile, triumphant. He had won.

Ezzie's words struck me, then, jolting me out of my stupor. Angel had paralyzed me, hypnotized me, like a cobra hypnotizing its prey.

I turned and ran.

I was more afraid than I'd expected to be, afraid of Angel and of myself, my uncertain ability to discern good from ill. I was afraid of Angel and I was also afraid that I was making the wrong decision by running from him. All I could do was stick to the plan—I could join Angel later, after I'd thought more carefully about what he'd said, but if I went with him now I wouldn't be able to stop Sir Tom from attacking him, and if Sir Tom killed him I'd never find Meritt—though Angel was probably lying about that—of course he was lying. I'd seen that secret smile.

How could I have come so close to ruining our plan?

I was supposed to distract Angel, but instead he had distracted me, and not for long enough. I'd bought the others hardly any time—only a minute or two. This had all gone wrong.

I ran for the rocky promontory, but the dragging sand slowed me, gave my flight that helpless surreal nightmarish quality, so that with every step I expected to feel Angel's hand on my shoulder. But whether Angel followed me, and how far, I don't know. I was afraid if I looked back I'd see him reaching for me, or else I'd trip and fall, so I didn't turn until

I was on the cliff top, at the very edge of the sea, escape within easy reach.

Then I did turn, and what I saw took my breath away.

Four black-clothed wardens were right behind me. They were close, very close—how had I not heard them? Their faces were hard and mean and they were coming on fast.

"You're going to pay," the one in front called. "No one kills a warden and gets away with it."

Me, kill a warden? I hadn't killed anyone.

Angel was nowhere in sight. The warden was almost within arm's reach, and I wasn't going to stop to argue with him. I swung straight over the edge of the cliff, where the terrifying ladder hung, and began to climb down.

The warden peered over the edge at me, then turned and flung one leg down, felt for the rung. He was following me—he was coming down the ladder, and it swayed as he put his weight on it. If he fell, he might take me down with him.

Someone up above shouted; a single shot rang out. Who was shooting? Was it Angel? Sir Tom? Or were the wardens shooting at my friends?

The warden kept climbing down after me. I sped up, counting aloud—one, two, three, skip the rung, one, two, three, skip the rung. But I had two feet, not one, and I began to be confused about which foot was on which number, plus I was waiting for the warden to hit a bad rung, one of Sir Tom's booby-trapped rungs, and come down on top of me.

An indistinguishable cry rose up above us, someone hurt, someone in pain. Who was that? I couldn't tell, not with other people yelling.

Then the warden did hit a weak rung and the ladder jerked violently, slamming me against the cliff wall. I held on tight and didn't fall, but neither did the warden; he caught the side rope and held on. The ladder swayed as he dangled from it, felt for a safer rung. And then he came on again, if anything faster than before, and now with a steady stream of curses and threats.

Dizzy, I clung to the swinging ladder, though it swung and scraped my knuckles against the rocks. As soon as the vertigo passed I started down again, unsure of the count, testing each rung but with no time, and eventually plunging on and trusting to dumb luck.

Finally I made it to the bottom, and the rock felt hard and unyielding after the rope, and the waves hissed and snapped.

Since I didn't know how to swim and didn't know how deep the water was beyond the ledge, I wanted to cautiously edge my way along the wet shelf of rock, but with the warden hard on my heels, I had no choice but to rush forward. I had never stepped on anything so slick. I went down on the second stride, and waves washed over my arms and legs, tried to pull me into the sea.

Warden or no warden, I would have to move carefully, testing each step and digging my toes into the rocks.

I heard the warden drop onto the shelf behind me, and willed myself not to whip around and lose precious seconds. I cleared the outer edge of the little peninsula and there was Farrell Dean in the tiny cove, watching for me. When he caught sight of me he began easing the little boat further into the water. Then he saw the warden.

"Get in the boat!" he yelled and began pushing through the waist-deep water, trying to get to the warden before the warden got to me.

But the warden was too close—only a couple of yards away. He lunged at me and I jerked away from his hands, losing my footing on the slippery rocks, falling with a splash into water so icy I gasped and swallowed a mouthful of salty sea.

As I came up, gagging and gasping for air, I caught a

glimpse of Farrell Dean grabbing the warden around the neck, hauling him down into the water, and then something else caught my eye.

The boat was drifting.

Swaying gently in the waves, bobbing slightly, it was edging away from us, toward the open sea. I hurried after it as fast as I could, but the water clung heavily to my legs, soaked into my clothes, dragged at me.

What if I lost the boat? We'd be trapped—more wardens could follow this one down—and the rocks were sheer, there was no escape from here but by sea.

I took a deep breath, bent my knees, and launched myself out toward the boat. I came down hard and water went up my nose, set me spluttering and coughing again. My fingertips touched the edge of the boat but as I scrabbled at it, it moved away, out of reach again.

Frantically I got my feet under me and lunged again. This time I caught the boat solidly with both hands—so solidly that it tipped up toward me and things fell out. I stood up—the water was only up to my chest—and when I did the boat leveled. Keeping one hand on it, I grabbed an oar floating nearby and flung it back into the boat.

What else had fallen? It didn't matter. I had to get back to Farrell Dean.

Getting in front of the boat I started tugging it after me, back toward shore. It was maddeningly slow, like moving through honey. Where were Farrell Dean and the warden?

There they were—oh, this was bad—the warden was on top of Farrell Dean. As I watched he shoved Farrell Dean further under, held his head under water.

I pulled with all my might, gasping with the effort. Farrell Dean's hands were around the warden's neck, but the warden was bigger, heavier.

Finally the boat wedged on the sandy bottom. I let go of

it and grabbed the loose oar. Taking three steps, I swung hard at the warden's head.

My aim was bad and the oar caught his shoulder, jolted out of my hands. He staggered and Farrell Dean came up in a rush, tackling him, knocking him off his feet.

But the warden came back up again, fast, and he came up swinging.

Farrell Dean ducked under the blow and then the warden saw me, lunged at me. He was too close—I couldn't get away—and he grabbed me by the shoulders, shook me so hard my teeth rattled, and then shoved me backward, hooking my feet out from under me. I struggled and kicked, managed to keep my head out of water, but then he was reaching for my throat, he was going to drown me—

Then he froze. His mouth came open in surprise; his grip on me loosened. His eyes rolled back in his head and he fell with a splash into the shallow water near the rocky cove.

Panting, Farrell Dean dropped the rock he was holding and grabbed the floating oar. He hurried to the head of the peninsula to see if there were other pursuers. Satisfied, he turned back to the fallen warden.

"Help me get him out," he said, bending over the man and catching him under one arm.

It was awkward work, he was heavy, I was trying to bear the brunt of it to spare Farrell Dean's injuries more trauma, but finally between the two of us we got him up on to the shore, high enough that he was beyond the tide line, and wedged him against a rock so he wouldn't roll back in and drown.

"Let's go," Farrell Dean said.

I clambered gracelessly into the boat, feeling it sway and tilt beneath me, and Farrell Dean pushed us into deeper water, leaning hard against the wooden front, finally heaving himself over the side and then shoving with an oar, sending us into the arms of a tide that pulled us away from beneath the rocky cliff and shot us out toward the open sea.

"You okay?" he said, breathing hard.

"They have guns," I said. "Up above. Someone was shooting."

"I heard." He slid his oar into a notch on the side of the boat and stroked it through the water. The boat jerked, slewed sideways. Farrell Dean reached for the other oar and slid it into place, slammed both oarlocks shut, then tried again. This time we moved smoothly, shooting out further, faster. It was windier out here on the water and my hair tangled in my face, blinding me.

Were the wardens on the cliff top pointing guns at us? We couldn't possibly be a safe distance out, not so quickly.

Farrell Dean was facing me, sitting on the wider middle bench rowing hard, his back toward the open sea, his eyes on the jumble of things in the bottom of the boat.

"Where's the gun?" he said. "Find the gun and if they start shooting at us, shoot back."

I crouched down and dug through the things in the bottom of the boat.

"It's not here," I said finally. "The boat tipped when I grabbed it. The gun must have fallen out."

"All right," Farrell Dean said, rowing harder. "Don't worry. We'll manage."

I crawled up onto the seat but my back was to the shore. I didn't want my back to the shore. What if the bullet was about to come, was about to hit me?

Hurriedly I glanced over my shoulder, bracing myself to feel the shot, the bullet piercing my body.

That quick glance relieved one fear and replaced it with another. No one was pointing a gun at us or even looking at us; but on top of the peninsula several figures were fighting, some in the black uniforms of wardens, two of the struggling figures in gray, while a third in gray knelt on the ground, on his hands and knees—a dark man—Ezzie.

Three in gray was too many—and where was Sir Tom, in his brown and green clothing?

Farrell Dean slowed our outward thrust, turned the front of the boat down the shore, south. There was no room for me to turn fully around on the little end bench; I twisted, straining to see what was happening back on the cliff top.

Was Ezzie hurt? Why was he kneeling like that, watching and not fighting? Had he been shot? As I watched he collapsed onto the ground, tried to rise, collapsed again.

The three wardens were fighting hand to hand with— yes, it was Cline, I could see his short blond hair, but who was the other? No one else was supposed to be out here. The others were all supposed to be at the stockade. He was small-er than Cline, most everyone was, but this person also was blond and I had a sick feeling it was Judd, who was just the sort to do such a stupid thing, trying to protect me when I had promised to protect him.

I turned toward Farrell Dean, fighting my hair out of my eyes. "Can you tell who it is?" I started to say, but Farrell Dean's gaze was fixed elsewhere, a short distance to the right, where two figures stood alone on a high precipice above the sea, watching the fight below.

One was easily recognizable, tall and well built, long pale hair lifting in the wind: Angel.

The other I would know anywhere, from any distance, day or night, dead or alive.

"Meritt!" I screamed, standing up. The boat tilted and a wash of water came over the side.

"Sit down!" Farrell Dean grabbed my leg and yanked me unceremoniously off my feet, then reached for a small metal bucket. He began bailing, his eyes still on the two figures. The oars jerked in their locks and the boat stopped moving.

"Meritt!" I screamed again, my throat burning with the effort.

On the big rock, Meritt raised one arm toward me in acknowledgement.

I kept my eyes on him as I untangled myself, got up on my knees, soaked through by the freezing water sloshing around the bottom of the boat, not caring, not feeling anything but joy that Meritt was alive, he was there, I could see him, soon I could talk to him, touch him.

"We have to row," I said. I climbed onto the middle bench, squeezing in beside Farrell Dean. Grabbing the oar on my side I rowed hard, gouged at the sea. It yanked back and the oar ripped out of my hands, clattered in the oar lock. I grabbed it again, caught it, held it more firmly as I dug at the water again, not as deeply this time, and in response the boat listed sideways, in the wrong direction—there had to be a better way, I had no idea how to do this—we needed to row back to shore, farther down, far from the wardens, where we could land and make our way to Meritt. Meritt, who wasn't dead—Meritt, whom I hadn't gotten killed.

"Angel was telling the truth," I said, gabbling, stumbling over the words. "He would have taken me to Meritt. I should have gone with him. Row, Farrell Dean! I can't do it by myself."

He didn't budge. He bailed water from the bottom of the little boat, shifting the items sloshing around—a spade, a leather canteen, various odd bundles—with maddening deliberate movements.

"Please," I said, grabbing his arm. "Please help me."

But though I ordered and pleaded and finally wept with fury, Farrell Dean wouldn't row, wouldn't move so I could reach the other oar, wouldn't even look at me.

He finished bailing the water out of the boat, then held his oar up out of the water and watched the two figures grow smaller. He let the wind and waves seize us and turn us outward, away.

I called him every bad name I knew while all the time keeping my eyes fixed on the figures high on the rock, figures growing smaller and smaller and, as they grew dark with distance, becoming silhouettes, becoming more and more alike—tall, broad shouldered, familiar and unfamiliar, safe and mysterious—

"He's Meritt's father," Farrell Dean said suddenly, sounding startled.

I should have seen it before.

Their coloring was different, and Meritt wasn't as perfectly beautiful, and he was thinner, hadn't yet filled out as a completely grown man, but the resemblance was there, not only in their faces but in their height, in the way they stood, in the timbre of their voices, in ways I couldn't put my finger on but knew were there, were true. Meritt was Angel's son. He was the son of a Guardian.

Surely Meritt knew—why else would he be out there with Angel? But why hadn't he told me? And who was his mother?

The waves rocked the boat and I clutched at the side, staring at the figures on the shore until my eyes burned. The gray sky rocked above us, the gray sea below. Farrell Dean sat there waiting, not touching his oar, letting the elements propel us.

"Why are you taking us out so wide?" I said, bewilderment beginning to drive out anger. "And we're supposed to circle round counterclockwise, toward the stockade . . ."

Farrell Dean didn't answer; he merely shook his head, his eyes fixed on Meritt.

It was the currents, I thought, or the tide, forcing us to take an altered path to the other side of the island, sweeping us out and curling us clockwise around the island.

No—not curling us around it—we were—

"Farrell Dean!" I said, panic flaring. "You have to row—we're getting too far out—we might not be able to get back!"

He looked at me, then, and I saw pain in his eyes, and something else, too, something that struck me suddenly frightened and desolate. And all I could manage was a single short sentence, terse and under my breath: "No more secrets."

Farrell Dean didn't look away, though it seemed to cost him. "There's another island," he said. "We're going there."

Another island?

Was he insane? We had to get back—had to get home. I couldn't jump out of the boat. I couldn't swim. And I could see by the set of his jaw that there was no persuading Farrell Dean this time. I was helpless, stolen away from everything I knew, everyone I loved, sent off over the edge of the world into some mad dream of that mad old man.

"You planned this," I said. Farrell Dean shook his head, but I went on.

"You didn't speak to me all day because you knew you were lying to me. Yes, you were—Cline knew you were going away."

Oh, yes, Cline had known—that was why he had attacked me. He had known that Farrell Dean was going to carry me off somewhere, that he wouldn't be seeing us again for—how long? And he wanted to chew me out before we went.

Seeing their deception, thinking it through, kept me from yielding to the blinding panic that swam just past the edges of my vision. The distant figures of Meritt and his father were tiny now, blurring together into one dark shadow.

Divided loyalties. That was what the Watchers had said about Meritt. Did they know about his father the Guardian, or were they thinking only of me, of our friends?

I got up from the middle seat, crawled to the end bench, as close to Meritt as I could get, and stared until he was gone, until even the rock he stood on blurred, became part of the island, indistinguishable from other rocks and ridges. I stared until the island itself was nothing but a low shadow on the surface of the water.

"Everyone lied to me." I turned toward Farrell Dean with a look so stony that he flinched. "Sir Tom. Cline. Your mother. And you most of all."

Farrell Dean ran one hand across his eyes. "Sir Tom misled you," he said quietly. "He misled you for your own good. But I didn't even do that. I was going to take you back. They didn't know it, but I was going to take you to the stockade."

When he dropped his hand and looked straight at me, I could find no trace of deception in his eyes.

"So what's stopping you?" I said. "We can still get back."

He shut his eyes briefly, as if my words hurt. "No," he said. "They were right, Sir Tom and my mother. They said it was too dangerous for you here, that you needed to get clear away. I thought we could keep you hidden in the woods, that that would be good enough, but ..." He broke off mid-sentence, leaned forward. "On the far side of the other island, Red—if they're still there, if we can get help, Sir Tom says—"

It was an obvious attempt to distract me. "Take me home," I said cutting him off. "I want to go home."

The island—my island, my home—was a distant line on the horizon now. I wouldn't even have noticed it, if I didn't know it was there. I looked the other way, looked all around, and saw nothing but open sea, gray waves, gray sky.

"I wasn't in danger," I said. "Angel wouldn't have hurt me. He's Meritt's father. Why would he hurt me?"

Farrell Dean was only eighteen, but at that moment he looked ten years older.

"What?" I said. "What is it?"

"I'm doing what's best, Red."

That was too much. "I should just trust you, is that it?"

Farrell Dean said, evenly, "I wish you would."

"And I wish you'd tell me what's going on!" My voice was shrill. "You of all people, after accusing Meritt of keeping things from me." I hesitated a fraction of a second, could have stopped myself, but I didn't want to stop. I wanted to hurt him.

"Do you know what this looks like, Farrell Dean? This looks like you saw a good opportunity to get me away from Meritt. You saw your chance, and you took it. But I don't appreciate being kidnapped. I won't forgive you. Not ever. I hate you."

Farrell Dean listened stoically to my tirade, the expression in his eyes growing increasingly distant. When I stopped he waited, eyebrows raised, as if to see whether I was truly finished.

Then he said, softly, "Hate me if you have to. I'm doing what's best for you, and I'll take you back home when it's safe. I promise." He took a deep ragged breath, the only sign that he wasn't perfectly calm. "And if Meritt's with his father, he'll be okay. He'll be waiting for you when you get back."

Cline's angry face swam before my eyes. The rocking of the boat made me ill, though it might have been the turmoil inside me that did it. I shut my eyes and tried not to let the panic in, the grief over leaving Meritt, the shame I felt for the way I'd spoken to Farrell Dean.

I almost wished that I could lose my mind.

Chapter 32

The waves bore us swiftly along for one hour, or two—all I knew was that behind the screen of clouds, the sun gradually was moving west. We were in a gray bowl, gray sky above us, gray sea around us. I had never seen so much open space, so much nothingness.

"When will we go back?" I finally asked.

"Unless we can find a boat with an engine, we'll have to wait until the currents shift. We'll need the current to get back."

"And when do these currents shift? In a day? A week?"

Farrell Dean looked away. "Around about the winter solstice," he said.

The winter solstice? That was more than two months away. I couldn't believe this. "And what if the current, or the wind, takes us straight out into the open sea? You've gotten all your information from a crazy old man."

I wanted to make him admit that he might not know what was best, wanted to punish him for taking me away from home, wanted to make him feel as unsettled as I was feeling. Maybe I succeeded. All I know for sure is that I ended up scaring myself, because the more I thought about it, the more the truth of it sank in. We were trusting a crazy old man.

A crazy old man, and I was the one who had led us to him. What if I'd chosen wrong? What if Angel was the sane one, the good one? After all, Meritt had been with Angel. And if occasionally I'd caught a glimpse of something hard, something calculating, in Angel's eyes, well—he'd been having to plot and calculate for years to survive around the old man, hadn't he? Because he didn't trust Sir Tom. He'd said so. And he'd said I shouldn't trust him.

But I had. And because I had trusted Sir Tom, Farrell Dean had trusted him, and now here we were, out on the sea, with only Sir Tom's words for a guide. The sea was unending, and we had never set foot in a boat until that morning. We could die, and the seagulls would eat our bones.

"We could die out here," I said aloud.

Farrell Dean considered this. "You've always wanted to see the sea," he said finally. "Why don't you try to enjoy it?"

It grew cold, out on the water. The wind was still blowing, skimming us along, and my clothes were still damp. I felt in my pockets for my black cap.

Several packs were in the bottom of the boat. One had dried fruit and meat. Farrell Dean tried to get me to eat something, but I wouldn't. Then he opened another pack, pulled out a blanket, wrapped it around my shoulders, and turned away, clearly intending to leave me in peace.

I didn't do him the same favor.

"You made me leave Judd," I said. "I promised to take care of him, and you took me away."

Farrell Dean nodded. "That's true. I'm sorry."

I didn't want to be blamed for anything else. "That promise was mine. I'm breaking it by leaving. But you're the one who made me break it. If anything happens to him, it's your fault."

Farrell Dean looked at me for a long moment without speaking. Then he turned, studying the horizon.

The sun was visible through a thin layer of clouds, and the waves were greener now. I stared at the sea outside the little boat, catching glimpses now and then of strange creatures that I knew only from Rafe's descriptions in biology class. Jellyfish. The fin of a shark. Farrell Dean hoped I didn't notice that, I could tell; he sat up and gazed with interest at a spot in the distance, where absolutely nothing was, as if I'd automatically look where he was looking.

I watched the shark.

"Farrell Dean?"

We had been sitting in silence for several hours. Now Farrell Dean leaned forward, rested his elbows on his knees, and looked at me warily.

"I appreciate your concern," I said. "But please explain how your secret about why you're taking me away is any different from the secrets you were angry at Meritt for keeping from me."

"I'm trying to protect you. His secrets were leading you blind into danger."

"Excuse me for saying so, but when you gave me your mother's stolen food, weren't you leading me blind into danger?"

Farrell Dean nodded.

"But I had to do that," he said. "Do you remember that winter when you were sick all the time? You were ten or eleven, and you were growing really fast. And one day you weren't in school, yet again, and Rafe said you weren't getting enough nourishment to get well. The Watchers weren't killing people back then, so it seemed worth the risk, considering."

"Notice who did the choosing. I didn't choose to take that risk. You chose it for me."

Farrell Dean stared at me for a heartbeat, then gave a short disbelieving laugh. "You aren't stupid," he said. "You knew I couldn't magically produce extra food."

I looked away. There wasn't much to look at—just the waves, the horizon. "And now you're carrying me off to some unknown land, all in the name of protecting me, and you won't even tell me what you're supposedly protecting me from."

"That pretty much sums it up," he agreed. The waves behind him were gray and cold.

"We can't go back now, anyway," I said. "The die is cast. The deed is done. I can accept that. I just want to understand it."

His face was grim. "Understanding it would hurt you, Red. More than you know. Best to let it go."

I counted very slowly to ten, to twenty. When a full minute had elapsed, I tried again.

"I am going to an unknown land," I said. "I want to know exactly what I'm leaving behind."

He shook his head.

I counted to sixty.

"You're going to an unknown land," I said. "As long as you don't keep secrets from me, I promise to always watch your back."

Still he said nothing.

Sixty seconds.

"I'm sorry for what I said before," I said. I tried to keep my tone light, but my voice wobbled a little bit, and Farrell Dean looked at me sharply.

"I don't hate you," I said. "More than anybody in the world, you always try to protect me. I know that. And I probably will forgive you, eventually, for kidnapping me."

Scooting to the middle seat so I could reach him, I leaned forward, touched his knee, and looked him straight in the eye. "But I will not forgive you if you keep secrets."

Farrell Dean didn't smile, but the tension in his face eased. "You're ruthless, aren't you?" he said. But he knew I meant the apology, even if I also intended to use it to get what I wanted.

"Is it because Meritt and Angel were together?" I asked. "Because you don't trust Angel and you think I'd be around him because of Meritt?"

No reply.

"Is it Sir Tom? Did he tell Alice something while we were asleep, something that worried her?"

No reply.

"Is it because Judd killed that warden—did you hear the warden shouting at me? He thought I did it."

"Those are all good reasons, Red."

"But they aren't the one you had in mind. Is it because Cline dislikes me, and you're afraid he'll yell me to death if we go back?"

"You aren't going to stop, are you?"

"Not ever. Not until you tell me. You're stubborn, Farrell Dean, but I'm more stubborn than you are. You know that. I will never let this drop. I'm tired of secrets."

He sighed and looked out over the empty waves. After a moment he turned to me, his face weary.

"Bear in mind I could be wrong," he said. "I hope I am."

I waited. He looked so very tired, and his face was filled with so much pain and dread that my heart sank and I almost relented. Maybe he was right—maybe I didn't want to know, not if telling made him look like this.

But how could I stand to not know?

"I can only tell you what I heard," he said. "The wardens in the prison were talking." He paused.

"The wardens?" I prompted.

"Last night. Before the city meeting. They thought I was about to die, so they weren't being careful." Again he paused, and I heard the unsaid words. They thought he was about to die, and so did he. What had that been like for him, to think—to be all but certain—that he was moments away from execution?

I put my hand back on his knee and absently he picked it up, traced the length of my fingers.

"One of the wardens said, 'He won't do it. He's fond of her.'"

My heart began beating too hard and I felt the slow hot flush creep up my neck.

Farrell Dean went on in a low voice, his face turned away, as if he couldn't bear to look at me. "The other warden said, 'That's just it. He has divided loyalties. He has to prove he's on the Watchers' side. What better way than sacrificing the little redhead? Anyone can be bought if the price is right.'"

So that was what the Watchers meant, that "one way or another" I'd be gone soon. Either I'd be "euthanized," or Meritt would hand me over to them.

"Then what?" I whispered.

"Then they took me out to the city meeting."

I leaned forward. "But Meritt would never betray his friends—not me, not you. He's the one who saved you from the city meeting."

Farrell Dean nodded. "I know. Cline told me."

"That was a terrible risk, Farrell Dean. We thought Meritt had been killed for helping you escape. Trapped in the watchtower and killed."

Again Farrell Dean nodded. "I thought so, too. He saved my life and risked his own. I'm not denying that. I'll owe him as long as I live."

"But."

"I didn't add any 'but.'"

I laughed, a strained, ugly sound. "I know what you want to say—that Meritt saved you, but you weren't the one the Watchers wanted. You weren't the price they wanted him to pay. He could afford to let you go."

Farrell Dean said nothing, sat looking at me as if waiting for it all to sink in, and in a moment it did.

"There on the beach—just now—you think he was coming after me. To turn me in."

He didn't nod, but I knew I had read his thought.

"You think he brought the wardens—that he came after me with wardens, with guns . . . you think Angel was helping him trap me."

The windswept boat pitched and rocked, and Farrell Dean shook his head.

"I don't know what to think, Red. But I had to make a snap judgment, and it seemed safer to get you away. To do what Sir Tom said. Like I said, I hope I'm wrong."

"You are wrong."

"I want to be. But what if I'm not? You know Meritt. He plays to win."

"This is real life, not a game."

But I shifted uneasily, remembering things I'd said to Meritt, things he'd said to me.

Farrell Dean said nothing.

A more solid defense occurred to me. "Listen," I said, leaning further forward, determined to make him understand, to make him agree with me. "If Meritt had come out to get me, why would he bring wardens? He didn't need them. All he needed was himself. I would have gone straight to him."

Even as I spoke I wondered—why *was* Meritt out there with wardens? Maybe he wasn't with them. But if he'd been out there alone, why hadn't he come to me on the beach? Why had Angel come instead?

"I'd have gone to him," I repeated absently, my thoughts fixed on untangling the logistics. "I would have done anything he wanted. Anything at all."

Farrell Dean flinched at my words. For a second I thought his feelings were hurt, that I had twisted the knife again, but then I followed his thoughts and saw he was thinking something worse.

I would have done whatever Meritt wanted, and Meritt wanted to save the city.

A wave splashed hard against the boat, rocking us, giving us an extra shove as if proving we were unmoored, without foothold.

"Meritt could have saved all those people," I said slowly. "All I had to do was go with him. The Watchers would have killed me and been satisfied, and then Meritt could have persuaded the Watchers to spare everyone else, could have come up with some other way to get us through the winter."

Farrell Dean said nothing.

"My old people," I went on, and my voice trembled. I looked up at the sky, trying to stop the tears prickling at the backs of my eyes. "Louie, Estelle, Mariella . . . and the food supplies, the winter coming on . . . So many people will die, and it could have just been me."

"Hold on, Red." Farrell Dean was shaking his head. "Don't get ahead of the facts. Everything you're saying—sure, that might have been going through Meritt's head. But I don't think it would have worked. The Watchers wouldn't have given Meritt any real power, not even in exchange for you. He'd be a token, a puppet."

I didn't believe that. I knew Meritt, knew how single-minded he was, how smart, how good he was at getting things done, how easily he could manage people—even

Cline, suspicious and cynical about absolutely everyone except Farrell Dean, liked Meritt.

He could have made it work. He would have made it work.

But Farrell Dean had messed it up.

"It should have been my decision to make," I said. "My choice. Not yours."

"Stop it, Red," Farrell Dean said sharply, shifting until we were knee to knee, looking me straight in the eye. "Think about what you're saying. A suicide mission is still suicide."

Was it? And if so, so what? It was just a word. Suicide, sacrifice, whatever you wanted to call it, the question remained: If I'd had the choice, would I have turned myself in, knowing I'd die, but giving all the others a chance to live?

"Maybe Meritt still can salvage the situation," Farrell Dean said. "He's good at that, at thinking on his feet. Maybe it will all come right after all."

"Maybe he was already planning to salvage it," I said. "Maybe he could have brought me to the Watchers and persuaded them that arresting me was good enough, that they didn't need to kill me. Or maybe he was coming out to get Angel to help him—to help us—and wasn't intending to turn me in at all."

I could come up with all sorts of possibilities, but how could I know which was the correct one? The waves slapped the little boat, waves that were cold and dark and gray. What had happened to the lovely sea, the water that felt like freedom, like hope?

"Red?" Farrell Dean waited until I looked up. "If you can't think of yourself, think of Meritt. For his sake, it's better we got you away. He might trade you for a chance to save the city—I hope not, but he might. Or he might let you trade yourself. And if that happened, Meritt would never forgive himself. It would eat him alive."

But when he met my eyes, we both knew he was describing how he himself would feel. He wasn't sure at all that Meritt would feel the same way.

"We're going to have to agree to disagree," I said, turning away from him. "I know Meritt. I trust him to do what's best."

Whatever that was. I no longer felt like I knew.

Chapter 33

"How far is this other island?" I said. The sun had set and we were in the long gray twilight.

Farrell Dean, who had been sitting facing away from me—giving me what privacy he could—swung his legs over the bench seat, turned towards me.

"I don't know how far it is in miles," he said. "Sir Tom thinks it'll take us less than two days. Maybe only one. It depends on the speed of the current."

I tried to hide my astonishment, and knew I failed. Two days in this little boat? Two days on the open sea in this tiny little boat, with only—I looked again—one gallon bag of water? We had plenty of dried food, but water . . . that apparently was part of what fell out when I tipped the boat.

I didn't want to think about it. We couldn't get back now, anyway.

As it grew dark the movement of the waves slowed. I dangled my fingers in the water; it moved, but I didn't think we were moving any longer. We were rocking, but not going forward. I dropped a small piece of dried apple in the water; it floated gently beside us for a long time before it drifted away. After a series of such small experiments, I was sure—at least as sure as I could be, out there in the dark, with no stable landmarks.

"I don't think we're moving anymore," I said.

Farrell Dean pulled something out of his pocket and studied it.

"What's that?"

He held up a short metal cylinder. "It's a compass. The little arrow points north."

"So does the north star," I said dismissively, looking up at the cloudy sky.

"Exactly," Farrell Dean said. "Sir Tom said that at sunset, when the current dropped, we'd need to bear west."

"You mean row west?"

"That's right. The current brought us this far in the right direction, but now we need to pull west before the next current picks us up. Otherwise we could miss the island."

Well, that was motivating. Wordlessly I moved back to the middle seat, beside him, and picked up an oar.

We rowed side by side, in silence, for what felt like hours. My palms stung and my shoulders began to ache, but there was no point in complaining. I didn't want to miss this island and end up lost forever on the open sea.

There was no moon and the clouds obscured the stars. There was only black night, black sea, the oar that grew heavier and heavier in my hands. When my arms started trembling with exhaustion and I thought I couldn't possibly row another stroke, Farrell Dean spoke.

"I think we've gone far enough," he said. "Let's take a break and eat something."

That sounded good to me. I crawled forward and felt around in the darkness for the bags of food, found some nuts and dried cherries, and passed some to Farrell Dean.

He paused just long enough to eat, then picked up the oars. "Drink some water," he said.

"We don't have much."

"I know. But we have to drink it sometime."

Cautiously I unscrewed the cap on the neck of the leather canteen and squeezed a little water into my mouth, then carried the bag to Farrell Dean and made him drink a little. He was still rowing.

"Move over," I said. "Give me an oar."

"Don't, Red," he said. "I think we're fine. I'm just making sure."

"What if we overshoot?"

"I don't think we can. The current will shove us back."

"Move over," I said again, and this time he did. I took an oar and started rowing, trying to ignore my protesting muscles. I didn't want to go to this other island, but I'd much rather go there than end up dying on the open sea.

"Are there people on this other island?" I asked.

"Sir Tom says there used to be. No way to know for sure, now. They could be gone, could be dead. But we're hoping they're still there. We'll try to find them and—"

"But if there are people, why have they never come to us?

Farrell Dean shrugged. "Maybe they have come. Maybe Jensen scared them away."

I nodded. "Or the wild men killed them."

"Or maybe they haven't come because they don't have boats. Or they don't know the way."

"Or maybe they just like staying home."

"Yeah," Farrell Dean agreed, his voice wry. "Would you want to go to Optica, given a choice?"

"Yes, I would," I said sharply. "Optica is home."

No matter what it was—an experiment, a death trap—still it was my home. Meritt was there, my friends, even my parents, whoever they were.

For a few minutes Farrell Dean was silent. I felt bad for

breaking our truce, but not bad enough to say something conciliatory.

Then Farrell Dean spoke. "We have traps and fishhooks," he said. "We'll be fine. We won't starve."

But his tone was less confident than his words, and I could read his thought: wouldn't that be great, if he'd managed to keep me from starving in Optica, then carried me away to starve on the open sea.

We rowed on in silence. I counted one hundred strokes, and my palms felt raw with blisters, but as long as Farrell Dean rowed, I intended to row.

He lowered his oar and looked at me; even in the darkness, I think he read my mind. "We're far enough west—we have to be, by now," he said. "I'll keep an eye on the compass to make sure we keep heading in the right direction. Why don't you try to sleep awhile?"

I wasn't sure what we could do if we went wrong—row wildly in circles in the dark?

Then we felt it—the boat swayed, bobbed a bit more vigorously, then pointed its nose and began flowing speedily along. Wordlessly Farrell Dean handed me the compass: The little arrow on the compass glowed in the dark, and it pointed, comfortingly, north over the bow of the boat.

"Sleep," Farrell Dean said again.

"Only if you promise to wake me later," I said. "It won't help us if you collapse from exhaustion."

There wasn't much room to rest in the boat, but by sitting on the damp floor of the stern and extending my legs under the middle seat, I could lie down flat.

I spread the blanket over me, and in the bow Farrell Dean reached down and pulled it over my feet; and before I knew it, I was asleep.

Sir Tom was sitting in his cabin, near the blazing fire. It was warm and bright, and my friends were all there, sleeping on the floor.

"It all comes down to loyalty," Sir Tom said, puffing on his pipe. "Some might call it faithfulness. A fullness of faith."

I awoke to a thick gray fog that had soaked straight through my blanket, my clothes. I wanted to close my eyes and go back to Sir Tom's warm fire, his snug cabin, my friends, but it was too late. I knew it was only a dream.

Shivering, I sat up.

"It's pretty cold," Farrell Dean said, watching me. He was hunched into himself on the little bow bench, wrapped in the other blanket. In the gray morning light he looked pinched with exhaustion.

"You never woke me," I said. My teeth chattered when I spoke.

"Here." He tossed me the bag of food and ignored my comment. "Eat something. That'll help warm you up."

I fumbled with the bag and managed to pull out some beef jerky and dried apples. Maybe they helped a little bit, but I was still shivering when I finished. I took a small drink of water—my throat cried out for more, but I was terrified of running out.

"Are we going in the right direction?" I asked. Farrell Dean nodded. The fog was so thick that, though he was less than ten feet away from me, he looked blurred.

"You look half frozen," he said, moving to the wider middle seat. "I think we'd better combine our body warmth."

I was halfway to him before I thought.

"What's wrong?" he said.

I was embarrassed, but I couldn't think of an evasion. "Cline says I toy with your affections," I said. "He says I'm torturing you, or something."

To my surprise Farrell Dean laughed.

"Cline's a mother hen," he said. "I'm not as delicate as all that. Besides, I don't think Cline would thank you for letting me freeze to death."

I didn't need more persuading.

We sat together for two hours, maybe three. We sat mostly in silence, huddled under the two blankets, watching the waves, the shifting clouds, the endless bare horizon. The boat rocked gently and moved steadily along. The compass pointed north.

Maybe it was the warmth from Farrell Dean's body, thawing my frigid limbs. Maybe it was the western wind that began to blow, lifting the fog, caressing my face. Maybe it was the sun peeking out through the clouds, sending thin gold fingers of sunshine through to streak the gray water a glowing green, a hopeful color. Maybe I was sick of fear and grief, anger and despair; maybe I had to let them go in order to survive. Maybe it was all these things, or none of them, but after a time I began to feel strength returning, and courage.

I was the same girl who had imagined other islands, other worlds, places where I wasn't confined in a circle but could go freely as far as I wanted to go. And now here I was, on the sea, going to a new world—a world of mystery, possibly of danger, but also a world that was outside Optica's walls, out of range of her cameras, beyond the Watchers' influence and command. What wouldn't I have given, just a few weeks ago, for this chance, this adventure? And now I knew what my city had become. Now I had good reason to leave, to find help. Maybe I'd even find answers. Maybe from outside I could look back in, and from that perspective understand.

Beside me Farrell Dean shifted, leaned forward to pick up the water canteen. The blanket slid from his shoulders. I saw the dark streaks of dried blood that stained the back of his shirt, welding it to his back, and I remembered my dream. Loyalty and faithfulness, Sir Tom had said. Fullness of faith.

Meritt had saved Farrell Dean from the city meeting, but—how could I have forgotten?—before that, Farrell Dean had refused to betray Meritt. He hadn't told the wardens that Meritt was up in the watchtower, and he hadn't told them that he had accepted stolen food not for himself, but for me. He had taken every strike of the whip on his own back, rather than turn the wardens' attention to us. He had been loyal. He had been faithful.

Reaching out I touched his back gently, just barely making contact with the welts across his shoulders. They weren't a dream, any more than the bruises on my arm from where the scarred warden had grabbed me were dreams, or the claw marks Ezzie had taken in order to help Sir Tom. All this was real. We were real. We were brave. We were willing to suffer if that's what it took to help each other, to help Optica. That was worth something, surely, in the overall scheme of things.

And if I could help my friends, if I had even the smallest chance of helping them by going to this island, by looking for whatever or whomever Sir Tom wanted us to find, then what could I do but go, and go gladly?

Chapter 34

The second day on the sea went faster than the first. Farrell Dean stretched out in the bottom of the boat and slept restlessly while I watched the compass assure us that we were drifting north. Then he climbed back onto the bench seat and I dozed in the intermittent sun while he watched the compass.

Eventually the fog burned completely off and it grew so warm that we rigged a tent from the blankets and sat in the bottom of the boat, in the wedge of shade. In my wildest dreams I'd never pictured anything like this—sitting knee-to-knee with Farrell Dean on the hard damp bottom of a boat, both of us sweaty and unkempt, not to mention bloody, with nothing but open sea around us, nothing but the inexorable sun above us, peering at us through the weave of the blanket, and beneath it all the rocking, always rocking, never ceasing rhythm of the sea.

"Farrell Dean," I said, holding on to the bench seat to keep from being rocked against the side, "There's something I need to tell you."

"What is it?" he said, but he reached up and adjusted the blankets, and I knew it was so he wouldn't have to meet my eye. He was expecting me to say something else that would cause pain. That made me feel smaller inside, and lonely. If even Farrell Dean wasn't comfortable around me, who was I, anymore? And I couldn't blame my hair this time; it was all my own doing.

Pushing that thought away, I said, "On the beach, right before we left, Angel said Optica was an experiment."

"An experiment," Farrell Dean repeated, his face blank. "An *experiment*?"

It felt like years since we'd had a full conversation. Farrell Dean hadn't heard about what Meritt and I had learned in the watchtower, and he hadn't heard what Sir Tom had told me when we were alone on the beach, about watchmakers and the care and feeding of ants. There was a lot to tell.

But we had plenty of time, rocking along in the middle of the ocean, so I told him everything, as exactly as I could remember it. Farrell Dean listened silently for the most part, his face intent, only interrupting now and then to clarify a point.

"And Angel didn't say what sort of experiment," he said when I'd finished.

"No. The wardens showed up and I ran."

"An experiment. And the Watchers said you were the best chance for future subjects." He grimaced. "You know they do keep a close eye on the bloodlines, Red."

"Yes, but I'd be a liability as far as that—you'll never get a bigger, stronger person using me."

"Maybe they're not going for brawn. You're smart."

"But not especially."

He studied me. "It has to have something to do with your hair. You're more likely to have children with red hair than anyone else is."

"Yeah, sure. A rage for red-haired Optica children. That's probably it."

He shrugged, acknowledging the point.

"Sir Tom said my hair had nothing to do with me being

watched. And the Watchers—they seemed to keep me around as a subject in spite of my hair, not because of it." I went ahead and told him the bit I'd left out before. "They said I was a joke. An un-funny practical joke."

Farrell Dean bumped my knee with his. "Consider the source, Red," he said. "An insult from a Watcher is as good as a compliment from a normal person. You're beautiful, and so is your hair."

Now I was embarrassed, as if I'd been fishing for compliments.

Farrell Dean didn't notice; he was too focused on sorting through the news about Optica.

"The Watchers mentioned Louie and Estelle, too, and other people," I said. "So it's not just me. It might even be all of us."

"But somehow you especially. You and your possible future children."

Farrell Dean didn't like that, I could tell. Neither did I.

"What sort of experiment could that possibly be?" I said.

He shook his head. "I can think of all sorts of experiments, but none that quite fits the bill."

"Whatever it is, it isn't going well. Not if the Watchers are talking about their life's work being all for nothing. Not if the watchmaker abandoned his watch. And Angel says Sir Tom backed a failure and that's why he's suddenly feeling guilty. We're not just an experiment—we're a failed one."

I didn't much like being a failure at anything, but maybe being a failed experiment was better than being a successful one.

Farrell Dean nodded. "That's why they aren't interested in keeping us alive anymore. Like Sir Tom said, the supply drops stopped. And the Watchers don't know how to keep us alive because they're just here to document the experiment. They don't know anything about running a city."

He broke off. "But that doesn't make sense either," he said, after a second's pause. "They've been abandoned, too. The Watchers and the Guardians. Would whoever is in charge really throw away their own people, along with the experiment? I guess if they're ruthless enough to experiment on people in the first place, then—"

"No, wait—" I said. "I just remembered. When we were all supposed to be asleep, Sir Tom was talking with your mother about the time of the ashes. He sent men to see what was happening, he said. The ones who got sick. Animal sick, I mean. Or contaminated or whatever it is—the things at the tree, you know—"

He nodded and I went on. "They went to where the black ash came from, and they came back saying everything was destroyed on the mainland." The word still felt odd on my tongue.

"So if that's where the supplies came from," Farrell Dean said, finishing my thought, "then they didn't stop sending supplies because the experiment failed. They stopped sending supplies because they were dead."

I nodded. "Or probably dead."

"Which means we might be a successful experiment," Farrell Dean said slowly, and I nodded.

For a moment we thought in silence.

"Who was it?" I said finally. "Who did this to us? Who was the watchmaker?"

"I don't know," Farrell Dean said. "But it might be a good thing if he's forgotten us or dead."

Our water supply dwindled. My tongue felt thick. In the middle of the afternoon I noticed that Farrell Dean was shorting himself and told him I wouldn't drink unless he did. It was frightening, but we reminded ourselves that, at the moment, we were fine—thirsty, and cramped from being in the boat, and sore from rowing and from our various cuts and bruises, but better than we'd have been if the Watchers had had their way.

Night fell. How long we sat silently in the dark, adrift on the waves, I don't know. There was no moon, and for a time there were no stars, only the sound of the water and the feel of the wind turning colder and colder on my face.

Then the clouds cleared and the stars began to shine. Out there on the sea, with no buildings or trees to block them, no electric blue lights to dim them, they were magnificent, astonishing. Farrell Dean and I leaned back against the sides of the boat, staring up at them, tracing patterns here and there.

Eventually, feeling dizzy, I sat up again. Farrell Dean had fallen silent and I felt no need to talk, either. I sat there in the starlight, watching the sea move past, feeling as if I were living in a dream.

I had been staring at the shape for some time before my brain registered what my eyes were seeing in the dim starlit night.

"Land!" I said, and Farrell Dean swung around.

A huge form loomed above the sea. It drew closer and closer and we watched, as if it might vanish if we blinked, as if it might be an illusion. But it wasn't. It was real. The half-insane old man hadn't, after all, sent us out to die on the sea.

Eventually the bottom of our boat scraped something solid. We were still a good ways from the pale stretch of beach, so Farrell Dean leaned way over the side, stretched his arm down.

"It's sand," he said. "I'll get out and pull us in. You stay put. Stay dry."

But after watching Farrell Dean work for a few minutes, after seeing him wince with the pain in his back, I climbed out too, the cold water wetting my pants up to my hips, and together we tugged the boat in, up the long gentle sandy slope. Then we kept pulling, tugging the boat beyond the tide line and into the shelter of the trees.

Afterwards we walked back down to the beach and surveyed our surroundings as best as we could by starlight. My legs felt funny after so long on the rocking waves; the ground kept either being farther away than expected or rising up to meet me faster than expected.

We walked a good distance down the beach in both directions, long enough for the ground to feel firm under my feet again. But we saw no buildings, no lights shining out of the darkness, no boats, no sign of any inhabitants.

"Great," I said finally, feeling deflated. "A deserted island."

"Maybe not," Farrell Dean said. "Maybe just this side is deserted. Sir Tom specifically said to go to the other side of the island. We'll look around when the sun comes up. Until then, let's get back to the boat and try to sleep."

We found our way back to the boat and sat down side by side on the damp floor, in the stern where there was more room. We ate some dried fruit and jerky.

"Let's finish the water," Farrell Dean said. "We can dig in the morning for more."

I looked at him. "Did Sir Tom tell you how to do that?"

"No. Old Louie told me, a long time ago. He said on a beach you could dig in the valley just after the first sand dune, and the hole would fill with fresh water. It shouldn't be too deep, he said—just to your elbow or shoulder. And we have a spade."

Sir Tom had gotten us safely to this island, but I had to admit I was glad to be trusting Louie when it came to our water supply. It made me feel as if I hadn't entirely left my friends behind. He'd be pleased if his stories and advice paid off; I'd be pleased if I got to tell him so.

Once we'd finished the water we settled down to sleep. We had no dry clothes but we pulled the two blankets over us, stretching our legs under the middle bench, leaning together against the cold. I pulled my cap more firmly over my ears, but still I shivered. After a moment Farrell Dean shifted so that his arm was around me and my head rested on his shoulder.

"I won't tell Cline if you won't," he murmured.

"As long as I'm not hurting your ribs," I said, and he shook his head.

My eyes already felt heavy. "Should we keep watch?" I asked.

"I didn't see any tracks on the sand," Farrell Dean said. "Nothing to suggest animals or people have been around here recently. And we're both exhausted."

I knew he was right; I wasn't sure I could stay awake if I had to, and he hadn't slept at all the night before.

Farrell Dean shut his eyes. After so many hours on the sea it felt strange to be in a boat that was steady, unmoving, especially since I could hear the waves lapping against the sandy beach. With my eyes shut I felt dizzy, as if my body didn't know whether it was moving or still.

"I'm going to dream of waves," I said, very quietly, in case Farrell Dean was already asleep.

"Me too," he said. Then, after a moment, "We might be warmer in the sand."

"But something might crawl on us."

He smiled without opening his eyes.

The boat was small protection, I knew, but it was our only bulwark at the moment, and in a strange land something bounded and familiar. A little while before I'd been anxious to find people, but now, thinking about how vulnerable we'd be asleep, I almost hoped there were no people—strangers with strange ways who'd have to be cautiously approached, who might help us or might hurt us, who would know nothing of us, nothing of Optica, nothing of the only things I knew.

I was bone weary, but I listened hard for a long time, alternately fighting back and indulging frightening thoughts. I never heard anything except the waves and the occasional hoot of an owl and, eventually, the deep steady breathing that told me Farrell Dean finally had fallen asleep. Somehow that made me feel safer. If he could sleep, it must be safe.

"Star light, star bright, any star I see tonight," I whispered, looking up at the vastness above us, at the bright beautiful stars beyond measure. "I wish I may, I wish I might, have this wish I wish tonight."

But then I couldn't bring myself to voice a wish because the rules said I could only have one, and how could I ever decide which to choose?

I wanted to wish that my old people, my friends in Optica, would somehow be rescued.

I wanted to wish that Ezzie would be okay, that he would live and be whole and healthy, with no ill effects from the wardens or from the wild man's claws.

I wanted to wish that Judd would be safe without me there looking out for him, that he would forgive me for leaving him.

I wanted to wish that Meritt had not been planning to betray me, but if I really trusted him, I wouldn't need to wish for his loyalty.

I wanted to wish that that Farrell Dean and I hadn't irrevocably damaged our friendship. We'd struck an uneasy truce, it was true, but would that be enough to carry us through whatever lay ahead? I had said terrible things to him, and he had kept secrets from me. But I couldn't wish for our friendship, not after Cline's tirade. And I couldn't spend my one wish on Farrell Dean and not on Meritt—Meritt, whom I'd left standing on a cliff while I drifted away. Against my will, yes; but it wasn't against my will that Farrell Dean's arm was around me now. Maybe it would have been more honorable, to freeze to death out of loyalty to Meritt, but I wasn't convinced.

What a tangle it all was.

I wanted to wish Rafe back to life, but I could see Rafe shaking his head: even a star couldn't grant that.

Most of all, perhaps, I wanted to ask the stars whether I would always feel alone. A spectacle, a freak, an outsider. But that question was too pitiful to say aloud, even to a distant star.

"Star light, star bright," I murmured again, and then again and again, until sometime in the darkness of early morning I turned my face into the crook of Farrell Dean's neck and fell asleep.

I awoke to a bright shining sun and a girl's voice.

"Hello?" she said. "Are you shipwrecked? Are you injured? Do you need help?"

I opened my eyes and tried to sit up, struggling to untangle myself from Farrell Dean's legs, the blankets, the bench seat.

He wasn't helping me. He was sitting up, but he looked like he was paralyzed—staring, white-faced, shocked, as if he was gazing at something more terrifying than any Guardian, any wild man, any betrayal. In all the years I'd known Farrell Dean, he'd never once looked anything like this.

Slowly I made myself turn to face whatever new horror had come.

This is what I saw:

I was standing outside the boat, on the sand. My flaming hair was loose, curling at the ends in the damp sea air, stirred by the gentle breeze. I was wearing a long tunic of blues and greens, thin rectangles and squares of beautiful colors all sewn together, colors like the sea, the sky, the grass.

And I was staring back at me.

Beside me in the boat Farrell Dean moved—reached over, fumbled at my head, pulled off my black cap. My long fiery hair fell loose across my shoulders and tumbled down my back, and the me on the sand grew wide-eyed. Her hand went to her lips, then reached toward me.

"Valentina," she said. "You're alive."

THE END, Book One

The Red Series

The Watch (Book One)
The Stolen (Book Two)
The Watchmaker (Book Three)
The Forgotten (Book Four)

www.amandawitt.com

Acknowledgements

All four books in *The Red Series* were family endeavors:

My husband—a professional writer and editor, and former creative writing professor—provided invaluable editorial feedback, copy editing, and proofreading.

My mother—also an English professor—served as another proofreader. Any errors are because I just kept on fiddling ...

My sister—yet another English professor—gave me a much-needed boost of enthusiasm at exactly the right moment, as did my sister-in-law Laura.

My father gave me a collection of Yeats poems for my nineteenth birthday, thus permanently fixing "The Stolen Child" in my psyche.

And my three (then-teenage) children not only talked me into writing these books to begin with, but also offered constant encouragement and insightful feedback every step of the way.

I am grateful to all of them for their help.